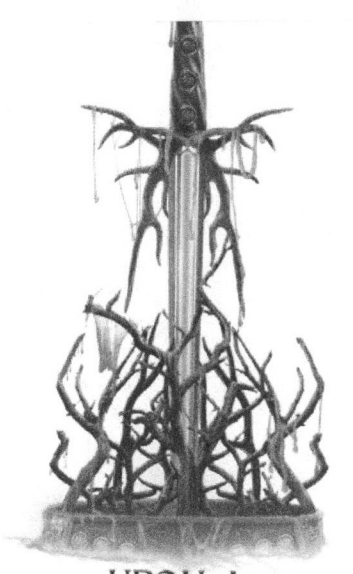

UPON A
KINGDOM'S BREATH

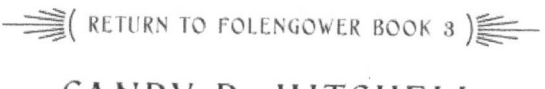

(RETURN TO FOLENGOWER BOOK 3)

CANDY D. MITCHELL

Candy D. Mitchell

This is a work of fiction. All names, places, characters, and situations are from the author's imagination and any similarities are coincidental.

Upon a Kingdom's Breath

Book Three of the Return to Folengower series

Copyright © 2023 by Candy D. Mitchell

All rights reserved.

No portion of this book may be reproduced in any form without permission from the publisher, except as permitted by U.S. copyright law.

ISBN: 979-8-9859927-1-7

https://thepeculiarfairy.com/

@thepeculiarfairy

Cover design by MiblArt

Edited by Lozzi Counsell

To all who have traveled to Folengower, may you make it through without being tossed to the depths.

The ELTRIST

Eltrists a.k.a. Twilight Breathers are mammals who are native to Folengover. They can communicate in a sort of telepathic way amongst non Eltrists. Despite their abilities, they are kind to those who wish to live in harmony with them. Magic bringers use to sing for spells.

Fig. 1 HORNS
Mass of tiny horns on head.

Fig. 2 STRUG
Glowing lavender ooze, expels from their mouths. It is created in their glowing bellies. Once expelled it melts flesh. They slurp up strug piles once their food is done melting.
* Plants also are melted.

Fig. 3 CAVE
They live in frigid caves of hard blended rock. It gleams like moonstone with carved jagged lines. They spiral and lean at the top.

Fig. 6 WINGS
They have powerful wings. Wing colors generally vary based on fur color.

Fig. 4 CLAWS
Their sharp claws have been known to lift folks in the air.

Fig. 5 BLOOD
They bleed a far-lite black.

Fig. 7 TAIL & FUR
Tails have bumpy protrusions that swell in spiral pattern. Can have many fur colors.

1

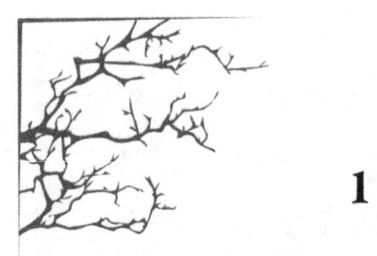

War is long, long like a perpetual snowstorm infecting every surface with its frigid hands. Folengower, now consumed and plump as a pig, sniffed at the air. If it could have, it would most certainly spit out the foul smell that comes with the death of a land. For now, it would burrow underneath the toxic layer, hopeful for the storm to end and its breaths to steady the seas. Perhaps someday that would happen, but war usually festered for decades, creeping until finally it would stampede and howl, with the eye of the storm at its beck and call.

The folks of Folengower slept soundly in their beds or beneath the moon's fading light, unaware that the course of history hung on a web at that very moment. Each silk but one contained lies, and Theodore learned of it, but Eliza sat before the truth.

At the top of Talkun's Tower, Eliza stood on her knees. Talkun enveloped her with his long warm fur, his large paws, and his wilted wings, which wrapped around her. Eliza rested her cheek against his. His hug was safety in a bottle. Talkun's wings loosened their embrace as Eliza backed up slowly and peered at him as if he were a lost friend. Except she had never seen Talkun other than in the few pictures and drawings that had slipped her mind until now. For an Eltrist, he was sickly thin. She'd felt and could see the bones of his paws, like shards of glass protruding beneath his skin. The sacks of skin that sagged with fur and no meat. A scar lived across his back and crossed to his wings, and there was another one under his belly. No hair dared to grow over them. The scar piled on his back in peaks as if someone had reopened it over and over again.

"*Bloodtress*, what is it?" Thorn called from below. There was a subtle shake that was only heard when she spoke the last word.

Eliza turned to the steps.

"Who is it?" Talkun spoke in her mind.

"Amarda's army," said Eliza in a hollow tone. A glare tugged at her eyebrows.

Footsteps clanked onto the steps as if each one stopped abruptly to suffocate the sound.

"Friends?"

"Not of mine." Eliza held up her arm. The rapture stone remained coiled around her arm, teeth and all. "But yours."

Talkun squinted. His eyes seemed to move through her. "Time has been unkind to me. Explain."

"We are in the middle of a war between the two kingdoms because of my father not following through with an agreement made after the last war. I was unaware until Amarda's folks captured me and told me of what he's done. Before truth lived in shadows, but I hope we can find the light together."

"The only light that will follow you is in death." Thorn scowled.

Eliza stumbled as she tried to stand, falling into Talkun, who caught her gently in his paw.

Thorn's eyes widened in surprise, if not fear. Her dagger, which she'd hidden behind her back, clinked as it hit the floor. She dropped to her knees. Her head bowed, though her eyes peered up at him. "It's true. You're alive," she whispered. "Please, let me save you from this prison."

Talkun glanced at Eliza before turning to Thorn. "It appears safety is right in front of me..." Talkun spoke to them both and put his paw on Eliza's shoulder. "From my cassus."

Thorn's scorn could have melted Eliza if she'd had any magic to do so, and her back stiffened. "Very well. We will both release you from your prison." She stood confidently but indignantly. Leading the descent down, she focused on each step.

"A name?" Talkun's voice seeped into her thoughts, like smoke filling a windowless room.

"Oh..." Thorn froze. "Forgive me. My name is Thorn."

As if a window appeared, it unlatched, and Talkun's voice slipped away. Then, Thorn continued at a slow pace down the steps. Her head stayed turned to the side, as if she were unsure if Talkun was planning to harm her, or perhaps it was Eliza she hoped to keep an eye on. Light licked at the last few steps from the door that hung ajar.

Kinsington stood between Aylo and Esna. The morning glow lighted the back of Esna's fur like a golden campfire, and Aylo's fur looked ethereal and the opposite of Kinsington's never-ending darkness. O stood on the side, scrutinizing the door with his eyes, while the rest of the folks stood breathless.

Thorn jumped down the last two steps and out the door with an unrestrained grin and a grand bow that confirmed their suspicions. And then, like spring's return, winter aged. Its bones turned brittle, its muscles threadbare until even its skin—too thin to be anything—drowned into the soil. Talkun was spring. First, the crowd's jaws, almost in unison, nearly unhinged from their skulls. Talkun scrunched his eyes shut and held up a paw to shield the light.

One man from the side sang, "Above and below, watch them soar, hear them roar and speak, their magic runs deep, a bringer of gifts, a synchrony unlike others, we breathe together, we rule as one. Talkun returns!" The others joined in. Thorn rose her fist over her eye and chanted along.

Eliza stayed hidden behind Talkun on the last step of the tower. Her mind overgrew with escape plans until she felt Talkun's fur press into her. She backed up into the tower. Kinsington made soothing noises that caused him to stop. Eliza petted his back and hoped that whatever Kinsington spoke would calm Talkun.

O stepped to the side and locked eyes with Eliza. His eyebrows narrowed and his arms crossed at his chest. She frowned as she searched for what his expression meant. Then one man hurried towards Talkun. Thorn reached out for him. The smell of drunkenness seeped off his breath. She fumbled to snatch his shirt as he slipped past.

"*Talkun*," the man shouted.

Kinsington locked into his mind. "Halt, or you shall take your last step."

The man ignored him and shouted again. Other folks followed behind him. Kinsington raised his paw to swat them like flies, but Esna grabbed it.

"Wait," she said with her mouth clenched into his mind. "They all want to meet him. We don't want any hostility."

Eliza crept out of the tower, her back glued to the cobblestone wall. She shuffled to the side, watchful of the crowd's movements and listening to their shattering voices. Bits of stonework on the tower had dips and broken pieces, and she dug into them as if rock climbing around it. With her chest heavy as a brick, she stared off into the distance at the castle.

"Where are you going?" Thorn whispered.

Eliza's body jolted and turned around. Sunlight beamed onto tiny specks of pollen that swept towards the cliff like bumblebees. Thorn flicked a piece out of her curly green hair.

"Did you really think you could just leave?"

"I did as you asked; Talkun is alive. Shouldn't you be with your king?"

"You will come back with us, Bloodtress." Thorn grabbed her arm.

Eliza yanked away and punched her in the jaw.

Thorn's head shot back. "You cursed scum!" Thorn rubbed her jaw and then, with eyes full of hate, she wrapped her hand around Eliza's throat and lifted her off the ground. Eliza flailed and bashed her legs against her torso. Her face paled, and she lifted her hand. A black flame chewed at the air. Just as soon as it animated, her other arm bled from the rapture stone's teeth slicing her skin as easily as if it were pie. Eliza shot the black mass into Thorn's cheek. Thorn let out a sickening scream as she threw Eliza to the ground. Thorn stumbled backwards, her legs soon giving way, her cheeks wet with tears.

One more bite on Eliza's wrist like from the teeth of a mangy dog. Shreds of skin dangled her hand from her wrist. The rapture stone, bloodied, landed on the ground. Eliza frantically tried to push her hand back in place, but she only managed to rip the last threads, releasing it altogether.

"What is happe—" O gasped as he caught sight of the dismembered hand. He rushed over and picked it up with two fingers, holding it out as far as his arm could stretch. Eliza's eyes rolled to the back of her head, white as frost, fainting half in O's arm and partly against the foly weeds. Blood speckled the pink flowers.

Thorn shivered in and out of consciousness.

"*Thorn, Thorn,* what happened?" O scooted his way over to her. Eliza slid down him, and he kept having to hoist her back up while he held her severed hand squished against her back.

"Cursed soil." O said in disbelief, covering his mouth with his hand.

Thorn's cheek held a black hole, but no blood pooled, as if the skin had seared shut. He gently lowered Eliza and placed her hand next to her before crouching down to Thorn's shaking body.

"Thorn?" He tenderly touched her shoulder.

Thorn pushed O's arm away as best as her shaking hand would allow. Slowly, she dug her hands into the foly weeds and stood. Her body moved chaotically like electricity.

"Let me help you," O breathed.

Thorn reached for and failed to grab her dagger several times before she held her hand in place and tore it from her belt. With each step, she shook, demented, as if possessed, over to Eliza. Her teeth shone and clinked against each other and her copper eyes were now plagued. O reached his arm out to stop her. She pushed it away, but O held firm.

"You aren't well. Let me take you back to the others. You need healing magic now." His tone was barely below a demand.

Thorn rushed at Eliza, and O's arm flung forward. Eliza's head twitched awake just in time to see Thorn's dagger hurling at her chest. She rolled, Thorn's dagger stabbing into the foly weeds, killing several clusters of pink blooms.

"*Stop*," O shouted.

Eliza stood with pure adrenaline, grabbed her hand and fled to the castle.

Thorn shook too badly to follow. "*Kill her.*"

O watched Eliza reluctantly.

"*Now*," Thorn yelled. "Get her."

O groaned and leapt after her. His hooves rose and fell with ease against the uneven ground. For a moment, Eliza peered back at her executioner. O shook his head slowly. Blood dripped in a come-find-me way.

They'd left the castle with doors wide open like an invitation, though she would hardly say the castle would be happy to see any of them. The inside looked much like she felt—torn to shreds and on the verge of being forgotten. She ignored it all since danger sprinted quite literally behind her.

Heaps of shredded curtains were piled all over in uneven lumps. Eliza reached down for a handful of fabric, ripping what she could to wrap her wrist. She gagged as it touched her. Hooves clanked onto the floor. She looked over at the drips of blood that followed her and darted towards the staircase. O's hooves stopped. Eliza placed her hand over her heart and shifted her body to lay along the wall as flat as possible.

"Eliza?" O gulped. He knelt on the bloodied floor and touched a spot, as if he hoped it were old. The blood painted his finger dark. He stood, keeping his eyes on the drops.

Eliza shoved a painting to the side that rested lopsidedly and had a massive knife mark down the middle. The flaps of the canvas opened like shutters. O rounded the corner just as her leg moved behind the steps.

"Eliza... for moon's sake, I have not come to hurt you."

Eliza crossed her legs and placed her detached hand on her lap. The cloth sagged in her dark blood. She unwrapped it, tossing the soiled cloth next to her. Green light swirled above her palm. "Then why have you come at all?" Eliza cupped her wrist with the light.

O exhaled. He wiped the sweat from his forehead. "I want to help, but..." His head fell, causing his long sage hair to hide his expression.

"But?" Eliza winced and toppled to the side. The pain moved through her like a snake. Every few seconds, she removed her hand from her flesh to breathe and regain her strength before trying again. Her lips moved quickly and silently. The blood strung together encapsulated in frost as if they were snowflakes.

"Oh, Eliza..."

Eliza jumped but didn't struggle as O pulled her up and brought her against the back wall. She'd been concentrating on her magic so hard that she'd failed to hear his hooves gently moving nearer or feel his eyes on her.

"Can you reattach it?"

"I think so, but what will it matter when the spirit of death is before me?" Eliza met his eyes, and even though she knew he had to be her enemy, she felt nothing of the sort from him. She felt his pain, as she was sure he felt hers.

He ignored her assumption. "Come, you cannot stay here. Where can I take you to hide?"

"Up the stairs. All the way to the top." Eliza weakly pushed herself away from the back wall to start what felt like an impossible ascent in her state, but O immediately gathered her in his arms, making sure to also pick up her hand. Eliza opened her mouth to speak again.

O shook his head. "Save your energy. The spirit of death will come, but it will not be me, and I hope it will not be soon, Bloodtress."

Eliza watched silently and slightly less warily than she felt she should have been as O carried her up the many flights of stairs.

When they made it to the top, O asked, "Now where?"

Eliza simply pointed to the first door, which was barely held together. She slid out of his arms and touched the splintered mess. She peered through the diamond-shaped hole, then pushed the door open with hardly more than a finger.

O remained at the door frame. His head cocked to the side as he stroked curiously at his chin and held her hand in the other. "This is your room?"

"Was."

Eliza pulled open a drawer in her dresser that mainly contained shirts. She grabbed one and wrapped it around her bleeding stump before moving around the room like a mouse searching for a snack.

"What is it you've lost?" O stepped one hoof into the room. When she did not answer nor look up at him, he continued to her. She dropped to her knees and felt under her bed. "Can I help?"

Eliza pushed her hair out of her face as she peered up at him. "Shouldn't you get back to the others? Talkun lives; I assume a celebration is in order."

"I can't leave until I know you have a place to hide." O picked up a picture frame from the carpet. It was a picture of her and Theodore sitting on a tree branch, their legs dangling several feet in the air. O assumed they were only a decade old or younger. He placed it back on her desk. "But if you want me to leave so badly, I—"

O's head snapped to the door, his ears perking. Swiftly, he crouched to Eliza and placed his hand over her mouth. "Footsteps," he whispered.

Eliza frantically clawed at the floor with gray light until a round handle appeared beneath her bed. She pulled it open before turning back to O with wide eyes. "*My hand.*" She shook, her eyes full of fear.

O passed her it. "Be safe, Bloodtress." A flicker of sadness stared at her.

Eliza grabbed his arm and pulled him towards her to kiss his cheek. His eyes closed with a grin, and then she fell through the door. It faded back to a rug.

O hurriedly rose and flipped over a gray nightstand. "*Cursed scum. I'll find you,*" he shouted before flinging her mattress to the floor. Her dark blue blankets and pillows scattered around the room.

Thorn ran into the room with two other people. "Where is she?" She looked around with downcast eyes. A strug mixture dripped from the hole in her cheek, and her teeth stared out from it like a window.

O tapped at the floor with his hoof and punched at the nearest wall. His knuckles swelled. "She was here, and when I went to grab her..." O's eyes flicked around the room with no intent of truth. "She vanished. The secrets of the castle have defeated us again. Perhaps Talkun can fill us in."

Thorn's eyes bulged. "*Argh.*" She ripped off a chunk of the door. Her teeth rattled as she shook her head. She squeezed the wood, but unlike a can, the wood splintered into her palm. Smoky sawdust seeped out of the slits in her fingers. She hurled the piece down the hall, which landed almost completely intact. Thorn's left eye twitched and she breathed as if a magnificent beast lurked in her vocal chords. Micro splinters lined her palm. She glanced at them with only disgust. "He will. Let's go. Kinsington awaits your presence." Thorn stomped out of the room dramatically while the other two followed quickly after her.

Before O left, he stared back at the floor where she'd vanished and bowed solemnly.

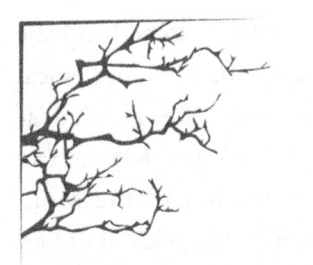

2

Skeletal vines climbed up the wall. Their spindly arms reached out and their heads wilted, their gray insides on display for any underneath to see. Many of the flowers lowered themselves around Eliza's body. Each petal opened, as if to see better. With each staggered breath she took, their heads moved as a metronome. For the sixth time since she'd fallen, the flowers excreted a chalky pink pus that smelled of a dying campfire.

With her nose twitching, her eyes flickered awake. She could see only a slit of an image at a time, but as the image focused, she shot up and scooted away to a wall. The skeletal flora jerked from the wall, unsuctioning itself from stability. They followed her, curious as a jumping spider.

A deep groan released from her parted lips. She stared at the stump of her arm, and for a moment, a tear streaked down her cheek.

"*Shoo.*" Eliza swung her hand around at the vines. "Leave me be, or I will rip you apart." Dark blotches of sweat formed on her shirt.

The skeletal things lifted their petals and shook in defiance.

"I'm already bleeding out, what more do you want of me?" she whispered. Her shirt, tied around her wrist, sagged in red.

Yellow covered the door behind her, seeming eerily too cheery to be in such a dark room. Eliza backed up to the door and grabbed the yellow handle. As she lifted herself up, the flowers gazed into her eyes close enough for her to touch them. She opened the door and slammed it behind her, leaving the skeletal things to crawl back onto the wall.

Bright light illuminated the halls. She squinted at the orbs above her. Agor vines climbed to the ceiling around the doorframe. Eliza ripped off a strand and bit it. Placing her hand between the strands, she balanced to tie it. Blood dripped onto her chest, and the hand was too loosely tied and fell at her feet. She lifted it back up and tied the agor vine tighter before placing it around her waist like a knotted belt. As she wandered through the halls with a stoic face, her severed hand slapped against her thigh. She moved as if jewels encrusted her belt instead of her severed hand bound by agor vines.

She passed several doors, and some she opened. One room smelled sickly sweet, another was cluttered to the point of blocking out anything beyond the first layer and the last one opened to stairs leading down. She poked her head in and leaned over to the point of her feet teetering. Not much of anything could be seen past the dark, but that didn't stop her from journeying down.

The room at the bottom of the stairs was at least twice the size of the room she'd woken up in. Forgotten things stockpiled along the walls and in between. She coughed, holding up her arm at the dust she'd startled until it settled back down. In the far back, a black armoire loomed over everything in the room as if it were in charge. She navigated around the random piles of armor that looked frail and bloodstained, goblets, stacked chairs and things she'd never set her eyes on.

Surrounding the armoire were lidded crates. She held her injured arm at her chest and pried the lid off one box. Dresses were neatly folded inside. Eliza set one on top of a crate and ran her hand down the middle of corpse-thistle-shaped buttons that branched off to either side at the waist. She gently set it back in and sifted through the other boxes. More clothes. She grabbed a shirt that looked moth-ridden and placed it under her armpit securely. She tore it to strips. Slowly, she unwrapped her makeshift bandage to replace it with another.

On the other wall, vials squeezed together on a leaning shelf that only remained upright thanks to a bookshelf that graciously offered its shoulder. All the magic inside was still and dull. Eliza walked over to them, sliding her fingers over a pearlescent jar in the middle of the shelf. Its small shape made it appear insignificant. With careful ease, she pulled it from the surrounding glass. The next vial slid down sideways to the other shelf, cracking the one in front of it. The scarred glass held in what it could, though a gray liquid trickled out of the cracks.

Lips parted, she picked through others on the shelf, swirling the mixture inside each one. She either glared or revealed a flicker of a smile before concluding if they were worthy of her one hand to hold. It became full quickly, and she set them down on the bottom shelf. She scanned the rest of the room and found a knife and agor vines.

In the corner beside her, more crates waited to be opened. Her stump of an arm lingered at her heart. For a moment, she reached it out as if her fingers were waiting to grab at the contents. Eliza kicked at the lid and cursed under her breath. She tore the cover off and sat on her knees. Inside, she found a mishmash of things that she threw to the side until she got to the bottom, where a very faded satchel that contained a broken bottle and crumbled leaves sat. She lifted it by the bottom edge and shook it. The glass pieces clinked together at the bottom of the box, the crumbled leaves floating down slower until they too settled. Eliza went back to the shelf to store the jars that she'd set aside.

Eliza pushed her finger into her temple, squinting as she wandered back up the stairs and into the bright hall. When the moon took its light away, Eliza found her way back to the inner wall of the castle. She placed her hand on one stone, which liquified. Soon, several others around it did the same, and she stepped through to the outside of the castle. The stones vibrated back into place shortly after. Her body lingered against the solid stone, and she envisioned Ben next to her in disbelief as they moved through.

Voices stirred from above, and Eliza's head shot up as she backed herself against the wall and held her breath to listen. She couldn't make out any words, but she could just about work out where the voices were coming from. With the silence of a rabbit, she hunched over and stalked around the castle on tippytoes. She peered above briefly, searching for who spoke, but she could only see small birds perched on the edge. Two folks stood on the far end next to the front of the castle. The taller one threw his head back and laughed. Eliza slunk back to the corner, her head lowered. Magic nipped at her hand, like a dog begging to play. She squeezed it into a fist. *Not yet*, she thought.

Nearby, a chackle stomped at the stump that held him captive, its reign wrapped tightly around it. Its nostrils flared after each grunt. Soon, the stump's roots flung out as the stump toppled to the side, and the chackle nudged at it with his wet nose. The stump rolled forward, taking the chackle with it. It dragged onto its side causing clouds of soil to poof out. A mix between a snarl and a whine sounded from the creature.

Eliza peered around. With the people now gone from sight, she sprinted to the chackle. She took another look all around her for any signs of anyone else before reaching into her satchel and taking out a dull knife. She awkwardly sawed at the rope that bound the chackle as he huffed and clawed at the ground.

"It's okay," she whispered comfortingly.

Strand fibers broke and were left like straw. At the last bunch, Eliza ripped it off, and the chackle leapt up with its tail swishing.

Eliza placed her palm on his forehead. He bowed at her touch and rested on the soil. She climbed onto its back and breathed into its ear, "*Halko*."

The chackle charged away from the castle with fire in his eyes. Eliza held on to his neck, her other hand flapping like a stone against her thigh. She rode with white knuckles. Freedom pulsed through her veins with every tree she passed. Her head rose high, her eyes alive and full of determination as freedom grew into a boulder.

Then all at once, the chackle flung Eliza from his back. Her body flung into the air, leaving the boulder behind. The grasses met Eliza's face first, then the rest of her flopped down on her belly. She could taste the earth on her lips as she glared at the chackle, bowed as if his front legs were sliced in half. His heliotrope tongue lulled to the side in constant bounce from his sudden breaths.

"And where do you think you are off to, little bird?"

A man stepped out from behind a tree as Eliza pushed off the ground and spit out the last of dirt and blood from her cut lip. Blood and dirt stained her hair, which draped like a curtain over half her face. A shadow covered the rest of her expression. The man patted at the chackle's back, who snorted and stumbled up before taking to the woods alone.

"Seems your ride has left," he whistled through his missing tooth.

Black smoke glowed in Eliza's hand as she stood. The flame danced in front of her wild gaze. "I remember you. Perhaps I should show you what I should have done the day you axed my door?" Eliza limped closer, and the flame swirled into smoke.

"Cursed scum." Fint looked over his shoulder and signaled something with his pointer finger, or so Eliza thought. "Little birds like you should stay in cages. Come back with me and—"

Through parted lips, she blew the smoke to his face. It swam into his nostrils, mouth, ears, and eyes in a sickening hiss. His mouth opened into an oval, his head rocking back as if someone pulled it. No air came out, and his bulging eyes spoke too well of the lack of oxygen. The man keeled over while his stomach convulsed in a rippling motion while his hands focused on his throat. They gripped it tightly, as if his esophagus were about to spill out.

Feet rustled nearby. Eliza scanned in between the rows of trees. Fint fell to his knees and gurgled something. He reached out to Eliza, balling her shirt in his grip. She tossed his body to the side despite his desperation for mercy. He toppled like an ancient tree ladened with snow.

A twig snapped, and she froze, her eyes darting beyond Fint. The sound made her stomach climb into her throat. She backed into the trees, her eyes glued to the castle. Fint stilled. *Two*, Eliza counted in her head. Another lost at her hand. Wyatt's desperate face flickered in her mind. She brushed the sweat from her forehead and wiped it on her pants. Now in the present, she descended the hill.

Another crack sounded, as if bones lined a path to her. Eliza breathlessly rounded a tree with a massive trunk and placed her back against it, sliding down to sit. Moss clung to her shirt. Eliza unraveled her hand from her makeshift belt and held it against her wrist. With the agor vines clenched in between her teeth, she lowered her lips to her dead hand and wrapped swiftly from it to her wrist as it balanced on her legs. The vines snaked between her stiff fingers and down to her wrist many times in an X shape.

Branches shook several trees away. Her head whipped around. A twig fell from above. She peered up and watched a critter with a red tail as it made its way above her. Leaves whirled down. Eliza gathered up any that were close enough to reach and pushed them underneath the agor vines until her hand shined like a waxy fern. Eliza gave a single nod to the creature with her hand over her heart.

A green light flickered from Eliza's living hand. It swirled up, and she coaxed it gently as she blew towards her severed hand. It seemed to nod at her and hid under the leaves. They aged and blackened like raisins.

Eliza flung her head back and closed her eyes, her good hand searching the ground blindly for a stick. Her fingers wrapped around one, and she pushed it into her mouth and bit down hard. She could feel her tendons tug and slither back into place. Tremors ate at her body as she struggled to still, struggled to keep her screams internal. Warm ligaments grew and wriggled back where they belonged. Eliza's teeth clattered against the branch. The leaves faded to gray, as if her skin absorbed the ghost of them. Sweat beaded down her forehead and down strands of hair.

Her cheeks were wet with silent tears. Under the skeletal leaves, frothy new skin crawled and popped until it cloaked the entire area. It dripped, slimy at first. Crack. Eliza gagged. Her lungs burned ruthlessly, her stomach contracted, and out spilled yellow acid from deep in her belly onto a stick that now swam in her vomit like a raft. Eliza coughed and wiped the foam from her curled lips.

The diaphanous skin layered together until it sealed and the slime thickened. Eliza, twitching, unwrapped the agor vines. Their blue coloring stained the peculiar slime. She poked at it, and it jiggled like a mushroom cap. Her hand tugged at it for a moment, but she retracted, as if she couldn't decide if it needed to stay on or not.

"Stand, Bloodtress," a voice hissed.

Eliza didn't flinch nor turn; she simply stared at her hand, almost threatening.

"I said *stand*." The person stepped closer on heavy feet. Every movement was like the end. And the world beneath her snapped like mouse bones.

Without moving her head, Eliza eyed the tree behind her. She rose like embers and clawed desperately at the trunk. She scraped off what she could of it and smothered it between her palms. The renewed hand's jiggly surface cracked and shed, leaving hardened skin beneath it. It flaked off in shards that surrounded her like a fairy ring. Both hands lit, fiery and fueled. "I dare you to even breathe again in my direction." Eliza turned to the mystery person, her face paled with sweat.

Her mouth parted before she could stop a tear escaping. Her magic shadowed over her eyes that glowed like obsidian. "Riven?"

Riven moved sideways. "I see you have a better memory than your brother."

"When did you become a warrior for Amarda?" Though her lips quivered, she raised her head strongly. Her eyelashes stuck together from all the moisture whenever she blinked.

"It's been a long time." Riven stepped forward, her hand out, as if she wished to dance. "Let me take you back—"

"So you can imprison me? My own friend?" Eliza extended her arms out.

"Another lifetime..." Riven moved behind a thin tree. "We were only children. Anyone and everyone was our friend then," she said, barely above a whisper.

Shouts came and someone wailed.

"I'll tell them it was an accident," Riven said. "We'll play nice."

"I would much sooner slit my throat. You know as well as I do that they... *you* care only if my blood spills. Now that you have Talkun, you should find your way back to my home. Leave me with the shadows."

Riven rubbed at the scar on her cheek that rested underneath her eye and ended under her lip. She followed the crescent shape like a nervous tick. "You know I can't do that." She held her hand out again. "Come, and I will tell you my story."

"*Riven*," Thorn shouted.

Eliza jumped.

"*Riven.*"

Riven turned towards Thorn's voice and walked towards it. Enough to see beyond the trees. "They aren't far now. Make your choice," she whispered.

Eliza gave a single slow nod. Black fed between her hands as they parted. It flowed and licked outward like Cerberus. Reds and blacks entwined and slashed at the air.

"I have made my choice. Run..." Eliza smiled a crazed smile. "Run, or I will kill you."

Riven's tongue slid across her top teeth, as if she could taste the hate of Eliza's words. She shuddered. Then a shadow blocked out the sky and stole her gaze. Eliza followed it too late. An Eltrist tore through Eliza's shoulder with its brown claws and lifted her up. Eliza screamed at the hot pain in her shoulder, her hands slapping together from the impact. Her magic expelled like a wormhole towards Riven. Thorn jumped out of the woods and tackled Riven. They rolled down the hill several feet in a ball, barely missing Eliza's magic.

Her hands ached as if frostbitten. From above, the treetops held a whole new world of nests, small twig built homes and fiery lichen and vibrant mosses. Eliza blinked, and her focus on the lively world atop them distracted her from the pain. The forest thinned the closer they flew to the castle. She squeezed her hands and released and then did it again until she felt the magic pulse through her fingertips.

"Eliza, stop," a voice whispered in her mind. She knew it to be her uncle Talkun. Reluctantly, she let the magic subside. "You have nothing to fear with me, cassus." The Eltrist tossed her to the ground beside Talkun who stood next to the garden. She winced as the claws forcefully slid out of her shoulder. Kinsington and others gathered behind him.

Talkun looked sickly, the kind that could never heal, at least not fully. A pile of strug deceased the plants and animals that he slurped, though it merely gave the facade that food would be enough. Eliza's eyes drooped, and her hands held her elbows loosely as she watched her uncle eat.

"Why such sadness, cassus?" Talkun asked her.

Her head bowed, and she shook her head, as if she couldn't bear to speak out loud in front of everyone. She wished he would understand and provide the same privacy that he could command every time he spoke.

He looked at Kinsington and groaned something at him. Before long, Kinsington commanded them all to leave except Eliza. They gathered inside the castle, including Kinsington.

"Now will you speak?" Talkun said in her mind.

"Yes, Kalus...?" she said, almost as a question.

"You still remember some of the old language? I am honored." Talkun grinned, and strug seeped down the side of his lips.

"Some; not much. No one speaks it often, just a few words here and there mixed with all the other languages we've intertwined it with." Eliza looked down and her lips drooped. "But I remember Mom singing and saying words that were used when Grandma was the ruler."

"Can you feel it?"

Eliza turned around. The forest, calm with its cornucopia of green, eased her. She wished to disappear into it. "Feel what?"

Talkun stopped feeding and placed a paw on her hand. "Sulint."

Eliza frowned, unsure of what the word meant.

Talkun let out a grunt. "They're all in mourning. If you listen, you will hear Folengower weep. Sulint. I ache to find the home I once had. Touch the ground, cassus."

Eliza knelt and placed her hands on the soil. Her hands eased the grasses to the side. "I'm not sure I feel what you mean."

"You will. Listen... not just with your ears."

Eliza nodded and removed her hands. "Is it true what they claim?" She gazed up at the castle, the stonework bare or close to it as strug melted down the once lively plants that curled up it. "You are an Ancient One?"

Talkun stiffened his back and raised his front left paw. Across the pads were lavender circles, and down on his metacarpal pad was an upside-down black triangle with smooth edges—the same as Eliza's forehead. "Does that trouble you?"

"No." Eliza's head twitched while she swallowed. "It's all true?"

"If you are asking if I killed her... my..." Talkun's neck twitched. "I watched Korrigan allow hatred to strangle his insides until that was all that remained." He sighed and slumped to the ground. "There is a lot more that I would never trouble you with, but, cassus, you must choose. Even I cannot protect you from this."

Eliza told herself not to cry, not to let the truth destroy her. She bit her lip hard enough to keep her tears at bay. "I don't know what to do. The people who freed you want me dead. And if my own father would kill his mother, I hardly believe he would listen to me or stop this war peacefully."

"Do not wait long. Kinsington hungers for war, and now that I am released, he will have more allies, which means a true battle will come like a fallen rock any day now."

A raucous noise echoed through the stones and then a vibration expelled, jagged yet straight, like a detonating cord. Pebbles sprung to life as bouncy balls, flowers wilted as if choked by nutrients, and then—

Talkun narrowed his eyes at the slithering lines. Curious, he stepped forward, and his mouth hollowed. Before Eliza could run, Talkun snatched her arm and swung her on top of him. "Hold on," he breathed into her mind. In one swift movement, he leapt into the air, his wings agonizing into existence. And like dynamite... BOOM.

Stones tumbled from the back of the castle, and folks screamed and sprinted, though some dumb but brave took to their weapons and sneaked around the back. Kinsington commanded them all to leave. Those who were smart mounted an Eltrist. Aylo and Esna flew to those outside and forcefully threw any on their backs. Kinsington flew up ahead with Thorn and O. He scornfully scanned the trees.

"Over there. Talkun has Eliza," Thorn yelled.

"Camp," Kinsington spoke to the Eltrists.

O peered over his shoulder. Smoke climbed in an animalistic manner and thickened. He believed a man stood beneath it, though he couldn't be certain who it was. He was certain that the person's head jerked, then their grimace bled through the blight. O shivered from the face that followed in every cloud.

"Do you see it?" O finally whispered to Thorn after too many clouds showed its silhouette.

Thorn frowned and peered over her shoulder at him. "What?" Her head tweaked to the side, as if she could feel eyes on her too.

"Nothing." O's voice cracked and fed the winds.

The camp glowed in the last bits of dawn. A chilling silence loomed over the camp until a man woke to piss on a rock, his eyes filled with the sandman's dust. The man tilted his head up just as Aylo landed next to him. The sky was full of Eltrists. Startled, he buttoned his pants and rubbed his eyes. Esna landed next to him, and Kinsington came shortly after. The man moved back and out of the way before any others squashed him like an egg.

"Folengower will soon be ours. The true heir to Folengower has returned," Kinsington spoke into every mind in the camp and, one by one, they rose from their beds and fled to the center. A chorus of ravenous heartbeats came with them, most of their breaths delayed.

Then, through the puffs of fog, Talkun flew in great strides above them. Eliza kept her eyes sealed and nuzzled into his fur. His appearance called for instant celebration.

A boisterous voice sang, "Above and below, watch them soar, hear them ROAR and speak." The voice halted until the others forced their jaws back in place and sang along. "Their magic runs deep, a bringer of gifts, a synchrony unlike others. We breathe together, we rule as ONE."

Kinsington stretched his head proudly into the sky. The voices chanted, some voices shook, and tears streamed down their faces. Once Talkun landed, his right paw slid, almost giving out beneath him. Just as he tried to correct it, Kinsington placed his paw on his. He steadied and let out a growl.

The crowd silenced, but the Eltrists could still hear their hearts. Eliza slid down, and Thorn yanked her wordlessly to the side. The hole in her cheek reeked of something that could have lived in the deepest pits of a grave. Eliza stared into it. Two of her teeth formed together like crystals—one teetered right and the other to the left. She wondered if her mouth smelled that foul on its own or if it were the healing potion that caused such a stench she could taste it in her mouth.

Talkun twitched his neck in their direction. "Leave her," he demanded to Thorn. Thorn squeezed Eliza's arm and narrowed her eyes. Eliza tugged her arm, and Thorn's lip curled. Again, Talkun spoke in Thorn's mind, "Now." She released her grasp and pushed Eliza away.

Eliza rubbed her wrist and narrowed her brows at Thorn. If it weren't for Talkun, who gripped Thorn's mind, she would have allowed her rage to consume her. Instead, she locked eyes with him and let out a breath until her face softened and her arms slacked.

Kinsington lifted his head, grinning broadly. "There have been days where I felt unsure if we would ever be here, if hope would die just as our forests, and yet here"—Kinsington, with glossy eyes, pointed his paw to Talkun. The folks clapped and rejoiced—"the true heir stands before us. *Alive*. Our truths are now reality. Though there are still distant clouds to go, tonight we join in revelry."

Riven grabbed Thorn's hand and led her through the crowd, lost to Eliza's view, though not forgotten from her thoughts.

The camp roared with life, and copious amounts of fermented ash leaves and carveberries sloshed around in their mugs. Not a mouth that danced didn't drip gray from their elated lips. A tinge of pink lost in the gray shined when the light hit.

Eliza joined Talkun away from the celebration. Her wrist burned as if sat above a burner even though she'd reattached it. Talkun watched the people jump and kick their legs up and down together, arm in arm as they spun around. Everything seemed well, but Eliza saw no comfort in Talkun's eyes.

Someone near them took out an instrument with latticed strings in the middle. The wood, which had small holes leading up, elongated up towards his mouth. The man plucked underneath, between the swirl and above, with his other hand. O danced next to one tent, his green hair moving like leaves on a windy day. For a moment, Eliza felt her throat tighten and her heart race. As if he could feel her watching, he turned mid-dance and smiled at her. His smile could have shattered any heart. It felt like the last sight of a loved one before watching them die.

O peered at Eliza from time to time, but she didn't return the looks.

"What are your plans for all this?" she asked Talkun.

Talkun kept his eyes fixated on the uproarious crowd. "I am new to this world. It would seem they have already decided my plans for me... much like yours."

Eliza glanced at his wings, which twitched slightly, as if he had a chill. "Did you not want to be rescued?"

Talkun turned to her. "A wish that I have made for as long as my brother locked me away. The vengeance is what I do not take lightly. Korrigan is—"

A circle formed in front of them. Riven took the center and shouted nonsense before they pushed her out, and Thorn caught her in her arms. She laughed even with the grimace of her hole. Another person took the center and shouted to the musician to play the song, Amongst Trees. He put his lips on the top and blew in while plucking the strings. The crowd clapped and listened to the person in the center sing, his arms expanding and contracting as his voice rang out.

"What were you going to say?"

Talkun swallowed and shook his head. "Vengeance. It will show the people of Nniar exactly what Korrigan has spoken about Eltrists and those that stand by us. This war could make things worse, which is what he wants. He wants us to show what we are capable of so he can do what he's done to me to all of them."

"You don't believe they can win?" Eliza glanced at O. He bowed his head towards her and rose his cup to his lips, which were already stained to stone.

"I think Korrigan shouldn't be underestimated."

Eliza frowned. "We have to do something, then. I have to find Theodore. He won't stand for our father's lies, and he, more than anyone, can stop the war."

"What does he know of Amardians? Has he sat amongst them and healed the forests? From what I have been told, Nniar has forgotten my fellow Eltrists unless they need our magic, and they do not welcome even the folks who live in Amarda in Nniar. What good will another Ancient One have towards a war that has already infected us all?"

"You forget that you are part of that line. If it is true, then you were... are an Ancient One. What would you have done? Do you choose to sit and wait for Nniar's army to take you again or kill you this time?"

Talkun eyed her, strug trickling from his mouth like a hose just turned off. "Look at me." Talkun moved an inch away from her face. He could have swallowed her whole. "Would you back me as the true heir of Folengower? When you look at me, do you see that glow of an ancient lineage that has blessed my body and mind?"

"I... I..."

"You see an old Eltrist neither alive nor dead." He shifted to the crowd. "They may not see it yet, but my time of ruling is but an empty hourglass."

Kinsington stomped towards them. His wings relaxed and his mouth parted in a grin as he passed the folks who sloshed their drinks as they danced next to him. His grin stopped at Eliza. "Is she troubling you?" Kinsington spoke to Talkun.

"It is a gift from the moon to speak to family, however dire the circumstance may be."

Eliza rubbed at her jaw, unsure of what they spoke of, but Kinsington bared his teeth at her. Talkun moved between them.

Kinsington snapped his mouth shut and bowed his head. "Forgive me."

"I am not the one who you wronged."

Another Eltrist flew overhead. One wing was smaller and flapped harder than the other. Eliza peered up at it. It came closer and closer until it landed a mere yard from them, its ashy-blue fur sopping wet, like a dog just come in from the rain.

"Sylin, where have you been?" Kinsington scanned above the trees. "And where are the rest?"

"The rest?" Talkun said.

Sylin breathed heavily. The strug inside him flickered. Strug bled down his chin. "We... we were attacked."

"Korrigan?" A storm swirled to life in Kinsington's face.

Sylin nodded, his wings finally resting.

"Where?"

"Just outside the divide. The Cursed Knights put corpse thistle powder in the river. It moved like a fog up to us and burned our senses. Several are back waiting in a safe area, but they can't see to fly. I got lucky."

"I will find them." Kinsington growled something loud and demanding after. Eliza jumped, and not a second later, Pavlyn tore through the camp, waiting for orders from Kinsington. "Another battle is here. You will come with me." He turned back to Sylin. "Find Aylo and Esna... tell them what you told me, and send them to help. Stay here and prepare a space for the healers."

"Of course." Sylin disappeared amongst the tents.

"Stay safe, my king."

Talkun's body stiffened, but he said nothing as he watched Kinsington and Pavlyn soar off to the clouds.

3

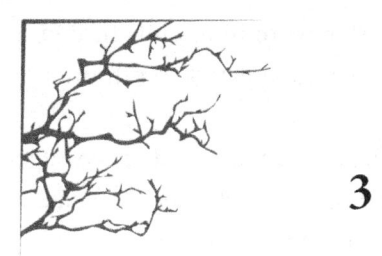

One would think that Folengower seemed but a nightmare in the midst of war, yet as Ben watched a finnix paw at a rock as if it were a ball, he thought it but a dream. Beams of white light seeped through the keyholes between the leaves. Even the finnix wasn't free from its blinding glow that dazzled onto its mauve fur as if they encrusted it with jewels. Its twisted horns blended in with the bark behind it. For a moment, Ben believed it to be the tree that spiraled out until the finnix gave up on digging the stone out of the soil and leaped deeper into the woods.

The night had come and gone in the Nniar woods. Theodore, Audrey and Ben had not.

Queen Agden had left under the canopy of darkness after she couldn't convince Theodore to choose a different path. If she were to linger too long, danger would pelt down like hail, and none of them were ready to answer to King Korrigan, so she left with a heavy heart. "If the only side you choose is yourself, then you must rally an army," she had said at last.

Theodore could see her last words floating between the trees, as if dipped in the blood of phantoms. The word army gathered together, smoky and hollow in large, moody letters. He could see them as clearly as he could see the sap slide down the crevices of bark next to him. Only he could see it, and when all the words dissipated, his thoughts remained heavy.

"Are you coming?" Audrey said. She stood at the edge of the creek. The branch behind her held her shirt like a flagpole over the sparkling water. She jumped in.

Theodore heard her, but a bird with a dull orange belly twitched its head below him as it gathered seeds from the forest floor. Theodore knelt, his hand outstretched to it. The bird twitched its head to the side and hopped into his hand. A thin smile shined on Theodore's face. "I understand," he said. The bird seemed to nod, and Theodore rubbed his thumb on the bird's head. Then, off he flew.

Ben blinked. "All birds, then?"

Theodore chuckled. "No. Some are quite... boorish to people." He shrugged. "I get it."

"What now?" Ben peered up into the sky. His fingers tapped on his pant leg.

"Hey, you both stink." Audrey splashed as far as the water could reach, which would have never reached Theodore, who stood closest to the stream.

Theodore grinned.

Ben lifted his arm and smelled. His nose wrinkled as he moved his face swiftly away. "She's right though, we do smell."

Theodore and Ben stripped down to their briefs and splashed into the water. Audrey roared with laughter.

The warm water eased their body aches. Theodore swam beneath the surface. Orangey strings floated as elegant chiffon, while moss-covered plants peaked their twilight oval heads through. Fishes swam by his face and other creatures walked on six and ten legs without a care, at least not one for him.

Down below, a cavern opened onto the side of the hill. It could hardly fit more than one person at a time. Theodore stared at it, his forehead tense. Bubbles blew from his nose up to the surface, and he followed.

Audrey shared a glance with Ben. "How long should we stay here?"

Theodore peered over his shoulder and down into the water, where sunbursts of light poked at the surface. A fish with verdant scales touched Theodore's hand as it swam past. His eyes fixed on it even as it blended into the rest of the underwater world. Audrey placed her hand in Theodore's palm, her eyes studying him. He kept his eyes on the memory of the fish.

"Theo—"

"I know," Theodore said bluntly towards the water, though he meant it in response to his nagging thoughts.

A croak sounded just beyond their dripping bodies, vibrating through the ground and then into the water like an earthquake. Audrey jumped and Ben placed a hand over his heart, but Theodore curiously looked up. He swam to the side of the ravine and latched on to a tangle of roots that reached out of the dirt like dead fingers.

"Stay here," he said with a glance behind him.

Audrey momentarily held a hand up as if to protest. Ben swam next to her and scanned what he could see of the land on either side. Another vibration came after another croak, and bubbles spread through the water like blisters and popped this time.

Theodore climbed up to the side. Water trickled down his chest and legs, grasses clung to his calves and pollen clung to his leg hairs in vibrant stripes of cherry and a fiery orange from the patches of flowers. He followed the sporadic croaks as if he were playing a game of Marco Polo. He stopped at a tree whose limbs caved into arches and whose leaves sank into pits on each branch as if they were dens for them. Beyond it, a swamp breathed, and a single croak quaked beneath him louder now.

He placed a hand on the trunk and steadied himself. "Who is there? I am not here to cause harm."

The croak twisted into raspy words. "Ancient One... time has not been kind since your absence."

"Saj? Is that you?" He peered into the swamp. Smooth rocks scattered about the surface. He watched each one, thinking one was her.

Theodore moved around the tree, and there, on the side of the swamp, Saj stood with water up to her waist. Green film collected onto her abdomen. She had a twig basket in the crook of her arm. Her other webbed hand carried a fistful of strands of a gray-bluish plant that resembled bipectinate antennae. "Ilums. It's the perfect time to harvest." She tossed them into the basket and dove her hand back into the swamp. She repeated the motion, her hand diving as her knees bent, pulling them by their roots and placing them in the basket.

"What do you use them for?" Theodore stayed where he was and curiously watched.

She pursed her thin lips together. A quick croak came out as if to chuckle. "Has it been that long since you bought soap from me?"

"It has, but I wasn't aware of how this plant looks or how you made them."

Saj smiled with her lips sealed. As she gathered more, she trudged closer and closer to Theodore until she was right before him. The stone earrings that cascaded down her pointed ears clinked together. A hollow and rhythmic sound.

"Have you decided what you will do?"

"Were you listening?" Theodore cocked his head, neither angry nor surprised.

She nodded. "I don't think folks realize how far away we can hear." She placed the basket down. Mud and water seeped out of the bottom and sides. "Now, an answer?"

Theodore rubbed his forehead. "I have an inkling of what I should do. I just—"

"Unsure of how to do it?"

"If I can do it."

"Not alone, of course. Should you get back to your friends? I can hear them anxiously murmuring."

Theodore peered back. "Come with me."

Audrey sat on the grass, her body slumped over with her legs pulled to her chest. Spears of grass clung between her wet toes. Ben leaned against a tree trunk, squeezing out the strands of his hair. The sunlight drained them of pigment in its white light.

"Audrey, Ben."

Audrey glanced over her shoulder, her hair falling in waves and dangling onto the grass. She shot up when she noticed Saj. Awkwardly, she tripped over a tree root and caught the tree branch, balancing herself. Audrey cleared her throat as she eyed Ben and Theodore, who snickered. She grabbed her shirt from the branch and pulled it on. Her bra, still wet, darkened the front into blotches.

"This is Saj. I've known her since I was a child."

"It's nice to meet you," Ben said, bowing his head.

"Yes, very nice to meet you," Audrey said.

"My, my. Cursed soil. You both have traveled a long way." Saj placed her hand on Theodore's arm and squeezed gently. "No wonder Folengower felt dark—our light left."

Theodore placed his hand on hers. "I didn't think my absence would be noticeable."

Saj smacked her lips together. "Even those who haven't met you have heard of your strength and kindness. Many of us have been waiting."

"For what?" Audrey blurted out.

"The next Ancient One. We all have."

Theodore fixated on her. "*We?*"

"Come. You all will be welcomed."

Saj guided them back to the swamp and beyond it. Towering flowers of fire bounced from their springlike stems. They stood in a line that carried on into another row, creating sides. Saj leapt in between the two. Theodore parted the flowers and went through before holding the sides apart until Audrey and Ben made their way in. Audrey brushed her hands down a stalk, her head tilted up.

There was no shape to describe what was before them or if the space ended at all. The ground splintered as if wood oozed moss and mud. The fire-like flowers bloomed over in parts that completely blocked out the sun. Those patches had larger cracks in the ground where mud flowed as if a stream. Stilted homes and shops peeked out from tall trees and shrubs that they hid behind. If it weren't for the colorful lights that beamed from the insects that circled, they would remain hidden. Many of the roofs sagged with black granite-like leaves.

Goling children with infectious laughs leapt around a massive mossy stump while adults stood and chatted, some holding babies wrapped in blankets of fuzzy mint-colored leaves. Other folk carried on shopping or enjoying company at what looked to be a small café. Smoke billowed out in rapid spurts of amber. Other structures spied behind giant plants. It was impossible to tell if they were shops or homes without being up close to them.

As they continued through the town, a roar sounded over and over. The closer they walked towards the sound, the ground puddled.

"Strange," Audrey mumbled as she patted her shoe into it.

The path continued in a decline and the puddle turned into a flood that eventually turned into a river with a waterfall shining below. It wasn't massive or impressively tall, but it did not lose its uniqueness on any of them as they watched the water flood and then float up the hill. They walked down and stared at it. Ben did so with his mouth agape and ready to claim any bug that made its way in.

"What is this place?" Theodore asked.

"You've never been here?" Ben asked.

Saj placed her basket on the ground. She held her hand up and dove into the water. Theodore sank his toes in the mud and edged closer to the pool of water.

Audrey grabbed his arm. "Be careful."

His shoes dug into the mud and his body slanted.

The water flowed as if void of anything beneath. Then a shape took form, then another and more, until they muddled together into a massive shadowy figure. Saj erupted out of the water with three more golings. Water splashed out and traveled up the hill. The largest goling swam towards Theodore. His ears were at such a point that they curled back.

"Ancient One..." He peered over his shoulder before continuing, "We have waited a long time for what's coming."

"I have heard. And your name?" Theodore stepped down into the water with them.

Ben and Audrey waited next to each other.

The golings formed a circle around him. Ben edged closer to the pool, as if he was ready for anything. Audrey stayed put with her arms crossed.

In a hushed voice, the goling said, "Some of us know the truth. Call me Rew." His eyes darted back and forth from Theodore's eyes, as if he needed to confirm that he knew the truth too.

Theodore cocked his head and rubbed at the strands of his beard, but he gave nothing away.

"You know the truth, right?" Saj said with desperation, trembling in her words.

"If you speak of my father's crimes..." His eyes closed when he heard them make a deep croak as one. "I only just learned a couple of days ago. It has been a shock... even to me."

"And?" Rew said.

"I will not involve you in my burden."

Rew shook his head. "It is not a choice. Not in a time of war. We have shared many burdens, not of our wants. I find that yours is one of justice, not a hunger for blood."

"You are right. But I have to warn you, I am not on either side. I hope to unify Folengower once and for all."

"A feat not done without allies. You're in luck. On this cursed soil..." Rew sank into the water until his mouth touched it. He blew into it, and rings of bubbles formed around them. The bubbles popped and calmed into a circular mound. He rose and said, "Our blood bound or corpse thistles, we will drown."

In unison, the rest shouted, "*Our blood bound or corpse thistles, we will drown.*" They formed a line in front of Theodore, their arms linked and their heads askew. Rew unlinked his arms, and his hands flipped as if he was performing an act of prestidigitation. They rested on his throat with his thumbs side by side above his sternum.

"I am honored by your loyalty. Allies may be hard to come by, but until we have a fighting chance, I will need any morsel of whispers brought to my attention."

Rew waded forward. "I speak for all of us, we do well at hearing secrets."

High above, a crash of what sounded like plates banged together. A cacophony of noise erupted followed by laughter and banter. Rew said something and snickered, but neither Ben nor Audrey understood.

Theodore placed a hand on his hip. "Who amongst you is willing to be a leader in my army?"

Audrey's lips parted as if surprised.

Saj stood next to Rew. "Rew is a leader amongst us." She said "us" with such emphasis that the others nodded or shouted Rew's name.

"Is this true?" Theodore raised one brow.

"It is."

"Is this what you want?"

Rew gave a single nod.

"We have much to discuss, then. Is there a place we can discuss alone, perhaps out of water?"

"Of course, Ancient One. Follow me."

The other golings dove except Saj, who watched Rew until he leapt out to the hillside. He peered over his shoulder at her. She gave him a look, one that he understood. Rew lifted one of his webbed hands up before turning and trudging up the watery hill.

Before long, they made it back to the stilted structures, to one that was nearly invisible had it not been for a raven that hopped across the roof. It croaked, "WHERE... WHERE?"

Ben jumped at the voice. Then he flinched his head back slightly, nudging Audrey. "Isn't that Elm?"

Audrey stepped closer and studied it before shaking her head. "I don't know. How could you tell?"

"He's right," Rew said.

Theodore waved his arms around. "*Elm*." Elm flew down and landed on his shoulder. He stroked his chest feathers. "My, my, I am happy to see you. What stories do you have to tell and..." Theodore turned his attention to Rew. His eyes narrowed. "And what on cursed soil has brought you here?"

"I called her." Rew licked his bruise-colored lips, as if he could taste what he last ate.

"How?" Theodore frowned. "This is Eli—the Bloodtress' bird."

"Come inside. I can answer any questions there."

Theodore turned to Elm, uncertain if he should trust him. Elm clicked three times and flew back to the hidden house.

Floating planks curved into an 'S' shape up to the balcony of the home. Ben scratched his forehead at the tip of his scar. An echo came and went of his screams and Eliza's cries as Taylor cut into his skin. He shivered. "How are we supposed to get up that?"

Rew leaped up to the first plank. Moss beaded down the sides while hints of glowing slate shined through, as though animal eyes gazed back. Rew ignored his question and continued to the top, where he waited for them. "I can offer a place for your, uh, friends to stay while we talk."

Theodore held his hand up. "I don't think you understand. They will be joining me." Theodore reached down into the cracked soil and scooped up a handful. It was neither mud nor sand nor dirt. Bewildered, he rubbed it around all his fingers. Then, as if he remembered why he had grabbed it, he clasped his hands together. Light floated between his fingers. He pulled them apart and threw them back and then towards the floating wood. More shadowed in between the empty spaces.

He motioned his hand forward, and Audrey shrugged and stepped on the first and the next. Ben and Theodore followed to the top. Mud layered over the balcony, some parts cracked like the ground below. If you looked close enough, you could see a fern-colored stone with black zigzags breathing underneath. Even through their shoes, the chill of it licked their toes. A giant leaf fawned over the door. At the top, the leaf parted into hornlike structures. Bushels of burnt orange fruit that looked like melting stars were attached to the sides.

Rew moved the leaf to the side. One fruit jiggled loose, bounced off the porch and splattered a green goo down below. Rew motioned them into the house. Ben leaned over the railing and stared for a moment at the squashed fruit. Audrey tugged at his arm. Theodore had already vanished behind the leaf.

The room welcomed them with the smell of sugared butter and petrichor before their eyes could even adjust to the dim light and see the dried corpse thistles hanging from the ceiling. Theodore smiled with his lips closed.

"Sit," Rew said. He wandered around the room, with his fingers tapping at the hanging orbs that reminded Audrey of an anglerfish. Each one illuminated at his touch, and the room brightened considerably.

Mushrooms sprouted out of every crevice, sticking to the walls like vines. In the center, there was a circle rug and moss-infected stumps that were carved to look like proper chairs. to the side, a quaint kitchen opened behind them. A smudged window above one counter gave the view of a leaf half covering it, while the rest of it gawked at the river. On the opposite side, a ladder made of branches led up to a dark loft.

Elm flew around the room before eventually landing on Theodore's arm.

"Sit," Rew repeated. He sat down on the marbled colored rug. His ears drooped back, and he stretched his feet before relaxing. The webbing was almost thin enough to see through and wrinkled as he moved.

In clumsy unison, they all chose a spot to sit. Ben almost sat on the same stump Audrey moved towards.

Rew stared into each of their eyes in order, not uncomfortably, just sincerely and curiously. His eyes intensified in the light, so much so that they were opaque with a pale pink glint. He had sunspots of brown against his pale green skin that showed on his bare chest.

"Where would you like me to start, Ancient One?"

"How were you able to call Elm?" Theodore raised his left eyebrow.

"Ah... Elm." Rew placed one of his hands on his cheek and rubbed at it. "I found her just beyond here in Nniar's forest. I had been caring for my child at the time, and he came across her wounded. I saved her, and for it, she gave me a feather." He looked away as if in thought. "I believe it was shortly after you and the Bloodtress left."

"A bond formed." Theodore stared off and nodded. "Elm, I need you to find Eliza. Has she not called for you?"

Elm shook her head and ruffled her feathers.

"She might not know the birds are back," Audrey said.

Ben nodded.

"Find her." Theodore lifted his arm. "Rew, do you have anything I can send a message with?"

Rew leapt up and wandered over to a side table. He pulled out dried-out leaves, the same kind that adorned his roof, and a long, skinny pointed bone. He rummaged through a drawer, clinking things that sounded of glass against each other before settling on a glass jar of muddied-looking liquid. "Here."

Theodore walked over to him. Rew unscrewed the lid of the jar and dipped the bone in. Theodore held it over the leaf and took a breath. The ink blotched onto it, and he cursed under his breath. He wrote, *Branch, be brave. The moon has seen me, and I have found the truth*. Below it, he signed the word, *Storm*.

He quickly rolled it up and Elm, who was standing patiently on the shelf next to him, snatched it with her beak. "Make sure she reads this. Fly swiftly back to us." He lifted the leaf, and out she flew.

Theodore walked back over to them. "I believe you had more to tell?"

Audrey slid her hand under Theodore's. He squeezed it gently.

Rew stared at their hands strangely. He licked his lips and said, "Have you heard of The Choke?"

Theodore cocked his head. "Once. I do not remember who they are. Enlighten me."

Rew smirked. "After Queen Callum was murdered and the war left Folengower forever divided, folks like me have kept in touch. We knew when the smell of blood returned that we would only stand by a leader who would heal Folengower. The leader of The Choke will be pleased to hear from you."

"Why haven't you reached out before or done anything in providing the truth?" Ben said.

Audrey's nudged Ben in the side with her elbow.

Theodore rubbed his index finger on his bottom lip and patted Ben's shoulder. "I am curious to know the answer," he replied.

Rew frowned. "Time."

"What do you mean?"

"Truth cannot be given to those who are deaf."

"I understand, but what has changed?"

Metal vibrated loudly behind them. Rew leapt up and took to the kitchen. He snipped petals from a hanging plant and tossed them into a mostly silver pot with two dangling handles. The contents of the pot sputtered, and steam flooded the room. A humid warmth cradled them, and a smell seeped into their nostrils. It smelled of nostalgia, the kind that can never fully be caught and remembered.

As Rew stirred the liquid, he squinted his eyes and said, "What is it for you?"

Audrey held her arm up to her mouth and coughed.

"What... do you mean?" Ben managed to get out in raspy breaths.

Theodore moved his arms around, like a child chasing bubbles. "Calund juice?"

Rew chuckled. "I'm surprised, Ancient One. I never thought you would've tried it before."

"I may have grown up in a castle, but I had many friends who were kind enough to let me explore the world beyond."

"Kind of them. This comes from a creature that has the magical ability to trick its predators by leaving trails of goop. It does this most of the day, leaving a matte black goop that eventually turns to silver." Rew stirred at the contents before sipping the liquid from the spoon. He smacked his lips together. "Mmmm... Once it is satisfied, it stops excreting and goes to its home. Once there, it waits for any animal to follow a trail. The smell is unique for everyone. It is always a scent that means something. The calund must have magic to alert them when they have an admirer of what they left behind because the calund will come back and eat them. The creature who stalked the trail gets stuck in it and has no escape. Sometimes I find a helpless creature stuck, and I move them off of it. It seems a terrible way to die." He paused and grabbed a set of oval wood bowls. He lifted the pan and poured some into each. The steam flooded again and dissipated quickly. "It is the perfect ingredient, especially for new guests."

Rew made his way back over to them with his hands and arms full of bowls. Theodore helped grab one that nearly slid from him. Rew hopped back to the kitchen and picked flower petals from the vase on the counter. He placed one in each bowl and sat on the floor with his long legs crossed. Audrey gazed at Theodore, who took the flower and stuck his lips into the trumpet-like shape and breathed in. Ben twirled the flower in his fingers. Then, as if the flower were a straw, Theodore swallowed.

Audrey's eyes lit up. Theodore, amused, put his mouth back in and slurped. Ben choked back a laugh.

"Have I done something wrong?" Rew rubbed his throat.

Theodore wiped his lips with his arm. "Cursed soil, no. They have been exposed to a lot of new experiences." He motioned to Ben and Audrey to drink. They did so quickly.

"If you suspect where they are from, it will be a danger to you and anyone to make it known," Theodore said with a glare, and his body stiffened.

Rew gazed at them, and for a time, the only sounds came from their mouths. "The strug depletion changed everything," Rew said dryly.

Ben slurped up the last bit of the liquid. It reminded him of blackberry pancakes Harper used to make while they camped. The warmth clung to his tongue and even the seeds of the berries felt stuck in one of his teeth even though he'd seen no seeds floating in the bowl. He'd eaten it fast at first until realizing it would all be gone soon. A memory he could taste. "This is amazing."

Audrey searched her thoughts for what she smelled. It was an old memory, and one she was unsure she wanted to remember. She tasted potatoes first, then roast with homemade gravy. Her grandma flashed in her mind. She had forgotten the dinners and long nights playing games with her grandma and grandpa when they would watch her. It was a love she'd never had at home, and yet here it came, flooding into her. She sipped from the straw more. Her lip twitched. "It is wonderful," she said, her voice quaking.

Theodore had already finished first. He rubbed his finger over his lip. Rew, delighted, waited patiently for him to say more.

Rew continued, "Folks are whispering for a change, but none of us knew when to make a move."

"A move? Did you mean to overthrow my father on your own?"

"Some of us want that... but then there is The Choke. We would rather unite Folengower than burn it down with no obvious way to move forward."

"When can I meet with the leader?"

"I can arrange a meeting tomorrow."

"Good. I have some things I need to take care of. Should I meet you back here?"

Rew grinned. Two of his pebble-like teeth showed. He leapt up and wrote something down from the table. He rolled up the leaf and handed it to Theodore. "Read it later."

Theodore ran his finger along the veins. Rew bowed.

4

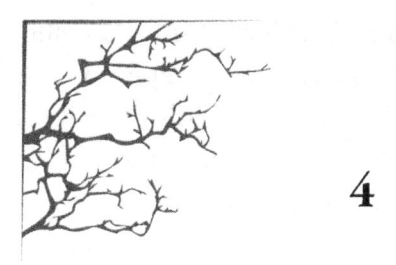

They stood at the edge of the forest. Conifer trees' shadows striped the ground in never-ending lines. Audrey stepped forward, and a twig cracked beneath her foot. Theodore put a hand in front of her waist, halting her. She raised a hand to signal Ben to stop as Theodore put a finger to his lips. They turned their heads up as if to listen. Ben eyed the towers. Though they were still far from them, he felt bumps rise on his skin, as if he would turn into a toad at any moment.

"Wait here." Theodore reached down and gathered the dead from the forest floor—twigs, dirt, leaves and insects. He squeezed them tightly in his hand, and when he opened his fist, black fire gnawed out of his palm. Each step was with great care and stealth in the same way luna moths use their long tails to confuse bats from eating them. A slow wind tunneled around the castle at him. Theodore shielded his face with his hand and held in a cough. His saliva pooled in his mouth, tainted with the smell the breeze brought. Reluctantly, he swallowed.

Stench beckoned him to follow the path beyond the castle's moss-infected bricks. The garden screeched before he made it. A shard of stone from the once beautiful fountain scraped against another, and when it did, the stone rocked as if it were a rocking horse before tumbling onto its side and splitting in two. The culprit, a lone creature, bolted on top and scurried towards the towers, flitting its spiky brown tail. Theodore barely had time to turn his head. It dove into the foly weeds, letting the tiny pink blooms hide it.

Amongst the excitement, he breathed in, and the air sickened his lungs, forcing him to focus on why he walked in that direction in the first place.

Ben followed Audrey, who inched closer and closer to the clearing. "Wait, Audrey," he whispered.

Audrey swatted behind her without so much as a glance in his direction.

"*Audrey.*"

Audrey breathed in and turned around. A harsh glare landed on Ben. "What?"

Ben bit his cheek. "We really should wait."

"What if he needs help?" Audrey crossed her arms.

"He escaped Kinsington without us." Ben shrugged.

Audrey crossed her arms. "I know." She stopped walking. "I just don't want him to have to do everything alone."

"I think we need to let him do what he thinks is right. As much as I want to pretend that I know what I'm doing in this new world, I don't and neither do you."

"I know I am not much help in this world, you don't need to tell me. It pounds in my head like a coffin nail every day."

"I didn't mean to—"

Audrey held her hand up. "I know. I just..." She crossed her arms and turned away. "I just need to have a purpose here or else—"

"You'll want to go back to Harthsburg?" Ben raised his eyebrow.

Audrey shook her head. "No, of course not. But the facts are that we have no magic, hardly any fighting experience, and definitely not to this magnitude. I just wonder what we will do when we are in the middle of battles."

"What do you want to do, then?"

Audrey's lips parted. She shook her head and rose her hands, as if done with her very existence.

Ben lowered her hands and wrapped his arms around her. She weakly pushed him away, but after several of these same moments living together, he knew better than to let her go. "We will figure everything out. The important thing is that we are here, and we aren't as useless as you think." His nose wrinkled. "What is that smell?"

Audrey swatted at Ben. "How dare you."

Ben chuckled. "No, not you. Take a sniff at the air."

"The cave." Audrey pulled the collar of her shirt up to her nose.

Ben shivered. "Flesh melting." They thought back to Harthsburg, to the bodies of their fellow townspeople slowly melting away covered in strug.

"We need to find where Theodore went."

"Aud..."

Audrey ran out to the clearing and looked towards the towers and then back to the castle. Theodore was hidden from sight. She followed to the rancid trail. Ben creeped behind.

Audrey found Theodore hunched over on the east side of the castle just outside of the forest and standing as if he were about to propose. He held his arm up when he heard the footsteps approaching.

"Wait," he said with trembling breaths.

"What's happened?" Audrey froze midstep.

Theodore rubbed his mouth and backed away. Beyond him, a pack of finnix gnawed on what was left of a pile of bodies. Strug dripped from their lips and fur, their mauve color now a dirty purple. One clutched a bloodied, deteriorating finger in its jaws, and another licked and clawed at an eye socket that was plump with muscle. The last finnix prodded a skull around with its paws as if playing with a ball. Muscle fragments clung to parts of it, and every time the finnix growled, he bit and shook it violently before passing it back between its paws.

Ben arrived breathing heavily and immediately placed his hand over his mouth as he gagged.

"Who are they?" Audrey said, wide eyes unable to look away. Her hand rested on Theodore's shoulder as much to steady herself as to provide comfort to him.

"I don't know. Cursed Knights, I imagine. I found some armor in the mess."

Audrey reached out her hand. Theodore exhaled and gripped her hand. She helped steady him as he rose.

"They must have left in a hurry; the Eltrist aren't known for leaving their food unsupervised. There's a chance that someone else is here. Although, if it were

Cursed Knights..." Theodore peered over his shoulder at the castle. He scanned the spots he knew they watched from and frowned when he saw no one. "They would already have found me. It's more likely that we just missed Eliza." Theodore's palm flickered to life with magic. He walked next to the castle's wall. His hand graced the brick as he went. "Unless she managed to stay behind."

"They might not have even brought her here," Ben said.

They followed him to the front of the castle and stepped inside.

Inside the castle, faint echoes haunted the halls. Ben continued through with rigid strides. Audrey crossed her arms snuggly as if cold. Theodore kicked the glass out of the way while his body hunched with wolflike movement. The staircase shined dully in darkened smudges of mud, yellowing grass stains and dark blood spots. Almost too dark to realize that's what it was until Theodore knelt to the first step, put his index finger on it and rubbed it like a dusty window. He couldn't deny the musty smell of strug and copper laced together.

Up they went until they reached the hallway. The remains of Eliza's door contorted as if it walked limp. Theodore stopped at it. His eyes trailed up and through the holes.

"Well, that's one way to break down a door," Audrey said.

"Eliza," Ben gulped. He gripped at his chest.

"Huh?"

"This is Eliza's room," Theodore said.

Ben nodded.

"Oh, shit." Audrey's eyes lit. "Were you two in here when they attacked you?"

"Yeah, I tried to stop them, but..." He shrugged.

Theodore placed a hand on his shoulder. "You did. A broken door is but little concern to the life inside it."

"They still got her."

"Not on your watch."

"We will get her back," Audrey said.

"I have no doubt that she is alive; fortunately, she is a Bloodtress. She is worth more alive than dead." Theodore turned his gaze to the end of the hall. "Until their twilight bodies find me."

"They won't... at least not when we aren't ready for it," Audrey said. "But what are we doing up here?"

"I need to retrieve some things from my room. That is if everything is still intact."

The crimson door had no scars of torture like the other door. Theodore turned the knob. His body jolted as a flood of energy seared through his hand. "Someone used magic to open it." He put his hand in front of Ben and Audrey and waved them away as he peeked through the slit. He pushed it open all the way, half expecting someone to jump out, though it was hollow of life.

Theodore walked over to the side of the window. His hand brushed against the wall. A long line cracked in its place, as if it had come to life and moaned open.

Audrey muttered, "How many secret doors are in this place?"

He reached in and pulled out a sword. The pommel had an obsidian stone carved into a triangle with the point facing the tip of the blade, and the grip had four sunwave stones down it. The guard mirrored corpse thistle leaves, spindly like an insect with thornlike wings. He set it on the bed, and the light shined on the sharp edges. He pulled out a black tunic, pants that matched, a carved belt that resembled bark, and his armor, the same as the Cursed Knights. He gently laid them out on his bed ceremoniously.

He took his shirt off and placed the tunic on. The top was embroidered with the mark of an Ancient One—circles started at his collarbones and an upside-down triangle with smooth edges was in the middle. Corpse thistles and leaves surrounded it. Theodore moved his fingers across it.

Ben stared out the window, brushing his brown hair out of his face. "Weapons for us?"

Theodore paused as if surprised. He proceeded to put the pants on and wrap the belt around his waist. He placed his armor on, careful to not get the many intricate spiderweb-like strands caught on his head. The obsidian-colored armor blended in with his attire so well that it tricked the eyes that it didn't exist.

Theodore clawed at the top of the armor that rested at his neck, as if it were a noose. "There is still time."

"For what?" Audrey put her hands on her hips. "Don't. Even. Say. It," she fumed.

Ben frowned and sighed. "Save your breath and please finally get it through that head of yours that we will be right here beside you."

Theodore averted his gaze. He sucked in his breath, almost unable to let it out, and when he did, it sounded like a hiss. "Then we have one more room to stop in." He walked back to the closet and pushed aside a box to get to the very back. He leaned inside of the narrow space and retrieved a dyed carf flower sheath as black as the rest of his clothing. Audrey stared at Theodore and placed his hand over her heart.

"Why is it racing?" Theodore's eyes lit up.

Audrey tenderly rubbed the back of his hand with her thumb and whispered, "When we have some time alone, I would very much like you to leave this on."

Theodore almost purred, "Oh, really now?" He pulled her closer and gently kissed her lips.

"I can go." Ben shrugged.

"No... no. We really must be moving." Theodore grinned at Audrey. "No matter how much I would rather be doing something else."

They left the comfort of Theodore's room and went over to and up the other staircase, to the top. Two halls forking one way looked similar to the one they'd just been in. The other one was abundant with moss and an entire mass of life, from insects to what could have been a toad croaking, though they could not see one.

"Wait. This is a test of sorts." Theodore took one step onto the spongy floor. He looked over his shoulder at the other two before walking carefully and strangely across the floor, as if his limbs were now that of an arachnid. He lifted his leg at times and squeezed his body against the wall. After about six feet of his arachnid-limb walk, he stopped and knelt. A stone carving of a mouth sick with a black tar-like substance opened to his touch. The lips parted and forced a key drenched in the black stuff into his hand. Theodore clenched it, and the mouth shut tightly with its teeth bared as if to bite his fingers off.

"Almost finished," he called back. He pulled the substance off of the key that clung to it like glue. Finally, it sprung off, and he flicked it several times from his fingers until it landed on the lips.

The corner of the hall had two doors edged out like two corner shelves meeting in the middle. They were neither short nor tall, but both at the same time depending on the angle that you looked at them. The crimson gloss on them bared no distinction from the Cursed Knights' eyes. Theodore slunk to them. Keyholes mirrored one another.

Theodore moved the key to the left door, his hand shaky.

"Everything okay?" Audrey said, lifting her leg to step onto the mossy floor.

"*Don't, don't*," Theodore yelled.

Ben grabbed her and moved her away from it just in time.

"Dramatic much?" Audrey said to Ben.

"I'd rather you live. We don't know what all this is."

"A sort of booby trap," Theodore called back, now with his other hand holding his trembling one. "I said to wait," he said with a sharpness that he usually reserved for enemies.

Audrey frowned, and a heat started in her cheeks.

Ben rubbed her shoulder and whispered, "He is trying to keep you... us safe."

Audrey nodded. "What's the problem?"

Theodore coughed. "I don't remember which door it is. They randomly switch, and before I would be told, but..." He eyed each one, trying to sense which one was correct. He mumbled, "But I've been in Harthsburg."

He shoved the key in, his eyes shut tight as a clam, and his heart followed in an aching pause as his breath did. The door clicked in a mechanical sort of way before igniting a black light. Ben and Audrey scrunched together to the side, though their gaze could hardly see what had begun even with them on their tippytoes nearly falling over one another. It wouldn't matter if they could see the thick black light that pulsed before Theodore, they would hear it.

One, two, three, Theodore counted in his mind. On three, his heart resumed, his breath released, his eyes widened, and for a moment his lips bowed in a smile. *Four*. His expression soured, and he threw his body down hard enough to bruise his ribs in the process. With a growl, he screamed, "*Get down*."

The black light whipped back and propelled like a catapult past Theodore's body. Ben, in shock, stood still as Audrey landed on her stomach. She hooked her arm around Ben's legs, and, like a scythe, toppled him. He moaned as his back hit the hard floor. Light barreled past them, not stopping until it hit a wall and exploded. Their bodies, the walls, the floor all vibrated as one.

Theodore's fingers gripped under the mossy floor. Bits of it stuck under his nails and a sharpness from something in the mixture of the verdant space cut into his index finger. Blood dripped onto the springy phyllids.

Audrey stretched her neck and peered over her shoulder at the wall that had exploded. The black light extinguished, leaving behind a hole that opened like a portal to the outside, its edges seared in an ashen paste. Ben frantically patted down his body.

"Your limbs are all intact," Audrey grumbled as she cracked her neck.

Ben sighed. "Are you unscathed?"

Audrey nodded. "Theodore?" she called.

The end of the hall filled with silence. Audrey pushed herself up and called him again. Theodore hovered his hand long enough for her to see it dripping onto the forest floor. A moan escaped his lips.

Ben sat up, his eyes flickering. "Are you hurt?"

Theodore tried pushing his body up, only to have his arms give out. Heaviness filled the air. Not smoke. At least not the smell of it, but a lick of it perhaps. But that wasn't all. The other, more pungent smell lingered and prodded and leapt as soon as it started to smell familiar. Then, poof, it vanished.

"Not by the magic at least..." Theodore let out an uncomfortable laugh. "The floor is not kind to me, I'm afraid. I just need a minute."

Theodore pushed up again, though his arms wobbled as he stood up. Needle-like things protruded from his palms, chest, torso and legs.

Audrey gasped and covered her mouth.

"It's like acupuncture," Ben said. Audrey shoved her elbow into his ribs. Ben swatted her hand away.

Theodore shakily backed into the wall. Below him, a haphazard pile of the needle-like things netted onto the moss.

"Well, at least I know which door it is now," he said with a fake smile.

Audrey bit her lip. "There's no more?"

"Balls of killing light?" Theodore chuckled. "No, there shouldn't be." He placed the key in the other door. It let out a whirl of a sound. He pulled it open and stepped inside. "See." His hand waved. "No trap."

Inside, organic-shaped metal hooks lined the walls. The metal, nearly black and pounded into form, had craters and lines, as if they had been forged by a herd of chackles running over them. At the back, mountain-like cupboards joined at each branch that prodded out of the sides. Most were left with nothing, though a few hooks carried sheaths with swords left, but most were cleared out. The fronts had carvings over the arched window doors. One door gaped open. Theodore peered inside. A single piece of chest armor remained. He pulled open another cabinet and another that had once held jars upon jars of strug mixtures. They were all bare of contents.

The branches in between carried nothing, though Theodore knew they had held potions before battles and blood knocked on the door. He wondered why there was anything left at all. Could it be that the last person had been too late to retrieve the rest?

Whatever the reason, it couldn't matter now. He collected the remaining items on the hooks and the lonely piece of armor and locked the door behind him. With his hands full, he balanced the key in his hand and knelt at the mouth. He tapped it with the tip. The lips parted, and back in went the key to be choked on until the door would need to be opened again.

Audrey and Ben helped grab what was in his hands.

"I never thought my home would attack me, yet here we are." Theodore shook his head at the now giant hole. "Well, at least no one will suspect I was the one to cause damage this time."

"What would that matter now? This will soon be all yours." Audrey smiled.

"We shall see." He leaned over and kissed her forehead. His smile couldn't last, not when it barely shone and his mind lived in the future, off on its own missions to figure out how to lead an army when his insecurities latched on to him like a thousand ticks. There would be times when he felt in control and confident, a fleeting feeling at best.

Downstairs, they sat on a cushion sliced every which way. The innards puffed out in a viridescent mess. Ben twirled his fingers in between them, as if the softness comforted him. Theodore sat in the middle of Ben and Audrey, his legs arched, lazily holding the leaf scroll that Rew had handed him.

5

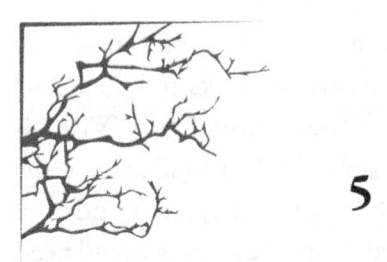

Glowing orange light streaked above the Sea of Calip. Dawn's eye was watchful over the fish, the sea calmed as usual for the early hours when The Moon, Esmeray, made her slow form of invisibility to the people below. While the folks below believed her to sleep too, it was a falsehood, for The Moon never sleeps.

Folly's blue feathers were too bright to camouflage amongst the coppery browns, dazzling greens, angry reds and dirty yellows; instead, they stood out like spring in the dead of winter. She pecked at the ground and pulled up a slimy creature that she happily slugged back into her mouth before searching for more. In the middle of her search, a noise echoed. Her head shifted and her eyes peered at the coming dawn. The new light created a swarm of rays that crept in between the Anorphus' branches. In the lighting, she could see a faint liquid in narrow cuts that the gigantic tree had received over the years. The liquid was black and shiny. Fatal. Folly's eyes lingered on it until the noise came again. She spread her wings and took flight away from the poison and her slimy food.

Queen Agden held Folly's cage, which resembled a draped crystallized web. The little door was open and waiting. Folly dove into it. Queen Agden closed it, sealing the crystal door back in place. "We have work to do," she said.

Folly responded with a querulous tone.

"You'll see."

A Cursed Knight bowed with his fist in front of his right eye to her as she passed. Queen Agden tightened her jaw and returned a single nod in his direction. A shiver ran down her spine. Her hand gripped the handle on Folly's cage harder, causing the rawness of the crystals to print into her skin.

"And where are you off to?" Korrigan rapped on the cage three times.

Folly puffed up and hopped to the back. Agden tensed and stepped to the side.

"I thought you were off doing more important things than sneaking up on me."

Korrigan scoffed. "Answer my question."

"If you haven't heard, the birds are back... and work is inevitable during war, is it not?"

Korrigan lowered his gaze, his eyes wandering to the crowd hardly a tent away. "I have." A smile cut through his tight jaw. "But did I give you something else to do, or have you forgotten that orders come from me?"

"I am the queen of Nniar and..."

Korrigan raised his hand to her lips in such a way that it appeared to onlookers as a loving moment, but his eyes never met hers, and she could taste the poison on his fingertips, ready to strike if need be. "What are you up to?"

Agden, too scared to turn her head, let her eyes scan. Folks moved about the tents, and the taste of fish moved back up her esophagus. She focused on the Anorphus' leaves hovering several feet above, swaying occasionally when the wind felt the need to release a bout of chaos. She glared at it.

"Cursed soil." Agden huffed a laugh. "What paranoia has struck you?"

Korrigan whispered in her ear, "My very words can change the course of your life, though I would hope that we would rule together like it's always been." He gripped her sides and his lips touched hers soft at first, but the harshness came and quickly faded except for the taste of his scorn. She would taste it for days.

Agden, subtle in her discomfort, swallowed and felt her body instinctively relax. She even managed to crack a half-decent smile in case anyone was watching. "Bruthren mentioned corpse thistles needed to be extracted for battle. I assumed I would stay working with him until I am needed elsewhere."

Korrigan raised his head with a glint of something—confusion or self-doubt. "Of course. Don't let your duties make you late for dinner." He released her with a huff.

"I would never miss such an important part of my day." Her hand was still curled tightly on Folly's cage. She hit her shoulder into his as she passed and walked away. He stilled, his hands clenched at his sides for a moment, before walking in the opposite direction.

Queen Agden entered a tent. She scanned all the folks who worked, but she lingered on Kalien. An instant smell of sugared butter and petrichor made her take a deep breath. One of her eyebrows raised as she focused back on Kalien. He stood off to the side of the table, his face tight, his eyes far from bright and in deep concentration on something not in the room. Cressa stood out with her short, phoenix red hair, and when Kalien hardly acknowledged her when she asked him something, she continued to sweep the floor with placid composure. Today, she had on a belt with several containers attached and a rag that hung off the side.

"He's quite unusual," Bruthren said behind Agden.

Agden, startled, stiffened her back. "Bruthren..." She said it with exhaustion in her voice, like a mom having to repeat herself for the tenth time in five minutes. "You will do well not to spy on your queen."

"My queen, I am appalled that you would think such of me." Bruthren rubbed his glasses on the end of his heather gray shirt. Fog-like glaze moved about them, streaking to the other side. "It is merely an observation." Bruthren placed his glasses back on and bowed in a curtsy-like stance. Agden looked at him sternly and motioned for him to stand back up.

"How is he healing?"

"Kalien?"

Agden gave a single nod.

"Well, Craven checked on him the other day. His bone is back where it should be." Bruthren took a deep and dramatic breath in and out. "So wonderful. And I have yet to find him fiddling with his arm as though it's foreign today."

Kalien's face twitched as though he heard their conversation, and he poked at his arm, as if the bone still stabbed out of his flesh.

"Not everything lasts. Perhaps it's a new game with him? He's but a tadpole in a river of predators."

"Of course." Queen Agden tapped her foot and scanned the room.

The table's contents had changed quickly after the success of the birds returning. Five large wooden contraptions rested on the table next to a heap of wilted corpse thistles. They tossed their ultramarine petals and long green tendrils in such a way that they bent and curved in strange ways. The workers placed handfuls into the contraption, ready to be crushed and left with only the sticky innards. The person on the end of one placed a wooden board over the top and, with a glove on, pressed it down. Goggles protruded out from her eyes as if mini fishbowls were suctioned to her. The sides of the goggles were made from carf flower, stronger than chackle hides. She then used the handle on the side to crank in a circular motion. The corpse thistles made a sickening slurping sound as they drained. Hollowed-out sticks let the liquid flow into a round bucket on the floor. Its blue color carried into the nectar covered in a toxic milky sac. The contents jiggled as more plopped into it. The worker added more corpse thistles and repeated at a constant speed.

She reached for more corpse thistles and forced the wood board down. Her muscles flexed, and she rose on her tippy-toes to add more pressure to the overabundance she'd placed inside. Nectar squirted out at her, landing on her lip. Her eyes bulged and, without thinking, she wiped her lip, only to spread it into her mouth.

"*Don't*," a worker yelled to her.

She fell to the floor with her legs up at her chest. The apron she wore, made from carf flower hide, wrinkled like linen, and her goggles cracked. Everyone stopped what they were doing to help except for Bruthren, who pulled out a pouch of clawnuts. He grabbed a single nut and bit each claw one at a time, as if he wished to savor the chaos that ensued. Eventually, he grew bored and scooped out a handful of the green nuts and plopped them into his mouth. With all the cacophony, Nia ran into the tent, her sword raised from its sheath. Queen Agden pointed to the woman on the ground. Nia shoved the sword back and moved through the crowd.

Kalien slid under her, resting her head on his leg as he carefully removed her goggles and called for a clean rag. Cressa unclipped her rag and tossed it over the frantic folks around Kalien. He caught it and carefully wiped the woman's lip and asked her to open her mouth. He dabbed it inside the best he could before removing the cloth. Around the room, hands rose, ready to cover their gasping expressions, but they refrained from allowing their gloves to do the same.

"*Move*," Nia shouted as she picked Kalien up by his shirt and tossed him to the side. Kalien scowled. "Bruthren, what are you waiting for? Get Caven." She inspected the woman's lip. The inside speckled brown like a chickadee egg. In a single breath, the blotches raised like scars with a grotesque chartreuse hue surrounding.

Bruthren tipped his bag of clawnuts above his mouth. They plummeted onto his tongue. He slid the pouch back into his pocket and chewed.

"*Now.*"

"Surely, the queen can handle such a minor wound?"

Nia twitched her neck as if she were a snake about to strike. She jumped up and charged over to Bruthren, eyes narrowed in a crimson swamp. Her body stopped nearly an inch from his chewing mouth. Nutty and earthy smells flowed between his lips. "Has someone poisoned you?"

"What a strange quest—"

"Because if you haven't been, I can slit your throat so you won't have to remember how to speak to your queen. Apparently, that is too difficult for an imbecile like you. I asked you to get the healer, yet you stand here as if you are in charge."

Agden laced her hands together and watched silently.

Nia grasped his jaw with one hand and pinched until his mouth opened like a fish. Her other hand reached into her pocket. She rubbed her fingers on a cloth inside before catching his tongue. Heat scorched from her fingertips onto his tongue and illuminated his mouth.

"Wo...ah..." Bruthren squirmed.

"Laz, go get the healer."

One of the other workers quickly fled the tent.

"Laz understands orders. I bet..." Nia narrowed her gaze. "I bet they all understand that we do not force magic from the Ancient Ones." Nia squeezed his tongue, and a tremor roared through his body as the magic desiccated it.

Nia let go, a hole seared like melting fabric all black and hard cauterizing the wound.

A moment later, Laz returned huffing for air and placing his hands on his knees as he caught his breath. Caven entered shortly after, looking as frail as birch bark. He laid his eyes on Kalien, and Kalien nodded, as if to say his arm had healed from his magic. They stole Nia's gaze briefly before she turned back to Bruthren and said, "Just in time. After you assist her, Bruthren will require your attention. Take. Your. Time."

Bruthren sulked outside the tent on a stump, rambling to himself. It was only yesterday that Nia had desiccated his tongue, but his mouth looked perfectly well already despite a lingering rotting smell. Kalien walked past him, and this time Reed joined him. Reed picked two aprons off a hook and tossed one to Kalien, his eyebrow raised in suspicion. Reed shrugged in a neutral and void-of-emotions sort of way. Kalien took the goggles out of his pocket and adjusted them to fit his head. He looked crazed, like a bug. Reed fared no better, but Kalien snickered under his breath. They took to extracting corpse thistle nectar.

For hours, they squished down the sweet-smelling poison. Nia watched over them and the others who either cleaned, extracted corpse thistles or who stood at the silence table. At least that's what everyone in Kalien's tent referred to it as. The group peered over papers and hardly ever said anything, and when they would, it was only in whispers or written notes.

Strange, Kalien thought.

When Queen Agden arrived, the people at the table stood up with their arms behind their backs. Kalien watched, as he always did, with eyes wandering from his hands to the group, day after day. Over the days, the constant spying had made him hate himself. He would avert his eyes away and rub his ear on his shoulder, as if he could forget the "thing" in it. It had been days since he heard Thorn's voice in his mind. He contemplated whether she could have died when they'd opened Talkun's Tower.

Reed elbowed him and glared, though his face with his goggles on was questionable if it was intimidating or not. Kalien became more cautious of when he peeked over at the secret group huddled together.

6

The clouds billowed around them thick and roaring as their wings pushed through them as if the clouds were beasts themselves. Moisture stuck to each hair follicle like raindrops on petals. Bursts of light shot out several yards from them, and the clouds parted and groaned past. Kinsington peered over his shoulder at Pavlyn. He could barely discern her brown fur blowing in the wind.

"Did you see that?"

"Cursed Knights must be below."

Kinsington glided to the side, and Pavlyn mirrored. "The knights are hidden beneath the clouds."

"I will find what carnage they have unleashed."

Kinsington snarled. "Spare no mercy, for they will bleed as we have." Strug dripped down his sharp teeth. The lavender glow blackened as it swirled into the air. Where Pavlyn once flew became a silhouette of her form imprinted in the clouds.

Aylo and Esna came at a destructive pace. Aylo, with his white fur that could be mistaken for a cumulus cloud, slashed through the air. Esna was close behind, a permanent wry smile beneath his flared nostrils. He stuck out more than Aylo, as his gold-brown fur muddied the skies. Their tails whipped like a fishtail. The spiraled protrusions all over their tails could have been a creature of its own, especially when the fog swarmed them.

Aylo reached out his words to Kinsington's mind, "Have you located the rest?"

Kinsington darted over to them, his fur the embodiment of a void. "Pavlyn should be returning soon."

A cry gutted through the fog. Their eyes scanned below, but it was like looking into a murky pond. "For the true Ancient One." Kinsington plunged down.

Aylo snarled, cutting through the clouds. Esna licked up the strug stuck to the corner of his mouth and stretched his wings like someone would crack their knuckles before a fight.

"*Pavlyn*," Kinsington called to her mind. "Make yourself known."

The last layer of clouds moved on, and the fog let up enough to see the ground stained crimson and black. Chackles ran wildly with Cursed Knights atop or alone. They attacked Amardians on the ground, but they stayed away from the wounded Eltrists. Folks screamed, and faint Eltrists' voices of weeping and rage penetrated Kinsington's and the other Eltrists' minds.

Then, Pavlyn shrieked.

In a frenzy, Kinsington swooped down. Below, Pavlyn grasped on to a Cursed Knight. She dangled him like a doll, strug freely spilling out onto his helmet. It rolled down in clumps, like balls of yarn unraveling. It didn't take long for the dazzling glow of death to streak across his face and seep into his ears. Pavlyn plucked off his helmet as if she plucked a flower from its stem. The knight wailed, his hands trembling at his temple, careful not to touch. Pavlyn widened her maw, and in that moment, it appeared she would swallow the knight whole. Anyone who didn't know the eating habits of Eltrist would have shivered at the sight, expecting an unforgettable crunching sound to haunt them, but Pavlyn held her mouth above his head. The knight's lips parted as if to scream, and his face had a deathly pallor to it. She breathed harshly, and thick jelly-like strug flooded out of her cavernous mouth, drenching into his mouth, ears and nose. The knight kicked as his neck grew protrusions from inside. The lumps burst like a too-full kettle. Pavlyn tossed him to her growing strug pile, then pushed her wings back and forth to match her heartbeat.

Balls of fiery red light fired into the air. They exploded like flies zooming in all directions and then back together. Aylo tackled Kinsington right before a slice of the light landed where he was and shattered into the ground, sending shards of soil exploding up. Kinsington pulled away from Aylo. He slammed his front paws down like a bucking horse landing and released a roar that sent chills. For the first time since the fighting had begun, silence befell.

Cursed Knights stiffened. Amardians even gazed upon Kinsington with a flicker of fear.

"Leave them be. I would encourage you to run. Run or join the pile of strug," Kinsington's voice seeped into everyone's mind.

As their shock faded, one Cursed Knight shouted, "We do not take orders from the Eltrist." He spun his sword above his head and sliced it through an injured Eltrist who was already lying on the ground. He peered back at his fellow knights, who immediately charged back into battle.

Kinsington spoke to only Amardians, "Kill them!" He darted into the air, circling above the defiant knight.

The Cursed Knight battled an Amardian who carried a dagger and a handful of strug mixture. She threw the strug mixture in his face. Bits of it hit his helmet and dripped down. The knight flicked a bit off his cheek and grabbed her by her long silvery hair. She kicked at him and swung her dagger. It hit his armor as if it were a feather. Desperate, she reached for more of the mixture in a bag on her hip.

The knight grinned with his teeth showing. "Uh uh uh." He wiggled his pointer finger at her. Her face turned away in an unready grimace for what was to come. He moved his sword, ready to pierce through her belly, though it missed terribly as his legs lifted off the ground. He tossed his head back in pain and his eyes bulged. His sword fell from his hand, and he took to punching Kinsington's paws, which dug into his shoulder blades as easily as a knife in a pie.

Kinsington swayed in a wavelike pattern until the knight exhausted his arms. "Lead your knights away from here. If you choose not to... Look at all of them fighting."

The knight stubbornly turned away.

"*Look*." Kinsington's voice seeped into his mind and stuck like honey. "They will all be dead in a moment. Tell them."

"We do not win a battle by running," the knight said dryly.

Strug slid down Kinsington's chin. "That may be true, but your death will join the bodies that make up the vanquished today."

Kinsington swooped around, his black wings flapping harshly, and with a single movement, he let go of the knight. The knight flitted down and landed amongst the pile of strug, silent compared to the cacophony, silent compared to the screams, silent compared to the slicing of swords. Silent compared to Kinsington's voice strangling the enemies' minds.

"We are hungry." Kinsington landed with his wings spread wide next to the strug pile. "But even we can't consume you all. Run. Tell Korrigan we plan to stay."

A shiver pricked at their necks, and one person darted through the trees. More followed, slower, as they processed what had happened. Another left with a smug look on her face and her head held high as if they had won. The last four Cursed Knights held their swords out in a line.

Kinsington sniffed at the air like a dog. Pavlyn, Aylo and Esna landed behind them, while the other Eltrist stood beside Kinsington. No words needed to be exchanged. Aylo rose first, his white fur like a beacon of light. His jaw popped before he drenched the middle two with strug. Their bodies convulsed, but shock overcame them before any screams could come. Aylo ripped them from the line with his paws and tossed them into the ever-growing balls of dark lavender and blood. Esna and Pavlyn finished the other two in much the same way.

"Carry our dead and the living back to camp. If you are hungry, Eltrist, praise the moon for our nourishment before leaving. Do so swiftly. More may be coming," Kinsington said with a snarl in his words.

Kinsington prowled through the dead and distraught with purpose. He sucked in his breath, and the strug inside him sank to the bottom of his abdomen. An Eltrist lay on the ground a couple of feet from him. Her fur was the color of autumn, and her tail was curled around her body, hiding the majority of her. Kinsington raced to her. His chest heaved with angst and his fur stood on end as he pawed at her tail. He padded at the bumps that peeked through the orange fur, her eyes but a flicker.

"Haylin?" Kinsington said. He gently moved her over. Her chest bled black down to her ribs. A puddle of strug and tar-like blood dried under her. She softly smiled at Kinsington before her cheeks sagged.

"Haylin? *Haylin*! Wake, Fated of Souls. My breath and beat of my heart, *wake*," he sobbed into her mind. Kinsington placed his head down and pushed her over him and onto his back. Her body slumped down on either side. He soared off into the sky.

The moment for festivities drained just like an emptying tub. Folks walked around as if a chill had permanently bit at their spine. After Sylin coordinated the healers over to a vast space of meadow near the tents, he summoned everyone to tell them the news in a direct and stoic speech. Sylin slipped his words out of their minds, but Eliza studied him when he spoke more to only the Eltrists.

It made no difference, not when she didn't have that ability. Sylin stretched his wings, the smaller one fluttering briefly as if it needed to rid something from it. Behind him, Thorn glared at Eliza. She turned away. Folks and Eltrists scattered and moved like a storm carried them. Talkun even left Eliza's side and spoke with the healers.

Eliza moved her hand and watched it as if it wasn't hers. A thought tugged at her. *With everyone busy, would they notice my escape?*

Before Eliza could decide what to do, a gust of wind cycled down. Eliza peered up, her hand on her forehead brushing her cedar brown hair from her eyes as it flitted around. A hoard of Eltrists lighted the sky, their tails swaying like snakes in grass. Strug glowed marvelously through their furry bellies. When they were close enough, they descended and landed in the meadow. Some left the injured behind and charged back into the sky, returning with bloodied folks or hurt Eltrists limp in their claws.

Sylin charged away from the healers and stared up at the darkening sky. Kinsington floated down, his fur cold with tears. When his paws touched the warm ground, he collapsed not just from the weight of exhaustion but one of grief.

Sylin's tail swatted frantically. His eyes, for a moment, cemented on Kinsington and Haylin. Then he swallowed and latched onto every healer's mind. "Save her!" He sobbed. "Haylin our queen is wounded."

Many dropped everything they were doing and ran over, while others, stunned, kept working on their current patient. The two folks who arrived first grabbed Haylin off Kinsington's back and called for takthorns. Kinsington nudged his muzzle against the back of Haylin's head lovingly.

A woman in tight brown pants and a loose asymmetrical top charged over with a pile of takthorns clutched in her hands, the points long and skinny as a needle and resembling a twig. She immediately fell to her knees when she got to Haylin and placed the pile of takthorns in the grass. After scanning over them, she plucked a slightly gnarled one. She shooed Kinsington with her hands and shouted for help to roll Haylin onto her back. Her eyes concentrated as a surgeon's eyes would. She placed about eight inches of the point into her wound, then meticulously added another takthorn until it led all the way down her wound. The takthorns wiggled and expanded in places before deflating back to their normal shape. The healer took out the takthorns and replaced them with new ones in a continuous rhythm. She mouthed something, her lips quivering with anger, and the takthorns in her grip tightened.

Kinsington never shifted his gaze off Haylin, standing as if cursed to stone. Folks and Eltrists peeked from behind him to see who needed such an important treatment. Many gasped or clasped their hands together at their heart, tears coming to some. Though only the Eltrists were communicating with each other, the folks knew what they meant by their growls and howl-like sobs.

Talkun made his way through the crowd and stood next to Kinsington. "Who is she?" he asked.

Kinsington gritted his teeth, strug blobbing and dangling between them. "The night will bleed without her. I will bleed without her... she ruled Amarda."

"I thought you were their ruler? Why was she amongst the last to arrive?" Talkun asked. His voice was neutral.

Kinsington's gaze narrowed on him. "Her ruling has always been with all of us. She refused to travel without watching over the last group to join us."

Talkun nodded. "Understandable."

"If she dies, I need you to help lead with me." Kinsington sucked in his breath. "They need you. Another loss will be a sentence."

Talkun rubbed his paw in the grass, just like he would do against the cold floor of his prison. Claw marks etched across the floorboards there, but here only grass limped with each stroke.

"Is it not loss that brought them here? Loss is etched into our souls. It may have started with me, but I am at a loss for how to end it."

Kinsington cocked his head, his eyes narrowing even further. "You have forgotten your place in Folengower." He turned around and pointed to the right, to the shadowy shape of the castle. "That is your rightful place."

7

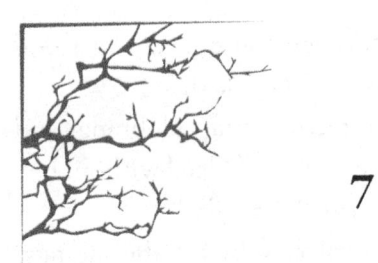

Pantries hung open next to an enormous slab of black stone that covered a frame beneath it. It had a single shelf with a pile of ash below. Audrey sat in the middle of the kitchen on a wavy counter that divided the room. The translucence of sea-foam color made her green eyes shine. Her legs dangled over as she chewed on a dried petal the size of her palm. Not much was amiss in the kitchen, not like most of the castle, though there were a few drawers pulled open and random kitchenware pulled out or broken on the floor.

"You know, I just might turn vegetarian if all petals taste this good."

Theodore chuckled.

Ben ran his hand over the counter she sat on. A wild, curious look struck him. "What is this?"

"Huh?" Theodore turned his gaze from the black stone. "Oh, just a rock from the Sea of Calip. I forget the name. Eliza and I used to play a game to find them. I don't want to brag, but I usually won." Theodore winked.

Audrey rolled her eyes. "So, you are good at finding things?"

"I found you," he said sweetly and snatched a kiss as he walked past. "I didn't peg you as a rock enthusiast, Ben."

Ben chuckled. "I'm not, but this is quite stunning." He wandered over to Theodore. "So, how can I help?"

"I haven't cooked in here before, so I am just as lost as you." Theodore crouched beneath the big black slab. "Though, I am sure down here is where I can light it."

Ben knelt beside him. "What would you put in there?" He dragged a finger through the soot.

"Hopefully, it works like any standard oven in Folengower." Theodore pulled out a white sack that rested on the shelf. "Ah ha." He opened it and grabbed a fistful of wishbone-shaped dried plants. He sprinkled them on top of the onyx rock, then patted his hands together to get the last pieces off. "Time to rummage."

In the corner next to the oven, an arched structure extended high to the ceiling. The frame was a deep brown, the inside too dark to see inside.

"What is that?" Ben said. "It's kind of freaking me out."

"This?" Theodore pointed at it, then shrugged. "Oh, it's like a fridge. Nothing to worry about," he said in a blasé way before going inside it. From the outside, he was unseen, as if zapped out of existence. A bright light lined the curved shelves. He grabbed a cut of silken blue meat and ghostly white stacked vegetables from a lower shelf. He then grabbed another vegetable that looked like weeks-old spinach and spiraled like fusilli pasta.

"'Scuse me, beautiful." Theodore nodded for Audrey to scoot. She jumped down. "Now, there has to be a knife around here somewhere." He plopped the food onto the counter on one of the hill surfaces.

"You can't just prepare it with your magic?" Audrey joked.

"That would be rad," Ben said.

"If only." Theodore sighed.

Theodore pulled open the first drawer under the counter. About twenty jars of luminescent strug filled the entire space. After four drawers, he finally found knives. He chopped and sliced away. Each piece rolled down the curved counter and slid into a crevice. He sliced the meat on another hill to slide down on the other side. He continued until satisfied enough to magic the heat on the slab and toss the food onto it.

The wishbone-like plants popped with an arched bounce, the abruptness appearing as a white rainbow. The plants moved around the food, and as the food browned, the pieces would burn out and wither into nothing.

Ben eyed the bouncy things. "We don't have"—he moved his hands in circles in front of the plants—"whatever these are back in Harthsburg."

"No, you do not," Theodore said.

"It smells good," Audrey said with an uneasiness in her voice.

"I feel there's a *but* to that?" Theodore raised his eyebrow.

"I think we should discuss it tomorrow."

Theodore tipped down two jars that hung above the food cooking. Seasoning shook down before springing back upright. "We will feast first."

"But—"

"We need this. This may be the last time we can sit down and enjoy each other's company without spilling blood."

Audrey stared down at her feet. "Well, then, if we are celebrating, let's fucking make it a good one. Where's the fancy plates?"

Theodore grinned. He pointed to the other side of the kitchen where cabinets hung on the wall as he shook seasoning over the grill. Bulging glass filled the middle of the doors while a curved wood framed the rest. Audrey reached for one of the aged silver handles. She pulled out three crimson and black ornate plates.

"Ben, a little help?"

Ben grabbed the plates and left the kitchen to place them on the table. Audrey reached the top shelf and grabbed the matching goblets before joining Ben.

"Someone take a knife to this?" Ben rubbed his finger on the slice marks on the table.

Audrey looked around. "Scratches are nothing compared to the rest of the place."

"True."

"I hope you are hungry." Theodore's voice, loud and impressed, took them away from their conversation. "Another lucmis meal, or... what is that word you Earth people say?" He carried a large black platter. The meat sat in the middle, now a dark blue with a blackened crust on the top. A honeyed sauce dripped down the sides and the vegetables surrounded it like a crown.

"Delicious? Scrumptious?" Ben held in a laugh.

"Although, I don't think I hear many people say that." Audrey laughed.

"I am not many people." Theodore set the tray down. "One more thing." He ran back to the kitchen and brought out a pitcher and silverware. He placed the utensils down and held up the pitcher. "For you, my love?"

"Please." Audrey sat down at the end of the table and held her goblet out to him. He poured a pink liquid with flower petals that swirled around the top into the goblet.

"And for you?" Theodore asked Ben.

Ben rose his glass.

"Don't be so polite on my account." Theodore chuckled.

Ben and Theodore sat on either side of Audrey. Though the table could seat plenty, they sat close together.

Before long, their boisterous voices carried throughout the entire bottom floor. Audrey ate with her legs hanging over the side of the chair, her plate resting on her lap, and Ben told jokes that he'd heard when he was still working as a mechanic. Theodore acted out the famous plays he had seen as a child. They were terribly bad re-enactments, but Ben and Audrey clapped, nonetheless.

The laughter slowly faded when their bellies were full, the drink down to its last drop and their bodies aching.

Audrey sighed and sat up. She rested her elbow on the table and leaned her cheek into the palm of her hand. "Well, tomorrow is nearly here. I think it's time to find out where we are going."

Theodore let out a soft laugh, pulled out the leaf and unrolled it. His gaze hyperfocused on it. "Well, at least we will not be traveling far. Only to the Rocks of Lunok, or it would seem that's what this means." He frowned.

"What is it?" Ben asked.

"It says follow me into the Rocks of Lunok before dawn." At the bottom, there was a small, smudged symbol of a long vertical line that had an upside-down triangle at the top and an open circle the opposite end. The middle had two half circles stacked back-to-back, facing up at either end as if they were mouths ready to feed each end.

Ben's eyes widened and he gently slapped the table. "Wait... Eliza and I were standing on them the day we arrived. She said there were stories about people falling in the holes on the top of them but no one knew were they went." I assume they would die." He swallowed, and a sad glint in his eye followed.

"Is it possible that this leader wants to wipe out all Ancient Ones?" Audrey said.

"Anything is possible now. I never thought my father would kill his own mother, but now I know the capabilities of others are far greater than I could have ever believed." Theodore stood and choked up. "Eliza and I have no idea what the Rocks of Lunok do, but none of the stories end happily."

"So, what now?" Ben said, seemingly stuck between reluctance and eagerness to leave.

"We will go." Theodore nodded confidently, decided. "I have no other lead on how to create an army on my own. With all the Cursed Knights gone, I hardly have a way to convince them to turn on my father." He peered down at the leaf again. "If I sense things are going awry, I will say, 'moon.' If you hear that, run back to the castle to hide."

"Does the letter mention the leader's name?"

"No, as mysterious as the stones."

Peace would not come for them as they waited for dawn.

8

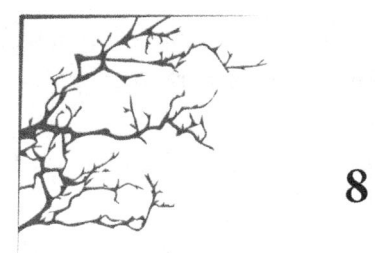

Silken white wrapped around the castle, its dreamlike being extending into the forest and beyond. The tip of Talkun's Tower protruded out ominously from the contrasting white. Dew drops speckled the ground with sustenance before the sun could rise to shoo it away.

The fog held on to Ben, Audrey and Theodore as if Mother Nature wrapped her arms around them. Theodore held Audrey's hand and Audrey held Ben's as they walked in a chain line. Their eyes could barely see three feet ahead, but Theodore assured them that he could make it to the Rocks of Lunok even if he were blind. There was no reason to not believe him; after all, this had been his home for a lot longer than they had even existed. If anything, that was harder to understand, especially since Audrey believed him to be close to his early thirties like herself. But age could hardly matter now when they walked together in Folengower and war festered on the tip of its tongue.

They passed the garden, still wilted, with cracked stones that had once portrayed art. Their lungs worked hard, each breath filled with too much heaviness. Every smell heightened in the fog. The piled bodies smelled as if they were eating the mud, flowers, grasses, and trees in the distance. The further they went, the more everything around them combined and morphed onto their tongue.

Ben coughed over and over.

"You alright?" Theodore asked, with his hand outstretched and swatting at the air.

"Yup," he struggled to say. He pushed his tongue out, rubbing it against his top teeth.

Audrey pulled her shirt up and let it drape over her nose.

Theodore spit. "Once we are further from the castle, I hope things will settle."

"It's not that bad," Audrey said in a muffled voice.

"Says the person with a shirt covering their nose." Ben laughed mid-cough.

Audrey snorted. "Fuck off."

"The banter can wait; for now, quiet steps," Theodore whispered. "We're close. Stay by my side and remember where to go."

The Rocks of Lunok took shape and so did another. He stood with his back to them, looking off into the forest. He was tall, and his brown hair looked wet in the midst of the fog. Theodore sidestepped to him. His hand let go of Audrey's, and he gave a glance to her and Ben to remember where to run if things went sideways.

"I believe you are expecting me," Theodore said with a steady voice.

The man stared off into the distance. "Indeed." He placed his hands behind his back and held them. "I must say, when Rew told me"—he shook his head and chuckled—"I believed it to be a joke."

Theodore leaned in closer. "You sound oddly familiar. Do you plan to keep your identity hidden even when I have not?"

"I wouldn't dare insult the next Ancient One." The man turned around, his glasses complete with a ghostly white film. He took them off and rubbed them on his shirt. "I suppose it is mad to wear glasses in the fog, but..."

Theodore gasped. He blinked and took a step back.

"As you know," the man continued, "I can't see worth a damn without these."

"Bruthren..." Theodore exhaled. "You are the leader of The Choke?"

Bruthren licked his lips. "Isn't it thrilling? I imagine you have a lot of questions."

"You know him?" Ben said.

"He is Nniar's lead creator. What you would call a scientist of sorts, but with our magical elements."

Bruthren gawked at Audrey and Ben, tilting his hips to the side and his neck to see them. "Why don't we discuss matters alone?"

"It won't be necessary; they are my most trusted confidants."

"Them?" Bruthren pointed at them. Audrey glared, and Ben crossed his arms. "Fine. I imagine Rew would keep his lips tight unless he believed himself to be amongst like-minded folks, but I have worked for many years to create a following. Folengower deserves unity. We deserve unity. No more hatred towards our sister Amarda."

"How do you plan to accomplish unity?" Theodore said.

"Distraction, of course."

Theodore rubbed his temples. "I don't understand."

"While Amarda and your father play a game, we will lurk as we always have."

"Do you intend to take both sides out?"

Bruthren giggled. "Oh, dear no. That would take worlds of armies. The Choke will take a much quieter approach." He paused. "Before I go on, I need to know whose side you are on. What is your need for this meeting?"

"I planned to build a separate army myself to recreate the world my grandmother created, but now it seems you are much further ahead than me." Theodore laced his fingers behind his head and paced. If you allow me to work within The Choke, spoil my father's plans and expose his lies, I would be indebted to you."

Bruthren's eyes narrowed. "Do you still want to rule?"

"That depends on what this new unified Folengower would look like. If there is a place for me in it, I will help rule."

Bruthren grinned. "It seems my opinion of you has always been right."

"And what would that be?"

"You are much brighter than Korrigan and you have something he has never had, at least not since I've known him."

Theodore frowned, not understanding.

"You have kindness in you. Now, if you are willing to risk everything, you should speak to the rest of The Choke." Bruthren crossed his legs and leaned against the rock. "I have arranged a meeting just in case my assumptions were correct, and my, are they."

Audrey's cheeks were flushed. She turned away.

"When?"

"Now." Bruthren impatiently beckoned for Theodore to follow him. "I don't care to wait for the fog to clear to settle everything." He climbed on top of one stone.

"You can't be serious."

"Oh." Bruthren turned back, his toes slightly hanging over the edge of the rock. "I forgot how much your father has blinded you to the kingdom you would inherit. Harm will not come to you under my watch. I promise you."

Theodore climbed up. He held out his hand to pull Ben and then Audrey up. Green slime stuck to Audrey's shoe. She tried rubbing it off by scraping her foot on the rock, but it only clumped it up.

"Now..." Bruthren scanned the many rocks for the correct hole. "Ah, yes, here it is." Without warning, he jumped in.

"Uhhh, where did he go?" Audrey backed up from a different hole, into Theodore's arms.

Ben loomed over the black hole, trying to work out where the other side would go, but it was impossible to tell.

"I guess we will find out soon enough." Theodore unwrapped his arms from Audrey, took a deep breath and stared into the hole. "I'll go first. If you don't want to do this, I understand."

"Enough talking. Let's meet who will end this war." Ben's words were confident, but the look on his face as he continued to stare into the hole betrayed him.

Audrey's eyebrows raised. "Well, if Ben is willing, so am I."

Theodore nodded and jumped straight through. He landed on his feet, crouched from the impact as a distant scream tunneled down followed by, "*Shit*." He rolled to the side just as Audrey landed awkwardly and yelled, "Ow." Ben kept his eyes closed even as his feet touched the ground, luckily not landing on Audrey.

"I see we've all arrived."

Houses lined beside them, including the one that Theodore had hidden in on his great escape from Kinsington. A woodpecker pecked at the same mustard yellow house that he'd spotted before.

"Amarda?"

"You have a keen eye," Bruthren said with a proud tone.

"I have been here... not long ago." Theodore spun around. A shiver ran down his spine, and everything felt twitchy inside. "Are you planning to cage me now?"

Bruthren darted a stare in his direction. "Curious. I know Eliza has always been the perspicacious one, but you must know that I could have ambushed you if that were the case."

Theodore glared. "Then, why are we here?"

"Amarda is almost fully vacant. Can you believe it? An entire half of Folengower is ours." Bruthren's eyes lit up, crazed with excitement. "Well, for the time being."

Ben walked down the trail between houses. "A ghost town. Reminds me of Croak Falls."

Audrey tapped on one of the houses. "A ghost town for a while by the looks of it. Where is everyone from Amarda if they aren't here?" She poked her finger into one hole rotting away on the frame.

"Nniar," Theodore said before Bruthren could answer. Bruthren's hand hung up, as if he wasn't sure what to add. "Though this town had already been cleared out when I was a prisoner. I think many of the towns here were abandoned long before the war started."

"Keen observation, Ancient One. Time is as devouring as a corpse thistle." Bruthren swiftly made his way past the many houses.

They followed quickly behind. They arrived at the last house, which looked like more of a shack than the others, before the road forked and twisted through the dead forest. Green paint remained untouched on the shack, as if it had frozen in time when all others crumbled. Bruthren opened the door and waved his hand to the side for them to hurry.

At least twenty people were inside, stood or sat in the main room. Quiet chatter continued until Theodore walked through the door and several eyes landed on him. The energy drained as if breathing seized collectively.

"*Surprise*," Bruthren shouted, his arms shaking on either side of his ridiculous smile. "With great honor, I present the next Ancient One, Theodore Lexington."

Someone dropped their cup and another nearly fainted.

Bruthren let out a boisterous laugh. "I do love surprises." He put the back of his hand to his mouth as if to whisper to Theodore. "Especially if I'm the one giving them."

Theodore waved him away. "I understand that my presence is quite a shock. I am only here to accomplish the same thing that you all have been working towards... for quite some time, it seems."

A goling with pearly white hair stood and spoke. "If you want the same thing, where have you been?"

"Someone only informed me of The Choke yesterday."

"And before that? What were you doing to unify Folengower?"

Theodore clasped his hands together in front of his chest. "The present and future are here. I believe that is what we should focus on, especially since I am not the ruler of Nniar."

"That may be, but you must know what is to come?"

"Now, now." Bruthren reached his hands out in a hushing motion. "I can vouch for him. Korrigan is not much of a sharer. Queen Agden may have a sniff of the truth, but even she is left to the mercy of the moon. This feud may have ignited long ago, but the reality bared no light." He took off his glasses and pulled out a cloth from his pocket to clean them. "Rew agreed to allow him in. I have also seen the kindness in Theodore's actions. He fights for unity, not loyalty."

The crowd murmured. Audrey moved clumsily to the right, and a creak escaped from the floorboards, as if to announce her presence to everyone. Ben grabbed her arm.

"And who are they?"

"They are—" Theodore began.

"Recruits," Bruthren finished. "The Ancient One found them for us. Now, enough with this paranoia. Where are we on securing the new grayden?"

A skinny male popped a handful of clawnuts into his mouth. "Consider it done. I went over there today, and Regan is devoted to the cause. He will allow us to use his property regardless of what shall pass."

"Delightful. Our recruits will stay there. Clay, will you set up the site and train the recruits? Assign jobs at once to whomever you must take."

Clay popped another clawnut into his mouth and made an "mmmhmmm" sound.

"There will be some changes in how we do things. Quiet until I finish." Bruthren stepped into the middle of the chairs. "Theodore will work closely with me."

Someone sighed just a little too loudly to not be considered rude. Bruthren met their sigh with a ghastly glare.

"For the first time, we have someone with more magic abilities than any of us, and not just that, someone who was taught to rule. If we want unity, we need a leader. We need someone who will—can make it happen."

"How would an Ancient One make Folengower any different?" a woman shouted.

Bruthren glanced at Theodore. He outstretched his arm and backed behind him.

"Before coming here, I planned on creating an army of my own. I have no intention of keeping things as they are. My father does not rule with the best of intentions, as you all know. I will do whatever it takes to create harmony again. I have empathy for Amardians and for those lied to in Nniar."

"I call for a vote," another person shouted.

"If you want a vote, I will allow it," Bruthren said. "If you'll be so kind to step out until the vote is done," he told Theodore.

Theodore gave a single nod. Before Audrey and Ben could turn to follow, he held his hand up just below his waist. Audrey reached for it, but he slipped away and out of the house.

Ben nudged her with his shoulder and mouthed, "It's okay."

Bruthren cracked his knuckles all at once with one loud pop. "I must say, I am bored with this. On this cursed soil, stand if you will allow the next king of Nniar, the announced Ancient One, to aid in our mission of unity. Sit if you reject his aid."

The goling with pearly white hair was one of the ones who remained seated, regarding Audrey and Ben through glaring eyes. Ben moved from foot to foot as other eyes focused on them with suspicion. Clay stood slowly, with an agitated sigh at having his snacking interrupted. Others were quicker to get to their feet. There wasn't much in terms of numbers between who was sitting and who was standing.

Bruthren disappointedly counted those who sat. His long legs stepped over their heads as he shook his. They ducked as if they were hit. "Now, those who stand," he said as he pointed his finger to each and ended on Ben.

"Paranoia is defeated, after all. Those who object, outnumbered *again*. What a delight."

Ben wondered what else had been objected to.

Bruthren clasped his hands together and squished them against his chest. "Stand. Up. Up. The decision is final, so I expect you all to remember that."

"Theodore," Bruthren called from the door. "Please rejoin us."

Theodore came in, his head held high. "Well?"

"Congratulations, your army." Bruthren bowed. "Well, a tree's worth at least."

"Folengower will be whole. I will fight beside you."

The room was silent as air. Some nodded, but many gave a sense of shock. Bodies stiffened, eyes narrowed or widened. Even those who voted for him seemed uncertain of what they had agreed to. But then Clay crossed his legs and gave a slow clap, with his bag of clawnuts still in his hand. His gray hair dangled slightly to the side of his pale white cheeks, enough for him to twitch his head.

More claps filled the room with the synchronized sound. Bruthren, amused, clapped with them. "Do not give them reason to betray you," he whispered with a wide smile.

Theodore swallowed, his jaw tightening. "I have other matters to discuss."

"Busy, busy, are you?" Bruthren whispered. He turned to the crowd and shouted, "No more surprises today. We will meet again in two days. I want a report of training and conditions of the graydens." Everyone followed his motion except Theodore, Audrey and Ben, who watched with confused gazes.

"May our enemies choke! May we choke if we fail!" the room shouted in unison.

Folks left shortly after, but Clay waited behind and walked over to Audrey and Ben. "So, I guess I will be taking you to the new grayden."

Theodore eyed Bruthren.

"I have other plans for them," Bruthren snapped. "Other recruits will arrive your way tonight. Get a move on. We wouldn't want them waiting."

"Even her?"

Audrey held her breath, as if she assumed that wouldn't be the end of it.

"We don't want them waiting," Bruthren replied.

"No, we wouldn't."

Bruthren held his finger to his lips until the footsteps faded.

"Did you know that Eliza was captured by Amardians?" Theodore said.

"Was she now?" Bruthren's expression didn't change.

"You don't seem that surprised."

"Well, they had to take someone when you escaped." He shrugged quickly before a smile returned to his face. "Oh, bravo, by the way."

Theodore shook his head. "I need help to get her back."

"Of course. Do you know if she has the same need to unify Folengower as you?" Bruthren tapped the back of one of the chairs.

"She would."

"Ah. So, this hasn't been discussed before?"

Ben threw his hands up. "Why would that matt—"

"They took her before I found out the truth and crimes of our father."

"I will see what we can do. Allow me some time to create a possible rescue plan and to hold a vote on whether to save her."

"A vote?" Theodore clenched his hand.

"Eliza may be your sister, but she is not our responsibility. War has already begun its reaping. We must decide if saving her life would endanger us."

Bruthren led them out and down into a cave just beyond a ridge. The dark followed them, but Theodore opened his palm, letting a white light guide them. The path appeared to vanish a few steps in front of them.

Theodore stopped abruptly. "Is this a trick?"

"Trust will serve you well." Bruthren sighed. "This leads to the main grayden. Your new life awaits below. Jump."

And they did.

9

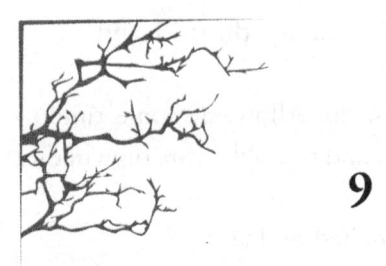

The wind had scurried through the Anorphus island with such foreboding that even the heaviest of sleepers woke. Many in the camp feared for their safety as a poisonous stench invaded the tents, and they prayed to the moon for protection against the Anorphus.

Korrigan sat up in his bed. His lungs were heavy and struggling, as if someone had just sat upon his chest. "Commander Glaslin, what does the wind speak of?"

Glaslin came in from the outside of the tent, with his long black hair blowing in first with billows of fog. "Ancient One." He placed his fist in front of his right eye and bowed his head. "The wind speaks of something foul. I can smell it. I have sent off the birds to bring word from the exterior."

"Has anyone returned from the Divide?"

"Not yet. I sent Polt before sundown, and I have yet to see his black wings return."

Korrigan sighed, his left eye twitching. "I call for a meeting with Lore."

"I will fetch him," Glaslin said and hurried back out.

Korrigan stretched his arms and let his legs dangle over the side of the bed. When his feet hit the floor, he winced. He rubbed each foot with scorn, as if their age disappointed him. At the end of his bed, he reached into a rounded chest, tugged out pieces of clothing. With ease, he pulled off his shirt and pants and replaced them with a stiff black buttoned top that angled at the bottom, dangling down his left leg. The buttons were crimson and shiny. His pants were of the same shade. He sat on the edge of the bed and waited.

Lore entered soon after. In the darkness of the tent, he could have been mistaken for skeletal remains that animated to life. "Knights have returned from the Divide. Glaslin ran off to meet them a mere moment ago."

"They have? It must be grim news; otherwise, the wind would not make such dread."

"I fear it too."

They stared into each other's eyes and waited.

Two Cursed Knights walked with Korrigan and Lore to the west of the island. Up on the knoll, Glaslin and several other knights whispered to the others who'd returned.

Korrigan scanned the knights. He cocked his head one way and then the other just to make sure that what he was seeing was right. The grim news he'd expected hadn't been this grim. "Four?" The knights tensed and one glanced over at her fellow comrades.

Glaslin gazed over his shoulder. "Ancient One." They all bowed with their fist in front of their right eye. "Only four have retur—"

Korrigan pointed to a female knight. She held her helmet, the bloodstained lavender plume stuck to her knee.

"Am I to believe that ninety-six of you died, or do my old eyes not see the rest?"

She averted her eyes and swallowed. "You are correct.".

"Glaslin, did you hear that? Ninety-six. Ninety-six..." Korrigan paced, his fingers tapping on his lips as if playing a piano. "Ninety-six."

"They outnumbered us. Eltrists came from another location to aid."

"And? Tell me something... something of victory."

The knight's crimson eyes darted to Korrigan and then back to Glaslin.

Glaslin nodded to the woman to continue. "That thing... the Fated of Souls is dead. I witnessed her stomach gutted with my own eyes. She bled black."

"Haylin?" Korrigan narrowed his gaze with scrutiny written all over. "You understand that if that is true, then they have lost a queen amongst them?"

The woman gave a wry smile. "Amardians will crumble before the chilly winds come."

Korrigan laughed, boastful at first, before sighing with his hand over his heart. "What wild thoughts you must keep up there." He poked at her forehead. "I hadn't planned on setting their hearts aflame, at least not yet. Do you know what vengeance can do to someone?" When none of them said as much as a whisper, Korrigan swatted his hand in the air. "Fire. One unlike any that you have ever seen. Haylin was not only a queen, but she was loved as the moon."

Glaslin cocked his head. The red swirled in his eyes. "I believe the order was to send a message, not anger the swarm."

"Casualties were bound to happen," Korrigan said. "We need only change plans. Now, you all run along to your tents. And don't even think about gloating or speaking a word about this meeting or the battle at the Divide, or it will be a fire unlike any that will feed on your insides."

Glaslin shooed the knights away with his arms as if they were stray dogs.

Lore did well to remain as a shadow. "In this new world you envision, what will it be like?" he asked, his hands held together below his navel.

"It has not changed." Korrigan sniffed at the air. His nose wrinkled and he spit. "The Eltrist at our behest for all to see and know that strug is a right to us all. They will breed only when our supplies need to replenish. Magic will be reborn. Imagine the new spells we can create with an endless supply of strug. We'll have rivers of it."

"Of course I know this, but Nniar needs to know. You need the support of the folks here, not just us. Soon, they will talk about how war is too bloody, too long. Give them a reason for it to continue," Lore said. A streak of light cast on his face in a ghastly way, almost as if his face were an X-ray image.

"Not all the folks would be too keen for this new world," Glaslin interjected.

Korrigan's head snapped towards Glaslin. "What have you heard?"

"I have heard whispers of a group that wishes to unify Folengower. They want it to be the same as when Queen Callum ruled."

Korrigan's eye twitched. "The Choke."

"You've heard of them."

"I never ignore whispers. They are nothing in this war. A tarbug is more of a threat."

"I wouldn't be too quick to ignore them." Lore raised one eyebrow and laced his fingers at his abdomen.

"Perhaps." Korrigan tapped his chin, then as quick as the gusts of wind that rushed at them, he gripped Glaslin's shirt. "What do you know of them, Glaslin?"

Glaslin stiffened. "Not much."

Korrigan stabbed his index finger into Glaslin's chest. "Find out, or it will be all our heads."

They parted ways with the wind, wild as a whip.

"Cursed soul, get up. *Get up*."

Kalien shivered and wrapped his sinewy arms around himself. At first, he thought it was the wind waking him again into an in-between state. He would have welcomed that instead of seeing Amarda's camp.

"Ah, there you are."

Kalien peeked around the tent. Reed lay on his side with the blanket draped over his legs; Cressa appeared to be curled in a ball, like a squirrel asleep; and Indigo had their pillow over their face, as if something or someone had bothered them. Kalien wondered if he had been snoring.

He jumped out of his bunk and made his way out of the tent with nimble steps. "What do you—"

"Enough. Did you know about the attack?" Thorn asked.

"What attack?" Kalien whispered.

"I told you to watch them."

Kalien rubbed sand from his eyes and groaned. "I can only do so much unless you prefer I die a terrible death."

"Tell me everything you have done since the last time we spoke." Thorn faced the river. Kalien could see fog lingering above it and beyond.

"Well, let's see." He held up one finger to begin counting. "I broke my arm. What a time that was. It still doesn't feel right—"

"*Kalien*, I swear to the moon I will break every bone in your body and dump you in the forest. Tell me something important so you may live."

Kalien crept around the tent with his hand covering his mouth. "I'm already dead, and you will be too."

"I am *far* from dead, you cursed scum." Thorn cracked her neck and then popped her fingers one at a time, loud enough for Kalien to hear as he watched her hands as if they were his.

Kalien huffed a laugh. "You don't get it. I can choose to help you, and in the end, I'll be killed by my own people, or I refuse to give you more information, and I know you will hunt me, so, really, what's the point?" Thorn stood and turned her back to the river. A chickadee whistled up on a branch where Kalien could see Thorn looking. "Why should I give you anything when you've taken my life already?"

If Kalien could see Thorn's face, he would have seen the sickly look of her cheek and how her tongue prodded at the gash as if she had already developed a new habit.

"Poor Kalien. What a hard life you have now," Thorn spat. "You have *no* idea what it is like to have your life ripped from you. I am fighting for a life. And you... well, you will see me every day whenever I feel like it. And I will see all the secrets you refuse to give me."

Kalien blinked hard as the view of Amarda's camp disappeared. He crawled back into bed with bumpy arms from the cold and fear, Thorn's last words echoing in his mind.

"Leave," he whispered, hoping to release the damn thing that trapped him to Thorn. "Remove," he tried desperately, but still it remained in his ear, sealed like a clam. He tried other words too, none of which worked.

The night dragged, as if walking limp through the heavy wind with a sword three times the size of it. Kalien felt the heaviness as if it were he who held the sword.

Reed woke, his eyes drooped, and when he lifted his arms to stretch, Kalien could smell the stench of his armpits. Kalien shut his eyes.

The wind had not calmed; if anything, it had become more boisterous in its plea. A gush of wind punched at the tent, rattling their beds. Cressa jumped as she woke. Indigo yawned and hit the tent wall, as if that would silence the outside.

Reed's face soured. "The wind woke me up all night. Did any of you sleep through it?"

Kalien rolled onto his side. He eyed each of them, the comment making him sweat, and he wondered if Reed had heard the conversation with Thorn.

Indigo stumbled over to the door and opened the flap. Fog puffed in, as if someone was smoking a pipe and donut rings were pulsing into the room. "I hardly slept," they said.

Cressa yawned.

"Kalien?" Reed's gaze met his. "And your night?"

Kalien fiddled with his thumb before saying, "Same as everyone else. The wind moves with vexation."

"I thought I heard you talking to someone at one point," Reed said. He sat up with a hunch, and his arms rested on his legs.

Kalien made sure to keep his face expressionless. "No, it wasn't me. Cursed Knights must have been checking on things. I'm sure I heard them too, unless I dreamed it."

"I could have sworn it was you." Reed's voice was that of someone coaxing a dog out of a corner.

Cressa threw her pillow, hitting Reed in the face.

Reed huffed and grabbed it. "What was that for?" He scowled at Cressa.

"Leave Kalien alone. You're so paranoid sometimes. Besides, it's time to get to work."

Reed bit his lip, but to everyone's surprise, he didn't retort, not even during the walk to the round tent.

The round tent was almost completely covered in moss and other tendrily plants caused by moisture. Bruthren stood outside, staring at his feet. The regular worker next to him had a rag and a mixture on his belt, which he used to clean the windows that were covered in green and yellow film.

Cressa led her bunkmates to the door.

Bruthren held up a hand to stop her. "Something is stirring in there. If I were you, which of course I could never be, I would wait out here until it settles." His gaze never left the ground, but the strangeness in his voice was as if he'd told them a secret, one that they should be happy to know.

Reed shrugged. Indigo crossed their arms as Cressa backed up to stand next to them. They exchanged glances, but nothing more. Kalien poked at his ear, unable to stop his finger from protruding into the cavity, like an unwelcome spasm. The movement stole Bruthren's attention.

"And what's that?" Bruthren tilted his head and peeked inside Kalien's ear, like a curious fox finding a den.

Kalien placed his hand over his ear and edged away. "My ear has been bothering me. Probably just dirt or wax buildup."

Bruthren's eyes lit like winter lights. His fingers danced on each other's tips. "It appears we both have secrets," he whispered. "Who's on the other—"

A ripping noise shook the tent, and Nia tossed out a man by the collar of his shirt. Reed flew back with the man's head pushed into his belly. They landed a few feet away, with Reed getting the brunt of the damage. Reed lay on his back, the man half on top of him.

"*Get off*," Reed shouted, lifting his neck to glare down at the man's bald head. The man struggled to gain his footing, but he did so after much scurrying. Reed pushed himself up and wiped his back and butt. Mud and moss clung to his hand. The man ran off.

Cressa ran over to him. "Are you alright?"

Reed ignored her. "What on cursed soil was that about, Nia?" he groaned. He patted at his clothes, with no end in sight to rid the caked-on earth.

"Focus on your spoiled clothes. Get changed and hurry back," Nia said.

Reed stomped his feet, like a tantrum rising to the surface. He turned on his heel and left. His entire backside dripped in mud. Even his hair was coated with dirt.

"Now, get to work. And I don't want to hear any questions pertaining to this." Nia held the flap of the tent open with her body, with one of her hands on the hilt of her sword.

Bruthren, his face nearly at the nape of Kalien's neck, said, "I'll come for you tonight."

Hairs prickled all over Kalien's body, and his eyes swelled, ready to cry. It seemed the accident with his arm, Thorn's words last night and his lack of sleep were getting to him. Bruthren was just another to add to his list of reasons he wasn't coping. He didn't even really believe Reed was done with his interrogating just yet. He followed into the tent as if everything was normal. To his surprise, Bruthren didn't join.

A few things were in disarray, like the corner that Kalien had previously watched for days with no idea what they discussed. Then, it clicked who'd been thrown out. He didn't know his name, but he was a part of the silence table.

Kalien rubbed his jaw.

"You okay?" Indigo asked. They handed an apron and goggles to him.

He shook his head, as if a fly annoyed him. "Mmmhmmm... just a strange morning."

"Very."

Nia hastily rearranged the corner while she ordered several others to do the same. They moved like bees, readying for their queen. Just as Laz placed the last chair back in place, Queen Agden entered with Bruthren close behind. Folly rocked on the swing in her cage.

No one sat at the table until Agden took a seat in the only chair with a filigree design on the back and front. When she sat down, Nia sat, and then the others. Bruthren, for the first time, sat at the table, claiming the seat that used to be taken. The secret table had never scared Kalien before. It was a curious thing, but never had his heart beat as it did now.

Bruthren peered over his shoulder at Kalien and mouthed, "Tonight."

Kalien gulped.

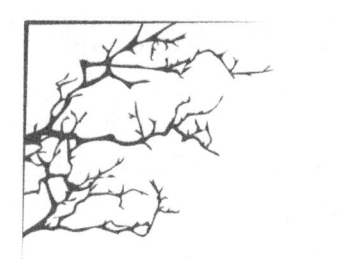

10

The end never came. Not as they barreled through the narrow space of a black hole and deep underground. Great dins echoed all around, and flakes of dried strug flitted around the room as workers wielded three-headed axes into the walls. Someone moved past them with goggles resting on their head and an ax-like tool resting against their shoulder. They pushed carts full of some sort of rock from the walls down a dark hall. Folks wandered with stern faces behind their goggles.

Above their heads, bare soil hovered with roots dangling, as if withered crooked fingers reached out to them. Fungi wrapped around pebbles and boulders in strands of thick, luminescent pink cords. There was no Esmeray to watch over Theodore, only insects that cared not for Ancient Ones, or any folks for that matter, and the occasional harling or other critters that dug too deep and plopped onto the ground below.

"What is this place?" Theodore said as he rubbed his head.

"Isn't it exceptional?" Bruthren breathed in the soil air and tapped at a root hanging in between them. It swung from side to side, as if it were a swing. "The main grayden.

We found a home underground to be able to work in secret."

"What are we underneath?"

Audrey scanned the room with her dry lips parted. Ben reached up to the ceiling and gathered bits of soil between his fingertips. He rolled them into a ball, as if he was unsure if it would feel different from Earth's soil. Oxygen inside the grayden felt suffocating and hollow at the same time, like hiding underneath a blanket. It wouldn't kill them, but it would take time to learn how to cope with the uncomfortable feeling of breathing with less.

"Finnix forest, though we have graydens all over Nniar and Amarda. I present to you a fraction of our army." Bruthren put two fingers in his mouth and whistled a melodic tune. Everyone halted what they were doing and turned to him, some breathless and grateful for a break from the monotony of ax against wall, others seemingly irritated at being interrupted from their routine. "This is your chance to shine."

Theodore stood next to Bruthren and cleared his throat. Nearly a hundred eyes landed on him. "I haven't planned a speech," he said loudly, yet uncertain of the voice that came out, "but I stand before all of you as not just an Ancient One, but as a folk ready and wanting to unite Folengower. I have seen what my father has done. I know it was him who sliced our beautiful soil in half long ago. That's a wrong I must make right. Though it is not my sin, it is my burden." Theodore patted Bruthren's back. Bruthren acknowledge him with a nod. "Bruthren has graciously allowed me to help lead us into a new breath. Amarda and Nniar will breathe as one, as they once did."

A goling nudged his way closer to Theodore and placed their webbed hands on the front of their neck. Theodore stepped closer and realized it was Rew.

Rew gave a subtle bow. "Our blood bound or corpse thistles, we will drown."

Heads turned and axes were placed down before everyone around mirrored their hands on their throat. Soft voices shuddered off the soil walls.

For as long as a lightning strike, a faint smile rested on Rew's lips. "Pick up your tools. Our work is hardly complete." Cacophony erupted through the space once more.

"The Choke council voted, then?" Rew said to Theodore.

"They did," Bruthren answered before Theodore could. "We missed you there."

"Good. I already alerted the folks down here of the change in command if he passed."

"Very good. I would love to gab and curse the soil with you all day, but as you know, my leash is being pulled in too many ways to count. Show him all he needs to see," Bruthren said. He placed a hand on Rew's shoulder, and Rew placed his hand on his.

"Until next time."

Bruthren clapped while he walked down another tunnel. Rew watched him until there was no sign of him left.

"Our new leader needs a tour... and his companions," Rew said in a hushed voice. "Be careful with them; not everyone wants them here." Rew pointed to Audrey and Ben.

"You sound like my father."

Rew's neck twitched. "This way." Rew leapt into another tunnel.

They hurried after him. The cavity moved as smoke, or at least every move from the folks and their drab clothing made it appear as though smoke lived throughout it.

"What are they doing exactly?" Audrey said.

"Under Folengower is—" Rew started.

"Dead magic," Theodore finished.

"Dead? Like necromancy?" Ben said.

Audrey laughed. "Not that, right?" Her laugh faded.

"No, it's all the magic that anyone has ever used throughout history. After it's used, it settles back into the ground and 'dies,' but not entirely. We can process the magic to be restored, but that takes a long time. Ancient Ones have thought about cultivating it, but the means were never worth it. Usually, you will find folks who will do the process for themselves if they are low on strug or need more. As far as I was aware, most folks do not know how to do this or at least not the complete process, but"—Theodore held his hands out and spun to the left—"look how wrong I was."

"Not exactly wrong." Rew shook his head. "Only a small handful of us knew how to do it. We have taught many. Dead magic is just one of our weapons. We are successful in collecting it in areas that have high frequencies of magic used, and once we bring its pulse back, we store it," he said with his head held high.

Rew led them down a corridor of sorts, but the walls were different here. They were lined with brightly colored wood planks, as if someone had taken paint and stamped it with a sponge over and over and then filled in the hollow spaces with something shiny, such as gold foil. Lights hung from the ceiling as amber orbs that reminded Theodore of the Eltrist's cave that they'd held him in. At least in here, he wasn't freezing. Every few feet, there were old paintings of folks and landscapes hanging slightly off-center.

As they neared the hall, herby and sickly-sweet smells funneled towards them. Ben's stomach growled. Around a curve, a steep set of hanging steps hung down about twelve feet into a room. The heart of the whole grayden. They followed Rew down the shaky steps.

Audrey sucked in a breath. The air felt whole and clean at the bottom of the steps. On the far wall, a line of chefs worked at an open kitchen not much different from the one at the castle. Theodore placed his hands on his hips.

"Bruthren made it a priority to have a feeling of home in every grayden," Rew said.

"And home it is," Theodore replied with a childlike gaze.

"Food is available all day and night. I imagine you haven't eaten in a while, so, eat. We have a lot to discuss after."

"We will be here."

Far above their heads, pinholes cut through the soil and let light in. Ethereal light beamed down in what appeared to be random places, but once Ben's gaze traveled from one to the next, he stood back and moved Theodore to the side.

"What?"

"The light is creating—"

"A symbol. The same one Rew put at the end of the letter," Audrey finished.

"It must represent The Choke," Theodore said.

There was an upside-down triangle connected to the center line right by the food prep counter. The line continued through two back-to-back crescent moon shapes that rested on each other, making it look like two sets of spidery legs sticking out. The middle line continued down to the entrance, where it ended at an open circle.

"Are the circle and triangle to represent Ancient Ones, like your tattoo?" Audrey asked.

"It's a bit more than that. The triangle represents Eltrist's eyes and the circles for magical beings... Ancient Ones included. The tattoo traditionally was to show respect for both halves of magic. Obviously, the tattoo is tainted now and is more of a reminder of the promises we refused to keep. The middle part must be for The Choke or the unity of them." Theodore cocked his head.

Pebbles snuggled tightly together on the floor in a mosaic pattern of dark and light stones. On either side of the room, wood-slabbed tables rested in between chairs. A few workers sat at them, their mouths full of meat and stringy fungi that would stick to the side of their lips every time a new mound was pushed in, as if it had suckers like an octopus. An arched entryway was hidden away in the back corner, with no visible light coming from it.

Theodore approached the counter.

"Orb fish or falen meat?" the folk behind the counter said, his back to them, gaze remaining on the stove in front of him.

"Falen and..." Theodore peered over his shoulder. "What do you feel like, fish or meat similar to what I cooked for you?"

"Fish," Audrey said.

"Falen." Ben shrugged.

The chef turned around with three plates stacked along his arms and placed them on the counter. Each plate had a heaping pile of stringy fungi, the same kind that grew on the walls in the grayden. "All yours."

Theodore sniffed his plate as he picked it up off the counter. "Smells delicious."

The chef bowed his head, as if to end a play he starred in.

They sat at an end table to not disturb the others. More folks came to eat as others left while they ate. It was quiet for a while, and once they'd all finished, they waited for Rew to return. A woman came down the ladder, and made a beeline to the chef. She said something, handed him a note, and then left.

"Ancient One," the chef called.

Theodore stood from his chair and spoke with him. Audrey and Ben turned, hopeful to hear the conversation, to no avail.

Theodore returned with a note. "Rew wants us to meet him somewhere."

"Where?" Ben said.

"Through that archway." Theodore pointed to the corner. "I guess there are rooms for people to sleep. Not everyone returns home often."

Through the archway, the dark remained for several feet until a light above them sprang to life. Theodore unrolled the note, which had a six inscribed in the old language with Rew's signature underneath. The hall was narrow, so they walked single file, with Theodore in front and Ben last. Doors were only on the left side.

"Those are numbers on the doors," Theodore told Ben and Audrey as they passed the second door. "They start at the highest number."

Ben and Audrey just stared at the doors, unable to read the numbers.

They followed a precise straight corridor that felt unpredictable with its dips every few feet or none for several and up at times.

"Here." Theodore stopped at a door and knocked three fast knocks and one slow.

The door rattled open.

"Hello?" Theodore called out. No one answered back. "I guess he wants us to wait for him here." He shrugged.

A bed faced them on the far wall. The walls were packed with dirt, smoothed in well and mixed with some sort of dye that made them look a pleasing sage color. Against the wall on the right side was an old dresser with a missing knob. The ceiling had three orbed holes the size of oranges that opened to the sky. Glass, or something similar, covered them.

"This feels off." Ben's chest rose and fell faster than before.

"At least there is a bed inside. Let's just relax for a minute. I'm sure everything is fine," Theodore said. He sat on the bed, which was stiff with thick padding. Audrey sat down next to him and patted the bed for Ben to join. "Come on, my dearest friend. Join us on this... very mediocre bed," Theodore said with a chuckle.

Ben picked at the door with his fingernail, like a kid peeling off paint. His face was deep in unsettling thoughts.

"Do you plan on staying?" Rew's voice came from behind him.

Ben tensed and quickly pulled his hand away. "Uh, yes. I just. Nothing."

"I forget how odd... never mind." Rew shook his head and pushed Ben inside as gently as he felt the need to before closing the door suddenly. "The room is the best I could do. I can give you another room if necessary for your guests. We can discuss such things before I leave." He paused and shifted his weight. "A battle has already taken place at the Divide."

Theodore tensed. "Was The Choke present?"

"No, we knew it would occur. And we will not be a part of the next either."

"Then, when?" Theodore pushed himself up from the bed to stand.

"Though we have many folks ready for our moment to unify in battle, it would be foolish to not wait."

Theodore's heart pounded. "What happened? Is Eliza alive?"

"Amarda handled it well... That is, except for Haylin." Rew hung his head solemnly. "The Fated of Souls is critically injured. As for Eliza, I don't believe she was present for the fight."

Theodore, Audrey, and Ben all let out a sigh of relief.

"Haylin? Kinsington's mate?"

"That's the one. Her abilities are"—he raised an eyebrow—"curious. Could you enlighten me on what she is capable of and if more Eltrists have it?"

"As far as I know, she uses slivers of souls to control the ones she took from, but I have heard whispers that it is not just used for protection. I have no inkling what that could be."

"Wait. Wait." Audrey held up her hands. "Kinsington took part of my soul. And Ben's. Could that mean he has the same ability to use us?"

"You?" Rew cocked his head. "That is a curious thing, isn't it? Kinsington cannot harness that power. He can take bits of souls, but they are useless to him... unless he transferred them to Haylin." He paced the room like a detective watching all the pieces of a puzzle slot together.

"Could she do that by touching me? Remember when I crashed the car and something called to me? I never fully saw what it was, but it made me feel a tug. One that I tried to scratch away." Ben shivered.

"They can put a small dose of strug inside you. It can make you go insane. It's possible that he could transfer the magic to Haylin, but it wouldn't make sense to use non-magic beings' souls. Especially ones not from here," Theodore said. "The souls must fuel her or be useful outside of battle."

"I'll ask around and see if anyone knows of her power," Rew said. "You never said if other Eltrists have the same ability."

"I know of only one other, believed to be dead long ago."

Rew put his webbed hands together. "Talkun?"

"Yes."

"Ancient One, you are wrong. Talkun lives and breathes."

Theodore blinked. He rose his hands and shook his head in disbelief. "How?"

"I have word that he lives and was released recently by Amarda; in fact, our informant spoke of the Bloodtress releasing him from Talkun's Tower, where he has suffered all these decades."

"That would mean..." Theodore stumbled back onto the bed. He placed his hands on his stomach, as if he had just been punched.

"Your kalus lives." Rew nodded and smiled. "The true heir to Folengower."

"Kalus?" Audrey murmured.

A heaviness weighed down the room. For a while, they all remained silent. "Uncle. It means uncle," Theodore finally said. "What does Amarda plan to do with him?"

"I have mixed reports. Some say that they want him to take the throne as he was meant to, and others want Kinsington to rule while Talkun helps."

"Which do you believe?"

"Before, I believed Kinsington to want the throne; now, I am unsure." Rew gazed up into the holes in the ceiling. That same faint smile appeared. "I think we will know more once we find out if Haylin survives. A death like that could bring out an ugliness we haven't calculated for."

Theodore nodded, his hand on Audrey's knee. "Do they know of The Choke?"

"Long ago, one of our people reached out to an Eltrist in secret. They weren't keen on a united Folengower. I will say that some of them now are, and we are doing what we can to turn that blade and have Eltrists join us, but…" Rew sighed and leaned against the door. "Kinsington is not willing to."

"Have any joined?"

"Not yet." Rew bit his lip. "The news of the Divide will not help."

"How am I to lead? What will be my role?" Theodore stroked the hairs on his ever-growing beard.

"We can't have you acting as if you aren't cursing the soil for anyone who doesn't bleed for Nniar. Bruthren has a plan to bring you to Nniar's encampment."

"Bruthren wishes me to join my father?" Theodore crossed his arms and huffed a laugh. "He can't believe that wouldn't spoil the plans for unity."

"Not if you act the part."

"A dangerous part. One that I have yet to agree to."

"Think about it. In the meantime, saving the Bloodtress is our top priority."

Now Theodore gave an incredulous stare and leaned forward, his crossed arms quickly uncrossing. "Why? I want nothing more than to save my sister, but why would The Choke care? You were unsure they'd want to get involved."

"Our informant believes she is following in your footsteps. I imagine you know that."

"I know if she knew the truth she would, but I am unsure how she would know that."

"Well, however the truth came to her, we believe having the Bloodtress on our side will strengthen our cause even more so. The next heirs of Folengower fighting for unity. Can you see the reaction in your mind?" Rew clasped his hands together and gazed up as if in a daydream.

"I want to be there to rescue her." Theodore clenched his teeth. "They wanted me, not her."

"And you will. Bruthren will send word tomorrow if it is safe enough to chance it. So far, we plan for the night and our informant to help. With the chaos around Haylin, it should be easy to make her disappear. Then, you will return your father's owl and your sister to the island of the Anorphus. No one will question where you have been."

Theodore tapped his finger on his thigh. "It would seem Bruthren has thought of everything."

"What about us?" Ben said.

"Unfortunately, you two have no roles to play in the plan. Not when Korrigan has made it known what he feels about outsiders."

"So, what, they will stay here?" Theodore said.

"They can work for unity like the rest of us and will have a home to go to in between. We have someone that is willing to prepare them, or"—Rew looked from Ben to Audrey—"you may return from where you came."

"They should be with me." Theodore frowned and squeezed Audrey's thigh protectively. "Eliza brought them here. She can convince my father that she wants them with us."

Audrey put her hand on Theodore's. Her eyes were serious in all the ways of heartache. "We will help from afar. I will not be the woman who ruins what could be. The healing of this land needs to happen, and you are a huge part of that. Not me. Not Ben."

"She's right," Ben agreed. "At least this way, you know we will be alive for the time being."

Theodore bit the inside of his cheek in thought, then focused back on Rew. "When Bruthren gets here, I will save Eliza, but these two must be protected at all costs."

Rew lowered his gaze from Theodore's. He was happy to keep them protected, but he wasn't sure about the "at all costs" part. "I will care for them just as I do the rest."

Theodore nodded, with his hand clutching Audrey's. "I want updates on them when I'm gone."

"That can be arranged. I will leave you three for now. Would you each like your own room?"

Ben looked at the only bed in the room. "I would."

Theodore opened his mouth to protest, to ask for another bed to be moved into the room, to say or do anything to keep his friend as close to him as possible.

Ben squeezed Theodore's shoulder and chuckled. "No, really, I will be fine in my own space."

Rew handed a piece of paper to Ben. "It's the room before this one. Knock like this." Rew rapped on the wall for him to hear. "For now, please relax in the communal space or the rooms, and, Ancient One, get to know the folks here. They demand a like-minded leader. Do not let us down."

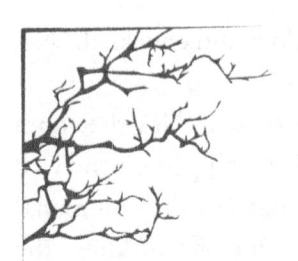

11

A monster could have charged into the camp and most would have ignored it or simply killed it and tossed it to the side as if it were a fly. Nothing could keep their attention except if the Fated of Souls would live another day. When night fell, they kept their eyes open, for exhaustion would have to wait. Even when the sun ate at their skin with its heat, they stayed busy. Busy waiting outside the canopy they hid her beneath.

Hundreds of people sat in the grass, most with their legs crossed, some playing music. Many had arms around one another. Others sat alone, their faces downcast in ways that only true heartache could cause. From time to time, folks and Eltrists brought gifts between training like flowers, rare nuts from the dead forest, stone chips of the same cut as their caves that sparkled like moonstone, hallowed nectar poured around her tent, as well as some more peculiar things like rotted teeth from small critters and ground-up scales.

A calm melody started from one mouth. Before long, they all hummed with a passionate yet painful expression. Kinsington exited Haylin's canopy, careful to not step on any of the offerings. The humming melded into a single held breath, their eyes begging for news. Kinsington had no want to look at them. His head hung.

"The Fated of Souls still lives... for now. Her life thread is thinning. We must stay united as we await the news of what is to come," Kinsington said into everyone's mind.

Tears streamed down many faces, others hummed once more and hope held on to few. The hopeful stood to gather more offerings because that would keep her heart beating, they thought.

Kinsington left the eyes of the many and searched for Thorn's mind. When he felt nothing of her, he wandered to Riven. He found neither.

"Sylin," he called.

"I'm here," he replied.

Kinsington realized Sylin was just beyond the crowd. His small wing twitched. The crowd parted as Kinsington made his way to him in slow, somber steps. "Find Thorn. I need her."

"Of course."

Sylin searched at Thorn's tent first and called to her with his mind, gently at first, but his voice grew when he received no response. He pawed at the fabric door and put his nose in. It smelled of her, but he could tell it was only from her belongings. Sylin sighed at the empty space and backed away. He wandered through the campsite, calling to other Eltrists to ask if they knew where she was.

"Check Riven's tent," one replied.

At the far end, Riven's tent stood darker than the surrounding ones. She had painted it with mud and crushed berries one day when boredom consumed her.

Splotches of lighter color stood out any time the moonlight or sun hit it just right.

"Thorn?" Sylin called out to her mind. His patience was like a broken cup, the water draining ever so quickly. There were only so many places she could be now that he already traipsed through the campsite. He sniffed at the tent just to make sure she wasn't there before he left to look elsewhere, but he the pungent smell of her was there. With a huff, he pawed the flap open, barging his eye in. Thorn was facing his way, but her eyes were shut and she was sitting on the edge of Riven's bed with her head tilted back. pawed the flap open, barging his eye in.

"What the..."

Thorn's eyes opened and she shot up, practically pushing Riven to the side. Thorn charged out of the tent. Sylin backed away just as Riven joined her.

"Sylin, since when do you just peek into our tents?" Riven shouted, hands on her hips. Her usually sandy blonde ponytailed hair looked as if she rolled around in the meadow.

"Kinsington needs Thorn now," he said unapologetically.

"Next time, knock or find me up here." Thorn pointed to her head.

Sylin bared his teeth. "I tried."

"Try harder," Thorn spat. She stomped off to Haylin's canopy, without as much as a backward glance. Many were still gathered in wait outside and inside. Kinsington was waiting next to Talkun, and Aylo snarled at her as she approached. Thorn, still feeling irritated, shot Aylo a glare.

"What does the boy know?" Kinsington asked, raising his head.

Thorn halted before him. At first, she frowned, and then, as if what he meant clicked, she asked, "Kalien?"

Kinsington nodded, his paw tapping on the ground. "Have I asked too much of you?"

"No... no, of course not."

"Rid your distractions, then."

Thorn's jaw tightened. "Kalien has been difficult lately. He wants to be freed from this, but he will do as I say."

"What news does he have? Did he know of the ambush?"

"He did not."

Kinsington spat out a blob of strug at her feet. "What is the point of him, then?"

Thorn shuffled back from the strug. "I will watch him more."

"Find the time."

"I will."

Kinsington shooed her away with his paw. "I would hate to replace you."

Thorn's head hung as she paused mid-step over a puddle of strug. "That won't be necessary."

Eliza could see everyone from the camp from the boulder she was sitting on. And that included the Eltrist with dark fur who lurked just outside the boundary of the camp whose warning glances prevented her from journeying any further. She'd spent the last few hours contemplating what to do and if she should risk running when the Eltrist would make its way around the camp before getting back to her. Her ashy and cold hands clawed at the stone.

The sun finally heated the rock enough for her hands to warm, and she lay down atop it, a golden glow cast onto her skin.

"Eliza," O whispered. "I have to speak to you now."

Eliza kept her eyes closed and sighed. "What?"

"Come down here. It's important." O peered over his shoulder as he rubbed his hands nervously.

Eliza sat up and jumped down from the boulder. "What?" she said with a shrug, as if she doubted that anything he could say would matter to her.

O grabbed her hand and fled into the copse. Eliza stumbled behind him. All the warmth she had disappeared beneath the emerald trees. A chill made her hairs stand on end as they ran amongst shadows. Even in the shade, Eliza could see his chest move at a quickened pace as he stopped and turned to face her.

"What is it?" Eliza pulled her hand from his and crossed her arms.

O swallowed. "You are leaving."

Eliza narrowed her eyes. "Is this your way of telling me that Thorn still wants me dead?"

O shook his head, taking time to catch his words and release them to her. "No, no. Your brother is coming."

"H-h-how could you know that?" Eliza stared into O's trustworthy eyes, his hair a lighter shade than the leaves on the trees behind him.

O placed his arms on Eliza's shoulders firmly, keeping her in place. "Trust me, he is coming to save you. All I need you to do is stay in here."

"I don't understand. How would *you*"— Eliza poked at his bare chest—"know where Theodore is?"

O squeezed his hands together and lowered his head. "I don't want to involve you, but I told you I wanted to help and so here's the proof."

Eliza's brow furrowed as she tilted his head back up with two fingers and studied his face. "Who are you?" she asked softly.

O struggled to make eye contact despite Eliza's persistence. "We all have secrets. I should leave all this for your brother to explain. There isn't much time."

"Why would you do all this?" Eliza pressed.

"You're innocent. I've told you before, I had and have no plan to harm—"

"No, tell me. You are releasing a Bloodtress, not a folk you just found. Someone who bleeds with the same disgusting blood as the one who tore Folengower apart. They will kill you for this." Eliza's backed away from him.

"Eliza... I..." O paced, kicking up pebbles with his hooves. His amber eyes brightened like flames.

"Tell me, O." Eliza's voice cracked.

"Your life matters to me." O averted his gaze from her and cleared his throat. "Your life matters to many people."

"If there is truth in your words, I feel that I am too lost to find it."

O gazed at her pensively. A flicker of something caught his eye, and he stared at the sky or what little he could see of it in between the tree branches. A split second later, O stormed at Eliza, snatched her in his arms and rolled to the ground under a bush. He hovered a hand over Eliza's mouth and said a breathy, "Shhh." His hand trembled as their hearts pounded together.

"What is it?" she whispered.

"Eltrist."

O tried to keep his hand steady as he held his weight barely above hers. Eliza grabbed his hand and motioned for him to lie on top of her. He lowered himself, with his head hung to the side of hers. The bush's thick stalks netted together, leaving little room for him to shift.

He lifted his head. "I don't think anyone saw us."

"I hope not." Their breaths were fast and hushed. O smiled and stared into her eyes. Eliza's lips parted, as if surprised. "Why are you helping me?"

His heart thudded against hers. This time, it felt different. A different type of scared. "Bloodtress..." O let out a soft sigh and bit his lip. "It is part of my job and a foolish dream I have held since we first shared our truths. If only that dream would come true in another life."

"A dream?"

"One where I would not hold you as you fear what's coming, but one where you would wrap your arms around me with love in your eyes."

Eliza grinned with her lips closed. She placed her hands on his cheeks and pulled his face closer. He hesitated, unsure if she could truly want him as he wanted her. Eliza met his lips with hers, and O groaned at her touch. Even though his mouth stayed hungry for hers, he lifted his head away. His body shook.

"What?" Eliza pulled him back to her. She kissed his neck, causing him to walk through the fog of bliss once more.

"No, no. Eliza. This can't happen."

Eliza wanted to protest, but she knew he was right. She steadied her breaths.

O rolled off of her and out from under the bush. He stood and scanned between tree branches for any more Eltrists. "It's clear," he whispered.

Eliza crawled out from under the bush and wiped the dirt and twigs off her clothes as she stood. She resisted the urge to pluck a stray leaf from O's hair. "When will he come?"

"When the moon rises. For now, act normal and return here tonight."

O turned to leave the copse behind, but Eliza called to him. "O?"

"Yes, Bloodtress."

"I plan on continuing this." She pointed to him and then to herself. "But that means you need to stay alive."

O smiled, all his pearly teeth showing. "For you, anything."

Eliza waited beneath the conifers. She stared at the beauty of them, of the giants they created with their shadows. She tried hard to not smile, to not let her mind invent stories she was sure would never surface. When she was sure O would be far from her, she emerged and wandered back to the boulders.

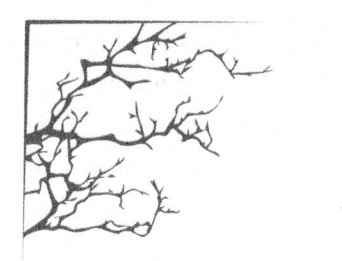

12

The entire camp could hear the echoes of waves crashing beneath the Anorphus inside a cave that howled with deafening breaths. The sea had only gained in its strength since the night waved its goodbyes.

Folks moved through the camp like frightened felines. Even in the round tent, Kalien and the rest of the crew were visibly on edge. Kalien had a befuddled mind already, and the repeated echoes only added to his distress.

Reed carried a tray of corpse thistles to the side of his contraption. His hands moved to set it down, but just as he went to let go, a howl shook through the tent and his hand flicked the tray. It jumped and landed on the floor. Reed slammed his fist into the table and cursed the soil.

Queen Agden rose from her seat. She laced her hands together and eyed all the workers one at a time. Some bowed to her and others did a half bow, unsure of what the etiquette would be in this situation.

"The wind speaks of foul things. While it may be unnerving, we must work. We work to end this war with haste. During times of good, we work as one. During war is no different, if not more vital."

Cressa had already begun cleaning up the mess, and another folk with gray hair helped. Reed gave a sigh as he knelt to collect the tray. Cressa rubbed his back for a moment. Reed, without thinking, placed his hand on top of hers, as if to thank her for it. Then, like Mr. Hyde, he shook his shoulder for her to leave him alone. Cressa scowled and backed away. She snatched the tray from him and set it back on the table before leaving him and the other person to gather up the corpse thistles.

At the end of the day, Kalien left before anyone else for the first time, with his head down and his footfalls as quiet as a reaper. Bruthren haunted his thoughts. He knew he would come as he had said and then he would know everything. Kalien's heart hurt and flowed into his throat, as if something had grown and was waiting for him to either vomit it up or swallow it back down.

"Kalien," someone called as he was about to round the next tent.

Kalien's eyes widened, and he considered pretending he hadn't heard his name being called, but he knew he would have to face Bruthren sooner or later. With all the assertiveness he could muster, he swung around as if he were ready to fight.

Indigo's eyes widened in return as they held their hands up defensively.

Kalien's face softened. "Oh, it's just you."

"Uh... yeah. Who else would it be?" They tilted their head and frowned. "You forgot to leave your apron and goggles. Here, I'll take them back for you."

"Huh?" Kalien felt at his chest and head. "I... I guess I forgot."

"For moon's sake, are you alright? You seem off today."

Kalien took off his apron and goggles and handed them over, unsure of what to say. "It's been a strange day."

"The"—Indigo twirled a hand in the air—"wind is unsettling."

Kalien nodded, his hands in his pockets.

"See you later?" Indigo said, eyebrow raised.

"Yeah," Kalien replied before racing off.

Crowds traversed down to the tables where dinner took place. Some would take plates back to their tents. Kalien assumed on a night such as this everyone would. No one wanted to hear the howl, though he noticed that Bruthren never startled or even held an unsettled gaze from the echoes that only fattened in its range.

Kalien stepped into his home. His three bunkmates were nowhere to be found, though he assumed they were still down the hill eating. Kalien wasn't hungry even though his belly was empty.

He stared at anything and everything in the tent, as if he'd stumbled into an antiques store. Part of his mind told him to pack his things and run, but where to and how far could he truly get without being captured, and what if Bruthren had no intention of harming him but wanted to help? It was true that Bruthren had previously not cared if he had died, nor cared that bringing the birds back had cost him a broken arm and migraines that he still suffered from. In the end, he sat on his bed, the lump in his throat feeling like a death sentence.

Reed, Indigo and Cressa made it back with windswept hair and plates of food wrapped in cloth. Their breaths could have instantly fogged up a car if they had been in one.

Reed looked Kalien up and down. "No dinner?"

"I'll go down later."

"I should have brought you a plate," Indigo said, as if they could have known Kalien didn't get one for himself.

"Are you alright?" Cressa said.

"I'm fine." He lifted his hands and let them fall to his lap. "Just a strange day."

Reed unwrapped his plate, and a sea of scents whirled around the tent. He picked at the flower ball that squished into his fish, which drowned out some of the fishy smell.

Cressa placed her fist under her chin and glared at Reed.

"What?" Reed glared back with a mouthful of fish.

"Kalien is going through something and you decide to just eat?"

"What would you like me to do? Let my stomach growl until you are sick of hearing it?" Reed tore off another piece, edged close to Cressa's face and chewed slowly without blinking.

"Go eat with the chackles, you animal," Cressa spat.

"Maybe I will."

"Please, just ignore me and eat your dinner," Kalien said.

"See, he doesn't care."

Indigo frowned at Kalien, but they did as he said.

Cressa followed, taking a bite of her fish. "I can share, if you want." She shrugged.

He waved. "No, really, I'm fine, but thank you." He lay down on his bed, listening to munching sounds that he feared he would never hear again; after all, the night had reclaimed the land already, and soon he would have to answer to Bruthren.

A sharp poke in the ribs stirred Kalien, and he groggily swatted whatever it was away. Another poke, then another. Kalien jolted up like a zombie escaping his grave and threw himself off his bed. Bruthren caught him in his grip as if he had done it before and gently placed his hand over Kalien's mouth.

"Calm now, friend." Kalien could smell his nutty breath. Bruthren motioned him out of the tent.

Reed had his body turned to face his "wall," with the blanket wrapped around him, as if he wished to turn into a butterfly by the morning. Cressa's arm was hanging out of the bed, her eyelids fluttering as she dreamed deeply. Indigo slept with a frown on their face, the almost-exclusive-to-Reed one they'd burned into his memory. Kalien's eyes darted to them, his forehead wrinkled with desperation, as if he thought about waking them.

The last step out of the tent felt just as painful as following Thorn back to Kinsington had after joining her at Talkun's Tower. Bruthren moved as if floating through the tents and over a knoll. A shrieking howl shook leaves from the Anorphus. They cascaded down like snow. Kalien dodged them the best he could in case the leaves could poison him too.

Bruthren peered over his shoulder at him. "Pay no worry to the leaves unless you plan on swallowing them." His grayish green eyes spoke of madness, and his grin started under his eyes and appeared to swoop down, from the moonlight casting on him. He looked more monstrous than usual. "This won't take too long."

Kalien gulped. The lump in his throat felt all-consuming. The blanket of verdure rolled, as if it would break away from the soil as a tumbleweed. For now, it held strong. Bruthren covered his mouth and eyes the best he could with a curved hand as he lifted his legs as if he trudged through a swamp. Kalien fared no better in the great air. His hair whipped wildly, covering his face. He tried sweeping it to the side with a shake of his head, as his hands were busy wrapped around his stiff body.

Up ahead, a mass of roots slithered in front of them like Medusa's snakes. The fallen tree, despite its death, had healthy, whitish roots. Kalien wondered if someone had ripped it from the soil or if the boisterous wind had reaped it. Bruthren waved to him to follow him beneath it.

The hollow below had a faint ring of dark purple, like a bruise that swelled before the deepest depths. Bruthren ducked his head. Swaths of roots brushed into his hair and some pricked at his cheeks. Bruthren snickered like a child tricking someone.

Kalien peered up at the wavy bunch, his eyes squinting. He thought of many things before following Bruthren under, all chaotic and depressing, as if he knew this was the moment a rabid beast would eat him face first. Kalien rubbed the sweat from his hands onto his shirt, pinching his skin as he did so.

"I can't," Kalien said, on the verge of tears.

Bruthren had already been consumed by the ghastly hole.

Kalien teetered the top half of his body in. "I can't," he repeated, even shakier this time. Kalien's brows furrowed. "Bruthren?"

When no response came, he turned to run back down the knoll. As his feet moved, something grabbed at his back. His face grew grim, and he screamed. He scratched at his back and found Bruthren's hand plucking an overzealous root from his clothing.

"My... you scare easily. Take my hand."

Kalien stretched out his hand like Bruthren held a rattlesnake in his. Bruthren sighed and latched on. He dragged him under like a crypt keeper. Kalien's wails came in rasping breaths. He squeezed his eyes shut. Then, with a thud, Bruthren let him go. Kalien tripped, catching himself with his hands out, landing on all fours.

"If I had known you would be so... so dramatic, I would have placed you in a sack and hauled you up here."

Kalien groaned. "If you would just get to the point."

Bruthren raised his hands and threw something speckled into the air. The soil above them shook with pebbles and dirt pelting them. A dull light pulsed into existence as the tree closed like a ring box. When it snapped into place, Kalien rushed to the trunk and struck it desperately with his fists.

"Where did you get a vision meld from?" Bruthren said, calm and collected as usual.

Kalien spared a single laugh, as if he couldn't believe what his life had become. His hair dangled over his face, wet with sweat. He peered at Bruthren between the strands, bent over, with the side of his head resting on the tree, out of breath. "What?"

"The vision meld. That thing in your ear." Bruthren poked at it.

Kalien grimaced. "Someone put it in me. I have tried taking it out, but it will not leave."

"What an extraordinary being you have turned out to be. I thought there was something strange about you, but this... my, my. Who put it in you, and what do they want?"

"If I tell you, will you tell the Ancient One?"

"*Ha*. These types of secrets are better kept, aren't they?"

Kalien stood up and gave him an incredulous gaze. Bits of dirt rained out of his hair. "A woman named Thorn from Amarda. I was at the castle when they came, and she took me as a prisoner to watch Talkun's Tower with this." He pointed at his ear.

"And that's when a knight found you in the forest and brought you here." Bruthren adjusted his glasses. "So, this Thorn person is still watching when she pleases, then?"

"Yes, unfortunately."

"Is she watching now?"

"No, not since yesterday."

Bruthren paced with his hands held behind his back. "Tell me, Kalien, what do you think of Korrigan?"

"What does that matter?"

"I wonder if you want to help Amarda... or if it is just a sad tale for you."

"My beliefs about our current Ancient One did not put me in this situation."

Bruthren tapped his fingertips together. "Cursed soil. You disapprove of our leader? Say it." He hovered over Kalien's face, only an inch away, with a sickly smile.

"I didn't say that."

"Oh, here we go." Bruthren reached into his pocket and clasped something. He blew on it, and smoke stirred from his hand in a stringy rope shape. It floated to Kalien and wrapped around his torso as if it were a hand, then it squeezed. "Tell me how you truly feel."

Kalien squirmed. "My grandmother worked for Queen Callum, and I know Korrigan is deceitful," he said through clenched teeth.

Bruthren rubbed at his palm. The smoke recoiled back into it. "Queen Callum?"

"Yes."

"We have a mutual distaste, then."

"What do you mean?"

"Have you heard of The Choke?"

Kalien shook his head.

Bruthren put his arm over his shoulder, as if they were pals. "Let me paint you a picture." He flicked his hand in the air. "When Queen Callum died, so did Folengower. It's been a slow and painful death. You may not have been alive then, but let me tell you, life was..." Bruthren sighed. "Exquisite. I was only a child when things took a turn, but I remember. I am the leader and founder of The Choke. We plan to unite Folengower once and for all by secretive and tactical means."

Kalien backed up. He wrapped his arms around his body protectively. "Do you work with Amarda, then?"

"No, dear folk, no." Bruthren snorted and moved from him. "Aren't you listening? I am on neither side, yet both. Folengower will become a corpse without us reuniting Amarda and Nniar." He danced around the space for a moment, his knees reaching his chest like an odd spidery thing. "Will you join us?"

"I don't want any part of this." Kalien dug his fingers into his forehead. "I don't want to be a spy."

Bruthren swatted away his words with his waving hands. "Do you not understand how wars work? Everyone takes part. Some may stand on the sidelines, waiting for others to drown in their own blood, but you... you are a survivor. Survivors have fight in them. And whether you like it or not, your web has already been woven. Thorn recruited you for a reason."

Kalien scanned Bruthren's every movement in the faint light. Bruthren moved as if he were leading him in a play. A frightening one at that. "Even if I agree, I still am a spy for Amarda."

"Oh, I know exactly how to take that out un—"

"How?"

"By feeding it."

"What do you mean feed it?" Kalien poked at his ear, his lip curled up. "How do you even know that?"

Bruthren raised a finger to his lips. "So many questions. I invented them, of course." Bruthren chuckled and shook his head, as if this was common knowledge. "Have you not heard of my prowess as the greatest mastermind behind some of the most brilliant and chilling magic in Nniar? Apparently, Amarda has heard of my legendary creations," he boasted, boisterous in his capabilities.

Kalien's shoulders slumped, unimpressed. "Can we take it out now?"

Even in the covering of the tree, the howling wind traveled through the craggy space. The sparse light flowed in a circular motion, like a fox chasing its tail.

"What if we left it?" Bruthren beamed. He grabbed for Kalien's hand.

Kalien recoiled. "I would rather—"

"Not. I know." He squeezed Kalien's shoulder in a show of support, but it felt fake to Kalien. "BUT what if we use this to our advantage? I already have watchful eyes on Korrigan, but having another set of eyes on Kinsington's army too could be a significant advantage."

"How do you suppose I keep all of you happy if I'm to report to Thorn whenever she chooses to pop in?"

"I have a delicious idea. Oh, yes... yes." Bruthren balled his shaking fists tightly at his sides, as if trying to contain his excitement. "Report to Thorn the information that I give you on my fellow Choke members. That way, she will think you have given up on trying to distance from her."

"Won't that make her suspicious?"

"Not when you tell her you've taken their side after seeing a horrible display from Korrigan. Be convincing. Wake her at night in a crazed manner and declare allegiance to Amarda. Over time, she will trust you as you check in with more information."

Kalien bit his lip, uncomfortable with the idea of going behind backs and freely giving out information that wasn't his to share. "Will I be telling her truthful things?"

"Of course not." Bruthren looked genuinely offended that this had even crossed Kalien's mind, and then his face softened as he seemed to rethink. "Unless it helps The Choke, of course."

Kalien felt his body numb as his last question reached his lips. "Do you really believe that you can unify Folengower?"

Bruthren grinned cheerfully. "On all the dead in this cursed soil."

"Fine." Kalien crossed his arms. "I'll do it. Just don't get me killed."

"War guarantees no souls left untouched, but I will do my best." Bruthren stepped in front of him. "Now, to join The Choke, I need you to mirror me." Bruthren flipped his hands onto his throat with his thumbs side by side above his sternum as he had done hundreds of times.

Kalien hesitated to place his hands upon his own neck, but he did so after Bruthren nodded persuasively.

"Repeat after me: our blood bound or corpse thistles, we will drown," Bruthren said slowly and then again in unison with Kalien.

"Welcome to The Choke, Kalien. I will alert the others that we have a most special recruit." Bruthren shook, as if dancing with insects crawling on him. "Now, get back to your bed, and when the moon steals the sky, tell Thorn that

Korrigan is showing his true self to the people of Nniar. Say whatever you must to convince her." Bruthren gazed up in thought. "And if she ever pops in when she shouldn't, close your eyes."

Bruthren whispered ancient words to the walls, and the tree lifted from its cushioned home in the soil. Its roots sprang out, bouncing as it reached the surface. Kalien ducked underneath and made long strides to return to his bed. Bruthren patted at the trunk of the tree, watchful of Kalien as he sped back down the knoll under the fading moonlight.

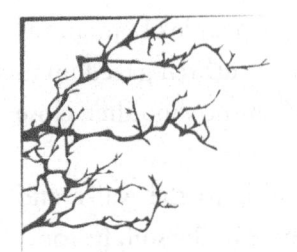

13

Theodore climbed the stairs back to the top of the grayden while Ben and Audrey sat at a table together, staring up at the light that shined down. Audrey sat with a wooden mug that she insisted on prodding with her index finger, as if she wished it to do a trick. Ben rapped his hands on the table in a beat.

"What do you think of all this?" Audrey whispered.

Ben lowered his head and peered around. The chef at the end moved on swift feet, gathering more seasoning, which he tossed over his shoulder, perfectly covering the slab of meat. The oven belched a dull roar as he seared the other side.

"I think we are in over our heads, to be honest. I don't mean to dampen all that Theo has done, but this is heavy."

"Fuck... I know."

"Are you planning on staying here?"

Audrey bit her lip. She took a moment lost in her own thoughts before answering. "I wouldn't leave Theodore. It may sound stupid, but I will follow him into battle regardless of the part of me that is screaming of danger. I see home when I look into his eyes." Audrey closed her eyes as if she could see him. "I could never walk away from that."

Audrey paused as a person passed. Ben smiled a wistful smile. "Is the heaviness enough to return to Harthsburg?"

Ben shrugged. "I'm scared, I truly am, but I could never turn my back on him or you or Eliza. That scares me more."

"Awe, Ben. It sounds like you love us?" Audrey snickered.

"I wouldn't have come if I didn't consider you family. Good enough?"

"I'll take it."

They laughed as if they were in Harthsburg sipping on tea and having an ordinary day.

Theodore had taken Rew's words earnestly. The grayden had many cavities and pockets of space where folks collected the dead magic. A pyndin balanced her hoof on an uneven rock. Her hooves shimmered in dust and flakes of dry strug as if it were gold dust. She reached her arms back, with a three-headed ax. Each head had serrated teeth different from the other two. She swung into the wall with the sharpest side. The wall cracked like glass. The webbed fissures reached to the ground.

Theodore watched her work with vehement swings. After a few minutes, she placed the ax down and pushed her goggles on top of her waxy-looking hat. "Did you come to stare or partake?"

"Both, I suppose. May I?" Theodore pointed to the ax.

"An Ancient One doing cursed work? Of course." She gathered a pair of goggles and a protective hat from a wall. "You'll need these."

Theodore gladly took them. "And your name?"

"Camis. You can call me Cam if you'd like."

"Beautiful name." Theodore placed the hat on, a dusty gray like almost everything else in the room, and snapped on the goggles. They were wide and stretched to the sides of his eyes. He lifted the ax, reached his arm back and swung.

Camis clapped excitedly and laughed. "Well done, well done, Ancient One."

The wall split into a ravine, and balls like geodes rolled down in the middle, pinballing against each side. Theodore set the ax down and bent over, reaching to claim one of the rough balls. It puffed between his spindly fingers like a balloon being squeezed. He poked at a piece with his other hand, and the ball crumbled. Theodore tried to put it back together.

"Dead magic is unstable; it can't stay together for long once we release it from its resting place."

"I see that. Should I put this somewhere?" Theodore said, his hands cupping what he could.

Camis grabbed a metal bin with handles made from chackle bones. It pounded the few steps it had to roll. Theodore tossed what he could from his hand, the dust sticking to him, as if he planned on finger painting. Theodore reached back into the gap and carefully gathered the rest that had fallen and placed them in.

"What happens after we extract these?" Theodore said, examining the ax.

"Well, after the cart is filled, we roll it into the reviving room." Camis waved a greeting to another worker as they rolled by with their newly empty cart.

"How do they revive it?"

"You will not find the answer with me, but I can lead you to the area, and Argwen can explain to you what they do. He, along with a couple of other folks, were the ones who gave us the knowledge to do all this. I have heard that when he was younger and still with his parents, they would recycle their magic. A rare thing, of course, but quite fascinating."

"Indeed, it is. I have never known anyone who's reused their magic."

"Of course you wouldn't. It's usually out of desperation."

Theodore took his goggles and head covering off. He handed them to her and frowned. "I didn't mean to offend."

"Someone of your lineage would not know of the misfortunes of the poor."

"You speak truths. I have not spent enough time with folks of every vein, though I hope you know my lack of understanding is not from a malicious place. I will help fix this."

Camis bent her knees and bowed. "I can see that."

"Now, where is Argwen?"

Camis led him around a massive rock formation of cuts that moved up to the ceiling like a brick spiral. "He's just on the other side."

"I hope to have the honor of swinging an ax beside you later."

"It would be a pleasure to."

Around the rock, a jagged entryway stood in the form of a rectangular piece of wood attached to a post. He swung it open and went through. He stopped at the entryway, placing his hand on the rough surface. Even in this room, everyone had the same drab clothing. It made Theodore stand out. He brushed his hand on his shirt, as if he felt uncomfortable. There was a large rectangular wood piece with an intricate weave throughout the frame, made from carf flower and agor vines that hung several inches deep. They shoveled the balls and sandy remnants of dead magic into the sieve-like frame. Underneath, a massive wooden bowl waited to catch all that came through. It resembled the same shape as a curved bathtub.

A stout person watched meticulously as the flakes fell, and as if he could count them, his head moved up and down. Another folk ran their fingers through the top as another worker shoveled more in. Theodore stepped into the room quietly, with his hands held behind his back.

To his surprise, the room went far back to the left and four more of the stations were set up. Another person with fair skin rushed over to the first sieve with a belt of many tools that clinked together when she moved wrapped around her waist. She pushed her wavy hair back in place from her crooked glasses and unhooked a toothed brush from her belt. Another worker set a step stool in front of her. She climbed atop the sieve, dragging the teeth across a small area and inspecting it.

"*Burn*," she shouted.

A person on either end summoned light to their palms and threw it over the sieve. They burned the dead magic until the weave appeared clean in its blue and brown. The woman, satisfied with the burn, staggered back down the steps. She quickened her steps back down the long room to another sieve as fast as her short legs could take her.

"Are you Argwen?" Theodore asked an older man, who watched as the next pile was loaded on top and the fine pieces cascaded down. He didn't peer up or answer to the name. Theodore assumed it was not Argwen.

As he moved through the room, out of everyone's way, he stopped at the last sieve. A goling sped past him and opened a door that was nearly invisible to anyone who didn't know of its existence. Theodore tried glancing into the room, but she closed the door too quickly for him to see anything.

"Come to see the great work of The Choke?" a voice said behind him.

Theodore turned around. "I am. I am looking for Argwen."

The man was slightly shorter than Theodore, his arms muscular from all the years of hard work. His face was kind and his skin the same shade as the rich bark from Nniar's ancient conifer trees. "Argwen is my name. I've never been in the presence of an Ancient One before, but I hear you're one of the good ones. Is that right?"

"Indeed. I am making my way through the grayden and hoping to get to know as many folks as I can and understand how the dead magic gets revived. I was told by Camis that you were the person who made this all happen."

"Oh, Camis. When I heard of The Choke, I thought what better way to have enough magic to fight than to do exactly what my father taught me." He chuckled.

Theodore listened with enthusiasm. "Could you walk me through the process? This is all very fascinating."

"Cursed soil." Argwen placed his hand on his heart. "An Ancient One interested in this. My... changes are coming, aren't they?"

"I plan on it."

Argwen led Theodore to a sieve. "As you know, the first part is getting the magic out of the soil. This step is... more delicate." Argwen raised his left eyebrow and stepped over a rock that protruded from the ground enough to trip over. Theodore followed his steps. "I call this the sorter. When dead magic is placed on top, I have a scrapper come and help with the last bits that are active while the rest will be removed by being burned. In here—the pot, we call it." Argwen crouched down so his head was peering over the tublike bowl. "This... this is all the good stuff. Dead magic that we can reanimate back to life without having fresh strug or matter of Folengower."

Argwen motioned him to the pot. Theodore crouched with him. The pot sparkled in strug dust. Bits dropped through the sorter until the entire frame had a thin layer left. They placed steps next to it, and the same short woman rushed over.

"She is very thorough with the scrapping. We don't have many bone brushes, so we make do with what we have. At this grayden, we have six workers who can do the scrapping. It's very important that we get that part right."

"What happens if it's not?"

"Well, we waste good magic. You need a keen eye to make sure what is left is unusable. This is a tremendous advantage since many of us cannot fight with our magic or wield a sword well enough to win."

"*Burn*," the woman shouted before rushing off again.

"Is everything in the pot live magic now?"

"If only. No, there's one more step, and it can take days to bring it back to life."

"Where is that done?"

"Some graydens do not have an area or expert for it, but this one has both."

Argwen opened the secret door behind them and held it for Theodore to go in first. Darkness surrounded them, and a strange smell followed. The smell grew, and so did the loss of familiarity of what it could be. The ground winded and felt as though cobblestones were beneath it.

Theodore held his hand out, and a white light emitted from his palm. "That's better," he said to no one in particular.

"I've gotten used to the dark in here," Argwen said as his footfalls sounded behind Theodore's. "Don't worry; in just a moment, you won't need that."

Luminescent fungi tore through the stones and dirt. The faint pink light ran underneath their feet and over their heads like vines. The deeper they went, the more fungi filled the crooked corners.

Theodore closed his fist, killing the light within it, and gazed at the masses of fungi. He felt as if he were back in Harthburg in winter, underneath dazzling lights for the winter festivities. "These are quite remarkable."

"When we first broke ground on this grayden..." Argwen scratched his head. "Oh, ten or twelve cycles ago, these fungi popped up everywhere. None of us had seen such a thing before. Then, one of us got brave enough to savor a piece. No poison, but mmm. They are a blessing of light and food for us."

"What do you call them?" Theodore ran his fingers down one. It felt wet and smooth, but when he rubbed his fingers together, it was dry and cold, as if he were playing with slime.

"Many names. Some say harmony spores, light strings, and so on. I like to say harmony strings because of when you do this." He took a strand, pulled it like elastic and let go. It snapped back, hitting the two next to it, causing the reaction to continue on down until there were no more left to react. A wondrous beat echoed off the walls, as if a faint xylophone had played.

Theodore's eyes lit like that of a child. "I imagine these make underground work a lot easier."

"A truth."

The cobblestone-like ground smoothed out. An archway and beams of light, like the dazzling sun, surrounded them. A burst of energy flooded through Theodore's bones and stole his breath.

Argwen cocked his head, unsure of what he felt. "What has taken you?"

"Magic, it would seem." Theodore breathed out, long and tingly, through his throat.

"The energy is powerful. I should have warned you."

"I wasn't expecting such a reaction."

Throughout the room, bags drooped like wasp hives on every wall, about five feet off the ground. There had to be at least three hundred strung about. Under them, a black and blue speckled stone basin followed the wall around until a gap divided them at the archway. Drips from the bags came steadily in their thick, goopy state. The magic was darker than strug, as if they had mixed it with charcoal. It shimmered as gossamer wings. Folks moved to them with long mixing tools that had a large circular shape on the bottom and a serrated edge. It cut through the magic like claws. Kinked ripples drifted until it collided with the next mixer's waves. It was a serene scene, as if they glided along a river with oars under a moonlit sky.

In the middle, they used a slab of rock as a table. Workers in this room had no protective gear. They sat at the table with sacks of cuttings from plants above ground. They sorted through them and rotated out the hanging bags with new cuttings while placing the rest in a stationary bag in a corner.

Argwen grinned without showing any teeth. "All the folks in here have limited magic. Hardly enough to do much with without strug. The magic feeds our being."

"It's quite overwhelming for me. I can feel what they were used for all at once. It's disorienting, which..." Theodore thought for a moment. "Which could be helpful against Cursed Knights and the Eltrist or anyone who possesses higher magical abilities."

"Bruthren has mentioned the same. He hates this room."

"I can understand. Is that finished revived magic?" Theodore pointed at the basins.

"It will be. Live magic takes time and courage to come back. The mixers are like mothers soothing a crying baby. See how they gently move in circular motions. It's calming, and once the magic moves through the basin steadily and without being stuck to the bottom, it can be used once more. Over there is where they bottle it and send it off to graydens to be stored. We have a storeroom here, just like the rest. Better to have stock throughout in case one is discovered."

Several folks gathered on the opposite side of the mixers and placed their bare hands into the basin. They lifted what they could and placed it into jars. When they were full, another placed the lid on, screwing it tight.

"How many jars have been stored?"

"Hard to say. Last time we did a mass counting, it was in the thousands."

"Is a plan in order on how we can distribute the magic to each fighter once we join in battle?"

"That is still to be calculated."

"I will see that it is a top priority. In the meantime, I would very much like to leave this space; my bones are numbing."

Argwen stepped out towards the tunnel. "Oh, come, come. I should have spoken faster."

Thoughts rolled through his mind on how to harness the magic efficiently and what else he could do to win such an astronomical feat as Argwen graciously led him back to the main chamber.

Theodore stretched his arms and legs while the numbing sensation slowly faded. He followed back down to the communal space. Audrey had her chin on a mug, her hair draped over her shoulders, while Theodore could only see Ben's back. The sight of them placed him in better spirits, but the thought that in just a few hours he would be gone indefinitely made his heart skip. A storm cloud of guilt hovered over him.

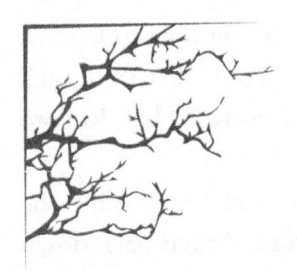

14

Dust danced down in the thin beams of light. They stared up at the three holes that offered a glimpse of the outside world. The light thinned before them as the night crept.

Audrey, Theodore and Ben lay on the ground with their heads touching one another's in a starlike shape, holding hands as if part of a coven. They had exhausted all there was to say and hadn't said the things they wished they could. Audrey squeezed their hands.

"It's almost time," she said. A tear streamed down her face, silent and fast.

Theodore bit his lip. "I know, my love."

The cold ground numbed their chaotic minds and kept their bodies frozen in place.

"Take care of Eliza," Ben said finally.

"Would you like me to put in a good word for you?" Theodore gazed at him.

Ben nearly got up, but Theodore and Audrey squeezed his hands. "No, I think we both just want friendship. I just want her to be well and focused so we can all make it out alive."

"I plan on it."

"Will we be able to send you notes? Do you have a bird?" Audrey said.

Theodore turned his head to her and kissed her temple. "I don't know what will happen, but I plan on keeping you safe. And no, I don't have a bird... at least not anymore. I have more."

"What does that mean?" Ben said.

"I have many eyes on both of you. If you need me, just ask the leaders here, though I know you will manage without me until I can return."

A subtle knock silenced them. Audrey gazed into Theodore's eyes. She took a breath in and held it until Ben got up. Theodore pawed at his leg to wait, though Ben caught his arm and dragged him up.

"The sooner things move forward, the sooner we can go on a real vacation." Ben gave a soft smile.

"Will you miss me at all?" Theodore said jokingly.

Another knock came. Theodore pulled Ben in for a hug, patting his back as they parted. He turned to Audrey, who bit her quivering lip. She wrapped her arms around him, and he placed his hands on the back of her head and kissed her lips softly.

"If either of you changes your mind, please tell Rew to take you back to Harthsburg. I can find you there after all this passes."

"I won't."

Theodore sighed. "I love you. A world without you is not one I could bear."

A bang sounded, one done with being polite. Ben opened the door. Rew stood with another folk. Audrey moved from Theodore's arms.

"It is time to save the Bloodtress."

"I assumed as much."

"It appears you've said your goodbyes. Shall we go?"

"Yes." Theodore got close to Rew's ear. "Don't forget what I said about keeping them safe and whole."

"Trust me."

"Good." Theodore stared at his friends one last time. He wanted to say goodbye, wanted to say something of importance, but he knew nothing could make this any better, so he gave a solemn wave and tried his hardest to smile. As if they were let go floating into the void, they managed to wave back. Audrey held her breath. No part of her felt like she could survive. At least not in the moment.

The door shut, and Rew, Theodore and the other folk rushed down the hall.

"Now would be a good time to tell me exactly what the plan is."

"Once the moon moves east, Eliza will be waiting for you in a copse that borders the outside of the camp. Once you find her, grab her. Follow back the way you came, and Fulin..." Rew pointed to the folk next to him, whose jaw was chiseled by the goddesses, her skin the embodiment of the deepest color of autumn and her hair silvery and tied in intricate braids.

Fulin stared ahead in deep focus. "I will take you through one of our graydens, and there you will send word to Nniar's camp to let you and the Bloodtress into Nniar's camp."

"How will I send word?" Theodore asked as they climbed up the ladder to the work floor.

"We have your father's bird."

"Polt? How did you manage that?"

The sound of axes pounding against the walls was deafening in some spots. Theodore cupped a hand over his ear.

"Bruthren has developed a strong bond with him over the years and has shown loyalty to them both," Rew shouted over the cacophony of tools slicing into the soil and stones. He stopped at a cavity in the ceiling and grabbed on to a rope ladder. Climbing, he said, "Follow me up."

Theodore climbed up and out to the surface. His lungs had forgotten how freeing open air truly was. It delighted him until he thought of where Audrey and Ben were. Fulin jumped out after them, her weapons swinging at her hips like wind chimes. Her longest weapon nearly scraped the ground. She gazed at the moon and mouthed something. Theodore's lips parted while he watched her, wondering if she knew Esmeray.

"Ancient One." Fulin gave a slight bow, interrupting Theodore's thoughts. "This way."

"Praise the moon that the depths leave you be," Rew said. He dove back down the hidden tunnel into the grayden.

Theodore followed Fulin through the Finnix forest. He spotted several pellucid eyes hidden beneath the verdant surroundings. Theodore heard the chackles' smacking lips just beyond a circle of trees before he saw them. They munched on the fungi sprouted from the ground, tugging and swaying to get ones out of reach of the agor vines that bound them to the tree.

"Choose one and we may be off. We must ride with haste."

Theodore ran up to the larger one and, kneeling, rubbed his cheek. "I need to borrow you."

Fulin untied the agor vines from around the other chackle and climbed atop. "Ready?"

"Indeed." The chackle nudged at his hand before he untied him and jumped atop. "Lead us," he commanded to Fulin.

"Halko," Fulin shouted to her chackle. They both took off darting through the forest, bounding past mossy stumps, leaping over fallen trees and rocks and scaring away any critters who neared their path. Air rushed past them, and the cold paled them. Through a meadow, they slowed, and Fulin gazed above. She unhooked a jar from her belt and held it in front of her.

"Watch for Eltrists. We are in the open, and they will not take kindly to anyone being close to their camp."

Theodore lit his hand. Black fire licked out of his palm, waiting for anything to appear in the cloudless abyss. Time elongated. In the distance, trees coupled together, spreading their branches lovingly to all close by.

"There. The Bloodtress is in there."

"Halko." Theodore's face hardened as he leaned forward.

Fulin charged next to him. "We will need to part ways. Leave your chackle over there." She pointed to a massive tree that stood alone.

Theodore patted the chackle's side, and it slowed and halted at the tree.

"Head into the woods. The Bloodtress is inside, waiting. When you find her, run back out the same way you came. If you need help, send your magic up."

"Easier than reigniting dead magic."

Fulin squinted. "Be quick," she said stoically.

Theodore took off to the copse. A faint chorus of voices flowed through the trees. Two massive fallen trees blocked the entrance to the forest, so Theodore held on to the bark, pulling himself up as he clawed into it. Bits of bark broke off or cracked in his grip. He lugged himself over the top and jumped down on the other side, landing in a crouch. The voices continued, fragmented.

Spirit wings fluttered together as if in dance, their iridescent wings hitting the moonlight like apparitions appearing and disappearing. An alliance of them landed on Theodore's arm, covering his entire sleeve. They sat in a row, with restful wings, their footprints leaving shimmery dust on his sleeve. They stayed only for a moment before flapping away to a cluster of flowers.

Deeper in, the trees' branches joined, blocking out the vastness of moonlight like an umbrella. The chill caught Theodore swiftly, making his body hairs prick up with a furtive step. The ground was blanketed in shadow beside the few speckles of light that gasped for air.

Theodore refrained from lighting his way—that would surely cause someone to spot him. Under his feet, rocks and soil mounded. It would randomly smooth out in patches. Theodore slunk around a tree, and his hand slipped on the bark, making a piece tumble down, subtle as a coin falling, but enough for footfalls to start towards him. He remained like a block of ice, in an awkward stance, with one hand on the tree.

"Hello?" a voice whispered.

He waited. It would be easy for someone to trick him into thinking Eliza had made it safely into the copse, then bag him. Crunching sounds over twigs and dead leaves grew closer to him at a quickening pace. He slunk behind the tree and listened. A bird rustled in the branches above and there was what sounded like an animal gnawing on a nut, but the singing voices were just loud enough to drown out the rest.

The footfalls reached the other side of the tree. Theodore pulled his sword out of his sheath. He spun it, bringing it close to his side. Stepping over the mass of roots with his knees bent as he crept around the tree, he proclaimed, "I plan on sparing your—"

A figure stood peering the other way. They had dark hair, longer than his. "When you come to save someone, you really shouldn't threaten them, Storm." Eliza turned around, her arms crossed loosely.

Theodore put his sword away and sighed. "I wish you were never here to begin with."

Eliza ran to him with open arms. He hugged her back. "Next time, I won't slip away thinking I can help."

"I blame myself, but now it's my time to shine. Saving a Bloodtress is a big deal, you know?" Theodore chuckled, taking Eliza's hand, hastening back to Fulin. The singing voices drained from existence with every tree they passed. "Why are they singing?"

Eliza stepped over a branch. "Haylin, their queen is dying. They are doing what they can to keep her alive, so they sing for her life to prevail."

"Do you think she will—"

A whizzing sound cut through the trees. Theodore placed his arm in front of Eliza, stopping her from stepping further. A dagger flew past them and stabbed into a tree. The dagger poked out, its silver edge shiny even in the dark.

"*No one leaves*," Thorn yelled. She twirled a rolled-up note.

Theodore lit his palm.

"Not happy to see me again, then?"

"Should I meet with Kinsington and tell him how you let me escape? Or are we playing a game of finnix and harling that never ends?" Theodore retorted.

"You are the harling, and I will catch you in my jaws." Thorn stepped on a cracked stump. As she jumped off, it split in two.

"A finnix never releases its prey, but you are doing a splendid job of that, harling. By the way, why are you alone?"

"I knew you would come, I just wasn't sure when, Storm." Thorn narrowed her eyes and unrolled the note. "By the way, have you found Elm?"

"What have you done with Elm?" Eliza snarled.

"She's still alive somewhere. Maybe." Thorn shrugged.

"*Enough*. I have already shown you what my magic can do, and that was when a rapture stone was on me. We both could kill you with a single movement. Run... run, little harling, with your tails between your legs," Eliza grimaced.

Thorn covered her cheek. Her glare burned into their minds, as if she wished it had powers of its own that could take them out. Thorn let out a murderous howl and lunged towards them. Theodore took his sword out and swiftly cut into her other cheek, slicing effortlessly. Another line to remind her of her failures. She stumbled back, crashing to the ground.

Theodore edged to her face, where she could feel the warmth of his breath. "Next time, this will go through your heart. I am only repaying the kindness you once gave me."

Thorn, disgusted, turned her cheek to him. Theodore united with Eliza and ran under the cover of darkness.

Fulin bowed when they jumped from the fallen tree trunk.

"We were spotted," Theodore said, out of breath. Heat from his mouth swirled in front of him. He climbed atop the chackle and grabbed Eliza's hand to pull her up.

"Then we must ride before a battle unfolds," Fulin said.

The chackles pounded their hooves on the cold ground. Even though they rode for a short time, it felt like hours passed. Finally, Fulin halted them and slid down her chackle.

"Here." She pointed to a bush. "Go inside. I will erase any trace of where you've been. Hurry."

Hidden beneath the bush, a hole was carved out. Eliza went down, with Theodore following behind. They landed awkwardly and almost on top of one another.

"What is this? An abandoned home?" Eliza said.

"I'm not sure. It looks too small to be a grayden." Theodore scanned the space. It was hardly big enough for more than five people. "Different from the other one I've seen."

A slow drip thudded off in a direction their ears couldn't pinpoint. Eliza lit her magic in her hand, the ball of light illuminating the room. Jagged red rocks stuck out from the soil walls. It was completely empty of anything else.

"And what exactly is that?" Eliza said while placing her hand on one rock. "This is odd."

"I have officially accompanied an army separate from Nniar and Amarda." Theodore wiped his hands. "They fight for Folengower's unity and so will I. It is a group that birthed after the last war called The Choke, so I count us lucky to have found such a group."

Eliza studied his mouth as if she didn't speak his language.

Theodore's shoulders drooped. "Look, I know when I left you, things were different. But, Eliza, our father has done unforgivable things. He killed—"

"Our grandmother."

Theodore's mouth gaped open. "How... how did you know that?"

"Someone from Amarda's army. I thought at first he was lying, but then I thought back to when we were kids, and I remember seeing him beat you. You were so little then. We were little then." A memory flashed in Eliza's mind of her peeking in a room to find Theodore lying on the floor with bloody slashes across his back and their father looming over him. She winced. "I feel awful for not saying something, but I didn't want to believe it then either. I had forgotten the memory, locked it away I guess, but after O told me, it flooded my mind like ice water." Eliza's body shook.

Theodore wrapped his arms around her. "Oh, little branch, why would you hold such guilt over something you had no power over? Either way, all wrongs will be righted, but you may not like my plan." Eliza wiped away her tears and let her arms fall away from him.

"What is the plan?"

"We will go to the Anorphus, where Nniar's army is, and—"

"Infiltrate," Bruthren said, his eyes aglow.

"Bruthren?" Eliza frowned.

"Awe, I will miss when no one says my name in such a surprised way. Greetings, Bloodtress. I am glad to see you alive and well. It's unfortunate you find yourself in another dire situation, but Folengower will cease to breathe without it."

"Stop talking in riddles."

"Riddles? Never. I simply mean you will need to pretend to be the favorite once more. I am here to take you to the Anorphus and so are a couple of Cursed Knights. I want no whisper of our little group said to anyone. Your job is to be true to who you were before you knew the truth. Once Theodore can 'grow'"—Bruthren put his fingers up to quote—"and show an interest in ruling Nniar, then we can destroy your father from within. He'll never see the betrayal coming. Oh, how I hope to be there when he gets gutted and his eyes are petrified with shock." There was genuine happiness on his face when he smiled, as if he took pleasure from the thought.

"So, we are to pretend to be supportive of the war? And then at some point someone will"—Eliza swallowed—"kill our father? And what happens to Amarda?"

"Not anyone," Theodore said. His gaze locked with hers.

Eliza's eyes grew wide. "No, you can't."

"Now, now, I thought you two were…" Bruthren took them both on either side of himself and placed his arms over their shoulders. "Like this." He locked his arms together. "I understand these things can feel—"

"Overwhelming," Theodore said.

"I was going to say dramatic, but what a great story this will be. Imagine your brother, the uniter of Folengower." Bruthren let his arms slip away from them. "What better way to start the turning of our cursed soil."

"With blood. Specifically, Theodore's." Eliza said with downcast eyes. "Are you certain you could live with yourself after?"

Bruthren waved his hand around. "Your brother's conscience is not what's important. Blood has already stained our land, and soon that stain will spread far and wide like veins."

Theodore gave her a sincere look. "I am willing to live with the weight that comes with it. I cannot live with knowing that Amarda and Nniar will remain deceived if I do nothing. Will you do this? There's no changing your mind later, or you will endanger not only my life, but everyone else fighting for unity."

Eliza felt her cheeks grow hot, like the fiery eyes of Cursed Knights. She felt the pit in her stomach, like a sword had sliced deep in her belly. She felt her thoughts race like a storm eating the sun. "I'll do it."

Bruthren clapped. "What a monumental night this is. Now, the fun part." He rubbed his hands together. "Keep up."

He took off down the only opening that they could see. With the ceiling low, Theodore and Bruthren tilted their heads as they moved through the tunnel. Shiny bronze reflected off of the light they cast. Rows of rocks splashed the color back.

The end of the tunnel came after several twists and turns and aching feet and a brief rest before a steep incline. Until then, there had been no reason to talk. Bruthren took a suspicious deep breath, as if even he was nervous, which, before this moment, neither Eliza nor Theodore had ever known him to have even a slither of nervousness in him.

"At the top, we will meet the Cursed Knights, who will have Polt. They will say to Korrigan that they rescued Polt and found you saving Eliza. Understand?"

"What if he asks questions?"

"It's quite simple, really—most of it is the truth. Amarda took you, as your parents already know. He thought of what to do about it, but so far nothing. And, Theodore, they already knew you were on your own and the knights were already on a mission to find Korrigan's bird and bring him back. If you choose to tell more of where you've been previously, I would be cautious of the details."

They walked the rest of the way tired from the days of stress and lack of sleep, but they made it, and at the top, two folks were shaded in seafoam and crimson. The Cursed Knights stood with the landscape like great tors that represented the night and day, with Polt on Cassin's arm as the keeper of darkness. Only Polt's orange beak could be seen in the dead of night.

"Cassin and Palina, please take the next Ancient One and Bloodtress to their camp," Bruthren said.

Polt swooped down from Cassin and landed on Bruthren's shoulder. The owl sang a short song to Bruthren.

Bruthren rubbed his finger against his feathers. "I will see you soon. Follow them."

Polt flapped his wings, barely visible in the night, and landed back on Cassin.

"With that, I leave you. Remember our goal." Bruthren went back down the tunnel.

"We heard of your want to join The Choke. It is with great honor that we take you," Palina said. She had freckles on her peach cheeks that looked like constellations.

Eliza smiled, and Theodore said, "What is honorable is your desire to want better of our home."

They bowed and led them up a winding path. The path curved next to a nearly dried up creek. Smooth dull pebbles poked above the last drops of water. At the end of the creek's outline, Tarmist and Scythair stood tied to a tree's trunk.

Theodore patted Tarmist's back as Eliza too pet her chackle lovingly. "Hello, old friend." He wrapped his arms around the chackle's neck. The chackle twitched his small tail that normally blended in with its shaggy fur, and it nudged his cheek.

On the sides of both the beasts hung dark gray bags, the stamp of corpse thistle to represent Nniar missing.

Cassin swung his leg over Tarmist and held his hand out to Theodore. Theodore took it and sat atop the chackle behind Cassin. Cassin's hair was like staring into a vivid pond. It rested in between his shoulder blades, with four tawny braids over his loose wavy hair. The braids were clipped together with small animal skulls.

Eliza rubbed the sides of her arms to rid the many bumps on her skin.

"Would you like a coat, Bloodtress?" Palina reached into one bag, pulled out a folded black garment and handed it to Eliza. Eliza squeezed it as she would an old friend. It was long with angled points all along the bottom like an upside-down ridge line. The front had crimson corpse thistle buttons that ended at her hips, making the rest flow like a petal in the wind. Palina helped her onto the chackle before lifting herself up with her brawny muscles.

Cassin locked eyes with Palina, who lifted a finger towards him. Cassin grinned and shouted, "Halko." Palina did the same and, with great huffs, the chackles galloped with great speed.

A numbness befell Theodore as the wind whipped his face and tugged at his clothes. He focused on what was ahead in the far distance. The castle dominated atop the mountain, like a beast guarding the skies. The moonlight reflected off the stone walls like a thousand glowing eyes. It was then that Theodore knew they would return to the Rocks of Lunok and then every move he made, every word that slipped out, could mean an end to their grand plan for unity.

Eliza kept her head behind Palina's back and shivered. She combed at the chackle's thick fur, as if she took comfort in the softness. After they passed another town sign, where a young boy watched them race past, his mouth agape, Eliza sealed her eyes. She could hear the pounding of hooves and the smell of conifers deep in the cold air, and she knew that the seasons twisted again.

15

Folengower bellowed at the depths as if having an incessant tantrum. Creatures and rulers of the depths rolled over with one lightning glare. Even the deepest of beings felt it. Eagerly their eyes twitched to see the latest victim, who would soon fall into the chilly waters. The many eyes gazed to the land above waiting to hear the wails that would soon come.

Kinsington, the fiercest of all, bared his strug-stained teeth. Grief shows itself in as many ways as a chameleon, but for Kinsington, grief reared its head like the vengeful dead.

"Kinsington," the healer demanded his attention. Kinsington turned his head away. "She has passed," she said with almost no breath. She moved out of the way, revealing Haylin on top of blankets.

The light in Haylin's eyes held no shine, no sense of life anymore. Kinsington stepped towards her. He collapsed at her side, like two crescent moons together. Resting his head behind hers, he wept.

The healer packed up the takthorn, bandages and bottles. She placed a hand on Kinsington's shoulder. Her eyes drooped, and she mouthed, "Her heart... is with you."

Kinsington placed his paw over her. "My queen... the darkness is holding me where you should be." Grooming his paws through her fur, crusted black blood clumped and fell to the ground. He left larger patches of blood, not wanting to pull her fur off with it. Kinsington nudged at her ear that spiraled back, wishing to speak into it, though his words stilled, as if caged. His eyes shut.

Pavlyn sat in front of Haylin and Kinsington. Haylin's mouth hung ajar with the last bits of strug hanging on to her speckled black teeth. The healer stood behind Pavlyn.

"Kinsington..." Pavlyn coaxed. "Dawn is fast approaching."

Without opening his eyes, Kinsington breathed to Pavlyn's mind, "The dawn will never come again for me."

Pavlyn's eyes glossed over. "It will come for us all, but it will never be the same. We must give her to the depths."

"The depths can wait."

"They cannot, and neither can Amardians. We all must grieve together, or we will not make it out of the war alive."

Kinsington opened his eyes enough to see a horizontal slit. "Fine. We must take her to the river, but I want her hidden by all for now. I need time to hold her."

Pavlyn spoke to the healer to distract the others from them. She left the canopy and commanded all eyes to her. The crowd silenced, and folks hurried to the rows that gathered in the field to listen to the healer.

Pavlyn peered out the fabric. "It's time."

He returned to Haylin and lifted her up enough for Kinsington to wiggle under and rest her on his back. They wandered down to the river through the back of the tents.

Kinsington walked slowly, trying his best to not let Haylin roll down. Pavlyn stayed near in case she began to slide off.

Water flowed alongside them, calm and comforting. "Where do you want to release her?"

"Further down." Yellow fungi grew out of the bank in pairs. Their long needle-like heads swayed as they moved past them.

They continued on until they made it to the end of their camp.

Kinsington trudged down into the bank. The movement of the water caught Haylin, pulling her into it. Kinsington let her slide off. He turned to her with his paws under her. "I'm not ready yet," he called to the depths, staring at her belly, wishful to see her glow revived and move through her like a symbiotic being.

Pavlyn cried and placed her paw where Haylin's heart had once beat. Kinsington sang a song, one that she'd sung to their children. When he finished, he realized no number of words could mend this wound.

"Let the rest come."

Pavlyn opened her mouth to speak, but Kinsington cut off her words with, "Now is not the time to question me."

Pavlyn stormed through the camp. Every tree she passed could have camouflaged her with its bark. Folks waited outside the tent, quiet and restless. Some had noticed that something had changed. They scanned the crowd and outside as if they'd missed something too quick to catch.

"Follow me to the river," she said as a command.

Surprised looks darted to her before folks got up or tripped over others to follow. Chatter of what it could all mean grew loud and undesired. Kinsington growled at them to silence as they approached. Now, they could only hear the river. Groups formed on shore, and as their eyes followed to Kinsington, the pain of Haylin's death flooded stronger than any wave. He allowed time for the realization of her death to wash over them. Some Eltrists gathered in the water with him. Sickening sounds and hollowed breaths came.

"Fated of Souls, Haylin, our queen..." Kinsington began. The folks calmed enough to contain their emotions to listen. "Your death is of significance, and Folengower will weep till the moon dies." Kinsington stared up into the vast sky. A dark cloud moved swiftly over the water. Haylin's wings gently fluttered in the water as Kinsington's body shook. "If war wasn't in our presence, we could properly mourn, though we must fight, and that comes with sacrifices that we all must face." His voice wavered. "Take the night to mourn. Our sorrows will not be our ending, but more reason to fight. Haylin..." Kinsington nuzzled his face on her cheek. "Fated of Souls, I release you to the realms of no return. The dead will be ever so grateful to hear your voice, fly alongside you and be amongst your kind soul."

Kinsington asked the other Eltrists beside him to place their paws beneath her. Their eyes were downcast, their wings drooped and their bodies glowed like lanterns around her.

Kinsington backed up. "It's time. Our bodies live above so the depths can take us below, for the waters have waited long enough for us to return home."

The folks of Amarda went into the frigid waters to say their goodbyes. Many held her paw, gifted pieces upon her head, like leaves, flowers, nut shells or cones from conifers. The more they nestled into her fur, the more it made a striking crown. Many wept with distressed screams, their cheeks wet with their tears. Every Eltrist too had wet fur under their eyes. Even Kinsington, who never openly expressed such emotions except to those close, did nothing to hide his pain.

Riven searched the crowd as she waited to join Haylin for the last time. "Have you seen Thorn?" she asked a folk next to her.

"No, I haven't."

O stood nearby and heard her question. "What do you mean?" he interjected.

"I haven't seen Thorn since earlier. She never returned after she spoke with Kinsington."

"Maybe he sent her somewhere?"

"Maybe," she said, unsure.

O scanned the many mournful faces. His face matched theirs, but now fear slithered down his spine. He peered over his shoulder toward the copse. He could only see the tips of the trees from where he stood. A bird dashed out of a tree as if spooked. His heart sank as he walked back through the crowd.

"O, where are you going?"

"To find Thorn."

"Let me come with you."

O hesitated, but then he nodded.

Riven called out Thorn's name through the camp. O stood outside her tent and hollered for her. When he heard nothing, Riven went inside. As empty as Amarda.

"Now what?"

"Go to the exterior?" O said.

"She has to still be in camp. I don't think Kinsington would have sent her off with Haylin being in such a dire state. Haylin was like a mother to her."

"I know. She was a mother to many."

"*Thorn*," O yelled as they neared the copse.

"*Thorn*," Riven echoed with her hands cupped around her mouth.

"I am here," Thorn said faintly.

They took off into the trees.

"Where are you?" Riven shouted.

Thorn followed her voice and stood betwixt two trees. Fresh blood was on her face, but Riven couldn't see blood anywhere else as she ran over and scanned her, other than from what had dripped onto her clothes.

"What happened?"

"I tried to stop the Bloodtress from escaping." Thorn's face and voice were devoid of emotion, though she seemed mentally drained rather than emotionless.

"She escaped?" O said in the most surprised voice.

"Theodore came for her."

"How did you know he was coming?" Riven said.

Thorn held up a note. "I assumed this was from him. I've been watching her closely the last few days, but today she went in here for the first time."

Riven crossed her arms. "Why didn't you tell anyone?"

"I wasn't sure if it was anything."

Riven shook her head sternly. "No, I know you, and you aren't some sort of lone beast. When will you start trusting the folks around you? Kinsington made you a lead, and you spit on that too. When he learns that you let her get away, what do you think he will do? You could have prevented it if you weren't so secretive."

"She's right," O said. "This doesn't look good."

"I haven't thought that far ahead."

"Because you planned to drag her and Theodore back into camp single-handed like a hero?" Riven spat.

Thorn glared. "I'll figure out what to say, like I always do."

"Well, while you decided to run off on your own mission..." Riven choked up. "Haylin..." She turned her back to Thorn and covered her damp eyes.

"She's passed," O gently finished for her.

Thorn felt her lungs tighten. "They... they could not save her?"

Riven shook her head. "The takthorn wasn't enough."

"Come, let us say goodbye together. Then we can help you with Kinsington. Tonight, we mourn," O said.

Thorn's shoulders sagged as Riven let out a sigh and took her hand. Riven pulled out a white cloth from her pocket and put it on Thorn's cheek. Red seeped through the white until only her blood stained it.

A shimmering yellow glow reflected in the dark waters, offering a glimpse into the depths. A cluster of maroon plants swayed together, and a school of fish swam in a swirl pattern beneath Haylin while, below them, eyes stared up, serious and focused.

Thorn pushed aside the crowd that still waited. They moved without a thought, as if they had lost their sense of care and place. Thorn held on to Riven and Riven held on to O, who apologized after bumping into each folk they passed.

Thorn stopped abruptly, her hand suffocating Riven's. Riven tripped over her own feet and O nearly ran her into the water but let go of her hand just in time. His body hunched over and his hooves dug into the ground. Slowly, he slid into the water. A bystander placed their hand out in front of his stomach, and O sighed and gestured a thanks to them as he came to a stop against the bystander's palm.

Kinsington locked eyes with Thorn, transferring pain and disappointment. Thorn's cheeks streaked with tears like stars falling from the sky. Even with the tumultuous crowd, she heard nothing as she took tedious steps to Haylin. Thorn threw her arms around Haylin, her quiet sobbing turning to loud wails.

Kinsington put a paw on her shoulder. "Take a breath. Brighter days will come. We will make sure of that," he said in Thorn's mind.

"She's not going to the depths," she shouted, clutching Haylin's fur, using it as a tissue for her eyes and a comforting blanket for her head. "I won't let them have her."

Riven stumbled down to join her. "Oh... oh..." she choked on her words as she wiped a tear away. "Thorn, we have to let her go. She's... she's already gone." She held one of Haylin's paws. "Sleep deeply, our queen. Folengower has lost a light without you."

O moved slowly, head down, to the other side and stroked her fur gently from the tip of her muzzle to her forehead. "May you find peace in the depths, Fated of Souls. A mother to all, even as and after you're laid to rest."

More came and went to speak to Haylin as Thorn remained clinging to her. Many repeated, "Our bodies live above so the depths can take us below, for the waters have waited long enough for us to return home."

Thorn finally stepped away, her fists balled and her body hollow.

"To the depths you go, away from our sight but not from our hearts where ours will beat when yours cannot. In the end, we will join you with our sight restored. For now, we release you from the pain of this world." Kinsington put his claw in his ear, and a silvery strand floated out. He opened Haylin's mouth and placed it in. "Take a part of me with you, for it has always been yours."

Kinsington gave a single nod to the Eltrists who stood nearby. They each placed their paws on her, with Kinsington at her head. He kissed her forehead. "Remember me when I come."

In a single motion, they pushed her down into the water.

Thorn screamed and trudged through the water, her arms thrashing. "No! No!" She grabbed handfuls of

Haylin's fur, pulling as hard as she could to lift her out of the water. Haylin bobbed up and down, as if Thorn were playing tug of war with the depths.

Aylo flapped his wing at her back. "*Enough, Thorn.*" Another Eltrist tugged her arms away. O grabbed her and tossed her over his shoulder, her fists beating at his back. They tramped out of the water.

"I know... I know. Take it out on me," O soothed. He set her down on the ground next to Riven. Thorn stood, her arms crossed tightly.

Kinsington moved his paw from the back of her head. Her face submerged into the water, a memory that would never fade. The rest of her went like autumn, dying before their eyes for the birth of winter. The Eltrists submerged with her, their breaths held, bubbles floating out through their nostrils. Lavender reflected into the water like lanterns. Something moved beneath them, causing thick waves to swirl. The Eltrists let go, all except for Kinsington, who placed his head onto Haylin's. The thing underneath tugged, this time without remorse. Haylin sank into the spiraled waters. The spiral thinned and thinned as it enveloped her, and the hands of the depths held firm.

16

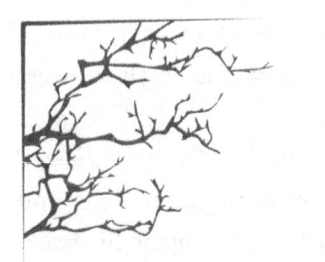

Blazing swirls of blue licked the sky, and the smell of fire flitted beneath the canopy of branches and leaves as if captive. Theodore had trapped it himself so that no one would see the fiery light.

Palina stood with her back against a tree and one foot on it while munching on roasted harling meat she'd caught when they first arrived. She bit another piece of its flesh and chewed rabidly to get the tough meat to break down in her mouth. Theodore sat across the fire from Eliza. She picked at the stump she was sitting upon, stripping it of its protection. Bits of bark stuck under her nails. She scraped away what she could without pushing it further in.

Cassin lay on the ground with his legs spread as though he were in the snow making a fairy. His eyes marveled at the fire as it tried to break the magic barrier.

Theodore barely moved, breathed or so much as acted alive. His eyebrows turned down, lost in thought.

"How did you do it?" Cassin said. The break in silence startled Eliza.

"Do what?" Palina said with a mouthful of meat.

Cassin sat up. "Not you. Ancient One, how did you create the barrier?" He pointed at the fire.

Theodore said nothing, as if he were part of the landscape. Eliza tossed a piece of bark through the base of the fire. It hit his shoulder. Theodore patted at it. "What was that for?" he said calmly, as if he'd just woken from a dream.

Palina and Cassin exchanged glances.

"Cassin asked you a question."

Theodore turned to Cassin. "Oh, what was the question?"

"Nothing, Ancient One. Forgive me for disrupting you."

"No, it's perfectly fine."

"He wanted to know how you trapped the fire," Eliza said.

Theodore glanced up. "It's protective magic. I used a feather from Polt and leaves from above. It's not a difficult cast, but without the proper space, it normally cannot be done. The trees being so close together made it possible. I can show you another time."

"It would be helpful to learn magic that isn't taught to us, that we can use to our advantage," Palina said.

"She's right," Eliza agreed.

Theodore nodded. "Perhaps you can oversee spreading our knowledge to the leaders of The Choke? You are good at teaching and being patient."

"I guess if I'm to have a role, that would be fitting."

"We will let Bruthren know," Cassin said. "For now, you two should rest. Tomorrow, we go through the Rocks of Lunok, and then there will be no turning back. We can make no mistakes."

"The Rocks of Lunok? We can't go through them," Eliza said.

"I've been through them myself," Theodore said, without making eye contact.

"No, you couldn't have." Eliza cocked her head. Theodore nodded. "What is through the rocks?"

"Different places, but we are going to the Anorphus," Palina said.

"How were we never told the truth about them?" Eliza looked at each person in turn, not really expecting an answer, especially not from Palina or Cassin. "I remember getting screamed at when we were kids climbing on them and pretending they were the eyes of monsters. It just..." Eliza shook her head. "It just doesn't make any sense."

"I think it's time to question what we've been told, but do so without setting off any alarms. We don't need anyone thinking differently, especially Lore or Dad."

Eliza wordlessly got off the stump and lay on the ground. She shut her eyes, and everyone grew quiet again. Theodore eventually dozed off slumped over, and Cassin fell asleep shortly after. Palina circled around them, scanning the expanse beyond that growled and emerged with life, from the ground to the glistening moon. The moon's purple ring appeared brighter than usual. Palina scratched her chin, as if she wondered what had caused it.

Twigs snapped on the outer edge of their camp. Palina stilled, only her eyes wandering. Besides small creatures that scurried up the trees or down in holes, she could see nothing of concern. She relaxed, continuing on her path. She had made it two rounds when whimpering stopped her mid-step. Something crunched and snapped behind her, then the whines dissipated. She turned around, her face stern and her sword out of the sheath. A few feet away between two trees, there were the remains of a furred tail.

"Cassin, wake up," Palina hissed. Cassin snored in response. Palina knelt, snatching a rock and tossing it at Cassin. It bounced off his leg.

Cassin jerked awake. "What is it?"

Palina's eyes remained scanning near the tail. "An animal, I believe."

"Cursed soil. You woke me for a beast walking about?" he scoffed.

"Not any beast. I believe a vorbin hunts near us. It ate something."

Cassin stood, brushing his disheveled hair from his face. "I don't believe vorbins to be in this area. It's probably just a finnix."

"Even a finnix has a stomach for us if it feels threatened."

Cassin stood next to Palina. "I doubt it would feel threatened by sleeping folks. Anyway, it appears to have left the area already, so nothing to concern ourselves with. And look." Cassin pointed to the chackles tied up against a tree. "They sleep soundly."

"I... I... you're probably right." She sighed.

"Take a breath. You're under a lot of stress," Cassin said sincerely. He reached his hand out to her, waiting for her to reciprocate.

She moved her hand over his, but her eyes grew, and her hand snatched his arm, swinging him wildly behind her. "*Vorbin*," she shouted. "Protect the Ancient Ones."

Cassin charged to Theodore and pulled him up. "Vorbin," he said before grabbing Eliza. "Stay behind me."

In front of them, piercing black eyes watched their movements. Its fur, like a layered pinecone, blended in with the forest floor, and they observed its top teeth draped over its bottom jaw with their braided prongs. It snarled at them, scratching at the soil with one paw. Palina held her sword out threateningly.

The chackles stomped and jerked their heads.

"Calm," Eliza commanded them, but her words were worthless as they twisted around the tree, trying to escape.

Theodore brushed Cassin aside. He reached to the sky with his palm open and moved his fingers as if he were crushing a can. Above, the fire dragged away from the treetops. The vorbin lashed from side to side, panicked, though Theodore held his grasp and the fire pounded down above his palm. It sniffed at the air with its velvet-like nostrils. Its nose wrinkled and its mouth opened before letting out a raucous sneeze. When it reached him, Theodore pulled his arm back before throwing it at the vorbin. The fire struck the vorbin's face, searing its nose. The vorbin bucked around as if it were a chackle before smothering its head into the ground. A high-pitched growl escaped its mouth.

"Halko, halko," Theodore called, as though he were only asking a chackle to go.

The vorbin stilled as if to listen, with fiery embers still lit on its fur blackening the shades of green. It ran in the opposite direction, with rolls here and there and rubbing against the bark of trees as it went.

Theodore slouched against a tree. "The night is still upon us."

Cassin grabbed the chackles' reins and sang them a sweet song. They continued to thrash their heads and whimper, only calming after he reached into his pocket and fed them a piece of dried fungi.

"I'm glad to see your aim remains as accurate as the sun's path," Eliza said.

Theodore huffed. "My aim has never wavered, though I had no idea if vorbins would be startled by fire. For all I knew, it would chew on it as it would flesh."

"Next time, let us handle any danger," Palina said, sliding her sword back into her carf flower sheath. "You should save your energy for what's coming."

"My energy is not wasted on such a minor task," Theodore replied with his eyes sealed.

Cassin made an uncomfortable face. "She didn't mean to offend—"

"Praise the moon, I am not easily offended."

Cassin took over guarding until dawn skies bled muted colors, like a dying rainbow. Eliza woke just as it came. She rubbed her eyes and rolled over until her back was flush with the ground. Polt took flight just outside of their camp, diving from a tree to snatch an unsuspecting rodent with its talons.

A new fire filled the pit, heating a stack of conifer cones. They bounced and sprung open like a jack-in-the-box with pale, fleshy insides. Cassin plucked the ones that popped from the fire and placed them on bark trays that were already filled with dull-pink, plump carveberries. He squished them with his hand and mixed in the fleshy bits from the cones. The berries created a sauce around it. When all the cones had popped, Cassin woke Palina. Eliza had already taken to shaking Theodore.

"No better time to eat than when the sun first shines." Cassin handed a bark plate to Theodore and another to Eliza. Palina sat next to Cassin and finished crushing the carveberries on her plate. Their fingertips were all stained pink, but their mouths were delighted and their bellies too full to care about such a trivial thing.

Polt landed next to Eliza. She rubbed his chest with her index finger. "What will you say to Father about where you have been?"

Theodore wiped what he could from his lips and his beard. "I don't plan to tell him the truth, if that is what you're asking. What do you plan?"

"Luckily for me, I was captive almost the whole time we've been separated. It wouldn't make sense to lie about much. Details, but not everything. If anything, I hope he will feel remorse for not having anyone come find me sooner."

"I don't think that will be the case," Theodore said.

Eliza turned to Cassin and Palina. "Why is that?"

"Oh... I think rescuing you was a low priority at first, or he planned to do it when it made the most sense. They gave us orders to come for you not long before Bruthren told us of his plan. Good thing both plans worked as one," Cassin said.

"Korrigan has his own methods," Palina said. "I imagine he didn't want to make any vast waves, and rescuing you would have been one, but when he heard about Haylin's condition, he sent the orders. I imagine he has plans that Bruthren will not know and that will be more of a challenge to manage. He is clever; I wouldn't underestimate him."

"I don't plan on doing such a thing, but I know his clever ways better than most." Theodore touched his back where a scar should have been if it hadn't been erased like the rest of his physical cuts that Korrigan had magicked away before anyone else could see them.

"We should head out. We could make it before nightfall if the chackles let us," Palina said.

They gathered their belongings and tied them to the chackles' sides. Before long, they headed towards the castle. The morning remained cold, a chill pinching at their spines. Steady wind clung to their cheeks, darkening them. The sun made its debut for less than half the day before the clouds rolled in and reaped the sky. Rain pelted down, muddying and flattening the chackles' white fur. They splashed into puddles without slowing, as if they enjoyed the rain.

Eliza shivered even with her warmest coat on, and Theodore's body felt too numb to react. Cassin and Palina acted as though they rode through clear skies, their crimson eyes like floating monsters beneath the slate background.

Above the clouds, the sun moved steadily and was only offered a breath when a cloud decided to move over for it. If only briefly, the rain calmed so the sun could warm below.

Theodore wiped his face of all the droplets that beaded his pale face and red cheeks. The town below the castle was as empty as a ghost town, one that was saved before the Eltrist came. Theodore scanned the houses, dark inside on this storm-ridden day. The chackles barreled through until they began their ascent to the castle, struggling to dig their hooves into the mushy soil. Cassin pulled the reins to direct which way the beasts should follow, but the ground sank in, as if a pond had been sculpted beneath them.

Cassin motioned his hand for Palina to wait. He jumped down, with mud up to his shins, and twisted the rope around his wrist before doing the same with Palina's chackle. He tugged with all his might to pull the chackles out. Cassin tripped to his knees, and mud caked up to his stomach, weighing him down. His knuckles, red and calloused, pulled harder. With another tug, he stood and trudged through the mud, up the steep road. He held on to stones stuck firmly in the soil and leveraged them with his weight. The chackles fought to keep moving and finally they hit a spot where the ground escaped from the downpour beneath a row of trees.

They made it up to the castle, drenched. For a time, they sheltered inside and warmed themselves. Eliza dried their clothes with a spell, and after Palina took the chackles to the forest shelter, she left the door open for them to feed, for when the rain stopped, they could graze. She found no other chackles there.

At the Rocks of Lunok, Eliza stared down into the endless pit.

"This is the one." Palina pointed. "I'll go first." Polt dove through before her, as if to show off. She jumped.

Eliza held her hand over her mouth. Theodore grabbed it and squeezed. Theodore jumped, and she followed after. Cassin jumped last. Eliza clenched her teeth together and closed her eyes. When they landed, the sky brightened with the dying sun and the smell of the sea wafted towards them. The entire camp was beyond the knoll they were stood on, and folks gathered in wait.

Cassin placed his hand on Theodore's back. "It appears your father wants to have a welcome home celebration."

"I doubt he has anything to celebrate besides the illusion he has created."

"That will change."

"Soon," Theodore said, placing his hand on his sword. "Eliza, stand with me."

They walked down the knoll, with Palina and Cassin behind. They kept their heads raised. When the folks below could see them clearly, they shouted and clapped with jubilant excitement.

Queen Agden waited in front of the crowd with Korrigan, their hands entwined. As they grew closer, she tugged to release her hand, but Korrigan held firm.

"What are you doing?" she whispered, careful not to draw attention, but Korrigan ignored her, a fake grin on his face as he stared ahead.

There were many things Korrigan could do to Queen Agden but keeping her from her children any longer was not one of them. She pinched his finger and tore her hand away. With haste, she crashed into Eliza and Theodore, her arms wrapping around them both.

"I feared you to be lost to the world," she said to Eliza and kissed her cheek.

Eliza had no words; she could only hug her back.

Theodore looked over Agden's shoulder at Korrigan as Polt landed on his shoulder. Korrigan glared at Theodore, and Theodore wondered how open he would be about the hate he felt towards him now that the several nearby villages appeared to be here.

"Come, everyone is relieved to see you both. I planned a modest festival," Agden said.

"Was the king happy about that?"

Agden gazed at him. "You haven't changed your mind, then?"

"Do not share what we spoke of with anyone," Theodore said.

"I would never endanger your life."

"Then go along with everything I do and say. I am playing a part now, as I assume you are too."

She nodded.

The crowd roared to life. Palina and Cassin blocked off folks who were a bit too excited to see them.

Korrigan grabbed Theodore's hand as if to shake it, though he pulled him closer and hugged him. "I assume you came to your senses about your Earthly friends?"

"Do you see them?" Theodore eyed him.

"It's better this way," Korrigan said emotionlessly before tossing him to the side.

"Eliza, little thistle. It gutted us to hear that the Eltrist had you." He placed his hands on her shoulders before embracing her. Eliza embraced him back like a scared little kid finally home safe. Theodore would have clapped for her performance.

Korrigan turned towards the crowd. "On this cursed soil, we thank the moon for guiding our children back home. We have already sacrificed so much, along with all of you. This was not one that I was willing to give. For Nniar, we gather as one, for this is a sliver of light that is much needed in such dark times. Hear my words, this sliver will grow with each battle won."

Folks jumped for joy, others cried with their hands over their mouths in shock and some looked as though they would faint. Cursed Knights directed groups to tables of food and drink away from where they were. The tables were lined with pressed leaves and corpse thistles hung from the Anorphus' branches. The scent drowned out the smell of fish. For once, fish wasn't on the table, but meat from other parts of Nniar that looked to be finnix meat. The tables were lighted with vials of strug.

When most of the crowd dispersed, Korrigan held on to Theodore's shoulder. "Before you go, we should talk."

"Can it not wait till after all this? It is for my return and Eliza's, is it not?"

"It will have to wait." Korrigan led him to his tent, away from where everyone moved to gather.

Theodore stepped in. "What couldn't wait?"

"Where were you?"

"That's a vague question. You left me and Eliza, or have you already forgotten?"

"Where have you been?" Korrigan tried to make himself taller, as if Theodore hadn't grown to his height over a decade ago.

"Wandering through Nniar to find Eliza. Something that only I believed to be doing."

Korrigan laced his fingers together.

"Were you not expecting me too?"

Korrigan smirked. "No."

"Sorry to disappoint you again," Theodore said sarcastically. "Though I'd already rescued Eliza by the time the Cursed Knights showed. We just happened to rejoin as we rushed out and they planned on going in. You should be thanking me for doing what you couldn't."

Bored of the conversation, Korrigan sighed and flicked his nails with his thumb. "You may be grown, but your words will get you killed."

"Is that your plan?" Theodore crossed his arms and leaned against his bed frame.

Korrigan paused, his jaw tighter than a hangman's noose. "You may be the next Ancient One, but time will burn slow. In the meantime, you will lead Cursed Knights in battle."

"And where will you be during the battles?" Theodore said with poison in his words.

"That is not your concern. The only thing you need to know is where you must wield your sword next."

17

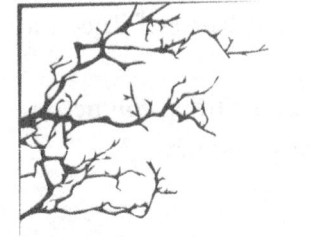

Theodore sat in a carved chair directly across from his father at the head of the table, while Eliza and Agden sat on opposite sides. He sat upright with his chin always turned up, even as he plucked morsels of food from his fork.

A wide eyed, young woman sauntered over to the table from the communal eating space, but a Cursed Knight immediately stood in her way with their arms outstretched to stop her from coming too close.

"Ancient One, please let me see you," she cried.

Korrigan waved her away.

She pushed at the Cursed Knight, who didn't so much as stumble. "Not him; Theodore."

Theodore glanced at his father with a devious smirk. "Let her come."

The Cursed Knight moved aside.

The woman knelt next to him, her hands clasped together. A flood of emotion struck her face. "I thought—"

"You can offer a gift another time." Korrigan huffed, disinterested and irritated.

"What is it?" Theodore said kindly, placing his hands around her clasped ones.

"They have separated me from my family." Tears began to fall from her dark blue eyes. "I need to find them, or we need to bring the other villages."

"How were you separated?"

"I was selling stones at the Market of Curiosity. My family is from Eten Hills."

"You traveled far, then. Alone?"

She nodded, a tear gently landing on Theodore's hand.

Glancing in his father's direction, Theodore asked, "Why have we not brought the other towns here?"

Korrigan rose from his seat, a fire gathering in his eyes. "This is not something we will discuss."

Queen Agden leaned back in her chair and tutted at Korrigan's lack of empathy. "It will take some time to help every town, and not all of them can be crammed onto the island. We will do all that we can to keep all of Nniar safe."

"My mother is right. Leave their names with the Cursed Knight, and I will see what we can do. We might reunite your family if there is no danger involved with doing so. On my travels here, I found the towns to be just as peaceful."

"Praise the moon for your kindness."

Theodore bowed his head to her. She stood and spoke with the knight before walking away.

Korrigan followed her with his eyes until she reached her table and sat back down. "What was that about?"

"Is it not my duty to care and assist the folks of Nniar?" Theodore challenged.

"Both of you, stop. This is not the time to be at each other's throats. And Theodore is right; it is our duty," Queen Agden replied.

Korrigan, now seated again, plucked a piece of meat from his fork and chewed harshly and slowly. Queen Agden ignored his blatant upset and chatted with her children as if they were back in the castle on a warm day, strolling through the garden with drinks in their hand. For that short time, all felt safe and well. Theodore laughed with Eliza despite the itch at the back of his mind of Audrey and Ben. He wished that they had gone back to the safety of Harthsburg.

Unable to ignore the itch any longer, Theodore stood and hugged Agden.

"Where are you going?"

"To my tent."

"Don't go; stay and dance with me," Eliza pleaded.

Agden patted his hand. He thought of staying and dancing amongst the folks, but he felt as if he were sinking. "Another night."

He spoke with the knights near the table, and two Cursed Knights showed up shortly after to escort him through the crowd of merrymaking folks. Many bowed to him as he passed, and Theodore returned the gesture with a smile and a nod.

His tent was near the edge of the island, at the back. Three corpse thistle flags swayed about the top, dyed in green hues at the top and blended to a dark lavender at the bottom. He walked inside to find a great wood chest in the middle with clothes and some other belongings inside. Off in the corner, a long vertical mirror framed with entwined branches caught his eye. He sat in front of it and poked at his face. His dark hair was speckled with the forest floor and grime. He ran his fingers through the thickness of his beard and pulled at his mustache. There was only one other time he'd let a beard grow, and that seemed like a lifetime ago, when he first became an adult. He combed his chestnut hair to the side, which waved down to his shoulders.

Next to him, a glass box reflected on a small dresser. Theodore cocked his head and stood up to take it. Inside, his crown rested, foreign and forgotten to him. He lifted the glass off and placed it next to the base. The crown rested on a nest of flowers and moss. Black twigs reached up from the base with crooked hands. When light shined upon the crown, dazzling obsidian shards could be seen set on the twigs. The crown had carvings throughout the band and three strug-filled stones on either side of an upside-down black triangle.

Theodore placed it atop his disheveled hair, as a reminder of who he was. Korrigan had a similar one, though he rarely wore it except for grand occasions. He gazed into the mirror, unsure of how to feel. He placed the crown back in its casket and crawled into bed. Music and laughter played like a lullaby.

Theodore's feet sank, his eyes sealed. He wriggled to escape, but the ground held firm in its capture of him.

"Wake," Esmeray said.

His body went rigid, and his eyelids opened slowly and cautiously. Esmeray was all around. The moon's surface covered his feet in gray, the ring around it glowing, as if lighted by the dawn.

Theodore walked in a circle, lifting his bare feet one at a time from the cold surface. Water flowed just beyond. A small scaly creature leaped out before diving back in.

"Why am I back here?" he called to anyone.

"You should ask yourself that question."

"I have no time for more games, Esmeray." Theodore stood; his body exhausted.

All around him, her voice replied, "You are dreaming. Tell me why you're here."

"Dreaming..." he muttered. He reached down and scooped up some of the surface, which then seeped out between his fingers. "It can't be."

Theodore trudged over her being. He felt eager to leave, yet captivated by a side of the moon he hadn't seen before. He stopped when he reached the flowing stream, which moved with agitation. Theodore knelt to it and let the water wash over his hands. Warmth surrounded them, but like with Esmeray, a piercing pain came, and he retracted his hands, falling on his back as he did so.

"*Fuck*. What was that?" he yelled. He stared at his shaking hands. No cuts or marks were on them even though it felt as if dozens of needles had prodded him.

Only the stream made noise. "Esmeray, what do you want from me now?" Theodore turned on his heel, with his hands outstretched as if they were poisonous. "Where are you?"

"I am everything around you," she said, void of emotion.

"Take me back." Theodore wandered over to a crater similar to the one he'd stood in to see his grandmother brutally murdered by his father.

"Wake up. This dream is not my creation, but yours."

Theodore dropped to the ground. He rested in the crater as if he were in a hammock.

"Theodore, where are you?" Audrey called.

Startled, he struggled to stand. "Audrey?" No one else walked on the moon. "Audrey?"

"Help me."

"My love, I do not see you." Theodore scanned all around and ran to where he thought her voice was coming from. Something tapped his shoulder, and he peered over it.

Esmeray stood, her long fingers wrapped around Audrey's throat. "I told you to get rid of her."

Theodore moved his hands to light his magic, though nothing happened. Then, he reached at his side for his sword. It too vanished. "Let her go," he demanded.

"Let her go, and I shall do the same." Audrey struggled in her grasp, her hand reaching out to grab Theodore's. "Folengower will die because of your love."

"No, she will help make it whole."

Esmeray squeezed harder. Streams of tears flowed down Audrey's cheeks. Theodore tried to get closer to her, but his feet were sealed in place. He pulled and cursed, but all he could do was touch her fingertips with his.

"Audrey, fight back. Please."

Audrey shook her head, her face matching the same gray that they walked on.

"*Fight.*"

"Let her go, you foolish king."

"No, no, no!"

"*Wake up.*"

It felt as though needles were pricking his hand again.

"*Audrey*," he screamed.

"Wake up," another voice answered.

Another stab to his fingers, and his eyes, which he'd believed to be open, opened in truth. Eliza knelt at his bedside, with Bruthren looming over him.

"Quite a dream?" Bruthren said.

Theodore's breaths pounded as if he had run for miles, and sweat beaded on him. "It would appear so."

"I can give you something to ease those."

"Why are you two here?"

Eliza sat next to him on the bed. "My tent is just there, and I could hear you rustling around as if someone was in here with you, so I came to see."

"And Bruthren?"

"When she couldn't wake you, she found me."

Theodore sat up. "Does anyone else know?"

"The revelry continues even without you," he said dryly. "It has not been that long since you slipped away. My, the dawn isn't even thinking about coming yet, though if it were any other night, this could bring cause for concern."

Theodore placed his hands on the top of his head. "I know. Give me whatever you have to calm my fears."

"Fears?" Eliza leaned in.

Theodore looked away like an injured animal. "Nothing."

"It would be apt to tell us." Bruthren adjusted his glasses and stared.

Theodore's neck twitched. "I was back with Esmeray." He pointed up. "On the moon. She had her."

"Audrey?" Eliza gave him a concerned gaze.

Theodore nodded. "She wanted me to get rid of her, just as she had told me before. It's nothing," he said dismissively. "I would rather not discuss this type of thing with you especially," he said to Bruthren.

"Love causes innumerable fears. You can keep your feelings to yourself but, dream or not, Esmeray is right."

Theodore glared at him. "And what exactly do you mean?"

"Focus." Bruthren poked at his own forehead. "Audrey will be a target, especially if Korrigan knows what she looks like. She should be..." Bruthren fluttered his hands to the sky.

"I've already tried to have her and Ben go back to Harthsburg, but it's not my decision. They have both proven that they can handle themselves." Theodore stood, anger flooding him.

"He's right; it's not our place to make decisions for people who have already made their choice. She and Ben know they can say the word and be out of here. Honestly, enough of this conversation," Eliza said, clearly irritated, with her arms crossed and one leg further out. "Bruthren, help him conceal any nightmares that may come. Other than that, leave him be."

Eliza left the tent without a goodbye, and Bruthren turned to follow.

"Wait," Theodore said.

Bruthren stood by the door. "Yes?"

"Who will train Audrey and Ben?"

"Morrow. I doubt you know her. She is exceptional. At some point, you two should meet."

"I want updates on how they excel."

"Keep your head above ground; we do not need it sinking in the cursed soil, for moon's sake." Bruthren opened the flap of the tent to leave.

"Last thing. Don't let them fight in the battles until there are not enough bodies to win."

"I wouldn't dare," Bruthren said, with mad eyes.

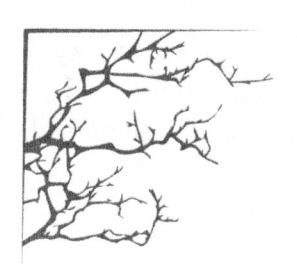

18

Water moved around Thorn's ankles, tossing and turning, as if it struggled to sleep. She dug her feet into the sandy bottom and gazed at her reflection. *Ugly*, she thought. The ghastly wounds on the sides of her face marked her for all the wrong she had done, a reminder that she was sure would send her to an early grave.

"You've had enough time," Kinsington said in her mind.

Thorn sank her body in the water, only her head staying above the surface, as if a guillotine had already chopped her head off. She blew a soft bubble out of her lips. "We should leave."

"We are fine to speak here."

"That's not what I mean. We need to find camp elsewhere. I fucked up."

Kinsington walked into the water. "What is it?" he said sternly.

Thorn gulped and crossed her arms tightly. "The Bloodtress escaped. Her brother took her."

Strug from Kinsington's mouth dripped into the water. Kinsington's wings flexed, agitated. He reached out his paw to her newly cut cheek. "Who did you alert about her escape?"

"No one." Thorn averted her eyes to the water. Kinsington dug his claws into her wound. Thorn tried not to react. Her stomach clenched as the pain soared through. "Kinsington, please... don't," she cried out.

"You are suffocating. A leader breathes life, but you have done no such thing. Once again, you have let your need to be a hero decay you. For this, you will not be a leader of mine. You may keep your spy, but if I find out you are keeping anything from me again, the depths will eat the crumbs of you I've left behind."

Kinsington released one claw at a time from her sticky cheek. "When did this happen?"

Thorn clenched her teeth, her eyes closed and moaned. Her arms hung limp. "Right before I found out Haylin died."

Kinsington glided out of the water and shook the water off his black fur. It cascaded down, as if he were a rain cloud. His leathery wings remained open for the droplets to slide off as he stomped away.

Thorn submerged her head under the water. She felt her insides squirm, as if rodents held her together. Her green hair swayed in synchrony with the plant life, and her dark skin shined under the surface, like buried treasure. She plucked a rock from the riverbed. For a moment, she clenched it in her hand, feeling the worn surface slick against her fingers.

O and Riven walked back down towards the water.

"Where's Thorn?" Riven placed her hands on her hips.

O stepped closer to the water's edge. "*Cursed,*" he shouted.

Bubbles surfaced and popped.

Everything went dark in Thorn's mind. With the stone against her jaw, she closed her eyes. Her lips parted, and she shoved the rock into her clenched teeth. Her body fought it away, as if her subconscious wanted to live. A flood of water flowed into her lungs. She swallowed, pushing the water in. Her face paled as moonlight sank beneath the water. While she waited for death to reap her, she saw the many eyes of the depths below her hungry for her to join them, but O was quicker.

O dove into the water, swimming feverishly towards the bubbles. Riven crouched down in the water, her hands trembled on the sides of her mouth. Disturbed insects crawled over her wet feet, but she only felt the pinch of cold.

He put his hands under Thorn's arms and dragged her out. Riven stumbled to stand. Her voice carried as she wailed for help even though O had already grabbed her. He whipped his drenched hair to his bare back and hunched over to pull her the last few feet to dry land.

Thorn lay dead as a fish on the ground.

Riven knelt to her and tapped her face. "No, no, no. Save her," she yelled to O. She reached into Thorn's mouth and threw the rock out while O placed his hand on her chest. With a single jolt, a forceful light illuminated her chest as if her skin were gossamer. The light shot up and out of her mouth.

"Try again," Riven begged, shaking her arm.

He placed his hand back down and violently shot the light out, quick as a dragonfly. Light held on to what it could and water sputtered out through her dull lips. Her face lolled to the side. O forced his magic again. Thorn lifted her head, and thin streams of water came out. She coughed for what felt like an eternity. O placed his hand on her back and pushed her to sit up. She leaned over and pulled her legs to her chest.

Riven wrapped her arms tightly around her. "What were you doing down there like that?"

"Our questions will have to wait; everyone is leaving within the hour. Grab your things and, you"—O put his hands on Thorn's shoulders—"stay alive for the sake of all our hearts."

Thorn's stomach convulsed as she coughed more water out. Yellow liquid spilled onto the grass. "Leave me." She wiped her lips with her arm, and her mouth stayed agape.

"You will not be lost to me. I won't let the depths have you." Riven pulled her to her feet. "We are all leaving together."

Thorn hung her head and swallowed her emotions. She wiped her wet face and wrung out what she could from her clothes as they hurried back to their tents. Most folks had already lowered their tents and folded them together with ties, and few sorted through their belongings or hollered at their children to move quicker. Thorn watched them as if she didn't recognize anyone around her. O parted ways, hopeful for Thorn to do as she should.

Riven came into her tent and grabbed the blankets from her bed. Thorn stopped her hand. "No, please let me do it. You need to pack too. I'll meet you at your tent."

"How do I know you'll be there?"

"You don't, but if you wait, you will lose all your things."

"I care more about losing you." Riven gazed into her eyes. "For moon's sake, tell me you will be there."

"I will be there." Thorn turned around, and Riven reluctantly left. She folded her blanket and took off the sheet that covered the pile of leaves, feathers and moss that made up her bed. She kicked the innards apart, leaving her presence to disintegrate over time. She felt hollow as a marionette. When her two bags were full and the tent empty, she took out the stakes to her tent and collapsed it. She rolled it up neatly to fit into its sack. Then, she headed to Riven's tent.

As she walked through, folks moved as if the camp were on fire. Thorn wondered how she hadn't noticed them moving about before or the great dins. She covered her ears until she made it to Riven, who was in the middle of shoving her last piece of clothing into a bag. Thorn stood outside the tent, holding the flap open. "Need any help?"

Riven exhaled when her eyes met Thorn's. "Help me take my tent down?"

Thorn did so without saying a word.

Eltrists swooped down while they folded the last piece together, each one speaking to a group of folks. It was all the same information: to line up to be flown to the next camp. Riven and Thorn would ride on Esna. She was easy to spot even at night with her shimmery brown and gold fur. Thorn peered over her shoulder at the river and wondered if she'd still wish to die or if she would be grateful for O's quick action later.

The line felt long, and most sat waiting for the Eltrists' return. They watched tens of them fly off and return for more folks to climb atop their backs. Thorn wondered if Kinsington had told the Eltrists of her treacherous act or if he would announce it to all of Amarda. A chill ran down her spine. The river looked more appealing every second they waited, even with Riven's hand entwined with hers.

"Everything will be okay. Believe me," Riven said.

Thorn squeezed her hand, giving Riven false hope that she believed her. In Thorn's mind, the battles to come couldn't compare to the disappointment she had caused Kinsington on the day Haylin passed, no less.

Esna returned to them. O had already left with another Eltrist. She ignored them and focused only on flying back into the sky. Thorn reached her hand out to the clouds, and it moved through the cold as if she moved through ghosts. Riven had her arms wrapped around Thorn, and behind her were two other folks holding on with all their might. Stressful energy radiated off of them like flares from the sun. It touched each of them and bounced back, charging each body with shaky insides, and Thorn could only think it was all her fault.

They flew towards a mountain deep in the Thornyarch Mountains. With the weather unpredictable no matter the time of year, it made the area a risk. Esna circled the top of the peak before landing. The ground had jagged strips of stones on the plateau. Just below the crest, a meadow smaller than the space they'd once had was in bloom. They would make do with the smaller space. Down below, a creek ran through.

Thorn and the others leaped off of Esna. They slid down the slope to the meadow, with their bags sliding ahead. Thorn watched the folks work to set up their tents and space out where they could. From this perspective, she could see more pockets of land that could be accessed by walking through narrow passages or flown into from overhead.

The sun's glow had reared its head, as if it were a nosy neighbor peering over a fence. Doses of adrenaline clung to every being, hastening them forward. After they had settled, the energy shifted to sluggish movements with spurts of hurried pacing. The last of them arrived just after the sun shined high in the sky, gripping Kinsington's back.

When they moved off, he hovered above them. "It is times like this that we remember what we fight for. We belong in every part of Folengower. We will not hide away like prisoners." Kinsington eyed Talkun. "We are the truth of Folengower, the hope of a new world. One that guarantees our existence as it had always been. This is not the end of our hardship, it is the start of it. For now, rest on this cursed soil and familiarize yourself with our new camp." He let his wings fall and his paws feel the rocky soil beneath.

Wildflowers tangled around their calves and some up to their thighs. O combed out seeds that had attached to his hairs. Rising tents huddled together as if on falling stilts, for the flora below was as mighty as the gods and hard to trample. The narrow passages led to another plateau and caves below. Above the plateau, where the Eltrist had decided to stay, lived a grassy hill with tangled trees. Rather than wrestle with the landscape, some opted for the caves. The brambleweeps cared not for their presence. They watched them with their weeping eyes, dragging their long arms on the ground. The light from the Eltrist felt welcoming to the folks who'd followed them.

Soon, everyone was ready for sleep as the night came. Some Eltrists slept with growling purrs, which startled the short brambleweeps more than their large frames and glowing bodies. Many hid deeper into the crevices of the cave.

Kinsington sank into the grass, as if he were on quicksand. The curls of the greenery devoured him. His back stood out like an onyx rock hidden beneath the verdant field. He wasn't alone, but he ignored most words, as if he wished he were.

"Kinsington," Talkun called to him. He stood behind him, his leathery wings draped down and his mouth hung open to catch his breath.

Kinsington peered back at him with one eye open. "Ancient One."

"Talkun," he corrected. "Korrigan knows these mountains well, and so do I. How long do you plan our stay to last here?"

"We have only just arrived. I barely have a thought outside of grief." Kinsington rested one front paw on top of the other and placed his chin over them. "Even I need rest. Speak to me of the mountain when my mind is able. Part from me, please; I cannot bear another conversation."

Talkun walked off, his wings lifted slightly off the ground, as if the feeling of grass against them made him uncomfortable. Light shined through the skin like a suncatcher.

Off in the meadow, Thorn disappeared in the flowers. She lay flat, with her eyes staring above. The flowers' stalks matted together, keeping her from reaching the ground. Riven could only make out her body because of the bare patch that she squished.

"Do you want to talk?" Riven loomed over her, blocking out the light.

Thorn peeked one eye open. "Probably not."

"What happened?"

"I don't want to talk about it," Thorn said, promptly closing her one open eye.

Riven sighed. "I have a right to know what happened."

Thorn sat up, with her elbows carrying her weight. "A right? What is that supposed to mean?"

"You aren't alone, Thorn. It's not fair to me to not know what's going on."

"Fair?" Thorn gave a bitter laugh. "I'm sure you keep secrets. Do I have a right to those, or am I the only one who needs to spill my guts every time I have a thought?"

Riven bit her lip and narrowed her eyes. "You can hide from our problems, your problems all you want, but soon you'll be all alone. If you just cared for those closest to you, you would see that we have your back. I've *always* had your back, and our dreams are still very real."

"The dreams we had back in Amarda are only that. Look at where we are and be realistic about what's coming. Haylin is dead..." She paused, her hands trembling. "If she couldn't survive one battle, what do you think that means for the rest of us?"

"You're avoiding my question. What happened between you and Kinsington?"

Thorn averted her gaze and let her back fall. "I've lost my rank. He doesn't trust me to lead anymore. If I mess up again, he told me the depths will be waiting for what's left of me."

Riven calmly nodded. "Maybe this is for the best. You've been so stressed and on edge even before we left Amarda. Reconnect with the folks around you and let go of the idea that you need to do everything alone, or"—she stared away—"I'll be left to live in the river to pray to the depths to not take you."

"The best?" Thorn raised her voice. "I find it hard to believe that something I have worked so hard to achieve has turned to dust before I have even fought. This only means that I am a failure, and when the time comes, I will be nothing more than a pool of blood. Nniar is strong, and now they have the next Ancient One and Bloodtress back and it's all my fault."

"It's not your fault, at least not entirely. It's Kinsington's fault that Theodore escaped."

Thorn let out a ridiculous laugh. "Kinsington's fault..." She mulled over the words as if they could be true. "That was me. I told Theodore he could leave if he promised to kill his father. Kinsington doesn't know, but I assure you, if you speak truths to him, you should have left me to kill myself."

Riven stumbled back and frowned. "You let him go? I don't understand. He got out from them fighting and tearing a hole in the splittlace. How could you have?"

"After that, I found him. I thought if Theodore killed him, there would be no war. He would restore our agreement with Nniar, and we could live like we are supposed to."

"Oh," she said with pity. "We've always known the war would happen and Kinsington would not spare Theodore's life even if he killed Korrigan. He has made it clear the death of them is the only way." Riven clutched her heart, as if making a silent promise on it to keep Thorn's secret. "You can never tell another soul this. Praise the moon you only told me."

Thorn shrugged. "A part of me just wants this all to end."

Riven sat next to her, the flowers felt springy. All around them smelled haunted and musky. "No, not like this. You can still earn Kinsington's trust back. All you need to do is include other folks. Stop acting like you are alone."

Thorn held her hands out, as if she didn't recognize them. "I feel the decay inside me, and I can't stop it. I don't know how to. It would be better to—"

Riven rolled onto her side and grabbed her hands. "It wouldn't be better. You helped free Talkun. Kinsington will let you back in, it will just take some time. And if he doesn't, then we will have much more time together."

Riven leaned over Thorn with her hands on either side. Thorn brushed a strand of hair out of her face and traced with her finger from below her eye down to her chin, tracing her old scar as if it were a map to better lands. Riven hovered playfully, smiling at her. Thorn pulled on the collar of her shirt, and Riven collapsed on top of her in a storm of kisses.

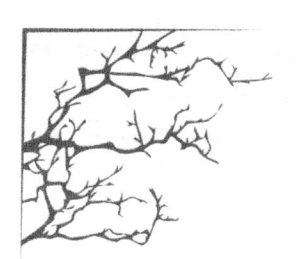

19

A buzzing sound came from the hall, hardly louder than a bee, though it sounded smoother, more like something pretending to be one. Light spied on Audrey from above. She rolled over on the bed and glared up at it before placing her arm over her drowsy eyes. Her body drowned back into a slumber.

The strange buzz pricked at her ears over and over until it pounded so loud that she woke violently, swatting her hands all around. "Ben, do you hear that?" she shouted, not knowing whether he could even hear her annoyance outside of his room.

She sat up, pushing her hair out of her face, tying it up in a messy crown with a hair tie she'd left and forgotten wrapped around her wrist like a bracelet. Audrey rubbed her eyes, but then she froze as she turned her head and the pillow stole her gaze behind her. She touched it as if she could feel someone else with her. For a moment, she grabbed it and held it to her chest. The pillow comforted her briefly like savoring a doughnut.

The buzzing came again, this time antagonizing at her ear. As she turned and swung her hands, the pillow fell. She sighed when she couldn't find the mysterious bug and crawled out of bed to begrudgingly put on the new clothes that were given to her after Theodore left. They were drab like the rest of them, with fitted cuffs on her legs and the top tight around her waist, though she welcomed the long pockets. They smelled like fresh linens dried above a flowery meadow.

She poked her head out of the door, then stepped out and closed it as if she had just put a baby down to sleep. She knocked on the door next to hers. "Ben? Are you up?" She knocked again, uncertain if he was even still in there.

Ben swung the door open.

"Well, that's an entrance. You look…"

"Awful?" Ben finished. He wore similar clothes, but they were slightly looser.

"I would never say that. I was going to say tired."

"Just like old times again." Ben chuckled. "Me and you annoyed in the morning at one another."

Audrey crossed her arms. "At least it's just annoyance and not murder yet."

Ben grinned. "I'm starving. I wonder what they have for breakfast."

"I miss French toast."

"Syrup in general."

Audrey laughed. "Syrup was something, wasn't it? They have to have something like it."

Ben wide eyed, stared up, as if he could see a pile of buttery pancakes drizzled in syrup. They wandered down the long hill-like corridor and found the communal space packed full of folks. Several folks huddled around one person, who told a joke before they let out a boisterous laugh while another sounded to be dying of laughter with their caterwauling. It only made them laugh louder.

Audrey and Ben observed from the archway. "Is this everyone?"

"I don't think so, but it's hard to tell," Ben said, with his hand on the frame. "Should we get in line?"

"You want to eat, don't you?" Audrey grabbed his arm and dragged him along behind her.

Ben brushed her hand off. "I'm coming."

They squeezed in between folks who stood together, and repeatedly apologized. Some folks gave them odd stares, while others moved, as if it were second nature. The line snaked up the ladder and out into the first underground space they'd come into.

Someone peeked down from the top.

"How many more people are up there?" Audrey called to them.

The folk peered over her shoulder and shouted, "A jarful."

Ben rose an eyebrow, bewildered by the measurement. "Is that a lot?" he whispered to Audrey.

She shrugged. "Doesn't matter either way." She grabbed the ladder and climbed up. Ben followed.

Light left them as they reached the top, leaving only a dim glow from the fungi. Five other folks stood lazily in line. They chatted now and again, small talk mainly from what they could tell, though some words were foreign. Ben thought to say something, anything, to the person in front of them, but his nerves got the best of him, so he stood with his hands in his very large pockets, wishing he had jeans on. Audrey picked at her nails and scanned the ground with a dusting of scrutiny. They made it down the ladder close enough to smell something nutty and sweet. Audrey tugged at her clothes.

"Strange, huh?" Ben said.

"What?"

"The clothes. Whatever fabric this is." Ben poked his finger out at her from inside his pants pocket.

"I hadn't thought much of it. At least it's not itchy."

"Yeah, I guess there's that."

Audrey followed Ben's gaze to Rew, who was making a beeline straight to them. His face was stern, feet slapping the ground with determination and quickness. She yawned in it's-too-early-for-this preparation for whatever earful they were going to get, wondering why he was staring at them as if they were children who had snuck out the window the night before.

"Why did you not stay in the rooms?"

Crossing her arms, Audrey asked, "Are you suggesting that we aren't allowed to leave our rooms?"

"You don't understand; Morrow is waiting for you. Did you not hear the buzz?"

"What are you talking about?" Ben said.

Rew took a deep breath, jaw clenched. "Morrow is the one who is training you. I sent a buzz to tell you where to go?"

"I heard a bug this morning, if that's what you mean," Audrey said.

"That was you?" Ben said, surprised.

"Not me. It tells you where to go. You didn't listen, apparently."

"All I heard was buzzing like a bee. I don't happen to speak bee, do you, Ben?"

Rew slouched his shoulders. "Never mind, let's go." He hopped off, zigzagging through the crowd. Audrey and Ben raced after at a confused tempo. Folks stood in the way and moved slowly, causing them to bump into one another here and there until they made it out of the grayden.

Fulin stood outside with her hands behind her back. "It's about time. I will take you both to Morrow."

"If you need anything, tell Morrow. She will be in charge."

"In charge?" Audrey said.

"Yes," Fulin replied. "Praise the moon for another day," she said to Rew.

Rew nodded and slid back into the grayden.

Springy moss helped them to not sink into the moist ground. The sun had already gone in the wake of great black puffs of clouds. They moved with sudden movements, as if they were horses being whipped every time they slowed. Fulin cared not to walk beside them. She moved with her arms dangling at her sides and her chin higher than could be comfortable.

They walked towards a great pile of salmon-colored boulders with dainty creatures that blended in like flora out of the crevices. Their tiny faces glared at them, their heads outstretched enough to sniff them, though they only looked like flowers blowing in the wind. Fulin led them around the back of the rock formation. Audrey peered down at the narrow trail, which was molded into cascading indents and packed with dirt. Pebbles were pressed into every step as a swirled mosaic. Alongside it, water trickled down into a thin stream.

The aroma of a windy spring day surrounded Audrey and Ben despite their uncertainty about the current season. Through the winding descent of steps, a sudden turn took them to the bottom. Trees lining both sides curved inward towards the middle of the trail like a canopy of ghostly purple leaves, their dull branches linking together.

Fulin stepped off the last step, triggering clusters of glowing orbs to float down from the branches as if alive. Ben ducked, and Audrey swatted her hand above, shouting profanities.

Fulin grabbed Audrey's hand. "What are you doing?"

Audrey jerked her hand back and pointed at the orbs. They stayed above, moving in a figure-eight pattern across the rest of the trail, to where a house stood at the end, lit and welcoming. "I thought..."

Fulin sighed. "Next time, I will offer a warning. I wasn't aware of your sensitivities."

Audrey glared deeply at her.

Deep green paint covered the bloated-looking house. There were no edges that made the frame; instead, it was as smooth as river stone. The black roof draped over it as if it were a snail shell. A bell-shaped door stood amongst the dark colors with its pulsing yellow stain.

A slender woman stood beside the door, wearing clothes that blended in with her home. Her top tied around her neck with many fabrics woven together that draped above her navel, and her pants were tight and looked soft. Two pale pink curved horns twisted to make up her hair. She looked younger than Audrey, and she would have guessed she was in her mid-twenties if this were back home, but in Folengower, she knew better than to assume someone's age.

"And here I thought they ran home." Morrow cracked her neck to one side with her hands and then the other. "But here they are, and now I'm wondering why my time is being wasted when you know how I get when my time is... wasted. So, I'm assuming..." She walked up to Audrey and Ben, her hands behind her back, hunched over, and cocked her head as she wandered around them, like a predator circling its feast. "It was your fault. And yours."

"We didn't know—" Ben started.

Morrow put her hands on his lips. "Listen, if you are staying with me, I expect no excuses." Morrow gazed at Ben through her russet-colored eyes. She grinned and moved her hands slowly from his lips. "You have soft lips."

Audrey scoffed. "He's single."

Ben glowered at Audrey.

Morrow patted his cheek. "Is that so?" she said to Audrey before peering back at Ben. "Get inside. I hadn't planned on this being a date." Morrow shooed them through the open door. "Fulin, a word."

Fulin gave a solemn nod. "What is it?"

"Is my time worth them?"

"It's not for us to decide. Our leader has decided they are."

Morrow crossed her arms. "Bruthren... yes."

Fulin's neck twitched. "And the Ancient One."

"Right, right," she said softly before turning from her and joining Audrey and Ben inside.

Fulin hastily left back up the steps.

Morrow closed the door behind her. She lingered at the door frame with a curious look on her face while she twirled her bracelet. Audrey and Ben gazed up at the spiral staircase.

"Stunning, isn't it?"

Audrey tried to steal her eyes away. "It's something."

"Mesmerizing," Ben said.

"There's more to the house." Morrow pushed at their backs into the main room. "I have two rules." She held up two fingers while walking backward. "One, don't move my things; two, never go in that room." Morrow pointed behind the staircase.

There was a fireplace shaped like a gaping mouth made of rock from Amarda. It shined like moonstone. Squished on the other side, carved bone reached to the ceiling—a beautiful impostor of two trees with dazzling branches that spread outward and to the sides of the ceiling with delicate leaves. Both of them were snug against the fireplace. A collection of taxidermy birds stood frozen in time on the mantle. A raven gripped a berry in its beak, while a woodpecker held on to a small tree stump as if it would peck any minute at it. Some flew above, hanging from shiny threads.

A black couch and a small side table stood facing the fireplace. The side table was draped with finnix fur and a drooping petal lamp.

"Sit," Morrow said.

Ben hesitated to sit until Morrow gazed at him and pointed down. Audrey plopped down as if it were her house.

Morrow bent over and rubbed her hands together in the fireplace. Audrey tried to peek at what she was doing. Fire birthed from the previous ashes, without any wood. Morrow slapped her hands together, dusting them off. She turned towards them and sat on the hearth.

"I only have one spare room, so either you can run back to the Earthen ground you left or deal with the arrangement."

"I'm assuming Theodore wouldn't have an issue." Ben shrugged. "I can always sleep on the floor."

Morrow hunched over with her legs crossed, resting her chin on her fist.

"Really?" Audrey tapped her foot on the floor.

"What?" Ben said.

"Theodore isn't here, and he isn't the only say in our relationship."

Ben sighed. "Of course. I didn't mean it like that. It's just—"

Audrey held her hand up. "No, it's fine. Just let me have a say too."

Ben nodded.

"And who's this Theodore fella?" Morrow said with both her eyebrows raised.

"The Anc—" Ben started before Audrey placed a hand on him.

"You don't know?" Audrey said incredulously.

Morrow straightened her back. "For moon's sake..." She shook her head. "You were about to say the Ancient One."

"What does it matter?" Audrey eyed her.

Morrow stood and paced. "What does it matter? What. Does. It. Matter? Well, a whole fucking lot."

Ben exchanged a glance with Audrey.

"No wonder having you two was a top priority. I'm just a babysitter. Lovely," Morrow continued. "What a curse this is."

Audrey shot up, her hands clenched. "No, we were told you could teach us how to survive this fucking war without magic. Don't baby me; I have fought Eltrists alone. We came here to save Theodore after he was taken, and I would do it all over again without such crass assumptions."

Morrow yawned a fake yawn into her hand. Her bracelet jingled with three stones—white, gray and black—surrounded by what looked like a ribcage. Ben's eyes widened as he took notice of it. Audrey only saw red, the kind you could bottle and use as poison. Her cheeks matched her rage. She stomped to Morrow and raised her fist, ready to punch.

"Wait, wait," Ben shouted. "Look, she is Earthen too."

"What are you talking about?" Audrey said, exasperated, dropping her fist.

Ben grabbed Morrow's bracelet. "See."

Audrey threw her hands up. "Who the hell are you?"

Morrow uncrossed her legs and tugged her wrist away from Ben's grip. "That's for another day. But, yes, I am not born of Folengower's blood."

"How are you able to use magic?" Ben said.

"I suppose that's why Bruthren wanted us to meet. He must not want you to die either."

"I doubt he cares. It's only because of Theodore," Audrey said, crossing her arms.

"Whatever the reason, I am here to teach you what I can, but I can't promise anything. I have never been successful at teaching other Earthen blood to use Folengower's magic."

"Great," Audrey said.

"I'd rather try than die helplessly here," Ben said.

"Isn't that warm and fuzzy? We can try with the first lesson today, but no fists. Rage." Morrow pointed to Audrey. "First, we need to go out. The clouds speak of more rain to come, which is a perfect time to learn."

"I hate to ask, but do you have anything we can eat before that? Rew swept us away before we could eat breakfast," Ben said.

"The kitchen is over there." Morrow motioned with her head behind them. A counter and a set of cabinets above blocked most of the view of the kitchen. "There is freshly baked bread wrapped in a leaf, with carveberries and crushed nuts on the top, and on the counter is the spread. Similar to sweet butter," she said, almost nostalgic about some memory from long ago.

While Ben and Audrey got to work on filling their bellies, Morrow went outside. Ben tried to watch her through the two windows from the kitchen, but he couldn't see enough since a bush covered half of the glass. In between bites, he could make out the tips of her horned hair, and he thought she was twirling or dancing due to the way they swayed and moved.

"What are you looking at?" Audrey said.

Ben choked down the last bite. "I was curious what she was up to."

"Leave the curiosity for now; we need to have our hearts and heads in this."

"I can do both," Ben said, snatching another slice of bread. The berries were just the right amount of sweetness. "Do you think she has syrup?"

Audrey rose her hands, as if to give up on the conversation.

"What?" Ben smirked.

She rested her back on the counter as she finished eating even though a perfectly good table stood at the end in front of the windows where Ben sat.

A gust of air wafted through the house. It hissed into every crevice. Ben leapt up. "What now?" he asked with his mouth full.

Audrey leaned over the counter to see into the living room. "Wind from somewhere... Morrow?"

Morrow charged over to the kitchen and bent her head to fit into the window right in front of Audrey's face. "Greetings," she said with a twisted grin. She moved her head out of the small space. "No time to waste. The rain is coming." Morrow motioned her hand for them to follow out the front door. "Since I doubt either of you can learn even the simplest of magic, I have to teach you how to fight with a weapon." Morrow looked them up and down.

"Unless you have been in combat and trained. Either of you fight in the military?"

"Nope," Audrey said.

"Well, even I'm not cruel enough to send lemmings into a fire, so let's begin." Three swords nestled in the grass. Morrow lifted one up. "Ben, honey, take this."

"Ben works just fine," he said while grabbing the sword.

Morrow held it firm and dragged him towards her. Ben scowled and tore it from her hands. "And here I thought Audrey was the fiery one. Glad to know you have a flame still... even if it's deep down." Ben walked away with it without a reply.

"Rage." Morrow moved her index finger for Audrey to come.

"Rage, huh?" Audrey grabbed the next sword.

"Any objection?" Morrow picked up the last sword and spun it around flawlessly, as if it were just an extension of her arm.

"Call me whatever you like," Audrey said with a sliver of venom.

Morrow smiled widely. "Good. This is one of the best weapons against any enemy here. I have put a protection spell on them to not harm if you are successful at besting me."

Ben pointed his sword at her. "How did you learn magic?"

"I'm adding a new rule: Do not ask me personal questions. Alright, honey?"

Morrow faced her hips towards them with one foot forward and one back, the sword held at the side of her chest. "Mirror me."

Audrey and Ben did as she showed. Audrey's arms were shaking holding the weight, and not long after, Ben felt his arms want to buckle.

"Every morning and before bed, we will do strength training. Your arms need to get used to using this as if it were a knife. Ben, come towards me and swing at me."

Ben let out a breath and charged towards her. His arms drooped with every step before he was close enough to swing. Morrow blocked his attack with ease and flung his sword from his hands. She then simulated how she would have struck the sword into his belly.

"Audrey."

Audrey charged at Morrow. Her long legs carried her swiftly, but even her determination couldn't keep her arms steady. She swung towards Morrow's head, who tripped her feet and swung. The sword hit her in the temple, but to Ben's astonished face, she was unharmed except for maybe a bruise on her leg.

Audrey rubbed her head. "It still hurts."

Morrow held out her hand. Audrey swallowed her pride and let her help her up. "I didn't say it wouldn't hurt, but it will not shed blood."

They spent the morning trying with all their might to win an attack on Morrow, but neither were successful. Bruises and welts mixed with muddied clothes and limbs were the only things they could accomplish. Rain gently patted down as Morrow led them around the back of her house. The stream that cascaded down the steps to her home pooled in the back like a pond.

Morrow knelt and dipped her hand in. She swayed it like a fishtail before bringing up a pool of water cupped in her hand and drank. "Join me in drink."

Audrey placed her hands in the water and sipped what she could before it seeped between her fingers. Ben rubbed at the scar on his head—a nervous tick that he loathed to have.

"Folengower speaks throughout its whole being. When you listen, that is when you can learn the songs of magic. My first encounter with it, I was submerged in water—drowning. The water slashed against me like a voracious beast, my body weakened from fighting and screaming, then I heard it. The first song." Morrow choked up on her words. She rubbed her nose with the back of her hand. "Melancholy really. But I knew what it wanted of me. It wanted me to fight. When I made it to shore, Bruthren found me. He taught me everything I know."

"Bruthren? He doesn't really seem like someone bent on teaching," Ben said, his hands now in the water.

Morrow shot him a glare. "Maybe not to everyone, but I had already run into him when I first made it here, and he was kind... strange, but kind."

"Strange that he showed up where you were drowning," Audrey clicked her tongue.

"I never thought of it." Morrow cupped more water in her hand, splashing it onto her face. "I'm grateful for all he has done. I wouldn't have survived alone without him."

Audrey nodded.

"Every day from here on out, remember to listen for Folengower's songs. But as I said before, no one else of Earthen blood has gained access to the magic, so let's not get our hopes up."

"That's encouraging." Audrey shrugged. "But there must have been someone else who could do magic. As far as I understand, this world is old, much older than Earth."

"Bruthren said there's no record of anyone else."

"Maybe they never tracked it?" Ben said. He sat with his knees up, leaning back with his palms on the ground behind him. He stared into the sky, as if to welcome the raindrops.

"You can wonder all you want, but if I were you, I would keep my thoughts on how many battles I could escape. I've seen firsthand where this war is heading... I find it hard to think that any of us will escape unscathed. Start thinking like a warrior, about how you can outwit your opponent. Be clever and bold." Morrow rolled her neck back and forth as if it was stiff. "Back to practice."

Ben stood up, his pants damp and stained green. Audrey fared no better, but neither cared about what became of their pants.

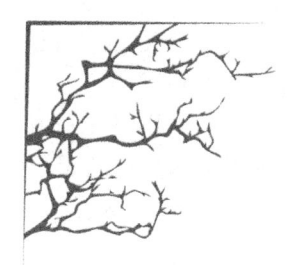

20

Everything blurred together in a smoky haze, and it only grew more suffocating as the days passed. Kalien's arms dangled at his sides. He was looking thinner than usual. Indigo, Cressa and Reed stood at the front of the tent waiting for Kalien.

"I need a minute. Go on without me."

Reed rubbed at his chin. "Why is that?"

"What does it matter?" Cressa said, putting her hand on his chest. "Everything doesn't need to be a fight."

"Well, I'm leaving," Indigo replied. "See you later, Kalien."

Reed lingered, his jaw tight. Cressa tugged his arm, pulling him away.

Since Theodore and Eliza had returned, reality felt stale. It was time in a glass bottle, and Kalien stood inside wishing to be freed while someone held it prisoner.

"Thorn," Kalien mouthed.

In one eye, he could see the top of a mountain with darkened clouds floating just above. "This better be good."

"Happy to hear you too," he said sarcastically. "I know I've been on the fence about helping you—"

"Fence?" Thorn snorted.

"At least at first, and yes, I haven't wanted to help, but you have to understand you forced me into this."

"Cursed soil, get it out already." Thorn walked over to an empty part of the meadow and sank her body in. Kalien could see the tall grasses, specks of insects that climbed on them, and sunshine dazzling onto the tips as if he were there with her.

"I... I mean to say that I don't want to fight this anymore. I've realized I want to work alongside you," he sputtered to say.

"Really?" Thorn said, with no faith in his words. "And why is that, Kalien? What could have possibly changed your stubborn soul?"

Kalien placed a hand on his head and gripped a handful of hair. "You were right," he said in a somber tone. "Korrigan is ready to slaughter us all if we question him. That's not the leader I want to be on the side of, and... fuck." Kalien took a breath. "My grandmother would have wanted me to fight for Talkun."

Thorn froze at his last words. She rubbed at her arms that had hairs standing on end. "What news do you have?"

"The next Ancient One has returned with the Bloodtress. I'm assuming she wasn't supposed to be here?"

Thorn bit her lip and tore out grasses beside her. "No, a hiccup is all. I want you to watch them closely. If you notice anything strange or what their routine is, call to me."

"I will."

"Be gone, Kalien. Don't let me down."

Thorn disappeared from his eye. He plopped onto his bed for a moment and breathed. The bed was too hard on his back and how he missed his everything about his home especially the sweet smells of flowers blowing in through his window on warm nights. He stood and followed the path, hoping no one would see his lateness, but now he hoped he had Bruthren's protection for such matters.

When he arrived, Nia was standing outside with a handful of berries. Kalien ignored her and placed his hand on the door.

"Kalien?" Nia said as if she were answering her own question.

Kalien's body went rigid. "Yes?" He kept his eyes focused on the door.

Nia popped a berry into her mouth. Once she swallowed, she continued, "It appears your bunkmates arrived before you. What is the reason?"

Kalien turned to her. "My stomach hasn't been feeling well since last night. I wanted to get here as soon as possible, but I needed some time."

"Your stomach?" Nia ate a couple more berries. "I suggest you see Craven after your shift, then."

Kalien nodded and reached for the flap. He lingered briefly, as he half expected more to be said, though to his relief she went back to eating the last of her handful of berries. Reed was sweeping along the walls of the tent, and Cressa and Indigo were working beside each other. Their goggles made them look mad. Kalien grabbed his gear, taking the last station to squeeze the corpse thistles. His muscles had finally grown used to the movements.

The secret table was empty for the first time. *Probably for the best*, he thought. He assumed that now he was a part of The Choke, Bruthren would let him in on all the details.

Nia returned just before their shift ended and watched each worker. She paced from one side and back again with her arms folded behind her back. Her chin never lowered, as if she were being tested by Korrigan. All seemed like a dull day, one that Kalien would gladly take.

Shouting erupted somewhere in the camp. Faintly they could hear a voice say, "*Run.*"

Nia held up her index finger to stop everyone as she listened. Her eyes alighted. She took her sword out and crept to the door. "Stay here. Hide under the table," she hissed.

Two of the workers shook as they dropped to the floor. Cressa grabbed Indigo's hand and pulled them down with her. Reed tossed his broom and charged under the table. Kalien waited, as if he couldn't bring himself to the reality of danger even if it came knocking. He felt a hand on his ankle.

"Get down," a worker whispered.

Kalien obliged and lay on his chest. Nia exited the tent and sealed it back up. Shrill cries vibrated past the tents along with the heavy sound of footsteps racing away. It all sounded too jumbled to know if they were all going in the same direction or veering off to different paths.

Their hearts pounded beneath the tables.

"Nniar," a booming voice seeped into their minds. "How I have wanted to speak to you all. Talkun has returned to us. His blood bleeds as every Ancient One would, as the true heir of Folengower."

The voice paused, letting their words sink in. Cressa and Indigo exchanged glances with Reed and Kalien with parted with gaping mouths.

"Do not fear us. Lies have shaped your world and ours, but no more can we allow them to tear our home apart. Amarda needs you to end the war. I ask for one thing... kill your king."

Everyone under the table exchanged the same hollow stares. No one moved, at least not voluntarily. Someone mouthed the words, "Kill Korrigan?"

Reed held up his shaking finger to his lips. "Shhhhh."

Nia charged into the tent. Indigo dug their head into Cressa's shoulder. Their bodies shaking. Kalien covered his mouth with his hand and bit down. With the back of his hand, Reed hit Kalien and pointed to Nia. "It's Nia." He exhaled and his shoulders relaxed. Cressa whispered to Indigo, and she too relaxed.

"Hide beneath the Anorphus' branches. Now. *Go*."

The table shook and flopped over as they tried to rise as one, like roaches scurrying as a light turned on.

One worker tripped, and Cressa pulled them up and pushed them forward. Folks pointed to the sky as they barreled into them. A man dripping with sweat ran straight into Kalien, and he stumbled, falling onto his back on the mud, the man lying across his torso. The man's hand dug into the ground, fingers raking at the mud, while his other hand pressed into Kalien's side as he scrambled to get up. As he did so, Kalien, motionless, saw what the man had been pointing at—three Eltrists hovering in the sky. They circled like vultures, long strings of strug struck down like pelting rain onto anyone unlucky enough to be underneath.

Wails turned into deafening screams. Kalien watched from the ground, as if time stood still for him. The man finally got up and took off. Kalien lay alone, his left cheek against the mud, watching Cursed Knights atop chackles direct folks where to go. Their swords were raised and some had magic in their hands to toss up into the gloomy sky.

"Kill Korrigan, and the nightmare will end," the Eltrists repeated in their minds.

It only made folks madder. They pulled at their ears or ripped their hair. The sound of them was too unsettling for most to hear. They believed that if the Eltrists could get inside their minds, they could kill them with their voice, though Kalien knew it to be untrue. It was just another lie that had been spread about them, but even he felt his chest tighten and a need to claw at his head.

Kalien pushed against the ground to get up, but folks darted past him, almost crushing his hands. As he got into a sitting position, a hand wrapped around his upper arm and pulled him violently up and atop a chackle in front of him. The Cursed Knight' forced his hand to hold on to the chackle.

"Get ready to jump off," she said.

They charged towards the underside of the Anorphus, the Cursed Knight hoisting two other fallen people up and atop the chackle on the way. They squished behind Kalien, the one directly behind clawing at his waist. Kalien's mind was too fuzzy to react to the cuts she had certainly made on him.

The Cursed Knight repeated herself. This time, her voice demanded. Her armor moved delicately in the wind. Other Cursed Knights shot up magical orbs, lighting the sky in puffs of destruction. As far as Kalien could tell, none of them succeeded in hitting an Eltrist.

"*Jump*," the Cursed Knight screamed. Kalien's heart pounded, but his arm stayed clasped around the Cursed Knight like the dead. She tore his hand off and tossed him down. "Halko! Halko!" she screamed at the chackle, and, like a harsh wind, they were gone.

Kalien sprouted up like a newborn fawn.

Reed grabbed his arm from the outer edges of under the Anorphus. "I thought you were dead."

"Not yet."

"Cressa and Indigo are over here. We should stick together."

"Glad I'm finally seen as one of the group."

Reed shook his head. Folks huddled and sat underneath the Anorphus, their breaths stinking of fear. Scrapes and gashes were present amongst almost every soul that waited for it all to end. They could track a trail of blood from those who had lost their shoe or snagged their hand and wiped them on the ground as they walked on their knees.

"Kill Korrigan," chanted in their minds again and again. Kalien kept his head down as they passed more folks and leaped over others who chose or couldn't bear to move.

Indigo and Cressa had their arms wrapped around each other.

Cressa peered out from behind Indigo's back. "*Kalien*," she screamed and held open an arm. "Oh, Reed, you found him. Thank you. Thank you." She kissed Reed on the cheek and pulled them both into their hug.

Every few minutes, new folks were thrown onto the ever-growing pile of limbs. Off to the right of them, in the distance, a growing group of voices bellowed, "Bring us King Korrigan. Kill him. Kill him for Folengower! You are cursed scum if you stand by him."

Kalien shoved his bunkmates aside to see around the tree's massive trunk.

"Where are you going?" Indigo shouted. Kalien moved alongside it, as if he couldn't hear them. Indigo moved to follow, but Reed halted them with his arm.

Beyond the trunk, the group of folks who yelled to others marched towards a Cursed Knight. The Cursed Knight spotted them before they could get close enough, and she shouted for their chackle to charge into them. The group threw themselves to the sides, barely making it before the hooves tore past.

Another Cursed Knight dismounted and stalked a few too slow to get away. He tripped them and called over to another knight to help tie their arms with agor vines. "You will be sentenced for your crimes, but for now, wait amongst your neighbors and listen to their scrutiny."

Kalien backed away, but something, a flash of light, stole his attention. Strug rained from the sky and landed on folks who were still running. One man fell to his knees with shaking hands as he tried to wipe it off his right eye, while another fell onto him. Kalien made out more and more victims. Many more than his mind could process. He saw boils forming on flesh before sliding off like snowmelt, uncovering forgotten atrocities below. Dirty and bloody hands reached for anything to grab.

The Eltrists glided in the sky, their wings darkening the light.

Kalien placed his hand on his chest. His jaw hung open, unable to close or do much else than quiver. His stomach churned, and he keeled over, puke projecting out before his knees hit the ground. Spatters of sick speckled his fingers, and he wiped them on the mud before using the back of his hand to wipe his mouth.

An orchestra of wails from the injured crawled under his skin, pricking every hair. A group of Cursed Knights rallied around them, creating a circle. One of the knights crouched and crept to drag the folks, one at a time, out of the center. They passed them down the line, then grabbed the next.

The Cursed Knights that made up the circle shot sparks of magic, animating lightning into the sky. Eltrists raced away in opposite directions, their bodies lit like ghosts. A spark struck an Eltrist's wing alight with embers, which seared a hole that spread. The Eltrist bucked around as if a beast had hitched a ride and spun in the air until the fiery magic went out. Smoke followed the Eltrist like a death trail. Bursts of light tore into the sky again, aimed towards the injured Eltrist. The Eltrist moved swiftly, dodging each sordid attempt.

The injured Eltrist darted at them, his wings flapping wildly before gliding straight towards the circle. Strug slipped down his chin, his emerald fur whipped back. He bared his many teeth, chomping at the air. Blobs of strug filled the circle, and the last of the injured screamed, knowing they would die slowly. Hands moved to wipe away the strug from their faces, though all they did was slide their skin off.

Cursed Knights trudged through the strug and out. Their armor protected what it could, but none of that would matter as the Eltrist collided with them. His mouth landed on a knight's head, and his jaw snapped and crunched on bone. Blood spewed out and squirted onto anyone close. The Eltrist spit out his head and crushed the helmet into the pile of strug. The body of the knight fell like a board of wood, blood streaming out of his neck.

The Eltrist darted a look at one of the other Eltrists, then tore back into the sky. Kalien knew the other Eltrist had tugged at his mind. The other knights scrambled to their feet and ran off towards the healers underneath the Anorphus' branches, leaving the remaining injured bodies for dead.

Kalien stumbled back to his group, falling to his knees. His breaths were so quick he couldn't speak.

"What happened?" Cressa gasped. "You're paler than bone."

Indigo embraced him and hummed a lullaby. Kalien squeezed his eyes shut as cold sweat beaded down his head.

"*Cursed scum*," Reed yelled to the sky.

"Don't attract any attention," Cressa said to Reed, her eyes welling up with tears. "I don't want to die."

"Oh..." Reed grabbed her hand and knelt. "Look at me."

Cressa drooped her head and shook it.

"Look at me," Reed repeated. After several moments, Cressa gazed into his gray eyes. "This is not how you go. You are going to be an old lady living in that beautiful town you told me about. Do you remember?"

Cressa nodded. "I don't remember the name though." She choked on her words. "My dad would remember. If he's even still alive."

Reed's eyes were sincere, and his hand cradled hers. "He's not here, remember? That means he's out there without a worry. He probably doesn't even know about all this. And when we leave, you'll forget too."

"No... no..." She shut her eyes tightly.

"I promise you are not dying here. Do you trust me?"

Cressa swung her head side to side, as if she wasn't sure, and then she opened her eyes and squeezed his hand as if to say yes. He smiled at her in a way she hadn't seen from him in a long time.

"Good."

"Kalien, tell us," Indigo said, taking them out of the moment and back to the original one.

Kalien focused on the ground, his eyes somewhere else. He didn't blink or say anything.

"You're scaring me," Indigo said, raising their voice. They placed their hands on his shoulders and shook him.

All around, folks cried and trembled. The healers moved quickly with ointments and jars of liquids to treat those with strug burns, while t

he others with minor cuts and scrapes waited.

"Leave him be," Reed said. "He's having a breakdown. None of us can heal that."

Indigo slipped their hands away and sat beside him, patiently waiting for him to come to. Reed took a seat on the bumpy ground next to them, while Cressa stared down at Kalien with a sorrowful face. Eventually, she too sat with them, her arms around herself. She wiped a single tear from her cheek and crawled into Reed's lap, who, without question, wrapped his arms around her. He whispered something, making her grin.

"*Kill him*," the voice flooded again, terrorizing every mind below.

Commander Glaslin led long rows of waving lavender plumes. He rode to the front, the only one upon a chackle. Their faces seethed as one, and the mass of their eyes together was nothing more than looking at a massacre. The backs of them created a massive web heightened by the seafoam color of their armor. The Eltrists circled above.

"The night will not greet them alive. *Fire*," Glaslin bellowed, his sword raised high. His chackle kicked its front legs up, with its mouth drooped open.

They held black fire and punched the sky, releasing the attack from at least a hundred hands. Death claps sparked into the sky, the noise vibrating into the ground. Crimson eyes glared up, expecting critical damage. Slate puffs blanketed above while an eerie silence cloaked the island.

The puffs dissipated at a crippling pace. Underneath the layer, clouds waited alone, and, beyond, the moon edged closer, as if to get a better view.

Glaslin whipped his head, his long obsidian hair moving like a crashing wave. "*Again*," he called.

Black fire erupted from their hands once more with precise movement, cracking into the sky and lighting it up with mesmerizing explosions.

Glaslin kicked at his chackle's side, who then raced away with him farther into the living spaces. Just as the next batch of smoke cleared, Glaslin returned with his hands both alight, one with red and one black. "They wish to deceive us. The skies are not free of them. Ready your magic."

Glaslin led the knights back where he'd come from, leaving the folks beneath the Anorphus' branches without them. A few knights hid nearby, like protective shadows, but most couldn't see them to feel any safety in their presence. They could still hear the eruptions and see through the leaves above each time light collided, but none could see the Eltrists. Some curious souls poked their heads out.

Kalien came to and collapsed in Indigo's arms. "Shhh," he repeated over and over. Indigo held him and did as he asked, feeling that instinctive call to manage even the sound of their breaths.

Time passed, and the screams came and went and explosive bursts shot into the sky less and less, signaling the battle would end soon, just in time for the dark to ripen. Folks moved with such subtlety that it was as if they thought the ground would give way. Cursed Knights rode back to them with Nia leading.

"The skies are clear," Nia shouted. "Please return to your tents."

The folks acted like stone.

"Go, get some rest. You are all safe," she said, her voice softer this time.

The healers took charge, corralling groups of folks together like lost sheep, though the shock of the afternoon's attack gnawed at the deepest parts of their bellies, sickening the reality they had believed to be truth. Someone swatted at the healer who tried to push them to the path, more soon joining in.

A Cursed Knight dropped from the tree like an assassin to stop the abuse. "Do as we say. It will keep you safe," he shouted, with his hand on the hilt of his sword. "King Korrigan will speak with everyone when the sun shines heavily upon us."

Reed, Cressa, Indigo and Kalien left promptly past the abuse, back to their tent. Even though the knights had assured them that safety would encompass them all, they stayed wide awake.

Reed stared up at the bottom of Indigo's bed, poking at the wooden planks. Indigo picked at their fingers, and Cressa tugged at her short fiery hair. Kalien, however, sat cross-legged on the top of the bunk, his head brushing against the roof of the tent. He rubbed his ear, as if he thought of reaching out to Thorn. So many thoughts rampaged through his mind, though the decapitated knight played on repeat. He would never forget the fear in his eyes or the helplessness he'd expressed. The memory infected his skin, causing shivers to come and go.

Kalien squeezed his eyes, hopeful that the image would fade. It only made the memory clearer. He punched his mattress.

Cressa peeked her head out from under the bottom bed. "What did you see?" She climbed a few steps up to his bed.

"You don't want to know."

Reed turned his head towards Kalien, still lying on his back. "We're all adults," he said, annoyed. "Stop acting like you're older than us."

Kalien glared at him. "Fine. An Eltrist dove, dousing folks in strug. But... when the Eltrist..." Kalien swallowed and stared down at his blanket. "The Eltrist bit a knight's head off. Clear off. Then he spit it out. He didn't eat it, just left it, like trash."

There was a moment of silence before Indigo clasped their hand over their mouth, as if vomiting was imminent. "That's fucking sick."

Cressa stared at him, sad and disgusted. She climbed the rest of the way and sat at the end of his bed with her arms held out. Kalien crawled to her and let her hold him. "That's awful," was all she said.

Reed rolled over, facing the fabric of the tent. Cressa held Kalien silently, rubbing his back comfortingly for a few minutes before climbing down and going back to her bed. Reed rolled back over, arms crossed. He glanced at her and then up at Kalien's bunk, green flooding his very being.

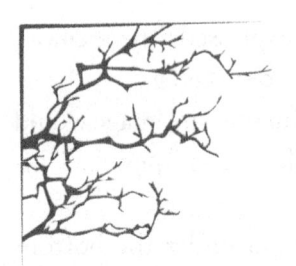

21

In the midst of the battle, King Korrigan hid away with the rest of his family in a cave below. The water sloshed up at the opening, and the wind swirled in and howled fiercely. Hargrove stood right before the mouth, another knight stood on a rock just outside and five others hid around the cave, watching the sky.

Theodore paced in the cave. "We should be up there with them," he spat at his father. The echo of his voice carried out to the sea. Bruthren glanced at him as if to offer a warning.

Korrigan smirked. His owl sat on his shoulder, preening his feathers. Korrigan took one of Polt's feathers, twirling it in his hand.

"Did you hear me, Father, or are you too busy being a coward?" Theodore said with a steady voice.

Korrigan rubbed Polt's belly with his finger. Polt hooted softly. "Even over the waves, I can hear your drivel. I would be careful how you choose to address me. You may be the next Ancient One, but I hold the crown, and it will be mine for decades to come."

"Not if you continue to ignore the innocents above." Theodore's hair was wet from trying to escape to the surface, but Korrigan had ordered the Cursed Knights to keep him from leaving, sabotaging his many attempts.

"This is not the time for us to be divided," Agden said. Nia stood by her. The cave was too dark to see that she was more than her levitating blood spots of eyes. All the Cursed Knights showed the same haunting look the deeper they stood.

"Then, when? When do we discuss important matters?" Theodore continued.

Korrigan waved his hand. "I will leave the important discussions to those I can trust."

Eliza sat on a barnacle-covered rock listening. "Why wouldn't you trust Theodore? He rescued me when you chose not to."

Bruthren gave a single shake of his head in her direction.

"Eliza, I am heartbroken that you would believe I hadn't planned on rescuing you sooner," Korrigan said. "I can't play favorites now, can I? Not when it's between the entirety of Nniar and my children."

"Hard to believe when we are down here and folks are being slaughtered up there," Theodore said.

"I will hear no more of this," Queen Agden interjected.

Theodore squeezed his fists, though he did as she asked, but not because she had asked it. He shared a look with Bruthren and knew that he would get nowhere like this.

Korrigan leaned against the cavern wall, whispering to Lore, with Polt on his shoulder. Agden took Folly from

Nia and held her fondly. Another knight, Calden, watched Theodore in case he ran for the surface again.

Disembodied screams siphoned down. Theodore could do nothing, so he sat in a jagged corner, drowning in his thoughts. He had little time to fix his already broken relationship with his father and hardly a chance to convince him otherwise.

The despair from above became white noise after a while, and when the air ran its frigid fingers to their bones even with a small fire going, no one realized the silence came.

Hargrove stood on the closest rock to the sea and called, "It's quiet."

Eliza stood up, barely, her body frozen in place.

The other knights cautiously made their way to her, and Theodore followed. "Nothing," he said, stretching his ear as close to the ceiling as he could.

Bruthren trudged along the side, keeping one hand on the cavern wall. "Either the Eltrists have been struck down or everyone's dead," he said with a slight laugh.

"Let's hope the former," Theodore said.

Hargrove stepped out of the cave, her swift feet balancing on the next boulder. The dark had blacked out everything from view, but the clouds seemed to have spread out enough that a glowing belly would surely stand out.

"What do you see?" another knight asked.

"Nothing," she said, without turning from the sky.

The knight made his way to the back of the cave, his sword pounding against his leg. "The skies are clear. They may have left knowing they couldn't win."

"Oh, I think they could win. They are clever and we cannot fly as they," Bruthren said.

"We may not fly, but the Anorphus will protect us. They cannot land in such a poisonous place." King Korrigan moved slowly towards the mouth. "Polt, find me an Eltrist."

Polt blinked and turned his head, as if to think about what he had been asked to do. Polt's wings spread and flapped hurriedly out of the cave. The ones at the mouth crouched down, ducking from him. They watched him soar farther from them.

"Hargrove, I want you to scout out above," Korrigan said.

"With pleasure," she said, curling her lip. She leaped onto another set of boulders to get close enough to the crag. Sea mist drenched the rocks, making them slippery at the first several feet that glistened in green, slightly darker than her armor. She reached out her hand and held on to a protrusion. Her hand felt like slipping, but she held firm, swinging her arm up to the next and the next without hesitation.

White clouds of her breath swirled in front of her, shining on the rocks like mirrors. She grunted with each movement until she reached the top, where she then crawled on top of the grasses and lay flat. Her head leaned up, and her eyes swirled with red, like the embodiment of hell. No one moved near the cliffs, so she crawled behind a tent.

She lifted herself up, still hiding in between two tents. She gazed out and saw folks looking dazed and wandering back towards her. Hargrove moved to the other side and peered up to where she knew they would station Cursed Knights. She could see the shine of the top of a Cursed Knight's sword in the Anorphus' branches.

Hargrove cupped her hands around her mouth and howled a whistle three times. The knight whipped his face to her and jumped down. He tiptoed through the crowd until he could break away to her.

"What is it?" he said.

"How many have died?"

"A heapful of folks and some knights."

"And the Eltrists?" Hargrove scanned to the right where the folks wandered.

"Gone. Vanished from the skies, like the sun."

"Vanished? They wouldn't just leave."

"Look for yourself." The knight bent his head back dramatically to gaze up. "No bubbling bellies lighting their way. Nothing but the black above."

"Why send everyone back to their tents if they still breathe?"

"You'll have to talk to the commander about that. If you've forgotten, he's the one that gives us orders."

"No need to be a cursed scum." Hargrove pushed him. "Where's Glaslin?"

"That way." The knight pointed to the opposite end. "Next time, howl for someone else."

The knight slipped through the crowd unnoticed by the dead-like folks who plodded by with their dark-ringed eyes and drooping melancholy rainbows for mouths. He climbed back up the tree.

Hargrove crossed through the crowd. They smelled of foul things, like urine and blood and, above all, fear. It carried even as she nudged her way out of their line. She crept through a trench on the other side of a knoll. Rocks filled most of the ground unevenly, which made it a perfect place to keep others out. With the night unkind, she found it hard to see every stone that could trip her. She kept steady and snaked around to a wider space.

She stopped mid-step, partly because she could see Glaslin and partly because it was rare to see him without his helmet on. He held it at his side, the purple plume brushing against his wrist. His hair was longer than she remembered. A group of knights surrounded him. The corpse thistles on their helmets looked like scratches in the dark.

He said something in a calm tone to the other knights, but Hargrove couldn't hear. She plodded closer.

Glaslin turned towards her footfalls. "Make yourself known."

"It's Hargrove," she said. "King Korrigan sent me to speak with you."

"Hargrove," he repeated as if he could taste honey. "Join us." He placed his hand on her shoulder, and she stared up at him. He was at least a foot taller than her and tanner than before from all the days spent in the sun on the Anorphus. "You have done well to protect the Ancient Ones."

Red crept across her cheeks and ears, richening her dark calla lily skin. "I'm here to report what took place back to King Korrigan." She swallowed.

Glaslin smiled as if he were watching a meadow bloom at nightfall. He shifted and sternly said, "Knights, take your posts. You know what to do if they come back."

The other knights treaded back or up the knoll to hide beneath the shadows until dawn.

Glaslin cracked his neck and sighed. "Three Eltrists came. They circled for hours, dripping strug onto folks for most of the time. It seemed more of an intimidation than an actual desire for battle. One knight died though in such a way..." Glaslin rubbed his cheek and down to his chin. "Gruesome really. The Eltrist swooped down and bit his head off."

Hargrove wrinkled her nose. "Did it swallow the knight's head whole?"

"Spit it out, like he was poison."

Hargrove's lip curled. "How many folks are injured and dead?"

"Too early to count. Caven has orchestrated the other healers to count the bodies and heal the ones that can be healed. By the looks of it though, not more than a heap."

"Where did the Eltrist go?"

"After we injured one, we continued to follow their paths and use corpse thistle to kill, but after the bursts of smoke cleared, they did too." Glaslin dusted his shoulder. Dried bits of blood and dirt rolled off. "If I had to guess, they will be back. I imagine this is due to Haylin dying."

"Haylin," Hargrove mumbled.

"I can't say I blame them. If they killed someone I loved..." Glaslin paused and stared down at Hargrove fondly before continuing, "I wouldn't hesitate to avenge their death."

"I would do the same." Hargrove stepped closer to Glaslin. "What do you want of the Ancient Ones below? Should they return to their tents?"

"Hard to say. I wanted the panic to mellow amongst the folks, but it's complicated to let them rest as if it was any other night."

Hargrove nodded. "Then, we should hide them away from the tents for the night, but if they stay much longer, they will turn to icicles." She rubbed her arms, as if she could push down the pricked hairs. "I am still frozen to the bone."

"The safest place will be below. Has no one lit a fire?"

"A small one. There was concern about the light attracting them."

"Light a bigger one and trap the fire. Bruthren can surely do that along with all the Ancient Ones if you cannot."

"They have not trained me on such things, though I imagine I could conjure it." She brushed a strand of hair back in place.

"I have no doubts; you've always been a quick learner." He tilted his head, gazed into her eyes and grinned. "Come back at dawn. I'll be waiting by the crag unless—"

"Unless they come back."

Glaslin turned his head to the sky. Insects zoomed past and others hummed or screeched below. The sound of them was comforting. "We are ready for them if they do."

Hargrove nodded and started back down the trench.

"Hargrove," Glaslin called. He placed his helmet back on. "Don't be a hero."

Hargrove stared at him pensively. "Isn't that the whole reason for being cursed?"

Glaslin shrugged. "At first," he said somberly. "Stray away from the depths, will you? I would like to look upon your face when the sun rises in the absence of bloodshed."

Hargrove froze, and for a moment, she lost her voice. "I plan on it," she called back before racing to the cave.

In the limited time she had gone, the sea calmed. She began the descent as surefooted as a cat. Sea salt settled in her mouth—an unsettling taste that mixed with her saliva like a pond beneath her tongue. Her focus remained on getting down, and at last she jumped the last foot and spit. She wiped her mouth and crossed back over the boulders, her muscular legs extending between them as she jumped from one to the next.

At the mouth, Nia grabbed her hand, helping her inside. "Good news?"

"Better than I assumed," Hargrove said, letting go of Nia's hand and walking past her.

Nia followed along with the other knights to the back of the cave, where Lore, Bruthren and the Ancient Ones waited.

"You've returned swiftly. What has become of the folks above?" King Korrigan said. He stood in front of her, his chalky eyes even more intense than hers.

"I spoke with the commander. There are some casualties, but not many from the looks of it. Caven is still helping the healers count bodies in between healing any that need it. A few Cursed Knights are dead, but the Eltrists have gone."

"Well, then, we can return to camp." Agden stepped forward to leave.

Hargrove placed a hand in front of her. "The commander thinks it best for us to stay here since no Eltrist bodies were claimed. He said one was injured, so it's possible that they returned home. He urges us to make a large fire and for me to return at dawn for a new report."

Korrigan snapped his fingers. "Bruthren, light the fire and protect it. I'm done with suffering through the chill."

Bruthren gathered a pathetic heap of driftwood from the mouth of the cave, but it would have to do for the few hours before dawn. He placed the wood in a pile in the middle of the cave, gathered up grains of sand and reached into his pocket for a tiny black bottle. He poured a few drops of strug and placed his hand atop the sand mixture. The fire breathed and floated like a shadowy being. Bruthren whispered something, and the fire clawed at the space, as if it had planned to grow but was stunted by his words.

Theodore sat on a rock near the fire, placing his hands out in front of it. The warmth made him sigh happily. Eliza sat next to him, and the rest followed except the Cursed Knights, who were expected to take turns in the warmth.

22

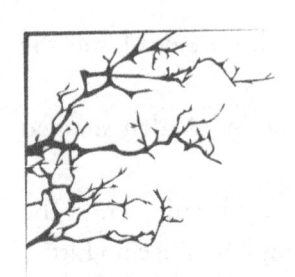

The moon positioned itself at the precise place to expand the shadows of dark tents into monstrous giants with unicorn-like horns, perfect for impaling. Any bird that flew overhead could see the immense shape and fled away.

Even Amardians felt uncomfortable in their presence, as if a curse or bad omen befell them. Many tried to jump over the inky-colored ground, but they soon found no way around it. Others laughed at the superstitious folks until wings morphed out of them in grotesque flares.

"Our young have returned," Talkun breathed.

Three Eltrists flew towards them, emerald, gray and orange fur swaying in the wind. Kinsington's mouth draped open as he peered up at them. They landed one at a time, smelling like salt and shaking the ground with their heavy paws. Lytha, the oldest of the three, landed first. Her burnt-orange fur was a rarity amongst the Eltrist. Rylog shook his shoulders, trying to rid the sea mist from his wings and dampened gray fur. The one with emerald fur, Tilion, landed last, his mouth dripping in revenge gold and his wing sunspotted with holes.

"I do not see Korrigan's head hanging from a paw." Kinsington narrowed his gaze.

"He was too cowardly to even face us. Cursed Knights shot at us from below with their fire magic," Lytha said.

Talkun lay down beside Kinsington. He still had little meat on his bones, and the amount of strug he could make was less than the others. "Did you land?"

"We wouldn't risk the poison. They put all the folks underneath the branches," Rylog said.

"Did you see any surface that was free of the Anorphus' grasp?" Kinsington's nostrils flared.

"Hard to say. The roots could hold on to the entire island, and the risk would be all ours."

"Then we must lure them out."

"How?" Tilion shook his emerald fur.

Kinsington snarled. "A flood is coming, one that they take for granted."

Talkun lifted his head, suddenly interested. "Drown them in strug?"

Kinsington nodded.

Tilion gave a wicked grin that stretched up to his eyes, revealing bloody teeth. "When?" he said, keeping his grin in place.

"Rushing into this is not the way. We must prepare for the greatest success. Rest for now... and, Tilion, go to Agatha for your wing."

The three Eltrists walked away.

Kinsington turned back to Talkun. "Are the healers not feeding you enough?"

"I need more than food to heal me... I doubt even a century of healing will manage it."

"We do not have centuries; we have slivers of time. Allow yourself to heal, or it will break all of us." Kinsington pointed his paw at the other Eltrists and the folks beyond.

"What would they have done if I wasn't in that tower? If the depths had already consumed me, then what would you have done?" Talkun stood.

Kinsington turned away. "You are alive, and that comes with responsibility. It doesn't matter what I would have done without you. I have..." He paused and looked down. "All of Amarda has fought for eternity for this and for your freedom, yet you sit defeated."

Talkun slashed his shoulder with his paw, black blood trickling into his fur. "My being is not written by you."

"It's still there."

"What?"

"That fire." Kinsington licked Talkun's shoulder. "Show Korrigan that you still have it, and clear your name of this stain."

Talkun's heart pounded. He had no words for the bubbling inside, the new rage that he thought had died long ago. Kinsington left him to join Esna and Aylo.

Kinsington gathered everyone together in the sunlight of a new morning. He stood in the middle, with Talkun, Esna, Aylo and O beside him. Thorn glared at O, as if he had caused her new position.

"We have a plan," he started, his words sweetly seeping into every mind. "The next several days, we will train with many of you who are able to fight. The Anorphus has met us with challenges and a delay in ending this war, but, fellow Amardians, I know we are many things, including masters of preservation. Now is no different. We will fly to the Anorphus with any able on our backs, and we will drown them in our magic." Kinsington stomped his paw. Storm clouds brewed in his eyes. "They have shown us how badly they want it, how much they abuse our very essence. If we cannot land, we will take to the skies."

"Drown them! Drown them!" folks chanted.

"Aylo, please take any able and strategize."

Folks, including Thorn and Riven, jumped at the chance to ride atop the Eltrists in battle. Thorn gazed in a validation-seeking way at Kinsington as she stood in line. He greeted her eyes with a look that a proud parent would give. She held her smile back and bit her lip. She knew she could repair the damage, and now was as perfect a time as any.

The ones who couldn't join got to work making what they could to help in battle. They bottled strug and placed poisonous plants, like corpse thistles, in satchels, with another satchel for healing and hollow nectar in jars. They sang as they did so, and hope washed over them once again.

Up the mountain, they assigned the warriors to an Eltrist. Thorn cursed under her breath when O stood next to Kinsington. Riven elbowed her in the side.

"What was that for?" Thorn clutched her side and frowned.

"Jealousy is how we got into this mess, and last I checked, I'm not dating Korrigan."

Thorn crossed her arms. "I thought Kinsington would take me back."

"Being jealous of a friend will not help. You need to give it time. He's going to test you before letting you back in. Have you forgotten how stubborn he is, or you are?" Riven watched the folks move through drills in front of her.

Thorn grunted.

"Uh, huh? Exactly as I thought. At least he's allowing you to fight."

"To die."

Riven shot a look at her. "We aren't dying this way."

"What do you think war is?" Thorn uncrossed her arms suddenly. "It may be for a cause that I believe in and honestly our only chance of survival, but we are being sent to die."

"You need to clear your mind." Riven lowered her voice and continued, "Is this you telling me that you still want to..." She ran the side of her hand flat across her own throat. She tried to say it, but she couldn't.

Thorn grabbed her hand and scanned the crowd. "No, it's not that." She closed her eyes. "This is all taking a toll on me, and it's spilling out."

"That's what happens when you keep everything locked away from everyone. It will get easier. Believe me."

"I'm trying. I am—"

"Thorn, don't keep me waiting," Aylo's voice growled through her mind, snapping her eyes open. Folks lined up to be taken where they would train. Birds watched them from the trees. Their heads twitching with curiosity.

"I'm your least concern," Thorn mumbled.

Aylo stomped over to her and snatched her with his paw. "Has anyone else in this camp allowed the Bloodtress and Ancient One to get away?" He shook her. "Answer me."

"No," Thorn whispered, deflated, wondering who else knew, who else Kinsington had told. Her body relaxed, as if she had given up.

"Then do not tell me what concern I should have over you. You may be a skilled fighter, but you have forgotten how to fight together."

Aylo dropped her, her legs folded under as she landed on her side atop weeds and small stones. Riven raised her foot, about to help her up, but Aylo snarled at her.

Thorn got to her feet and stood up straight as a stalk. She rubbed her side and it spasmed. "I will do... I will be better."

"We are going to another part of the mountain. Riven, you come too."

Thorn and Riven climbed onto Aylo, who charged into the sky before either of them had got into position properly. A glare cemented into Thorn's gaze the rest of the way as she clutched his white fur tighter than she usually would.

They flew just beyond the tallest peak and down to an expansive dell. Green sparkling water flowed closest to them. The folks below moved with weapons in hand or potions that exploded at stumps that they used for targets.

Each group appeared to have a leader if an Eltrist wasn't present. Aylo landed in the water, an uproar from the stream drenching them. Thorn cursed the soil while she wiped her face as Riven laughed. They jumped from Aylo's back into the water, which splashed up.

Aylo tugged on Thorn's shoulder. She stiffened. "Pick a group. The leaders know to be firm with you."

Thorn made it across shortly after Riven, rings in the water moving with each step.

"What did Aylo say?" Riven asked.

"Nothing."

Riven sighed. "Okay. I'm going to join O. You coming?"

"I'd rather not."

Riven shook her head and walked off.

Thorn felt as though she were slipping down a muddy cliff, her limbs unable to hold on to the surface, and soon she would be a ghost. She cracked her fingers and her neck and walked up to the first group. "Any room?"

The leader, a male with curly black hair and pearly teeth, crossed his arms. He was twice the size of Thorn in height and strength. He cocked his head. "It's a wonder you would ask." He smirked. "I thought you were Kinsington's top pick for every occasion. Folks wished to be you, including me."

Thorn rolled her eyes. "Do you have room or not?"

"If you can do as I say, I wouldn't curse the soil you crawled up from."

"I can."

"Sayone." The man put his hand over his heart. "My name is Sayone. We don't have time for mistakes. Now, get to it. Use a sword or strug magic with a partner. Remember, we will be in the sky. Magic will be integral for our swords to kill when the Eltrists cannot swoop down."

Thorn nodded and eyed the folks practicing their magic. She stared at them as if she felt pity. One folk chose blades over strug. He moved swiftly, cutting into a hollow tree. He turned and sliced into the bark. It cracked and puffed, with dust crumbling to his feet.

"I was told to find a partner," Thorn said behind him.

He caught his breath. "So, you've found me?"

"Everyone else has a partner to train with." Thorn peered over her shoulder. "By the looks of it, you are the only one without."

"I like to work alone."

Thorn groaned. "You've read my mind," she said under her breath. "Too bad." She snatched the sword out of his hands and spun it in the air before catching the handle.

The man clapped. "On this cursed soil, we praise the moon for your legendary skills," he said sarcastically.

Thorn glared, and her nostrils flared. "Do you know who I am?"

"Does it matter?"

"Thorn, get to work," Sayone scolded from afar.

The man cast her a look of curiosity or disdain. Thorn wasn't sure which. "Thorn, huh? I should have known. You look familiar and arrogant."

"You talk too much." Thorn took a dagger out of her hip belt and threw it past his cheek. It whizzed by into a stump several feet behind.

His lip curled. "Fight me, then. Pretend I'm a Cursed Knight."

Thorn stared at his eyes, which were neither crimson nor a deathly glow. They were opaque and yellow, like streaks of sunlight upon a meadow. A row of stumps varying in height stood next to them. Thorn jumped onto one, with the sword in hand. The man picked up a slightly smaller sword and chased her. She leaped onto the next one and the next until she ran out of stumps to leap to.

He swiped at her legs, but Thorn was more agile than him. She jumped up and came down, flying towards his forehead. His eyes grew wide as the hilt smacked him in the face. His body flew back, and his sword released from his grip.

Thorn stood proudly and chuckled. He pushed up with his hands against the ground so he was sat up and then he caught his breath. Thorn held her hand out, and he stared at it as if she were trying to give him a deadly animal, though he thought of her as deadly, especially now.

"Take it before I change my mind."

Sayone eyed her with scrutiny. His lips parted as if to yell, but then her partner grabbed her hand. Sayone wandered over to another pair, forgetting all about Thorn, for now.

The day continued in the same way until her partner leaped from her blade and knelt, swiping her legs out from under her. She fell hard on her back, and her legs fared even worse.

He stood over her, blocking the sun so its shining light traced around him, and held his hand out. "For you, our legendary fighter."

Thorn grabbed his hand and squeezed harder than was warranted. "It's about time."

"I wouldn't lie that you have a skill most of us wish for, but your arrogance will kill us all."

"Says the man who likes to fight alone."

He stared at the ground, rubbing his chin. "You're right." He peered around at all the other folks. "We have run out of the validity of our ways, it seems."

Thorn followed his gaze and stopped at O, who was in charge of a group. He captivated several of them with a ball of magic that he summoned from his hand. Thorn's jaw stiffened. She searched for Riven but couldn't find her amongst the sea of Amardians. She swallowed, as if scared of not finding her.

The man patted her back. "You look as if you've just been stabbed."

"Not by you, I hope."

"Is that what you think we are all planning? I think you missed the trail where we all left together to fight against Nniar."

"Just…" Thorn kicked a rock and grabbed the sword. "We can chat another time."

The man shrugged and swung at her.

23

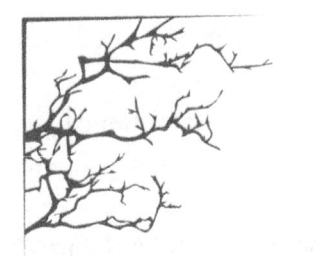

The drips, the splatters, the tapping beats drowned out all other noise. Even Morrow's voice couldn't carry as the rain pelted down. Audrey blinked rapidly, like clicking through a slideshow. She lay on the grass, wrapped in cold and drenched in shivers. She tried to clench her teeth, but each shiver was like a crowbar budging them apart. Water slid in, inviting at first, until it was more than she could swallow.

She rolled over, coughing up what she could. She rocked her head and breathed out through her nose, trying to rid the rain from seeping in. Snot gathered and dripped down. Her vision clouded. Morrow walked towards her. Audrey brushed her sopping hair out of her face and peered at Morrow, who still looked smudged.

Her mouth moved, but Audrey only heard the rain, and she was sure the water was clogging her ears. Morrow narrowed her eyes. Her pink horns stayed up no matter how hard the rain drenched her hair. Audrey stared at them, and for a moment, she thought they were cotton candy. She smiled briefly in delirium.

Morrow pushed Audrey back to the ground. Audrey's eyes vibrated under her eyelids. Her mouth hung agape, as if she were a fountain. Her body was numb. Theodore stood in front of her, his smile infectious. She reached out and put her hand on his cheek.

"Isn't it beautiful?" he said.

"What?" Audrey said without looking away.

"The ring?"

Audrey pulled her hand away, as if she couldn't remember how the ring had appeared. "Very."

"Though everything is quite dull compared to you, my love."

Audrey rolled her eyes. "Are we getting married?"

"Hmm... now, I thought when someone says yes, that implies a marriage," Theodore said, biting his lip. "Or is that not what Earthen folks do anymore?"

Audrey's eyes lit up. "We've won, then?"

"Won? What do you mean?"

"The war."

"I'd hardly call a disagreement a war." He let out a soft laugh.

"Your face." Audrey touched his skin where a beard had once been. "You shaved."

"I always shave."

"No, no. This makes no sense." Audrey turned around. Her surroundings were like partial images. "What's happening?"

"Audrey, look at me. Just stay with me."

"I can't. I can't. You're not Theodore."

"Are you feeling unwell?"

"I don't know." She drooped her head, shaking it. Theodore placed his finger under her chin, lifting it.

Audrey gasped at his hollow eyes, as if an artist hadn't finished their sketch. She stumbled back.

Theodore held his hands out. "What's wrong, my love?"

Audrey tried to run, but there was nowhere to go. She screamed at whatever was there keeping her.

Something plucked her from the scene, and her scenery became enveloped in black fog, pricking at her skin. Then a voice called to her. *Ben?*

"Morrow, fix this. Fix this now!" She heard Ben yell as clearly as she felt the needles throughout her body.

"Are you standing this close hoping for a kiss?" Morrow said with a lilting voice.

The shivers came and went at a slower pace as warmth blanketed Audrey. Her lungs felt too full to speak and her eyelids too heavy to lift.

"Audrey, can you hear me? Don't strain yourself. You're going to be okay," Ben said.

Her ears throbbed, and every sound made her body convulse.

Morrow had carried her inside and set her next to the fireplace several minutes before, and it roared with strands of angry flames. Ben sat next to her as Morrow rubbed a grainy translucent ointment from her belly to her neck. Morrow turned her onto her side.

"Grab a bowl from the kitchen," Morrow yelled at Ben. She raised a brow when he came back with a small one. "A mixing bowl from below."

He ran back into the room with it and set it down just before Audrey coughed water into it.

"Why didn't you just let me do CPR?" Ben shouted.

"This way is faster and won't break her ribs and exasperate you."

Audrey rolled back over.

"How are you feeling?" Ben said softly, leaning down.

Morrow shook her head and grabbed Audrey's chin. "And you are just too precious. How do you think she looks?"

Ben gazed at her. Her hair was knotted and wet, her skin pale and purple, but he could see the color returning to her skin. Her body was limp like a corpse; in fact, everything about her was like a corpse. He shot his eyes away.

"Mmhmm, that's what I thought." Morrow released her chin. "Don't worry, she'll live, but I don't know if you will."

Ben frowned. "And what exactly does that mean?"

"It's your turn now. Get outside before the rain decides it's done."

"You can't be serious. Audrey is barely alive because of this."

Morrow sighed and crossed her arms. "A bit dramatic, but we have to find out if you can use magic, like me. This is the best way. Do it for Audrey."

"You've lost your mind. Audrey would say the same. If she doesn't have magic, I definitely don't."

Morrow stepped over Audrey. "I promise I won't let you die."

Ben stared at Audrey. "It's not just death. Look at her."

Morrow cut off his view with her face. "Ben, honey, remember where you are. If you can use magic, you have a fighting chance." She pointed her thumb over her shoulder. "A much better chance than her. Don't you want to know?"

Ben tapped his finger on the side of his thigh and blew air out. "Fine. Let's get this shit over with."

"Ooo, I love it when you have fire in your words." Morrow walked her fingers up from his shoulder to his neck. "Lay down in the grass face up. I'll join you soon."

Ben sighed and walked to the door. His hand hovered over it, as if it were a hot pan. He clenched his teeth and turned the knob, leaving the warmth behind. Cold struck him, and he knew the second he lay down it would be unbearable. He picked a spot that had slightly fewer puddles around it. He took a breath and dropped to the grass. A fast breath came out of him, as if the chill had punched him.

The rain, relentless in its conquest, washed over him as if it sought to water him like a tree, though he felt that he would have come apart at his roots by the amount of downpour. He relaxed his shoulders only for them to spring back up, infected by the shivers. He tried all the same tactics that Audrey had while he'd watched from the window.

He locked his mouth shut and clenched his hands together atop his stomach. Rain beat down, sliding into his nostrils. Everything happened so swiftly that he couldn't believe how long Audrey had lasted in it. He moved onto his side, ready to give up, when a hand pushed him back down. Morrow gazed at him from above, upside down. For a moment, she blocked the rain, and he could breathe. He gasped and pulled her to him.

"No cheating." She hovered her lips above his, as if she was dangling his life before him. She moved away, leaving the rain to its own devices.

Ben shut his mouth and eyes. The rain seeped steadily into his ears and back into his nose. He breathed out as hard as he could. Morrow paced next to him, acting as though she were bored. Ben could faintly hear her feet in the squelchy soil next to him. His breaths came faster and his chest hurt.

Morrow shouted, "Can you hear Folengower?"

Ben didn't answer. His jaw stayed in place, but his eyes squinted. Morrow's silhouette stood before him, but something else flickered behind her.

"Concentrate and listen to her. She will guide you," Morrow shouted.

Ben tried to think of anything but the cold searing through his body. His lips parted. Morrow shouted for him to not drown, but water had already filled his mouth. His face was turning blue.

"So soon," Morrow muttered.

Squatting next to him, she placed a hand on his face. He welcomed the warmth and let his head rest on it. His shivers turned to convulsions. Morrow waited and waited till he was nearly dead. As his body went limp, she picked him up, and a light flickered from him.

Morrow dropped him and scanned his body as if she couldn't believe what she had seen. Her heart beat fast, and her face was more serious than it had been in a long time. She waited again for the light to return, but he only turned sicklier. Morrow lifted him up and carried him back inside.

Audrey was sat on the couch with a mug in her hand. The steam flowed like a stream around her, and a blanket was wrapped around her like a cocoon. The door flung open, and Audrey nearly threw her tea.

"Don't get up," Morrow ordered.

Audrey could barely move anyway, but she still wanted to. "Is he dead?" she cried.

"No, no. Just as dead as you were." Morrow dropped him onto the floor. The fire cracked and popped and turned as blue as him for a moment.

She tugged his shirt off and grabbed a jar that rested on the fireplace. She dug her finger into the grainy translucent ointment and spread it on Ben just as she had on Audrey. She moved the mixing bowl close to him and maneuvered him onto his side. He drooped over, and before Audrey could figure out what would happen, he coughed and threw up all the water.

"Fuck, is that what happened to me?" Audrey squeezed her mug. "And just to prove we have no magic."

"He does," Morrow said matter of fact.

Audrey shot a stare at her. "What do you mean?"

"He has magic. At least a flicker of it."

Audrey shook her head in disbelief just as Ben coughed up more water. A harmonious sound beat on the roof. The sound filled the room as it grew louder and harsher than before. Morrow peered out the window, with a smirk beaming on her face.

Black encompassed the outside of the house while the rain roared on and the ground puddled in every space in her yard. The flowers were sure to be ruined the next day, but still Morrow smiled, as though she could speak to the dark and its words filled her with curiosity.

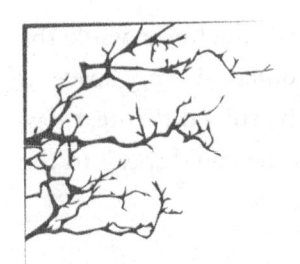

24

The morning never came. Puffs of fog ravaged the land, blocking out any sign of light. Chackles bit at the air, swallowing what they could. Cursed Knights sat atop them, creating a barrier around the Anorphus. A leader stood at each corner and middle with Nniar's flag grasped in their hand. They could barely see the vibrant blue corpse thistle in front of the lavender dye through the fog. Its movements were that of a deadly serpent.

Folks took longer to get to work, and some never showed from fear of the night before. Kalien woke with his hands clutched close to his chest and his clothes drenched in sweat. He pulled his shirt away from his skin and shook it. Cool air rushed up his back and down his chest. The tent smelled musty and like wet logs.

Kalien stiffened when he heard what sounded like a creature outside, but he soon realized it was a roar of snores from other tents. He climbed down from his bed, staring at the others. Cressa was facing the side of the tent, covered in a blanket, her hair reaching out in tangles of fire. Reed's left leg dangled over the side, and his mouth was agape, as if he were a toad catching flies. Indigo had a pillow covering their face and the blanket balled around them.

Kalien peered at the top of the tent. No light shined in as it normally did most mornings to greet him. He opened the flap, and a haze enveloped him. He shivered as his sweat turned cold.

Kalien eyed what he could as footsteps sounded with no bodies. He walked back into the tent, the cold following him. He snatched his blanket from his bed and wrapped it around himself. "Wake up," he said to no one in particular and clapped his hands.

Reed shot up, as if the claps were explosions. "What?" he yelled.

Cressa and Indigo rustled awake at his voice. They rolled over to see Kalien in the middle of the tent, now sitting with his legs crossed on the floor.

"I think it's morning. We're late for work," Kalien said, barely above a whisper.

"Work? I doubt anyone is working today, not after last night. Cursed soil. Most of us barely fell asleep." Reed wiped the sand away from his puffy eyes.

"It might keep our minds off things." Indigo shrugged.

Cressa rested her head back on the wooden support that ran up to Kalien's bed. The room was quiet, waiting for Cressa to speak. Reed glanced at her without turning his head. He could see the toll on her face, how the light in her eyes that could have once filled a room with warmth was now as dull as a broken bulb. He felt a tightness in his throat.

"Cressa, what do you think?" Indigo asked softly.

Her body stayed attached to the wood, as though she wished to become it.

"Unless a Cursed Knight comes and drags me out, I won't work today," Reed said. He crossed his arms, and a great growl came from his stomach.

"Eat at least?" Kalien said.

Reed glared at Kalien, as if he had caused his hunger. "If we go to eat, they will probably march us to work."

Kalien shrugged. "I can go and bring back food."

"Are you sure?" Indigo said.

"I need to stretch my legs. I'll be back." Kalien slowly stood up. He reached into his bag and placed a gray long-sleeved shirt on and dug his feet into his shoes. He sighed as he stepped out. Crisp air hit his face, and his shoulders tensed.

The gloom stayed thick and moist around him. He stared at his feet as he followed the trail. Footfalls sounded distances away. He wrapped his arms around his body, as if that would protect him from the growing fear he felt. The further he went, the more the fog lifted off the ground like a curtain being raised. As he proceeded, the visibility improved. He bent over and peered through the open space. Larger tents poked through, like shallow silhouettes in water. Near them, folks chatted softly.

Kalien turned off the trail and rested behind a tree. "Thorn," he whispered. He picked at the skin next to his nail that had started to peel off. One eye shifted to a sunny day and a man vaulting towards him with a sword. Thorn, distracted by Kalien's foggy surrounding, fell backward. She cursed the man heavily before shoving him off.

"I need a minute," she snarled.

The man held his hands up as though to surrender, though his smile was anything but defeat.

Thorn jogged away from all the folks fighting around her. "What is it?"

"Is there something I should know?" he blurted out. "I have folks here that I care about and who care for your side."

"Unless you have something to tell me, I suggest you refrain from reaching out to me."

"Still pushing everyone away?" Kalien retorted.

Thorn bit her lip. "I am in charge here; I don't have to tell you anything."

"You owe me my life. At least tell me if I should hide or help those who care for your side to escape the destruction. Last night, I saw folks die. I know you've probably seen worse, but I don't want to compare who's seen worse. I... I just want to live another day."

A long silence came. Kalien stood up and walked around the tree, certain that she would end the connection.

"Don't be in the crowds later today. Get off the Anorphus if possible or on higher ground."

"Another attack, then?" Kalien raised his hand to his lip.

Thorn cut the connection.

Kalien kicked the ground and cursed. He squeezed his fists and took off down to where they ate. He waited in line for breakfast in one of the many rows. Fresh bread, clawnuts, carveberries and fish that looked to be made of gloom covered the tables. A goling stood behind with a tall folk with a beard like a river in color and shape. The goling shooed the man to hurry as he sliced into a new loaf and plated it. She took a smattering of clawnuts, carveberries and slices of fish to the plate.

The man shoved a plate into Kalien's hands.

"Wait, I need three more. My bunkmates aren't well enough to come down."

"Three?"

"Yes, three more. One for me and three for my three bunkmates."

"And how do you plan to carry them all out of here?"

"Stack them?" Kalien shrugged.

The goling placed her hands on her hips, turned to Kalien and shouted, "Get moving."

The man sighed deeply and shook a piece of bread at her. "He wants more plates for the others in his tent."

"Then, sort it."

The man drooped his head and sliced more bread for the extra plates. Once he'd filled them with food, he stacked the plates as Kalien had suggested. Balancing the food took Kalien's mind off what Thorn had said, though the walk back to the tent was not long enough to keep his heart from racing.

Fog dispersed enough for him to see the tent clearly. He kicked at the flap of the tent and pushed his way in, nearly dropping the top plate. He gripped it, though a couple of clawnuts toppled off. Indigo rushed to him and took the top three plates, passing one to Reed, one to Cressa and keeping the last.

Reed sat on Cressa's bed with her. Her eyes were wide and lost. Indigo sat on Reed's bunk and patted the bed for

Kalien to come sit. Kalien eyed Reed with an unsure gaze, and Reed returned the stare with a harsh gaze. He sat next to Indigo anyway and kept his eyes on his plate.

Only sounds of chewing filled the space. Thorn's voice echoed in Kalien's mind. He zoned out of what was around him and into thoughts of where he could take them to be safe or if he should find Bruthren.

Kalien tore into the bread. He stopped mid-bite, holding the piece in his mouth, as if he was unsure if he should swallow it or spit it out. He suddenly swallowed quickly. "Wait, stop eating."

Reed frowned. "Why? What did you do to the food?"

"Nothing. Nothing like that. It's just... we should save it. Cursed soil..." Kalien stood and paced. "I need you all to trust me. Don't ask me anything about it, just trust me. Can you do that?"

Cressa placed her plate on the bed next to her. "Of course, Kalien."

Reed held his hand out, palm up, towards Kalien. "I knew there was something off about him. Don't you see it?" he said to Cressa mainly, but he glanced at Indigo too.

"We all have secrets, Reed," Cressa said.

"You know that's not what I mean."

"Just listen." Kalien took a deep breath, his hands shaking. "I found out something big is happening later today. We have to hide away without alerting anyone."

All three stared at him vacantly.

"Is this a joke?" Indigo asked, setting down their plate on Reed's bed.

"No, I wish. You can't tell anyone. I need you to follow me far up the island."

"What's going to happen?" Cressa edged closer to him and held her hand out. "Kalien?"

Kalien turned to her, wiping sweat from his brow. "An attack."

Cressa and Indigo exchanged looks of concern.

"And how would you know that?" Reed said, the only of the three to show any hint of unbelievability.

"I just need you to trust me. I can't tell you anything except to hide away with me until tomorrow."

Reed snorted. "How do we know this isn't a trap or something? Are you working for Amarda?"

"Has he not stood by us this whole time?" Indigo said.

"He has. Give him a break, Reed." Cressa put a hand on his. "I trust him."

Reed shook his head and pulled his hand away. "This doesn't feel right."

Voices came and went outside the tent as folks went back to their own.

"You don't have to come, but don't blame me if you are drifting into the depth's arms next time we see you."

Reed shot up. "Is that a threat?"

"It's reality." Kalien stood firm, refusing to back away from Reed. "I have no time to convince you, but I promise I only want all of you to survive."

A group of knights swept through the Anorphus, their voices chilling as they commanded everyone to get to their stations and not waste any time during the war effort. The hooves of their chackles pounded through the camp as they made their way to every tent.

"What should we do?" Indigo said, their chest rising and falling.

Reed peered outside. Folks rushed out of their tents and off to wherever they were needed. "If we want to win the war, I suppose we are quite integral in making the corpse thistle weapons."

"I'm telling you, don't."

Reed let go of the flap and marched up to Kalien. "I appreciate honesty."

Kalien's lips parted and then closed.

"That's what I thought."

Reed changed his clothes at the back of the tent as the other three sat in silence. Kalien knew there was nothing else he could do to get Reed to stay without telling the whole story. Reed strode over and stared into Cressa's eyes as if he could convince her to follow him, but she shook her head. He bumped purposely into Kalien as he left.

"Reed," Indigo called after him, but he kept walking, and the crowd soon swallowed him from view.

Kalien punched the mattress.

"Where do we go?" Cressa said.

"I have a place in mind, but we should wait until everyone has cleared out. I need to meet with someone first, if I can find him."

"What if you're not back before the attack?" Indigo said.

"Run up the hill. There's a massive fallen tree. It's hard to miss. Go under it. There's plenty of space for us all to fit."

Kalien left before they could ask anything else.

A stench of spoiled juice and rotted wood seeped from the Anorphus. At first, it came subtly, but by midday, folks gagged and covered their faces with rags. Folks shouted to the Cursed Knights to ask the Anorphus to stop. Some, believing they were being poisoned, bombarded the healers, though they assured them that the smell was merely a warning.

Kalien wandered through the camp, searching for Bruthren. He even silently and slowly used one finger to move the flap to the round tent open the tiniest bit, curious if Bruthren had returned to the secret corner, but he had not. He spotted Reed in there though, big goggles on, violently shoving down corpse thistles.

Kalien lifted his arm to block out the blinding sun. He could see Cursed Knights moving through the camp further away, rounding up any who had ignored them earlier. Then he heard the sound of chackles heading in his direction, Kalien darted behind a tent just before they rounded the path. He pushed his back against the tent, eyes shut, with his hand on his chest, as if he could stop the thrashing of his heart.

Kalien inhaled a gasp and stiffened as a hand covered his mouth. His heart felt stuck in his throat as a muffled "help" came out and he grabbed the hand. With the volume of his voice failing him and the hand like concrete over his mouth, he slowly opened one eye.

"Surprise," Bruthren whispered, moving his hand away. He smelled like salt and campfire.

"I was searching for you."

"Well, it's a good thing I found you, then."

"I have to tell you something important." Kalien peered around the tent.

"What is it?"

"Thorn told me another attack is coming, worse than the last. She said to hide."

Bruthren smirked and leaned in close enough to Kalien's face to see faint scars on his forehead. "Ooh, another surprise. When?"

Kalien edged away. "Today sometime. I think soon. What are you going to do?"

"Awe, you do care." Bruthren tapped his fingertips together and peered away. "But I'll be fine."

Kalien rolled his eyes. "What is the plan?"

"I will let The Choke know and see what we can do in such a short time. For now, hide yourself away."

Kalien tensed. "What about everyone else?"

"What about them?" Bruthren rubbed at a crease in his shirt, uninterested.

"A lot of folks are going to die," Kalien said a little too loudly.

Bruthren put his hand back over Kalien's mouth and a finger over his own lips. "Shhh. I can't save everyone, and neither can you. The sooner you realize that, the better. We have to be strategic about this. Did she say anything else?"

"Not much, just that I should get away from the Anorphus."

"So, higher ground for you, then." Bruthren moved his hand from Kalien's mouth and stepped back.

"Where will you go?"

"Far from the destruction, I assure you. I will have members help the folks if possible, but I will not throw away everything for one battle." Bruthren's eye twitched, and he took his glasses off and rubbed them on his shirt, like a bad habit.

Kalien nodded.

"Good, now go run off somewhere safe, and I'll find you later." Bruthren patted Kalien's shoulder before heading back to the path.

Kalien caught his breath before sneaking swiftly up the hill, back to his tent. Cressa and Indigo were sat together on Cressa's bed. They shot a frightened look at him and then let out relieved sighs.

"We thought you were a Cursed Knight," Cressa breathed.

"Thankfully, no. I found who I was looking for." Kalien reached into his bag and grabbed his cloak and placed a jar of hallow nectar into his pocket. "We should leave soon."

"Did you see Reed?" Cressa lowered her head.

"I did. He was working so aggressively that I thought he might break the contraption."

"Did you speak to him?" She bit her lip hopefully.

"No, I had to spy. He's made his decision, I only hope he changes his mind before it's too late."

Kalien, Indigo and Cressa walked up the path, crouching and listening for knights.

"Please can we wait a little longer, just in case..." Cressa shook her head, tears welling in her eyes.

Indigo looked at Kalien for an answer, who simply nodded. Cressa stared down the path as Indigo and Kalien stood behind her silently, watching sadly as her hopefulness ebbed away. She watched and watched until she too had to finally face that he wasn't coming.

They passed some folks on their way, none of whom seemed to notice them as they spoke about the attack from the previous day.

"Should we tell them?" Indigo whispered in Kalien's ear.

Kalien only shook his head without looking at them. His head hung for the entire walk until they made it to the fallen tree, which they dived under.

"How will we know when we can return?" Cressa said, sliding down one of the dirt walls to sit on the ground.

"I will go out and check."

"I imagine we will hear everything," Indigo said, picking at their nails.

Cressa covered her face with her arms on top of her knees. Kalien sat next to her and placed his arm around her back.

"We will make it through this."

"What about everyone else?" Cressa's voice came out muffled under her arms. "What about Reed?"

"I can't save everyone. If I could, I would. This is all very complicated, but I can't say anymore."

Cressa wept into her sleeves. Kalien felt his eyes growing heavy too, though he couldn't allow such a release when a wave of deaths was imminent.

It could have been the shock and exhaustion that caused them all to doze off, but Kalien sprung awake to a cacophony of screams. He scrambled to the entrance of the fallen tree and gazed out. Swarms of folks ran near his hiding spot, their faces in permanent terror. It wasn't the folks running that stilled him though, it was the sky lit up with fiery orbs and streaks of strug.

Kalien stepped out and hurried to the edge of the hill, his jaw dropping at the sight. Cursed Knights shot up fiery balls of magic while a fleet of Eltrists ruled the sky with snarling faces and folks riding them. Their glowing bellies and the waterfall of strug could mesmerize even those who knew what would become of them if they let it drench them.

Below, a stream of strug flowed between the tents. Kalien stared down at the folks of Nniar as strug moved quickly down the path towards a group of folks who stood in a daze. He searched madly for Reed, but he didn't recognize any of the faces.

Kalien cupped his hands around his mouth. "*Run*," he screamed.

The strug caught them, devouring their ankles. Kalien screamed again, his voice hoarse, then looked away quickly to a woman peering down at the strug she was standing in. For a moment, he thought she was going to run, but then another folk frantically trying to get away crashed into her. She fell in, her arms desperately reaching out to the closest leg. The man swatted her hand away, though it wouldn't make a difference because his feet couldn't move away, and the more he tried, the harder it was to keep himself up.

The woman's face paled and her arms weakened as others fell atop her, squishing her face deep in the goo. The man pushed off onto the pile of growing bodies to save himself, and he lifted one leg to find his foot melting away, his skin shredded like cheese. His eyes nearly rolled into the back of his head as he stumbled deeper into the strug.

Kalien's lip curled as he watched the limbs struggling to pull out, but from far away, it could have been a swimming lesson taking place, and from the looks of it, most would drown. Red streaked into the rising sticky river of strug, like strawberry swirl ice cream.

Kalien jumped away from the edge of the hill as a hand touched his shoulder.

"You were smart."

His hair stood on end and shocked, quiet tears began to streak down to his chin as he slowly turned. "Reed?"

There was no judgement or distrust in Reed's face anymore as he smiled down at him.

Kalien huffed a surprised laugh. "How did you escape?"

"I left right before it started. Something niggled at me that maybe I had been too quick to disbelieve you, and clearly that was the case. I hid down there." Reed pointed to a small rock formation off to the side, completely covered in moss. "Then I saw you up here, or at least I thought it was you. I'm glad I was right." Worry lines formed on his forehead. "Are Cressa and Indigo alive?"

Kalien nodded. "They are hiding, like we should be doing."

"I hope your hiding place has room for one more."

25

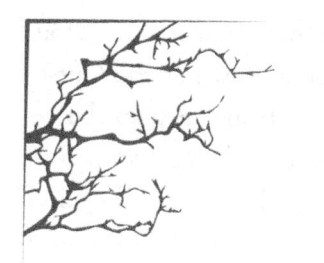

Pandemonium lived as a being, existing only because every soul on the island or above joined in on the wretched call. Folks knew the sounds would fade but never die, living instead in nightmares.

Folks searched for the portal to leave and soon they found one hidden in the doorway of the first tent below the knoll. Spooked chackles kicked off their knights and charged into the portal. Knights, too frightened to continue, joined them. When folks saw this, they too scrambled towards it, and the lucky vanished through without waiting.

Eltrists swooped down, spewing curved strug lines as they went. Their riders swung swords or tossed glass bottles at the knights. Deadly sparking light exploded out of the glass when they smashed. Knights followed close to the Eltrists who swarmed down, fighting against the riders or trying to stab the Eltrists. The knights struggled to use magic up close. Just as an Eltrist would charge down and leave its trail of strug, another would roar towards the knights, leaving the other Eltrist to fly back up freely.

Thorn rode on Aylo with her sword held at an angle casting light onto her face. It called attention to her ghastly scarred cheeks, and her wicked grin was an ominous sign of what she was willing to do to win. Aylo appeared as a cloud amongst the other Eltrists, barreling down at the Cursed Knights below who zigzagged away from the giant beasts. Thorn grimaced at the knight she edged closer and closer to. He peered up just in time to see her face as she sliced into his neck. Her sword caught on his web-like armor, and he yanked her down just as Aylo darted back up. Thorn released her sword and tucked her body in, rolling out of the knight's grasp, then sprinting away.

The knight placed a hand on his bleeding neck and shouted, "Halko." His chackle took off in chase, its fur muddied and now speckled with his knight's blood.

Thorn weaved through the crowd, hearing the hooves and the heavy breaths of her pursuer. She jumped over a thin stream of strug just beginning to expand, then ducked behind a bush. Crooked branches poked her back. She scanned her surroundings and spotted knights some trees over watching the sky. She tried to still her pounding heart and trembling body. The chackle stomped three times before charging to the other side of the bush where she was hiding.

"Come out, come out, Amarda scum," the knight said.

Thorn sprang up, as if she hoped to scare the chackle, but the knight snatched her throat and lifted her off the ground.

"I could crush you now, or you can be our prisoner. Which do you choose?"

Thorn's eyes diverted up just as strug rained onto the knight's face. Aylo crunched down, snapping his bones like a pencil. The chackle reared his front legs as the knight toppled to the ground, his blood pooling around his shoulders. Aylo held the knight's head in his mouth and lowered his face to meet the chackle's honeyed eyes. He opened his mouth. The knight's dead face stared back at his chackle between the slits of Aylo's teeth. The chackle tore off in the opposite direction.

Aylo spit out the knight's head, and Thorn climbed back onto him. Between shaky breaths, Thorn said, "You shouldn't have risked your life for me."

"Then you have forgotten why we are fighting," Aylo said, taking to the air.

Bloody strug streams veined through the camp, seeping under the tents on the lower ground and snaking off the cliffs into the sea. Commander Glaslin and a storm of Cursed Knights stood on higher ground. They were the lucky ones. The other knights fought below with their ankles deep in strug.

Glaslin had yelled *"fire"* so many times that he now only had to raise a hand to command it. Blasts of magic soared into the air. One blow hit an Eltrist's stomach, and they waited for it to fall, but instead it disappeared from sight. Glaslin clenched his teeth.

"We are nearly out, Commander," a Cursed Knight yelled to Glaslin over the caterwauling.

Glaslin locked his eyes below.

"Commander?"

"Let me think," he snapped.

Eltrists dove below, fighting any who were still willing. Glaslin's nostrils flared. His eyes followed each movement the Eltrists took. With each dive, they spilled strug from their mouths and swatted their tails, forcing the knights and folks towards the portal. They had moved everyone considerably to the other side of the island. Groups of folks jumped through the portal, where they hoped it would send them back through the Rocks of Lunok.

Once bellies of luminescence, now the brightness dimmed. Glaslin noticed everyone else moving with fear's hands clutched deep in their chests, though he knew what was going on. He kicked at his chackle. The beast charged through the remaining folks that were standing in strug or staring into the abyss above as if they were already dead.

They rounded a corner past the tents, Glaslin's cheeks reddening to almost his eye color as the frigid wind collided with his skin. He made it to the trunk of the Anorphus. The bark secreted a pale-yellow liquid. Glaslin covered his mouth and nose with his sleeve. His chackle galloped, kicking and groaning. Glaslin dug his heel into his side and rubbed at his throat.

"Death is not what I would offer you," he breathed in the chackle's ear. It flicked back, focused on his voice, as if it could understand. The chackle's legs calmed, and Glaslin stroked its neck one more time before leaping off.

He turned away from the trunk of the tree and stared at the knoll behind. The Anorphus' roots climbed under and over the wavy discolored hills. Glaslin placed his hand on the bark and said, "In times of desperation, I must ask for your aid. Will you allow me to harvest some of your roots? I have a plan to stop all this."

Glaslin tilted his head to the tree, as if to listen closely. Something snapped and cracked like old bones twisting. Glaslin searched for the cause and saw a root punched out of the surface up on the hill. It whipped around like a wild hose, moving up and down, and then another root broke through in much the same way until many moved towards him like an octopus.

The Anorphus bent its "legs," dangling them in the air before slamming them down onto a grouping of stones. The trunk seemed to squeeze and exhale. Glaslin snatched them up carefully in his gloves, placing them in a satchel on the side of the chackle. He gave a blessing to the tree as he rode back into the madness.

More knights were striding to the portal, and Glaslin snatched as many as he could by their armor. "You will not leave during battle unless you wish me to feed you to the twilight breathers."

Bruthren balanced on a broken table near him, playing a three-holed pan flute with strug and crimson liquid casing. He held it to his lips and blew a note, then stared at the thing and tried again. A song roared out, deep and unsettling. Bruthren twirled his hand towards Glaslin and bowed as he smiled, showing his teeth. He straightened up and placed the instrument back in his pocket.

Instantly, Glaslin and all the Cursed Knights stilled, their backs hunching like robots without batteries. As if life suddenly flooded through them, they snapped upright, and the red in their eyes moved like a whirlwind.

Glaslin fearlessly led the rest back into battle, leaping over the strug. He took out the roots and snapped them into pieces, yellow poison dripping from them. He waited for the next Eltrists to come for him as the other knights tossed magic into the sky.

"*Consume me*," Glaslin screamed, his body curling back.

Tilion snarled. "Gladly." He dashed down alone, his mouth wide. Just as he made it to the knight, Glaslin shoved a piece of root into his mouth. Tilion thrashed his tongue around and bolted into the clouds.

Glaslin didn't move. He had no trepidation about what might await him in the coming moments. A shadow in the moonlight covered him and then consumed several knights next to him and on and on until Glaslin could see the Eltrists falling.

"Cursed soil, move," he commanded the knights next to him.

Glaslin's chackle bucked until he staggered off it. It bolted away.

"*Coward*," Glaslin yelled after it.

A tornado of emerald swooped down, plummeting fast. With a thud, Tilion flattened several knights who didn't move out of the way quickly enough. Black blood drained from his mouth, and the glow from his belly vanished.

Glaslin stepped over Tilion's tail and traced a swirl of pointed skin atop his head. His lip curled while he sliced one protrusion off with his sword, then held it up, as if the moonlight would reveal a cluster of shiny gems. He placed his trophy in one of his pouches.

From above, the Eltrists could see the streams of strug, the bodies that floated in them, food too dangerous to eat on the island of the Anorphus and the many folks who left as they'd hoped.

Riven held on to Esna's fur as it swayed like a lion's mane.

"We have lost one of our children," Esna roared to all the Amardians present.

Like thunder, a chorus of growls released to the ground. They formed winding lines, their jaws nearly unhinged. Esna led them to the lifeless Eltrist. A flurry of magic from the folks on their backs came down in torrents. Their mass blocked out any light except the glow from their bodies.

The Cursed Knights closest held their swords up or used the wind to hurl poisonous corpse thistle orbs and black fire. Ultramarine puffed out like a bag of flour in between the flashes of fire. All around, reds, lavender and blues drenched the sky before shards scattered back to the soil in a beautiful annihilation.

O balanced on top of Kinsington, his sword raised, hoping to deter any more Cursed Knights from following Esna. His belt was heavy with satchels of magic powders. Kinsington's wings moved like great oars barreling upon Glaslin as Esna and two other Eltrists made it to Tilion's body.

"Don't land," Kinsington roared to the Eltrists. Esna hovered above Tilion, and Riven leaned over and covered her mouth. "We will come back for our dead when the time is right."

"Kill them all," Esna growled.

Esna rushed through the knights, sending them flying on either side. Riven tossed toxic powders as if she were standing on a parade float. The other Eltrists added to the strug rivers before darting back up. Knights stopped their advance, escaping the new gelatin-like death trails. Putting their swords back into the carf flower scabbards, they reached into their pouches for more corpse thistle orbs and tossed them up. They moved with such synchrony, as if a marionette controlled their movements. Corpse thistle orbs singed the Eltrists' fur, warriors toppling to their death as they inhaled or consumed the corpse thistle powder, though the bodies around the knights outnumbered Amarda's dead.

Glaslin locked eyes with Kinsington, giving a wry smile as he lifted another root. He shook it as if it were a dog treat. Kinsington neared and turned to the side, wrapping his tail around Glaslin. O raised his sword and sliced Glaslin's neck, his mouth opening, full of blood. Kinsington released Glaslin. His knees buckled and his head slouched into his chest, hanging on by one side of flesh. He toppled to the ground.

Strangely, the knights halted all fire and waited. Fifty crimson eyes transfixed on their dead commander. Pavlyn soared across from Sylin, drenching the knights with strug, and as if they came back to life from the pain, the Cursed Knights held up their palms of fire and shot into the sky. Another Eltrist wailed as they hit its chest. It thrashed around, trying to rid the pain before vanishing into the clouds.

26

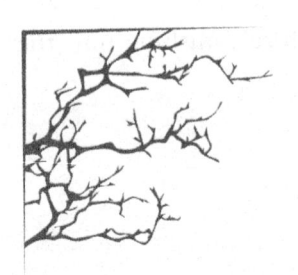

All the screams, all the clashing and bombing of weapons became white noise.

Bruthren drifted into their hiding place. "Leave now." His voice was clear as day, but he shielded his body in shadow, as if he were hidden by bat wings. "Go through the portal and wait in the Nniar woods. King Korrigan will not be arrogant enough to punish those too frightened to stay."

"Why are you here?" Reed said.

Bruthren huffed a laugh. "You were never the smartest one. Kalien..." Bruthren lingered on his name. "It appears a few spirit wings followed you, and you decided to bottle them up away from danger, so for moon's sake, you get them out. I have no time to argue or spill secrets. Either you want to die a long painful death by bucketloads of strug, or we can see how long the Anorphus can keep its poison hostage, or... or you get off this cursed soil and praise the moon for releasing you to nonlethal ground."

Kalien nodded. "Let's go," he said sternly. "I have no plan to die today."

Indigo immediately stepped behind Kalien, ready to leave, but Reed began pacing, as if he was considering dueling the depths.

Cressa pushed Reed forward and out of the hollow first. "Now is not the time to be stubborn."

Bruthren swooped in front of Kalien and placed his palm on his chest. "It is not up to you who joins The Choke. If I see that any of them are worthy of the cause, I will make it known to them."

"I didn't tell them anything."

"Repeat that." Bruthren turned his head and cupped his ear.

"I didn't tell them anything."

"Anytime you feel your secrets cannot remain that, remember this conversation." He held his arm out towards the exit. "Live another day."

Kalien hurried to the portal, all the noises clashing into his ears as if someone had removed headphones from him. The shock of it carried through his limbs. He wobbled as he ran, tripping as he went. Everything in front of him was too surreal to believe, too beautiful and grotesque at the same time. If only the brilliant colors that smeared the sky and soil were merely a sign of beauty and not destruction.

Indigo peered back over their shoulder as Kalien stared below at the many bodies floating in the strug. Some could crawl out, but parts of them never would.

"Hurry," Indigo shouted at him.

Kalien heard them, but he kept his gaze fixed as he ran sluggishly. There was too much to see and too much to imprint in his memory. Kalien rubbed his earring frantically, as if it were a djinn in a bottle, though he would have wished for his grandmother to float out alive and safely. With his gaze transfixed on the bodies, he tumbled down the hill. Cressa and Reed had already made it down, but Indigo had to jump out of his way.

Kalien placed his hand on his back and groaned.

"Are you okay?" Indigo said, their face looming over him.

He brushed off the dirt from his clothes. "Given the circumstance, I'm as shiny as a sunwave."

"Watch where you are going down here. We have to get past that." Reed pointed to a stream of strug with bobbing heads. They were far enough away to not have to see the grotesque details. "And if you fuck up because you are careless, I swear to the fucking moon I'll—"

"What? Throw him in the strug? Kill him with your bare hands?" Indigo said. "Hasn't he already proved himself?"

"I... It's just—"

"Let's just get the hell out of here," Cressa said.

Indigo walked past Reed, purposefully bumping into his shoulder. "I agree."

Cressa linked arms with Indigo as they crept into the chaotic space. Explosions sparked the sky near them, and the putrid smell of the dying reaped their stomachs with sick. Cressa coughed and pulled her sleeve over her hand, placing it in front of her nose and mouth. Indigo gagged. Kalien and Reed followed, neither escaping the foulness that lay before them. Reed turned his head and hurled. Kalien looked down and covered his mouth, worried that he too would vomit if he watched.

Disembodied voices wailed from the piles of bodies, begging for help and stretching out their hands. A woman ran towards one of the unlucky souls, her hair in a ponytail. She had high cheekbones and freckles. She knelt a foot away from the strug river and stretched her arm out to a sinking body. The person grabbed her hand, and the woman pulled. There was a disgusting sucking sound, and the woman fell backward, still holding the hand. For a glimpse of a moment, she remained calm, but then her mouth gaped and her eyes grew round like headlights as she hurriedly tossed the remaining flesh and bone back into the strug stream. The folk she'd tried to help let out a gurgle before their head submerged.

Cressa ran to the woman, who was now weeping, and reached out her hand, just as the woman had just done for the other folk. "Come with us," she said softly. "You did all you could."

The woman brushed her hand away with as much force as butterfly wings.

Cressa, not taking no for an answer, grabbed her wrist firmly and pulled her up. She looked into her eyes adamantly. "Run, we will be safe soon."

She shook her head but walked towards the portal with Cressa.

Two steps in, a blast of light rushed down. They fell to the ground, their bodies and everything around them hot. Their faces were dewdropped with sweat as smoke wrapped around them. Cressa and the woman reached for each other, fear clear and abundant in both their faces. Warriors atop the Eltrists hurled down more magic, caving the soil next to them. They flew apart in an explosion of dirt.

"Where are you?" Cressa coughed. She patted the ground all around her and wriggled her body, but only her top half moved. The smoke began to thin until Cressa could see more clearly, and her hand flew to her mouth as she screamed. The woman was lying on her side, a hole in her abdomen, as if a rock had crashed through all her squishy bits. Blood soaked her shirt down to her pants and trickled to the ground, but not enough to cover the exposed yellow of her ribs.

"No, no..." Cressa reached for her, dragging her legs behind her as she pulled herself closer.

"She's dead, let her go... Let her go," Reed shouted. He lifted Cressa over his shoulder and carried her away.

"She's not. She was alive," she cried, pounding his back and wailing.

Indigo and Kalien waited for them, and when Reed caught up, they started to sprint as death licked at their ankles.

There was no avoiding the streams of death—the luminescent lavender goo shined like glass in the coming of dawn, with limbs surfacing out, bloody and sagging what skin they had left. They could look away as they trudged alongside, but they couldn't do much about the stench.

As they neared the end of the tents, they could see the round tent not far away. The roof was caved in with strug, it also dripping down the sides, like a fountain. Other tents shared the same fate or had been toppled onto their side. The strug stream thinned the further they walked past the tents until they could jump over.

Shoving and screaming to go through the portal first gave life to unnecessary panic. Having seen hardly anyone on their way, they now knew why and where they'd been. Kalien peered ahead at the fighting. The Eltrists stayed near the portal, their glow dulling as dawn neared.

"Put me down," Cressa demanded.

"I don't mind carrying you."

"I don't care if you mind. Let me down."

"Cressa—"

"Just put her down." Indigo slapped his chest.

Reed gave them a deadly stare. "Fine." He pulled Cressa down in front of him and held her up, taking her full weight.

Cressa shook, tears running down her cheeks as she looked down. "I can't feel my legs."

Indigo shook their head. "Maybe they are just in shock... maybe you're in shock."

"Don't let go." She stared into Reed's eyes and gripped his arm, as if worried he would let go at any second.

"I'm not going to. It's going to be okay," Reed reassured her.

Kalien couldn't physically say anything, but his saddened eyes said it all. Reed carried Cressa over to a tree and set her down. They sat together in wait.

"Do you think she will heal?" Indigo asked Kalien, tapping their foot nervously.

"I don't know. I'm just glad she's alive, but we need to get through, or it won't matter. We will all die." Kalien huddled into the crowd, standing on his toes to see how far back they were. He could see folks following through and vanishing from existence. The shoving and fighting only delayed the line from moving.

Kalien rocked on his toes and bumped into the man in front of him.

"What are you doing?" the person yelled.

Before he could answer, the man pulled his fist back and punched his cheek. Kalien stumbled back a couple of steps. He was quick to reclaim his balance and, with all the pent-up anger and exhaustion he was holding, he rammed into the folk. They fell to their back, and Kalien immediately straddled him, punching his face over and over. The man's head flew to each side with every punch.

"*Stop*," Indigo shouted, tugging at Kalien's arms, but he was too far inside his emotions to listen.

Reed charged over and shoved Kalien off. Kalien scrambled quickly to his feet, while the other person clumsily stood, their face already swelling. They teetered forward as if they were ready for round two.

Reed stepped between them. "Look, look." He pointed towards the Eltrists. "They are staying away from here. We will all get through. We just need to be patient."

The folk followed his gaze and got back in line.

"I noticed that too. Why would they stay away from here?" Kalien said.

"Maybe they want us to leave the island."

Dawn came and went to birth the sun high in the sky, and by then, the sound of chaos had waned. The Eltrists had gone and the knights were holding fire. At first, the sun came as a blessing of warmth, but it only added to the stench of rotting bodies and vomit, which only amplified the need to escape. More fights broke out. They stayed huddled together on the cold ground until their turn finally came to go through the portal alive and hopefully to the Rocks of Lunok.

Reed carried Cressa through, and on the other side, the sun shined through the trees like lit lanterns. They stood on the top of the boulders, taking in the view of hundreds of folks spread from the towers to the castle and even in the forest.

"Hurry down already," a deep voice called. "Move."

Reed stared down at the Cursed Knight as Kalien jumped down and reached his arms out to grab Cressa. Reed lowered her into Kalien's arms and jumped down next to Indigo.

When the Cursed Knight was satisfied, he moved on to yelling at someone else. Other knights corralled the folks into groups. It was lucky that folks even listened after the Cursed Knights had abandoned their positions to run away. Reed took Cressa back into his arms.

"Now what?" Indigo placed their hands on their hips.

"I should return home."

"They will just bring you back," Reed said.

"What do you mean?"

"That's what they did with us. They came to our houses and forced us to evacuate with them," Indigo said.

"I don't live near the castle. They will leave me alone unless they care to evacuate other towns at some point."

"Then, how did you end up with us?" Reed said with a bite in his voice, as if he looked down on him for it.

"I was vending at the market, and Eltrists came. A knight rescued me and brought me to the Anorphus. I bet my family thinks I'm dead." Kalien stared beyond sadly.

"Then, go." Reed swished his hand.

"Stop being an ass." Cressa elbowed Reed in his gut. "It could be dangerous. What if other battles are happening in the smaller towns?"

"There might be, but I need to get home and now I can." Kalien shrugged. "Why don't you come with me?"

"Who?" Reed said.

"All of you."

"If only." Cressa smiled wistfully. "But I'm sure I will never feel my legs again."

"And I would never leave you," Reed said. "This is our home, and where else would we be safer if not with the Cursed Knights?"

"I think death follows them." Indigo crossed their arms. "But I want to stay near the folks I know. You should rest and get your bearings before you make the journey. Let's try talking to a knight and see if they can guide you back."

Kalien nodded. "I don't think the knights care much about what happens to us at the moment though."

They followed Kalien's gaze towards the castle. Cursed Knights had stationed themselves around it and above it, and he knew they hid in the trees just beyond too.

"Can we just... not talk about anything serious right now? I don't think I can

take much more."

"Does that include your legs? We need to speak with a healer," Kalien said.

"Especially my body. I know you mean well, but I don't want to know what I feel is true just yet."

Kalien gave an understanding nod.

"Why don't we have a celebration, then?" Indigo said. Reed squinted as if something bit him. "Kalien will be leaving tomorrow, and after everything, I think we need something to all remember that's good and happy."

"To life." Cressa chuckled softly.

"What is there to celebrate?" Reed said. "Look around, Indigo. Nniar is in a bigger mess than before, and now..." He stroked his chin. "Now we have nothing to protect us. At least before we thought the cursed soil would protect us on the island, but now what? No poisonous ground here to stop Amarda. No..." Reed shook his head slowly. "The strug rivers we saw back there, that is our new reality, and no number of Cursed Knights will save us. Pray to the moon all you want, but she's far away, and last I checked, she has no magic to help."

They all went quiet, and it lingered long enough to go from uncomfortable to expected. Indigo eventually lay on the ground, facing the moon. Kalien stared up at the great sphere too, examining the purple ring around it and how it appeared darker and thicker, studying the archedictyon-like lines throughout that appeared as though they were shedding off the surface. He wondered why the moon had changed, whether it was due to the destruction of the land.

27

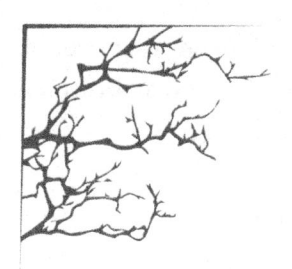

Sounds of battle ricocheted off the cavern walls, vibrating into their eardrums and rattling their bones. Salt water brushed into the mouth, like a painter darkening its canvas. For all the cacophony that pounded into the cave, the inside drained of any living sound.

All at once, they stood away from the warm fire as Cursed Knights returned from above. They balanced on the rocks and into the cave. Nia joined them at the mouth with Hargrove.

"How many have been killed?" Hargrove said.

"One Eltrist and a few of their warriors. I believe we've injured a few," a Cursed Knight with short silver hair said.

"One? And *may* have injured a few?" Nia guffawed. "*One*? What are you doing out there with your magic... your weapons?"

"Without them on the ground, we might as well be blind. Several knights left through the portal this morning before the curse activated."

"Are you telling me they left like cowards?" Nia snarled.

The knight nodded.

"Bring them back, Nia," Korrigan said.

Lore stood by him like any trained dog would. Theodore and Eliza stood by the fire with Agden. Bruthren was still gone. The knights joined by the fire.

"What has become of the Anorphus?"

"It's still breathing, but they infected the soil with strug. They have made our people drown in rivers of it. Most of the tents and kitchens are in a derelict state... and our commander is dead."

"Glaslin?" Hargrove's lips remained parted. Her eyes shifted as she felt a pain in her chest.

"Kinsington's rider killed him. A pyndin from the looks of him."

"A pyndin? I didn't know any of them lived in Amarda," Nia said.

"There used to be many long ago, but that's of no concern now. If the Anorphus cannot protect us, then we need to leave," Queen Agden said.

"Leave? And where would we go?" Korrigan said with his lip curled.

"I believe that's for the Ancient Ones to figure out."

"That's it; I'm going to help them." Theodore turned his back to them. Don't worry, I'll come back and let you know what a disaster the island is in."

"You can't be serious." Agden clutched her necklace. "You need to stay safe. Ancient Ones don't go into battle when such peril is at our doorstep."

"Maybe it's time that changed. What good are we hiding away?"

"Let him go." Korrigan waved his hand.

Theodore glared at him and bowed with a mocking smile. He turned around and walked towards the opening.

"Take Hargrove and the other knights with you who came down. Protect the Ancient One or throw yourself over the cliff," Agden ordered.

The knights' shoulders straightened and their heads lifted all at once.

Theodore gazed back at her and waved his hand over his head, leaving the cave with the Cursed Knights.

"Theodore," Eliza called after him but received no response.

"Let him go," Korrigan said. "He is old enough to decide for himself."

"If he dies, I will never forgive you." Agden's face hardened as she pushed her finger into Korrigan's chest.

Hargrove moved swiftly over the slippery rocks. Theodore followed with the other knights behind him. Hargrove scaled the rocks with ease. Theodore worked slowly, grabbing each stone and feeling for the best place to hold on. The knights below waited patiently.

As Hargrove advanced to the top of the crag, she yelled down, "Eltrists are still in the sky, not far from us. I have no plans of being their lunch."

Wings and the faint glow of bellies stole Theodore's gaze as the Eltrists moved through the clouds. A Cursed Knight tapped his foot, hoping he would move on without him asking so.

Theodore gripped the rocks tightly and made it to Hargrove, who held out her hand for him. She pulled him up the last foot. Theodore stretched his arms, as if he had a cramp. His hands were red and raw.

"Hurry," Hargrove called to the others.

Nia pushed at the knight in front of her. He cursed under his breath. One by one, they landed back on higher ground.

"May the moon save us," Theodore said as he tried to catch his breath.

Lavender moved through the flora like serpents all the way to the Anorphus' trunk and down to where the last tents were on the other side. Theodore couldn't see up by the hill where the smaller tents were, though from where he stood, no strug rivers had made it there. He stared at the Anorphus several yards away. Piles of leaves covered the ground beneath its crown, and even from a distance, the magnificent tree's branches looked cracked and seeping with its yellow poison, as if it could no longer control when and how much it released.

"Orders?" Hargrove said.

Few folks had stayed behind. One little girl sat next to a death stream, pulling at the plants next to her crossed knees. "Look, windcaps," she said to the person in the stream who looked like her mom. Her arm stretched out of the strug, but from her chest down, she was a blob of lavender jelly. The little girl reached for the pale green and orange zigzagged fuzzy bodies that hummed as they fluttered past her. She giggled when one landed on her nose.

Theodore watched her. "Take the last folks through the portal and all the Cursed Knights continue in the fight until they leave. I will speak with the Anorphus to see if there is any saving of this land. Oh, and if you find Bruthren, send him to me."

Hargrove nodded and motioned with her fingers for the others to follow her.

"Nia, come with me." Theodore walked over to the little girl and sat down next to her. "You know, when I was around your age, I would carry flowers in my pockets, and anytime I saw windcaps, I would take them out and hold as still as a stump."

The little girl rubbed her nose and sniffed. "Did they land on them?" she said in her little voice.

"Indeed. I would have dozens land—"

"Are you a Cursed Knight?"

Nia exchanged a glance with him.

"I do not have the honor of being a cursed one."

The girl wrinkled her nose and tossed her brown hair out of her face. "Why are you dressed like one?" She pointed to his eyes that lacked crimson for his grayish blue.

Theodore ignored her question and asked, "Is this your mom?"

The girl nodded. "She's tired."

Nia closed her eyes and swallowed.

"Would you like to spend time with a real Cursed Knight?" Theodore motioned for Nia to join them.

Nia hesitated but then slowly knelt beside them. "I can take you somewhere where there are other kids your age, and maybe we can find the rest of your family."

"I think my mom would like to come too."

"We should let her rest for now. I'll be sure to..."—Theodore choked on his words—"to bring her when she wakes."

The girl sat up and wrapped her little arms around Theodore. "I can't wait."

Theodore hugged her and patted her back. Nia turned away.

"Come on, we don't want to be late," Nia said, with her hand waiting.

"Will you play with me?" she asked Theodore.

"I will," he said with such promise that he knew he would find the time. "I just need to do a few things first."

She danced before taking Nia's hand and waving goodbye to Theodore. Theodore watched them wander away and hung his head, as if he'd killed her mother. When they passed a fallen tent, Theodore remembered where he needed to go.

Blood dyed the grass in blotches and puddles and pools. If a death stream was near, so was blood. Theodore gazed at the dissolving fleshy bits in the streams. Bones stuck partially out of the middle and some hands partially melted were just outside the strug. He could look down in it and faintly see the outline of the folks who were claimed by it as if he peered into a jar of jelly.

The stream looked to be older than others due to its expansive size in comparison to the others. Intact heads melted on the surface. Theodore paced at the stream, the width making it impossible for him to jump over. There was only one tent near him that was untouched by strug, and he peeked inside. No one was there, but there were still belongings scattered around from where the folk or folks occupying had left in a hurry. He dragged the bed out, threw the bedding off and pushed it into the strug. It wobbled and began to sink.

He climbed atop and ran across as bubbles rose and popped in the strug. He leapt off, landing on his feet. The bed sprang up a tad as his weight lifted.

Trails around the tents had dips and craters where magic had exploded. Theodore peered into each tent, hopeful to help any that stowed away. So far, they all were empty.

Up ahead, he noticed the corpse thistle flag bent and lying on top of his collapsed roof. Another tent blocked his way like it had been blown over to it. He pulled out the remaining stake and dragged it about a foot away from Theodore's tent door. He stepped inside and scanned above and below for any danger. Things were knocked over, but nothing seemed at a loss. Theodore's crown remained in the glass box. He eyed it as if unsure if he should grab it, then walked over and pulled the glass case off. He grabbed the crown and placed it atop his head. His eyes closed briefly, as if he thought it would strike him down. It nestled perfectly atop his hair, and he held his head high and left behind the rest of his belongings.

He continued his search through the many tents. "Any folks in there?" he called. For several tents, he heard nothing. As he passed to the next grouping, he heard someone weeping. He opened the first one. Tatters of fabric were strewn about and a side table split to pieces. Theodore tilted his head towards the hole in the top. On one side a single drip of strug landed on a piece of clothing. He left to the next tent.

He peered inside at a chest too short to completely hide the three folks jammed together in the corner behind it. "Praise the moon, you're alive." He smiled, finally knowing his decision to leave and search was the right one. If he hadn't found these folks, would anyone else have? "Let me help you to the portal."

They all stared at him, none of them moving from their clustered embrace.

"I am Theodore, the next Ancient One. Please, let me help. Are any of you hurt?" He looked them up and down but couldn't see any visible injuries, although they were too hunched for him to do a proper inspection and the third was practically hidden from view. He stepped closer, walking at an angle.

"You can't help," the young boy said, sniffling.

"Let me try."

He moved to the side, pushing the girl next to him out of the way. Theodore lost his breath as he finally got a full view of the third. The man was hunched over, the top of his head dripping with skin and hair down to his eyes. His eyes. All Theodore would remember was his amber eyes fixated on him.

"Are you two hurt?"

They shook their heads.

"Good... good. Come with me."

"We can't leave our dad." The young boy placed a hand on his dad's shoulder protectively.

Theodore gulped. "He would want you to leave."

The young girl covered her eyes with her hands. The man's eyes followed Theodore no matter where he moved.

"Come, please." He held his hands out to them.

The boy shook his head, tears streamed down to his neck. Gently the girl squeezed his hand and slowly they grabbed Theodore's.

He carefully wandered through the camp with them shouting for a Cursed Knight to escort the children to the portal. They leapt over certain spots using what they could find around them. When knights finally made it to them and left with them, he continued his search and found a dozen more, sending them off.

When he found no one else, Theodore placed his hand on his hilt. It pulsed to his touch, vibrant as strug. He squeezed it, as if it gave him strength to go on. He focused on the knights' formation several yards ahead of him as they held fire in their hands and fired their magic deep into the sky. The Eltrists maneuvered as if they felt the blasts several seconds before they made it to them.

"They're leaving."

Bruthren stood dangerously close to the Anorphus and the death stream that surrounded it. "Bruthren, there you are. What do you mean?"

"Look around, Ancient One." Bruthren sighed. "The skies bow to them. They have no reason to keep fighting. They will all be gone soon, back to their camp until the next one, but we won't be here then, will we?"

Theodore's lips formed into a thin line. "I should have killed him."

"The time isn't right. You would have been captured and sentenced before any work could be done. We also have Kinsington to fear. We need to meet with Talkun."

Theodore mulled over his words.

"Is the Anorphus dying?" Theodore knelt next to a death stream, watching the remaining body parts sink into the lavender.

"It's possible. It certainly smells as though it rots from within. Wouldn't that be something? Another old thing your father killed."

Theodore shook his head and rubbed at his beard. "I'll command the other knights to leave once the Eltrists are gone."

"You should be nowhere near the fighting; you are a precious commodity now." Bruthren tugged at a femur bone that stuck out of the stream, pulling it out and examining it. It was devoid of flesh.

"What are you doing?"

"Thinking. You should do it sometimes."

Theodore frowned at him.

Bruthren sighed. "Loosen up, Ancient One. There will be plenty of times to be serious. I'll command the knights to leave shortly. Did you notice their glowing bellies have dulled?"

Theodore followed his gaze. "I've never seen so much strug. They probably need time for their body to produce more."

"Indeed. Eltrist can develop ailments if they release too much."

"How do you know that?"

"I've had my share of Eltrists to... examine. For a while, it was my primary work. You have enough wit to know why your father would want that of me."

"And how much of all this is your fault, then?"

Bruthren smiled as if Theodore had complimented his clothes. "The infected helps the spread, but it is not the creator of the infection."

Theodore stared into his eyes. "I suppose it's pointless to speak of the past when the future is upon us. I still plan on fighting, regardless of my status."

"Then, go." Bruthren tossed the bone to the ground. "The Eltrists have waned and the battle will soon vanish."

Theodore took off to join the Cursed Knights. There were far more casualties in piles of strug, many of them knights, their armor now the only marker of who they were. He knew that any effects left behind would be priceless to those searching for a loved one.

Theodore lit the magic in his palms, his skin tingling as it flowed through his entire being. Thick black flames moved their spindly tips as if wanting to fly. As he exhaled, he flung his hands upwards, releasing the magic. It crashed through the air and, like glass breaking, the sound thundered. A warrior spiraled down off an Eltrist and down until landing with a thud. *"End this,"* he shouted.

The Cursed Knights turned to him, their mouths agape.

Nia darted towards him. She bowed low with her fist over one eye. "Your magic is not to protect us."

"Then who is it for?"

Nia stayed in position, at a loss for words.

"That's what I thought." Theodore walked a slow circle, arms out, palms facing up. "All this power for nothing. To hide behind all of you cursed and bound to us."

Nia slowly let her arm fall. "Be careful who you share your thoughts with."

He stopped, facing Nia. "I would hope you wouldn't be someone I'd need to be careful of."

Nia nodded.

"Good. Rise." Theodore pointed up. "They are leaving. Assign a group to move Amarda's dead into a pile. They will be back for them."

"You want them to take them?"

"They have a right to mourn, just as we do."

"At least their dead are whole," Nia said, spitting at the ground.

The last Eltrists flew into the clouds, leaving the Cursed Knights to cease fire. Bruthren crept over a narrow stream of strug and reached into his pocket, pulling out the flute-like object. He blew into it, and the Cursed Knights suddenly jolted and let out a breath as their true selves returned.

"What gallantry you have all shown." Bruthren clapped his hands. "Check the bodies for any life. We are leaving the island shortly. Gather up what you can that remains of the dead, like jewelry, clothing... anything that we can hand over to any loved ones searching. Nia?"

"Yes?" Nia stepped away from Theodore. "What is it?"

"Will you pick someone to gather buckets of water to clean off strug from any personal effects?"

"Is it important to do that now? Better to wait for the strug to melt into the ground or for the Eltrists to come back and eat it."

"They will not be back. At least not for days."

"Of course they will."

Bruthren took Nia's hand. "Details, details. Did you not see the dullness of their glowing light?"

Nia shook her hand away. "No, I didn't."

Bruthren rolled his eyes. "They need to heal first. Look around. All of you. Look." He paused. "Has anyone seen this amount of strug before? Rivers run through the island. The destruction that has caused will change the course of this fight. How many of their dead can we count? Can we count our dead? I doubt they could eat any of it without knowing the Anorphus is dead anyway."

Theodore rested his hand on his hilt and listened intently to Bruthren's words, as did the swarm of Cursed Knights.

"It is more important to gather what we can now so that the folks waiting on the other side of that portal know we still have souls. We do not need our own folks uprising." Bruthren eyed Nia. "Name someone."

Nia bit her lip. Calden stepped forward. Nia swallowed. "Calden, lead a group of knights on this mission." Calden smiled faintly at her. She couldn't smile back, but her eyes reveled in seeing him whole.

"I will."

Bruthren raised his eyebrows and stepped in front of Nia. "After we clear the island of survivors, grab your things and go through the portal." He waved his hands in a shooing manner.

Calden faced the knights and ordered a group to check the death streams. They linked their arms together with their fists raised and shouted in unison, "Soil, bless our blood." They said it as if the words would protect them.

"Bring my family up here," Theodore said to Nia. "I will be back."

"Ancient One, where are you going? I can have Hargrove go with you."

"I am going to speak with the Anorphus. Hargrove is busy enough as it is. Bring everyone from the cave up here."

Nia nodded and hurried to the cliff.

Theodore walked as if a gentle wind carried him. A group of chackles knelt in the grass and lazily chewed into it, probably searching for any morsel of fungi. Some slept or chewed and licked at their dirty long fur. As Theodore walked past them, he brushed his hand against the closest chackle's matted head. It huffed and nuzzled his hand before slumping back down.

The closer to the Anorphus he got, the deeper and wider the body of strug was. The Anorphus appeared as a castle surrounded by crocodiles. It wept angrily. Theodore could feel it all around, as if swarms pounded at his ears.

Theodore held his hands out, and a green fiery smoke danced upon his palms. "I think I can help ease your suffering." He moved his hands down to above the ring of strug. It tossed as if in a dome with heavy winds. He controlled its movement up and out of the deep hole it had made. He moved back, bringing both his hands close to his chest. A section of the strug lifted from the ground and swam towards him.

He looked around for somewhere to put the strug. A knight worked at the death streams a yard away.

"Bring me buckets," Theodore called to him.

The knight looked up and sucked in a breath. He blinked and scurried to stand up straight.

"*Now.*"

The knight quickly brought him his bucket and ran off to collect more. Theodore released the strug, which slopped into the container. The Anorphus let out a whining breath.

Before long, the knight returned with buckets dangling from their handles on his arms and another knight with a big basin. They set them down and watched. Theodore repeated his steps, moving the strug into the buckets, as if they were dolphins crashing into the sea.

"*Stop*," someone yelled. It was loud but too far away to know who had called.

Theodore ignored the voice, thinking it was for someone else. Then a crack like a whip hit him in the back. He moaned in pain, his magic immediately ceasing. The strug splashed down, bits of it splattering onto his pants.

Korrigan charged at him. "Do I need to remind you about everything?"

Theodore peered over his shoulder. "I thought punishments were meant to be secretive?"

"This is the last time you will go against our rules. You are not to use your magic for all to see." Korrigan stopped just in front of his face. Theodore stared at the wrinkles on his forehead, as if he hadn't noticed them before.

"Why do we have this rule? Not all Ancient Ones were cowards," Theodore spat.

"How would you know?"

"I have studied our history, and I know they helped their people and the land."

"Then know this: I am not them. You are under my rule, and you will demand the Cursed Knights to clean up this mess themselves."

"You demand it. I will not give such an order."

It was impossible to not feel the stares and silence as they argued. Bruthren even crept back over to them and listened.

Queen Agden ran behind Korrigan to Theodore. "It is not our way," she warned. She transfixed her eyes on Theodore and shook her head discreetly.

He glared at her. "The Anorphus will die if we don't help. Cursed Knights do not possess this magic. Unless you plan on training them in healing magic."

"I should have sliced your tongue when you were a child," Korrigan snarled.

Queen Agden frowned and crossed her arms, stepping forward towards Korrigan. She was trying to not make the scene any worse, especially knowing how Korrigan would react in private later, but it was hard holding her anger in completely. "How dare you say that to our child. Theodore is the next Ancient One, and you choose to belittle him in front of his army?"

"*My* army."

"Why don't I help the Anorphus?" Bruthren said, peeking behind Korrigan.

"Bruthren knows more than most. Why not let him finish what I already started?" Theodore said, cocking his head.

Korrigan licked the crease of his lips. "Bruthren, ease the Anorphus' pain in any way you can."

Bruthren bowed with one fist over his eye and took to the ring of strug. He walked around it to assess the damage.

"Come with me," Agden said to Theodore, grabbing his shoulder.

"Uh, uh…" Korrigan shook his finger. "Theodore needs to see what an heir to Folengower must do and how they should act. It seems he has forgotten."

"No, you have done enough," Agden said.

Korrigan's cheeks turned red, and his eyes looked as if they would pop out at any moment.

"I will go with you, but do not think you can punish me as before." Theodore stood next to Korrigan and whispered, "I could strike you down right here if I wanted to."

Korrigan turned to him and studied his face, as if wondering if the hate he felt lived inside Theodore too. If he had sealed his fate the night he murdered his mom, that his son would do the same to him.

28

Without healthy soil, nothing could thrive. Amarda was rotting not because the Eltrist lived for destruction, but because the price of magic needed healing. Folengower had known times when the healers would come and bring life back into the soil, especially when birth rates were higher amongst Eltrist and their babies needed more nutrients as they grew and stopped feeding from their mothers. Folengower had rejoiced at the births and the growth of them, and the healers had easily conjured life back. Yet, the magic of restorative life had become more and more scarce since Queen Callum's death after Korrigan made it so.

Now, Korrigan took the destruction in. It wouldn't be long before the Anorphus died and the majority of flora and fauna along with it. He knew it would look achingly similar to Amarda after several years, but it seemed a great plan to showcase the grim nature he hoped to paint of the Eltrist.

Theodore sat on the edge of the cliff. He had tired of his father's lecture and left with a smile. Few knights remained on the island. Night came like a thirsty horse, cloudless, with stars shining like jewels around the fullness of the moon. It was a comfort and an ill reminder for

Theodore. He thought of what he would say if Esmeray could speak back to him, or if she thought him foolish. He cared what she thought despite a stone of hate that rested in his throat. It would always be there every time he thought about what she'd done and her quest for Audrey's head.

"It's time," Bruthren said. He stared off into the Sea of Calip. Its waters were black and endless. The smell of the sea came in wafts, and they welcomed it over the corpses and the poisonous smell from the Anorphus.

"Did you save the Anorphus?"

"Unfortunately, I don't believe any of our magic can save such a life. The Anorphus is dripping with strug, and it's down in its soil, gnawing on its roots as the Anorphus slurps down its poison as if a treat. The Eltrists drowned it."

Theodore rubbed his head.

"Come, Ancient One. There will be more casualties, some bigger than this one, I'm sure, but the end of all of this will be worth all the loss."

Theodore stood up, gazing into the dark sea. Gentle waves moved with grace below, a glimpse of its stunning life shining from the moonlight every time it rippled. Theodore took a step closer. Pebbles trickled down, lost for eternity.

"Are you coming? Another step and the depths will consume you," Bruthren warned.

"The depths will have to wait." Theodore moved past him. "Who remains?"

"A handful of knights. The rest have gone through the portal."

They walked side by side towards the portal.

"It's clear that gaining your father's trust will be harder than I expected."

Theodore grunted. "And?"

"Perhaps we should take a different route."

"Did I ever tell you you're a genius?" Theodore said sarcastically.

"Actually, no." Bruthren sighed. "Your relationship is out of my hands. Do what you can, but choose your battles wisely, or you may curse us all. We need to look at the bigger picture. The fighting between you and your father is like a tarbug—they can consume stumps in alarming time, and so can that fiery hate you both share."

"Folengower will unite. I will not let that perish. Have a little more faith in me."

Bruthren tilted his head and gave a single nod.

As they passed the trunk of the Anorphus, Theodore stopped. He stood still, listening to the air for any wisps of words from the Anorphus. There was something, a rush of tranquility that pricked at his skin, and pain nipped at his insides.

"The Anorphus experiences death as we do," Bruthren explained, sensing Theodore's connection and empathy. "Pain and peace balled up together, sometimes in harmony and sometimes going back and forth between the two."

"Why couldn't you save it?"

"Could you have?"

"I wanted to try at least. With such an old being, I would imagine it would take more than strug to kill it."

Theodore whispered something and sent a wave of green magic that wrapped around the bark like lace.

Bruthren kept walking and tapped his foot. Theodore followed.

"There are so many forms of magic and ways to use it. Folengower has blessed us with the ability to manipulate it as we please, but it doesn't mean we always use the right process at first or ever. As I'm sure you have seen in your learning. I couldn't save the Anorphus because I did not find the right union to heal it."

"Maybe they are ready to die, perhaps even wanting to at this point, so it wouldn't matter what any of us tried," Theodore said.

"Won't we all feel that way at some point? Of course, my time is hardly near."

They rounded to the portal, which was now as empty as a graveyard. The folks who lived had accidentally scattered belongings about as they'd rushed through. Theodore reached down and picked up a necklace. It had three bright blue stones. He set it back down and stepped through, leaving the Anorphus to dream for eternity.

Theodore and Bruthren came through the Rocks of Lunok. Clouds settled over the castle grounds like angry giants. They were almost too dark to see, for the tar color was nearly darker than the sky itself. The thin streaks of slate gave them away. Folks looked to the sky, as if they wished to see stars, though there was no sign of the twinkling balls of light. Theodore's eyes adjusted to the crippling dark. At least before, he'd had Esmeray to cast her shimmery light down.

The Cursed Knights would be invisible if it wasn't for the crimson glow of their eyes. They came from the woods with piles of branches and sticks. They set them down into several heaps, all staggered from one another, and lit a fire with their magic. One by one, swirls of fire moved about the wood, dipping low at first like a curious creature, then rising high like a grown beast.

Theodore lit a white fire in his palm and jumped down from the rocks. Bruthren followed.

"Conversations are like ghosts—you can let them haunt you, or you can use them to your advantage. Don't let ours haunt," Bruthren said before wandering through the crowd.

"There you are." Eliza crashed into Theodore, wrapping her arms around him.

"Has that thing you call Father calmed down?"

"I would watch your tongue, at least for now." Eliza pulled away.

"What are they planning?"

"Have you forgotten? I'm a Bloodtress, not the next heir."

"You're the favorite. I imagine you could find out secrets I never will, at least not without force."

Eliza sighed. "I know that we need to be clever, and you..." Eliza poked her finger into his chest. "You need to stop openly defying him."

Theodore crossed his arms. "I don't know if I can."

"Try, or we will all be in mourning. And not just me. Audrey and Ben are still here. Have you forgotten about them?"

Theodore glared. "Of course I haven't. Do you at least know what he plans to do now that his safety net is dead?"

"No, I think good dad is still expecting the Anorphus to survive and we can go back to the island."

Theodore squinted his eyes. "Did he not see the damage or the bodies? He wouldn't even try to heal it himself."

Eliza put her finger over her mouth. "Keep it down. He's not thinking straight."

"When has he ever? I tried to heal the Anorphus, if you remember," Theodore squeezed his hands. Briefly a light beamed through the slits. He shook his hands and exhaled. "I'm sure Bruthren will find a solution. He has a knack for these things."

"Overthrowing kingdoms, you mean," Eliza whispered. She smiled as if she had told a joke.

"Exactly. Go off, Branch. I'll find you later."

Eliza bowed. "Storm."

Folks huddled in blankets near the fires in the giant campground. If only they had songs, smiling faces and marshmallows, their faces tinted in sunshine. Theodore walked by the fires. For so many folks in one place, there was hardly any noise above a whisper, not even from the children. *Children*, Theodore thought. He wondered if the little girl he'd seen with her dead mother had found a family member or friend to be with. He scanned the rows of Cursed Knights up high at the tower and down low for Nia. It was too difficult to find her in this darkness; he could barely see outside the stain of firelight.

Some of them noticed Theodore and placed a fist in front of their eye and bowed their heads. His crown gave him away, and he put his head down, as if he didn't want to be noticed. He walked till he made it to the garden. There was more rubble scattered about than the last time he had walked through, and Nia was there standing with another knight. She turned to him and said something to the knight before walking away.

"Where have you been?"

"Trying to be useful." Theodore shrugged.

"Aren't you always?" Nia shook her head. "You should be with your family."

"Where are they?"

"Inside the castle. For now, this is the safest place we have until we make new arrangements."

"Safe?" Theodore chuckled. "Look around." He kicked a piece of stone. It bounced once, then rested in a flowerpot of wilted flowers.

"Bruthren and Lore are holding a meeting in the morning. I'll let you know what I find out if they do not ask you to come."

"Will my father be there?"

"He always is."

Theodore nodded. "Praise the moon for you."

Nia smiled. "Go."

Theodore ambled down the path and rounded the corner. Vines had taken hold of many of the stones, and they only seemed to have grown since the attacks. The tall doors were cracked, but he could feel the surrounding magic. Theodore held his hand out. The air tickled him like a bee's feet. He moved through it and safely crossed into the front room.

"Oh, Theodore, there you are," Queen Agden called to him.

She sat all the way across the room at the grand table. He thought of Audrey and Ben sitting at that very table not so long ago. A grin crept over his face. Korrigan sat at the head of the table as usual, and Eliza was on one side and Agden at the opposite end of Korrigan. Theodore's seat was bare. Open and ready for him to leave them all and head to his room, he thought.

Korrigan laced his fingers and set his elbows on the table. He stared at Theodore as if to challenge him. Theodore pulled out his chair and sat down. The room felt too warm and stuffy even with the holes in the frame of the castle. No food covered the plates that sat in front of each chair. Only the glasses were filled with sustenance.

"Are you hungry?" Agden asked.

"I'm not sure." Theodore traced his finger on the lines of the table.

Korrigan cleared his throat.

Eliza frowned at him. "What are we having?"

"That will depend entirely on what was left," Korrigan said.

Theodore laughed, his eyes in a trance on the table.

"And what's so funny?"

"Even in wartime, you all are concerned about what we are having. Do we have food for all of them out there?" Theodore turned to point behind him.

"They will have food. The Cursed Knights are hunting and foraging as we speak," Agden said.

"Will we bring some folks into the castle?"

"Why would we?" Korrigan said.

Theodore opened his mouth to speak, but a server came in and placed meat on Korrigan's plate. Steam sizzled off of it. He hopped to the next plate, Agden's, and stabbed another piece before sliding it onto her plate, then the goling scooped sauce with an oversized silver spoon and placed it next to the meat. He did the same to Theodore's plate, and as he served Eliza hers, another server came out carrying another platter with vegetables and nuts seasoned together. She gave each one of them a helping before heading back into the kitchen with the goling.

While everyone else ate, Theodore poked his food with a fork. Eliza stopped to stare at him. She mouthed, "Eat."

Theodore cut his meat and took a bite. Eliza nodded, as if satisfied. He had forgotten how long it had been since he ate.

"You will join me tonight," Korrigan said while he patted the corner of his cheek with a dull, green napkin.

"Who?" Eliza said.

"Theodore." Korrigan put a forkful of meat into his mouth and chewed. "You want to help so badly, now you can. It's time you learn what it means to be an Ancient One by doing instead of observing."

Theodore studied his eyes, then his mouth. His lip wasn't curled, nor his eyebrow raised. "I want nothing more."

"Leave us," Korrigan said to Agden and Eliza.

Eliza finished the last vegetable on her fork.

Agden stood, waiting for Eliza. "Come, we have our own matters."

Eliza followed Agden to the staircase. They could hear the clanking of Agden's heels on the stone floor. Theodore turned to his father. Korrigan cocked his head, as though to listen to their fading footfalls.

"Now, we will discuss where to move our army and make camp. You being there is only to show that I honor your place in this kingdom."

Theodore leaned back in his chair, casually placing his arms on the armrests. "Honor my place?" He laughed with his lips closed. "Is anything not for show? Do you plan to gallivant me around?"

"You will do well to learn your place in this kingdom. You'll grow old before the kingdom will be yours to rule."

"I already am."

"Don't be so dramatic. When's the last time you partook in the ritual?"

"I've forgotten. What does that have to do with anything?"

"You have forgotten the magic that they owe us. Eliza partook not long ago, I gather. She understands that their magic is meant for us."

"Does she now?" Theodore put his hands on the table. "Well, I guess I better follow in her footsteps. We wouldn't want a Bloodtress more in line with the beliefs of our kingdom than an Ancient One."

Korrigan rose from his seat and walked behind Theodore's. He placed his hands on the back of his chair.

"No, we wouldn't. We can talk about beliefs another time." He walked away from the table and started towards the grand staircase.

Theodore pulled at his beard and made his way after him. Korrigan walked to the right side and under the stairs. He pulled out a key from his pocket and felt the wall for something. His hand stopped, and he pushed the key in. A door opened. Theodore joined him inside.

The room was large and unfamiliar to Theodore. A large wooden table made up the middle, and maps and old drawings adorned the walls. Against the left side of the wall was a long cabinet with magical trinkets on top. Corpse thistles were carved on the cabinet doors, and in between were carvings of Eltrists flying towards the thistles like cherubs shooting arrows at hearts.

Korrigan sat at the end of the table and stared at the thing atop it. Theodore eyed it too. It looked like a replica of Folengower, even with the moon hanging magically above. The sea moved, the wind rolled through towns, or rain pattered down depending on where you looked.

Theodore moved around the table until he found the Anorphus. The island had dark patches all over the ground that snaked through the island. The Anorphus was drooped over, its branches wilted to the ground, and its roots, which had once shown above the ground, had sunk into shallow holes.

"Sit," Korrigan demanded.

Theodore sat. "Is the meeting just us two?"

"No, the others will arrive shortly. I don't want your input, I don't want to even hear you breathe during it, I just want you to listen."

"That's always been a strength of mine," Theodore said sarcastically.

"You will make it a strength."

The door opened, and Nia walked in with Hargrove, Lore and Bruthren. They moved through the room and took a seat except for Bruthren, who plucked a chair out of the way. He placed his bag on the table, which looked like a stump lying on its side, and unbuckled it. His eyes were wider than usual, and he adjusted his glasses, as if he couldn't believe what he had. He unrolled his bag, which had many pockets with elegant stitching inside. They held dyed papers, small bottles, writing instruments and what looked to be bone shards.

Bruthren took out the papers and walked around the table, handing one to each folk in the room.

Korrigan held up the paper and scrutinized it. "What is this exactly?"

Bruthren slapped his hands together, his eyebrows raising. "This is the plan, of course. First, the Nniar residents we brought with us to the Anorphus will be sent back to their homes. Our focus should be on defeating Amarda, not protecting the folks here."

Nia crossed her arms. "We shouldn't protect our own people?"

"They are only slowing us down, especially now without the Anorphus to do most of the protecting. We should take some who are useful, but most are not. And can we be honest, we left the surrounding towns to manage the cursed soil alone. I imagine most of them haven't heard the call of war yet. What do you think they will do when they know we only took the folks from our city?"

"I imagine they would be angry," Hargrove said.

Bruthren nodded in agreement. "But what a turn of events. The Anorphus' death is a win to us."

"You are mad," Korrigan shook his head. "We have lost a great asset."

"Ah, of course, of course... but with loss, a new opportunity blossoms."

"For moon's sake," Lore said.

Bruthren placed his paper on the table. "It's clear, isn't it? What do they know of our land? We will use the towns we settle in to bring more warriors, and they will rejoice and praise you." Bruthren rose his hand to Korrigan. "They will see firsthand how deadly the Eltrist are, and that will make them fight to protect their homes."

"What is this part?" Nia ran her fingers over the paper. She looked up, her lips parted. "Are you expecting us to capture Eltrists and force them to fight against their kin?"

"Indeed. Any we capture, we will use. I am working on a serum for this. It will bind them similar to how our knights are cursed when times are volatile."

"A serum? When did you start this?" Korrigan said.

"I've been working on it for a few years. I'm very close to having it complete."

"Why?" Nia said.

"Because they deserve nothing more." Korrigan laughed. "Well, I've underestimated you. A weapon that will keep the Eltrist under our control for all our future heirs to come."

Nia swallowed. Theodore rested back in his chair, a wrinkle forming on his forehead.

"So, we shouldn't kill them, then?" Hargrove said with her head cocked.

"Of course some, but not all. We should focus on capturing at least a dozen."

"Why not more?" Korrigan's cheekbones raised as he smiled with his mouth closed.

"More is always on the table."

Korrigan stood. "Lore, make sure Bruthren has whatever he needs to carry this out. Nia and Hargrove, inform the other knights to not kill all of them at our next battle."

"We should discuss who should become our next commander," Lore said dryly.

"There's nothing to discuss; Hargrove, you will be our new commander."

Hargrove placed the paper down and glanced up as if she hadn't understood.

"Hargrove, *you* will be the new commander," Nia repeated.

"Me?" she said, surprised, standing up. "Praise the moon and the soil for such an honor." She placed her fist in front of her eye and bowed.

"We will have a ceremony later," Korrigan said. "Work closely with Bruthren. We need a collaborative effort if we want to shape Folengower for good."

"Indeed," Bruthren said. "I have more—"

"Indulge me at our next meeting. Focus on the serum, and you two keep our knights informed and ready for what's coming. Nia..." Korrigan turned to her. "Send the residents home when the sun rises. Give them a ration of strug to protect themselves if Amarda comes for the city. And has anything changed with that group... What was its name?" He searched his thoughts. "Choke, was it?"

"They seem to be quite silent in all this. I think the reality of war has sent them running," Lore said.

"Good. I don't need another group to deal with. Now, go." Korrigan shooed them out and stared at Theodore. "Except for you."

Theodore sat back down with a stiffness to his back. Bruthren rolled his bag back together, belted it and left. The room once again was left with Theodore and Korrigan.

"For the first time, I am proud of you," Korrigan said sarcastically.

"First time? What a monumental day it must be for me."

Korrigan curled his lip. "You will be watchful of Bruthren. He has a tendency to get distracted and work on other projects."

"And here I believed that you were proud."

"You don't want the job?"

"I'll do it. Better than having to disappoint you all day."

"In that regard, we agree." Korrigan let out a breath. "It's been a long couple of days. Get some rest. I can't have the next Ancient One not focused."

Theodore rose from his seat, bowed mockingly and left the room. Servants moved through the halls and rooms cleaning or moving furniture that was wrecked. The cushion was gone that he had sat on with Ben and Audrey. They moved the paintings into a pile against one wall, and a housekeeper cleaned the steps with a rag and a white powder that she let set before wiping off.

For a moment, Theodore watched them work without rest. They worked as if it were a normal day at the castle, exhausted yet moving faster than him.

"It's looking like home," he said to the man cleaning the steps.

The man's lips parted before he moved aside and bowed to him.

Up the steps, it was quiet and lonely. Eliza's door was gone and left bare for now. Someone dusted in her room with feathers at the end of a long black handle. Theodore walked past her room and down to the crimson door. He placed his hand on it, pushed it open, and went to the window to sit in the frame. His thoughts scattered like cockroaches when the lights turned on, while he stared off, wondering what would become of Folengower after all the blood had spilled. Would it be a better world, like Bruthren had been so keen on creating with him?

29

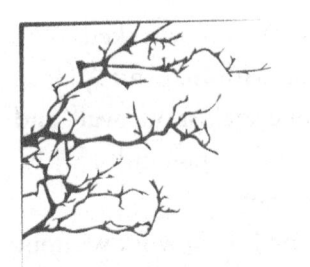

Great monstrous beings puffed through the sky as the fire died. Slate filled the sky, morphing from each campfire. The sun glared as the haze covered him just as he woke. A mutual feeling to all the folks being cast aside.

Hargrove sorted the groups and decided who would escort them home. They comprised the inhabitants of the four closest towns surrounding the castle—Tasslen, Cark, Pirne and Finor, except for those of Nniar's forest.

Hargrove stood in front of a stack of smoking and ashy wood. "This group is for Tasslen. If you are in the wrong group, please address that before we leave. I will not turn around for you." She held her helmet next to her hip and rubbed at the finnix fur plume. Her dark brown hair had loose braids that came together in a bun-like shape that created an x in the middle.

"Why did you take us from our homes in the first place?" a woman shouted.

A short boy raised his hand.

"What is it?" Hargrove said.

"I'm from Finor." He pushed out his belly and teetered on his heels.

"Calden," Hargrove shouted towards the next group over.

Calden strode over. "What is it?"

"This boy needs to go with you." Hargrove knelt beside the little boy. "You are going to go with this knight."

The boy looked Calden up and down.

"Go on," she said, gently patting his shoulder.

"You'll be safe with me," Calden said with a friendly chuckle.

The boy kicked at a blade of grass and walked over to him.

"Anyone else?"

Blank stares bombarded her. No hands raised, but some looked as if they would boil over or use their fists when the opportune moment struck.

Hargrove nodded, as if they'd said they were ready to leave, and placed her helmet back on. "Keep up, and do not wander off the trails. I will not come find you."

Many of the Folks walked in staggered lines as they tried to merge behind Hargrove. She walked on foot, unlike the other knights who'd mounted chackles. Blankets trailing the ground, whispers and children crying carried down the hill of the castle.

A man at the back with coppery skin picked up a rock and tossed it at the castle doors. He grabbed another and did the same until another folk with wavy red hair stood next to him. She took the next rock out of his hand and chucked it at the doors. The man grinned at her and grabbed another.

Hargrove heard the clatter and charged back up the hill, her sword in her hand. She grabbed the man's hair from behind and held the sword in front of his throat.

He gasped. "Tell me, are you planning on joining Amarda's army?"

The woman with the red hair set a rock down and crouched as she sidestepped away.

"You." Hargrove pointed the sword at her for a moment. "Stay."

The woman held her trembling hands up in front of her chest. "Please don't send me to the depths."

"I could send you to Amarda's camp. I'm sure the Eltrists will kill you quickly. Oh, wait... strug kills slow, doesn't it? First, your skin bubbles and burns. Then it melts right through your muscles. I can show you what's left of the bodies at the Anorphus. Bones and melted flesh."

"I didn't mean any harm," the man sniffled.

"I saw something different." Hargrove moved her sword away and kicked the man down. "You two will respect the Ancient Ones, or you will join the dead in the death streams."

The man nodded, his hands shaking. The woman nodded as well and slowly stood up straight.

"Get back in line, and I do not want to hear a single word out of either of your cursed lips, or even the moon will not shine upon you."

The man and woman hurried back into the group. Hargrove pushed past them and back to the front and led them down the hill.

To the right of them the market stalls dripped with the last rain's bounty. Some folks gasped when they looked in that direction, knowing it wasn't the rain that had caused the broken bits.

"What happened?" A woman with dark eyes said with her hand over her mouth.

"This was the work of Amarda before they stormed the castle and took our folks prisoner," Hargrove said matter of fact. She halted. "It may appear small compared to what we just left behind, but this was the beginning, and I plan on protecting Nniar to the best of my ability to keep this from happening in your towns."

Hargrove turned away from the vandalized mess and headed down a wide trail. Fresh wheel marks from a cart and chackle hoof prints imprinted the ground, though it appeared the rain had smudged them. Hargrove scanned what remained.

Curious folks glanced down and then up, wondering what she was thinking. Hargrove started off again before anyone questioned her. They trudged through the mud the entire way to Tasslen. Despite the short distance, they moved at a sloth's pace. The mud caused them to slip and fall into one another the entire way.

Tasslen could be seen by the bulbing houses like onions and slanted roofs that lived beneath moss. The windows were long and beautiful, with raindrop etchings on the glass, which made it impossible to stare into their two or more story houses. An enormous wood arch had "Tasslen" carved in it. On either side the wood bowed like two halves of a pumpkin with the middle cut out until they crossed at the top and wove into a helix formation.

A breath of relief came all at once in front of their forgotten homes. The sidings of many resembled cobblestone and had a shine that only the rain could provide over all the hues. Wild plants overlapped the walkways and loomed nearly half the size of most the trees. Hargrove stopped in front of the arch. Behind her, water dripped under it like a leaky faucet.

"This is where we part ways. We plan to check on all the surrounding towns and will offer aid if Amarda attacks. Otherwise, live as you once did." Hargrove placed her hand on the hilt of her sword. She moved out of the way, waiting for them to all charge in.

"What about the strug?"

Hargrove stretched to see who spoke. "What about it?"

The person moved past others to stand before her. She had a blanket wrapped around her and brown eyes. "We were told that we would all get strug to help protect ourselves."

"It will come later today by cart. Don't expect too much. We must ration our magic until the war is over, but I will make sure hallow nectar is also provided."

"Was there not enough running through the Anorphus to take?"

"Our friends and family died in that strug," someone shouted.

The woman turned around. "And what does that matter now, Relune? It will work just the same."

Relune shook his head. His forehead wrinkled and his lip curled. "I want no part of it."

A few whispers behind him said the same.

"I don't believe the strug will come from the Anorphus. Please head to your homes and watch over one another.

Send a bird if you suspect any Amardians heading your way."

The woman wrapped the blanket tighter around her body and cursed under her breath to Hargrove. Once everyone had entered Tasslen, Hargrove left.

Upon returning to the castle, she watched Polt soar across the towers and down towards the castle. With the castle grounds now emptied of Nniar residents, it felt eerie. Hargrove had returned first, and she made her way into the castle. At least three hundred Cursed Knights were in a row outside of it. When they saw her, they stood still.

"Commander Hargrove, the king is waiting for you," the knight in front of the door said. He opened the door for her.

"Where is he?"

"I wasn't told."

Hargrove walked past him into the castle. The floor shined as if new, and the piles of what to repair or throw out had shrunk. Nia stood outside of Korrigan's study.

"Is he in there?"

Nia nodded. "He's waiting for you. I'll tell him of your arrival." She knocked on the door. "Commander Hargrove is back."

"Let her in," Korrigan said through the door.

Nia opened the door and shut it after Hargrove stepped in.

Korrigan sat at a desk, shuffling through papers. Hargrove placed her hands at her sides.

"I assume Tasslen still stands."

Hargrove stared at a painting at the back of the room of Queen Callum posing in the garden with windcaps around her. She couldn't have been that old, as there was hardly a wrinkle on her face. She wore a lavender bardot dress, perfect to show the tattoos of her lineage that went from shoulder to shoulder.

"Hargrove?" Korrigan said sharply.

"It does. It appeared untouched, though I noticed something strange."

"What is it?" Korrigan made a mark on the paper he was examining.

"Someone went towards Tasslen recently by cart and chackle."

"A trader probably."

She rubbed her neck. "That's what I am hoping."

"Now then, have the other knights come back?"

"No, I haven't seen them return, but Cark, Pirne and Finor are further away than Tasslen. I believe Polt has returned. He was coming down from above the towers."

Korrigan looked at Hargrove for the first time. "*Nia.*"

Nia opened the door. "Yes?"

"Polt has been spotted outside the castle. Bring him to me."

Nia bowed and left.

"Anything else?" he asked.

"I will send strug rations off later today or tomorrow once it's all harvested."

Korrigan nodded. "That will be all."

Hargrove opened the door.

"Commander..."

She lingered in the door frame.

"I expect to see your war plans in the coming days."

"I will have them ready."

Korrigan nodded and gazed up as if to tell her to leave. She left and closed the door behind her, then left the castle walls and headed towards the garden. She stared at the knights standing there, wondering what they were all doing. Then Bruthren caught her eye. He was between the tower and her, with Polt on his arm and conversing with Nia.

"Commander," Calden walked up behind her. "That's like a symphony, isn't it?"

Hargrove turned around. "Do you always have to be so cheery?"

"Well, someone does. Maybe you should praise the moon more and find some cheer yourself." Calden chuckled.

"You're lucky I know you well, or else I would lock you up for speaking to a commander in such a way," she said harshly.

"Cursed soil, Hargrove. I'll lock my tongue away around you from now on."

Hargrove swallowed and bit the inside of her lip. "It's fine."

Calden patted her back. "I know it's a lot of pressure. You'll make the soil proud, I know it."

Hargrove slipped a half-smile and quickly rid her face of it. "Any foul things happen in Finor?"

Calden shook his head. "Smoother than a sunwave."

"Did you see any tracks?"

"Tracks? Are we short on food? We have hunters out—"

"No, did you see any cart tracks or chackles?"

"Hmm..." Calden scratched his chin. "It was too muddy in parts to tell. Nothing caught my attention."

"Next time, you should look harder. Our enemies could be anywhere. We do not know how many folks they have to fight alongside them. Did you already forget the grim death that many of ours suffered in the death streams?" Hargrove bent over and flipped over a small sculpture of a finnix that had been knocked over. "If any of the other knights are feeling as careless as you, I would remind them of what I—" Hargrove glared. "What King Korrigan expects of his knights. Making mistakes will result in the curse being cast on us more frequently. Is that what you want?"

He cleared his throat and played with his fingers. "Understood."

As Hargrove left towards Nia, Calden said quietly, "Soil bless our blood."

The clouds parted, and the sun shined down onto the grass and stonework. The statue on Talkun's Tower looked devious with the light upon it, as it accentuated the snarling beast. Bruthren held out something wriggling and dropped it into Polt's mouth. Polt swallowed it.

"Korrigan would like to see Polt," Hargrove said, interrupting their conversation.

"Of course. He just returned. What a journey he has had."

"Did he bring anything?"

Bruthren held out a yellow flower, wilted from Polt's talons.

Hargrove held it. "Thornyarch Mountains?"

"The almighty mountains indeed."

"There's only one other place that we know of that these grow, but it wouldn't make much sense to camp there. Too out in the open," Nia said.

"Should I take Polt, then?"

"No, no... I have to speak to Korrigan about other matters. I'll take Polt with me," Bruthren said before pulling out another treat for Polt. His black wings spread for a moment before eating.

Bruthren left with Polt on his arm. Nia stood in front of Hargrove.

"Where are we at on the strug rations?" Hargrove asked.

Nia gazed up at the fast-moving clouds. "It'll take some time, but I believe we can send someone out before the day's over."

"Report to me when they head off with them."

"Yes, Commander."

Hargrove headed back to the castle. Nia stayed behind, facing the forest, as if she was waiting for something or someone to appear.

30

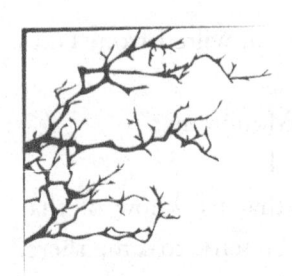

The floorboards creaked even in the dead of night. A single window let in an abysmal light that hardly could have been called that at all. Bugs circled next to it, probably from the dim light that hung just above the round window.

Ben sat up in bed, examining his hands. He poked his palm and curiously moved it towards the light.

"It's been hours," Audrey said groggily.

"Sorry, I know. I just..."

Audrey rolled over and held his hand. "This is a good thing. It doesn't matter how you have magic. Morrow is right that you have a chance to protect yourself."

"What about you?"

"Do you feel like you don't deserve it because I don't have magic too?" Audrey sat up on her elbows and brushed her thick hair out of her face.

Ben turned away from her. "Of course I do."

Audrey tossed her pillow at his face. "Well, stop. It's not your fault."

Ben grabbed it and chuckled. "It's a new guilt. Give me some time to deal with it."

"I have you and Theodore to have my back, plus I have already fought an Eltrist before." Audrey patted her back where her scar was.

"I don't think this is the same as what happened in the cave."

"We can worry about it in the morning." Audrey rolled on her side, facing the wall.

Ben stayed up for a while longer before succumbing to his nagging body to sleep. He tossed and turned and snored all night. Audrey woke up from it many times, but she didn't wake him to stop.

The sun shined through the little window like a flashlight spying. Audrey rubbed her eyes and yawned. She smushed the pillow down, propped it against the headboard and sat up. It rattled as if it would fall apart when she backed into it, the wood cracked and ready to splinter anyone who dared to run their fingers down it. Audrey glanced over at Ben, who slept face down on his pillow, with his stomach on the mattress. One of his hands hung off the side.

Audrey sighed and looked at her hands, her eyes puzzled. The doorknob jiggled, and Morrow popped her head in. Her hair horns could have been their own creature. She tossed clothes at Audrey. She reached her arm out and caught them by her fingertips. Morrow kept a pile of clothes in her arms for Ben.

"Get dressed and head downstairs." She tilted her head from side to side. "Is Ben still sleeping?"

"If I had to guess... it's quite obvious."

Morrow crept over to Ben, ignoring Audrey. She set the clothes down and rubbed her hand on his temple and hummed. "I bet he's fun to sleep with." Morrow raised her right eyebrow.

"You're welcome to sleep with him if that's what he wants." Audrey got up and changed, not caring if Morrow watched. Audrey tugged on her shirt, sniffed it and shrugged.

"Honey," Morrow said soothingly. He twitched but remained in his slumber. "*Ben*," she shouted.

Ben shot up. His face drained of pigment. "What? What?"

"Why the hell did you do that?"

Morrow forced a strand of hair that had fallen out of place back into one of her towers. "Good morning." She stroked his cheek. "Get dressed. We have work to do."

Ben caught his breath before pushing up with his arm to sit up. He stretched, twisting and cracking his back. "I barely slept."

Morrow pouted. "Oh, sweet Ben," she said, almost sincerely. "That's not my problem. My job is to give you the tools to stay alive, and, you"—she pointed at Ben—"are special, like me. That means the skills you need to learn will be much more time-consuming than Audrey here, but oh so worth it."

Morrow held her hand out to Ben. He slouched on the edge of the bed, his eyelids heavy. "Take it," she said.

Ben grabbed her hand, and she pulled him up. Ben took the clean clothes—a tight long-sleeved forest-green shirt with a low neckline; lightweight brown pants, which had something stitched on the waistband that looked like water flowing, cuffed at the ankles with the same design; plain gray underwear; and ankle-high socks.

"Put them on."

"Are you leaving first?"

"Audrey changed just fine in front of me. I assumed we could all chat while you got dressed."

Ben shrugged. He tore off the shirt he'd worn to bed and lay it on the blanket. Morrow whistled, and Audrey sighed. Ben had always been fit from the many adventures out hiking and camping with his stepfather, Harper. After the long days in Folengower, his stomach had become more chiseled.

Audrey ducked out of the room, heading towards the bathroom.

Ben turned away from Morrow as he removed his pants and underwear. "Are you lonely, or do you just enjoy messing with me?"

"I would never mess with you... well, maybe a little."

Ben gave a quiet laugh.

Morrow leaned against the bedframe and ran her finger across the bed. "And it's not every day that someone like you comes around."

"Like me?" Ben frowned. "No average guys in Folengower?"

"Average? Maybe in your world, but I haven't been there in a very long time." Morrow lay on her stomach on the bed and kicked her legs up. "Maybe when the war is over, you could take me out on a date?"

Ben pulled his underwear on and grabbed the pants. Morrow bit her lip. "I can't tell if you are serious or not."

"Cursed soil, Ben. I have no plans to lie about my wants. If we live through this war, what do you say?" The sunlight hit her eyes in such a way that she looked like an ethereal, horned goddess. Her eyes even shined like gold.

"If we make it out alive, I'll consider it, but I'm not making any promises." Ben grinned.

"Promises are for those who have never lived. Let's go. I have breakfast ready downstairs, and the sun is shining upon us. Perfect time to bask in the sun."

"Even after the storm? Won't everything still be wet?"

"Psshh... It's muddy, yes, but I have a lovely area set up that is completely dry." Morrow walked down the staircase. Her face turned back now and again as she spoke to Ben, who followed. "I may or may not have used magic to make it so. Either way, we will eat and then I'll see how much more that delectable body of yours can take."

Ben's cheeks warmed. He laughed, as if he didn't know what to say. They made it down the stairs.

Audrey stood at the window, peering out. "Finally."

"Someone who's ready to work. I like that. We are having breakfast outside this morning. I have to warn you though, after we eat, it's training time, and that will not end till the sun goes down."

Morrow moved to the door and wandered to the back. The trickle of a stream moved past the chairs and black table. The flowers next to the house stood firm and bloomed vibrantly. Hummingbirds and windcaps took turns drinking their nectar. Grasses were matted by their feet and in patches of puddles.

Morrow sat down and patted at the table for Ben to sit next to her. Two full platters of food sat in the middle, a cornucopia of color. Plump fruits, flaky breads, a chestnut-looking spread, clawnuts, some sort of cured meat and mini savory pies that had a corpse thistle etched onto the crust overflowed the platters. Three glasses with a pink tinge to the liquid sat on the table.

"Should I go grab some plates and silverware?" Ben began to stand, but Morrow, with her legs crossed on her chair, put her hand at his waist and forced him down.

"That won't be necessary. In Folengower, a lot of folks enjoy sharing a meal off of a single plate. Especially in the smaller towns. I partake in that way of life. We share together, we fight together," Morrow said, holding up her glass.

Ben raised his, and Audrey only lifted her cup when Ben kicked her leg.

"We share together, we fight together," Morrow repeated. "Eat till your bellies are full and ready for what's coming."

"A kick in the ass, I presume," Audrey said.

Morrow shrugged. "At least it will be me kicking your ass and not someone else."

Ben grabbed a slice of bread and slathered it with the spread. He took a bite and finished it off quickly. Morrow gave a genuine smile in his direction. Audrey snacked on a piece of meat and held one fruit in her hand. She stared at the green that resembled a huge acorn and peeled the outside.

Morrow chuckled. "Just take a bite. You don't need to peel moklins. They aren't oranges."

Audrey rolled her eyes and bit into the fruit. Sweet and bitter yellow juices filled her mouth and seeped down her arm.

Before long, only crumbs remained and their chatting ended. Even Morrow gazed at the empty platters, as if she longed for more to appear so they could go on as if a war wasn't festering.

Morrow leaped out of her chair. Her bare feet sank into the wet grass, the green over her toenail polish blending in like moss pebbles. "Who's first?" She placed her hands on her bare hips below her flowing yellow top that ended right above her bellybutton.

"Me," Audrey said.

"Splendid. While you sit there enjoying the morning, try to use your magic. I left a bottle of strug right next to the creek. Put Folengower's soil and a drop of strug in your hands and ask what you want." Morrow bent down to Ben. "And think of me." She put her hand in Ben's. He stared into her eyes and squeezed her hand for a moment before she pranced away to Audrey.

"Follow me. First, we will see how well you can aim." Morrow led Audrey to a small garden shed. The bottom of it had sunk into the soil. The shelves overflowed with jars of liquids of all colors. Some were bulb-shaped, while others were long or twisted.

Audrey peeked her head in. "What are we doing with these? This seems like something for Ben."

Morrow grabbed a basket from the ground and filled it with bottles. She crouched down to arrange them. "Audrey, my dear, you can use this magic without even a drip of it inside there." She poked Audrey's stomach.

Audrey narrowed her gaze. Morrow stood up, with the handle in the crook of her arm. She led Audrey past a row of trees. Audrey spun around, her gaze darting from the ground to up high in the trees. Oblong slabs of wood had been pinned to the understory of several trees with lustrous leaves. The slabs were painted with lined markings in red, green and lavender. Below, wooden dummies with what looked to be Morrow's old clothes on them stood or crouched in different positions. Some were just above the ground, while others were attached to the bottom of bark or stumps.

Morrow went to one that was hidden behind a tree and pushed it. It moved with speed on a ring track around the tree. Other targets floated from the canopy above like green bats. Audrey poked one of the carved people. It bobbed as if it were a balloon.

"So... I'm supposed to hit the targets, then?" Audrey said without moving her gaze from the dummy.

"Yes. Whether you can is another thing." Morrow tossed a jar at her. Audrey reached for it, but the bottle hit the tips of her fingers and bounced as she struggled to grab it. With her back bent, she managed to catch it.

Morrow roared with laughter. She clapped her hands and said, "You don't give up easily, I'll give you that." She held a bottle up and swirled the contents around. "The thing about these is that you don't want to be near them when they break. The magic inside can damage you greatly, so a general rule is that these are used for long range. That, of course, limits your protection, so a sword will be your new love, but these"—Morrow tossed it up and caught it in a showy way—"will kill without you having to do much except aim."

Orange and raspberry rocks surrounded the creek, with small florets the color of the moon sprouting in between. Ben knelt and reached for the bottle of lavender glowing death. He stared at it as if it could jump out on its own and start a plight for Ben to melt into nothing.

The creek made a pleasant, constant sound that calmed his nerves, just as the birds tweeting in the bushes on the other side of the creek did. Ben plopped down on the wet earth and dug out a handful of soil. Grasses clung to him, and he plucked them off. He took the stopper out of the bottle and tipped a drop in his handful of soil.

He felt his hairs stand on end. The strug sat in the middle of the soil like the yolk of a fried egg. It glowed and giggled in his hand. "Shit," he muttered, as if realizing he needed to ask the magic to do something. He scanned the bushes and then down at the stream, where his reflection peered back.

The amber in his eyes looked piercing in the sunshine, and the amount of facial hair surprised him even though it had been so long since he had shaved. His eyes didn't linger for long on his face, quickly moving back to the soil in his hand.

"What do I want? What do I want?" he repeated out loud to himself. Puzzled, he finally shouted, "Light. Bring light." He held his palm away from his body, his eyes squinting. After a few moments, Ben relaxed his shoulders and scrutinized his hand of soil and strug.

Trying one more time, he took a deep breath and then another before saying, "Bring me light." This time, when no light came from his palm, he hung his head. The hope of using magic felt like catching a star: impossible.

He dumped the soil onto the ground and knelt to the stream, moving his hands through it to clean them. The cold tingled his fingers, though he pushed them deeper till his forearms were covered and a chill seized his spine. He paid no mind to the uncomfortable sensation and lifted his hands out, drenching his face with water. He rubbed his cheeks and forehead.

Insects hummed, buzzed and made whispering noises above and deep in the grasses while the birds sang or bickered, creating a cacophony around Ben, though he only paid attention to the stream. It burbled and babbled ancient words, and the more Ben listened, the closer he sat to it. He couldn't understand the words, but, as if he could, he placed his hands back in the water.

Clear and pearly water moved past. Small beings swam under his hands and towards them curiously. Ben cocked his head as he watched them move in the small stream. He stared for a while, as if in a trance, but then a loud crash came behind him.

Ben shot up and bolted towards the sound. "Audrey? Morrow?"

Another loud sound, like shattering glass, sounded. He followed it, this time making his way into the tree line.

"*Run!*" Audrey yelled.

Ben stopped and stared in her direction, perplexed by what she'd said. Then his mouth opened as he saw a jar zooming towards him. With his body stuck in place, Morrow collided with him. They crashed to the ground. The bottle soared past and exploded a mere foot away, landing directly on a dummy's head. A burst of red smoke seeped out, and Morrow ducked and covered Ben's face while pulling his arm to scoot further away.

"Couldn't be without me, huh?"

"I heard a loud noise."

"Are you okay?" Audrey ran to Ben and held her hand out to him, but Morrow swatted it away.

"Well, you found it. I told you to practice your magic by the stream." Morrow stood up and dramatically turned her whole body one way and then the other, with her hand stiff and above her eyes like a captain peering out to sea. "I don't happen to see a stream anywhere here. Do you?"

Ben sat up and brushed bits of the forest floor off his back. "I'm sorry. Maybe next time you let me know what noises I should expect. Last I checked, we are now part of a secret army, and I assume we could get found out, or the fighting could come here."

Morrow held out her hand. Ben glared at it, but he took it nonetheless and stood. "Next time, do as you're told. If the fighting came here, believe me, I would know." She poked at her hair, making sure each strand could be put back into the horns she'd shaped. "Did you have any inkling of magic?"

Ben squeezed his hands. "No, nothing."

"Did you use all the strug?"

"You said to only use a drop."

Morrow scoffed. "How many times did you try?"

"Only once before I came running to you both."

"Is that it?" She raised a brow. "Well, since you are here, both of you get over there and practice your aim." Morrow walked over to the basket and tossed Ben and Audrey each a jar. "Choose your target."

Ben let his eyes wander to each target he could see before stopping at the dummy that moved around the tree. He rose his hand and lifted his leg like a pitcher for baseball and released. It spun and crashed effortlessly on the dummy's face. Morrow clapped, and Audrey nodded proudly.

They stayed most of the day practicing hitting targets. When Morrow felt it too easy for them, she left the area and told them to stay put. She returned just beyond the tree line with something on wheels. Audrey and Ben moved like an owl as they craned their necks to see in between the tree trunks.

"I didn't take you both for cowards," Morrow shouted.

Audrey scoffed and walked out of the copse with her arms crossed. Ben shook his head, smiling strangely, as if he was having another inner monologue about all the baffling things he had done in such a short time. He walked towards Morrow too.

Morrow held her arms out, showcasing the mini catapult contraption she was standing next to, which matched the rose-pink color of her hair. The throwing arm was carved to look like a real hand with long black fingernails waiting for something to fit in its bare palm. Morrow reached into the gray sack she'd brought with her and held a clay finnix about the size of a cucumber in her hand. She placed it in the hand, pulled it down, then shouted, "*Fire*" as the sculpture shot into the air.

Audrey and Ben tossed their jars at the clay finnix, but they both failed terribly at hitting it.

"Do you plan on our enemies standing still as a grave?" Morrow held her arms behind her back and strutted from one side of the catapult to the other. "Grab another bottle."

Audrey and Ben grabbed another jar each from the bag, and Morrow wasted no time launching another clay finnix into the air. They fared no better than the first time, but by the next hour, Ben had managed to hit two and Audrey had struck five. Neither number was enough to make Morrow have any belief that they would make it through a war, and she made sure to tell them that.

The next days were more of the same except the bottles were all empty—an unspoken disappointment from the other day. Ben could hear the water speaking more clearly now, but no magic lighted his hands. They improved as a week passed, and a friendly competition stirred.

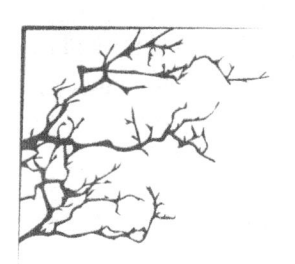

31

He smelled of campfire no matter how much the wind moved through his long dark hair, unable to cleanse the previous days from him. The further he trekked from the castle, the more he felt a tightness in his chest and a strange burbling in his stomach. He poked at his ear without even realizing what he was doing.

The mud would remember Kalien's footprints even after he'd tried erasing them with a stick. After a while, Kalien tossed the stick, realizing that the trouble and energy it took to conceal his whereabouts weren't worth it, plus the Cursed Knights had not cared when he left alone after saying farewell to Cressa, Indigo and Reed as they joined a group for the town of Pirne.

He paused and whipped his head back, his body rigid as a stump. Branches hung over the road and twirling leaves swayed in the calming breeze. Only Kalien and his poorly destroyed footprints stood in the road. He twitched his shoulders at the wind as if it had tried to spook him. For a moment, he thought he heard something, maybe the sound of cartwheels or chackles heading towards him, but besides the road, he saw nothing. The castle was hidden from his vision now that the road turned and the trees shielded the mountain it rested on. He wondered if he should have just gone to Pirne and then headed home later. He shook his head, as if to erase all the what-ifs he was now thinking about.

Kalien reached down for another stick, this time more determined to erase his steps. It curved on one side like a handle.

A small bird landed near him. It pecked at the ground, pulling up bugs.

"Have you seen anyone else?" he asked the bird.

It continued to peck without a care. Kalien sighed and relaxed his shoulders as he walked on. Curiously, a whisper of a noise no louder than the shaking leaves pricked at his ears. Without stopping, he peered over his shoulder to where he left the bird. It had flown off, perhaps causing the noise. He glared at the road behind him, empty as his stomach. His gut told him to run, but his mind told him to wait.

Leaving the road, he tried his luck in the forest. Staying near the road, he hoped to not stray too far and get lost. Beneath the verdant coverings, he could hear soft psithurism and birds singing, which calmed his distracted mind for a few strides.

The birds silenced and darted from their branches, shaking leaves that circled down to Kalien as he watched. He froze and felt a tug again of watchful eyes, and the feeling of his hair standing on end consumed his skin. As he peered over his shoulder, he gasped.

"Going somewhere?" Palina said. Her arms were crossed and her helmet hanging from her right hand.

"Home," Kalien said with a tinge of annoyance, and his eyes narrowed.

"I think you forgot something."

"And what would that be?"

"Bruthren tells me you are part of The Choke now." Palina twirled her hands and placed them on her throat as if her fingers adorned collarbone with feathers. Freckles on her cheeks brightened in the sun's rays through the tree's branches and, as she tilted her head back, her eyes were the same color as pumpkins.

Kalien sighed. "I'm a part of many things, it would seem, and none that I wanted any part of."

Palina ran her tongue over her top teeth. "I don't think any of us want war, but at least you will fight on the right side. It is an honor that Bruthren allowed you in. Where is your home?"

"I guess it doesn't matter to try to hide it. Carlen."

"You have a bit of a way to go. Did you pack some food at least?"

Kalien pulled at his pants and reached into his pockets to reveal nothing. "I can handle a few days without much."

"That is good, but lucky for you, the time to ration hasn't begun." Palina unwrapped a bag that hung from her waist and tossed it to Kalien. "Food for your journey. I will send someone from The Choke to watch you and make sure no one bothers you."

"You aren't coming with me, then?"

"Cursed Knights do not have the luxury to go on their own quests unless we are ordered by the Ancient One. We have many eyes from all places and types of beings in our community. Take care, Kalien, and get back to the road. It will be safer. There are vorbins in the woods."

Kalien cocked his head, as if he didn't believe her, but when her gaze held stern, he nodded.

Palina placed her helmet back on, and the lavender plume swished gracefully. "The Choke needs you just as much as you need it. Remember that."

Kalien said nothing, but her words lingered with him even as she vanished behind the trees.

Kalien returned to the road. The soothing sound of a creek wasn't far, and he stayed near the sound. He walked till the night reaped the sun, and he came upon a field with a cornucopia of flora in a state of nyctinasty. He touched the tops of buds as he passed, and they bobbed and swayed as if made of gelatin. When he found a spot neglected of stones, he sat down and rummaged through the bag that Palina had given him. He pulled out a moklin and sank his teeth into it. Yellow juice seeped down his arm, though he didn't notice.

He fell asleep without even trying, and his snores could have kept even a vorbin away.

The unrelenting sun woke Kalien, with its mass of light peering through the blades of grass and the open petals. Kalien sat up. He grabbed the bag and pulled out slivers of dried meat and a piece of bread. He placed the meat on top of the bread and took a bite. It was dry, but it would do for the time. Kalien swallowed every bite and moved his tongue, aching for water.

He could faintly hear rushing water. Kalien stood and walked towards it. He found it just behind where he'd slept. The meadow ended in a crevice that was a few feet down to where the water flowed. Hidden beneath the flora, Kalien jumped down and crouched. He dipped his hand in and scooped the water up to his mouth, then placed the water through his hair and over his face. When he was done, he grabbed his bag and headed back to the road.

His days were dull and his legs ached, but finally, after another night, he made it to a fork that read, "Shadowvale Ridge" in serious black lettering, the other town name nothing more than a scribble facing away from him.

He ran until his heart pounded too fast and his legs burned, then he took a breath and jogged the rest of the way to Carlen. The houses were just as he remembered—round, with thatched roofs and bright colors. The road was empty, but he could hear folks laughing and chatting up in the center of town where most folks went during the day to work or socialize. Kalien passed a few houses, and then another one that slanted slightly, but as he did, he heard the roar of a voice and a door opening.

"Praise the moon, is that you, Kalien?" Art said, stroking his mostly gray beard.

Kalien turned to him and smiled. "Art! Have you seen my mom?"

An open-mouthed Art jogged over to him. "Of course. We've been worried the depths took you." Art wrapped his brawny arms around Kalien before moving away and giving him a once-over. "All your limbs are still there. That's good." He frowned. "Where have you been?"

"It's a long story."

"Well, tell me later. Let's get to your mom. You don't know how upset your disappearance has made her. The whole town has felt like tarbugs have eaten us."

Kalien was speechless. Art chatted on about this and that while they walked together down a path behind the shops. They walked through the thicket, and there Kalien lost his breath. He could smell the flowers even from several feet away. The pink blooms wrapped their vines around the smaller house that used to be his grandmother's, and next to it, the larger home, his home, stood.

A lady stood out to the side of it, hanging clothes on a line. Her gray hair was in a messy bun with sewing pins to keep it bunched.

"Mom," Kalien tried to call, but his mouth only let out a whisper.

Art patted his back. "Luspy, look."

Luspy peered over her shoulder and only saw Art. "What is it?"

Kalien ran to his mom, colliding into her back and wrapping his arms around her. Tears flowed down his cheeks. Luspy grabbed his hands, and her body stilled in shock. She fell to her knees, and Kalien followed her to the ground. She placed her hands on his cheeks.

"It's you. Kalien. Kalien..." She sobbed onto his shoulder. "I thought the depths took you."

"I'm so sorry."

"Where have you been?"

Art waved his hand at no one in particular and snuck away.

"You can't tell anyone."

Luspy frowned. "What happened?"

Kalien rose and reached his hand out to steady his mom. "Let's talk inside."

A bluebird swooped down to their roof. It twitched its head and seemed to listen. Kalien noticed it. They went inside the house and sat on the couch.

He told his mom of his whereabouts, not keeping any secrets to himself. She sat silently and listened. When he was done, she finally said, "Did you meet the Ancient One? Theodore?"

"I saw him, but no, I didn't. Why?"

"He came here looking for you. He knows about the earrings."

"What earrings?" Kalien cocked his head.

Luspy pointed to the purple stone hanging from his ear. "That is not an ordinary earring. Your grandmother gave it to you to keep safe. I had the other one, and when the wearer has both, they can understand everything an Eltrist says, not just when they address your mind. They created it for Queen Callum because Talkun, as you know, was raised as her son. She wanted something to help her raise him before he mastered how to communicate with her, but Korrigan has wanted them for a long time so he can spy on them."

"What do you mean, had? Where's yours?" Kalien gazed out the window behind her at leaves that braided down from a massive tree like snakes entwined.

"I gave it to Theodore. He wants to unify Folengower just as his grandmother would have wanted. We were unified under her rule and even before that for a long time, but look at what Korrigan has done. He must be stopped."

Kalien's shot a serious look at her. His head tilted in thought. "He is a part of The Choke, then?"

"He didn't say, but it sounds like what you are a part of now."

"Then I must send this to him somehow."

"We'll figure that out later. For now, rest, and I am going to cook the best meal you've ever had." Luspy's smile radiated through the house and left a trail of good feelings. Kalien relaxed for the first time in a long time, and though he wished it would never end, this small comfort would be as fleeting as the wind.

Kalien shot out of bed at the sound of banging on the front door. Sunlight streaming through his window indicated the morning of a new day. He walked through the hall with his back against the wall and reached for an antique dagger that rested on a side table. He held it to his chest and crept to the door. Someone rapped again. Kalien moved his ear to the door and listened. It sounded like whistling. His eyes were scornful, and he held the dull blade towards the door as he gulped and burst it open.

"Surprise!" a chorus bunch rang out.

Kalien jumped back and dropped the knife. Not all saw, but those who did gave a confused smile.

Art was in front and gently grabbed Kalien's shoulder to whisper in his ear, "Everything alright?"

"I wasn't expecting anything," he whispered back.

Luspy came up behind Kalien. She wiped her hands on her red apron and smiled. "What's all this?"

"I had to get everyone together for a celebration. I hope we didn't ruin breakfast," Art said, stroking his beard.

Luspy smiled. "Thank you, Art. No, I was just baking a loaf of bread for later."

"Thank Claire. She coordinated everything."

Claire playfully hit Art's arm and blushed. "It is so good to see you again," she said to Kalien.

Luspy briefly embraced Claire.

"Well then, we have drink, we have music"—Art pointed to two females and one male who held instruments—"and, of course, we have Kalien back. We must celebrate. Praise the moon."

The crowd responded with, "Praise the moon."

Kalien danced and laughed and drank for hours and forgot all about the thing in his ear and all that had happened. Drunk and tired, he lay in the grass and stared up at the stars. "Praise the moon indeed," he said, with the biggest smile on his face.

"Kalien, right?" A man tapped his shoulder.

Kalien turned and stared at the man lying to the left of him. He had dark eyes and a sharp jawline. It was still dark, so he couldn't make out much else. "Who are you? I don't think we've met, which is strange considering I've known everyone in this town since I was a baby."

"We are going to get real close to each other, just like you have with all of them. Palina sent me. I have orders to take you to the grayden, but since this is a bad time, I'm waiting."

Kalien closed his eyes and brushed the backs of his hands over the tips of the grass around him, as if trying to soothe himself from the reluctance and distress building within. "What's a grayden?"

"You are new to The Choke, then." The man sighed. "It's where we work. You can come back home every night or morning depending on when we need you, but we all have to go there, especially now that battles have begun."

"What do I tell everyone?" Kalien said through gritted teeth.

"I plan to recruit them too. There are already six members of The Choke here."

Kalien's eyes opened wide as he sat up. "Six? Then why didn't one of them come and tell me all this?"

"News isn't as quick to travel. They will take over after today, but Bruthren has told me you have a vision meld from a leader in Amarda." The man paused as if to have Kalien confirm.

Kalien nodded.

"It's important that if the leader reaches out to you, you get somewhere that she won't see where you are, especially if you are in a grayden, understand? These are for you," he continued without giving Kalien a chance to respond. He pulled out rolled-up leaves from his pocket. "Things to say to Amarda's leader and things to learn from them. When you communicate with them, send word by bird of any important news. I sent a bluebird yesterday. Her name is Tassy. When you see her, hold your arm out to her and gift her a flower. Any will do. She will be our go-between when we are too far to communicate or the battles are near."

Kalien let his body lay back into the grass.

"Do you have any questions?"

Kalien chuckled. "What more could I ask when my fate is sealed?"

The man eyed him for a long moment before getting up. Kalien fell asleep after knowing that when he opened his eyes again, he would be taken somewhere new, but for now, all he wanted was to sleep surrounded by all the people he loved.

32

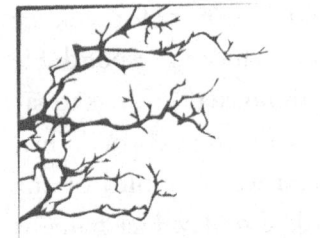

Dawn birthed over the horizon, blinding in front of the sunburst clouds. Riven closed her eyes for a time as the air carried them up and down, as if they were cascading through water. Thorn looked over at her and slid her head down onto Aylo. The sight of the mountains came slowly and with consequence.

The Eltrists lowered like feathers falling, allowing their wings to glide. Great tors stood out amongst the clouds, as if watchful of what was coming from the sky. The Eltrists fell through the clouds, the Thornyarch Mountains taking shape beneath them. Folks were just waking up and starting fires to cook what the early risers had caught. Fingers pointed up at them, and they could faintly hear shouts from their shocked mouths.

An injured Eltrist already lay in the middle of healers. When they saw more returning, they ran waving sun-stained cloths that moved like silk. The injured crashed into the ground. Takthorn was at the ready, though some hung by only a thread of life. O jumped off Kinsington as they landed.

"Help the healers."

O ran to them. Four Eltrists were waiting for care.

"How many have gone to the depths?" one asked.

"Enough," Kinsington replied. "Tilion and several of our brave warriors. We could not carry them back. The Anorphus' poison would have sentenced us all."

Pavylyn trudged to them. She moved as if she stepped on thorns.

"Tilion?" Pavlyn breathed. She collapsed onto his limp body.

Aylo stomped over to her and placed his head onto hers. "We will get through this."

"We shouldn't have allowed them to fight."

"What choice did we have?"

Pavlyn whipped her tail and pushed her head against Aylo. "*My* son was *my* choice. He should still be alive."

Kinsington stepped towards her. "Tilion was brave. We will all mourn his passing."

Pavlyn looked into Kinsington's eyes tearfully, desperate for him to feel her loss as she did, but she knew he couldn't. She whipped her body around with a loud cry and soared into the sky alone.

The day wore on as if the ground raged with fire. Two Eltrists were pronounced dead before the sun made its long descent. Not a soul walked through camp without a sense of dread and sorrow. It took three Eltrists to grip one of their dead down to the water and several days before they returned to the Anorphus to retrieve their dead.

After Haylin's passing, they could hardly breathe, yet some still believed peace would come. But then they stood face to face, with Amarda's army laid out in a row by the stream, they knew there would be no such thing, at least not in the coming weeks. Though if they had gone to the

Anorphus they would see the devastation of land and the swallowed bodies and know that Amarda had won.

Kinsington and Talkun stood in the water, with Aylo and Esna close behind. O and other leaders waited on the other side of the stream.

"Speak for us," Kinsington said to Talkun.

Talkun glanced at Kinsington. Soon, all eyes followed his fern and dark twilight fur. His wings drooped, the tips gliding through the water, leaving eel-like ripples behind him. "These are the souls of change. The ones brave enough to mend Folengower regardless of the cost. I do not see their bodies and rejoice for what they have done; I see them and understand the true cost of what it will take to achieve what Kinsington and you all started. I stand before you all as the heir of Folengower, the fallen ruler, resurrected from my prison, and I plan to unite Folengower—"

Kinsington's words interrupted Talkun's mind. "We are taking over Folengower. Uniting the two without our reaping of it is not an option."

Talkun shot a look of disappointment at Kinsington. "Then you are not seeing what I see in these faces." He stared down at the bodies again and continued back into the minds before him. "We must unite Folengower, or we will allow others to rot just as Amarda has." Strug dripped from Talkun's lip. "Decide if you want enemies over family in this new era. Will you stand for a new divide or a united whole?"

Aylo cocked his head. The spiral at the end of his ear pricked up as if it would straighten. Esna stretched her wings uncomfortably. The folks listened, Talkun's lilting voice carrying like a forgotten melody of kindness and valor.

Talkun made it to the first body and, peering down at him, he placed his paw upon the man's head in the cool water. He sang, "Our soul bound, for as you rest, your soul will fight with me even as you are taken to the depths." Talkun placed his paw under his head and opened his mouth with his other. Sticking one claw down his throat, out leapt a sliver of his soul. It was iridescent and green and no bigger than a dragonfly. Gasps erupted from the many who stared, and some even fell to their knees, unsure of what to think. "And when we defeat our enemies, your soul will follow, making you whole at last." Talkun swallowed the sliver and continued down the line to all folks regardless of species until he had swallowed a piece of all the dead.

One by one, a shimmering glow mirrored in the waters, and Talkun could see the eyes of the depths peer up and snatch the bodies. They followed him until the last body was taken, and their light extinguished.

Talkun made his way back to Kinsington. The many Eltrists watched him, unable to believe what had taken place, for Haylin had never shown such magic, especially on such a scale. Kinsington, for once, had nothing to say. He stared in awe at Talkun, though fear rested close behind it.

Talkun glowed brighter, and he stretched his wings out.

Finally, Kinsington breathed and seeped into every mind near him. "We take today to mourn, but in times of war, it is a privilege to do so. Ready your mind for more losses and for a life worth living at last."

Folks gathered in the water or sat on the grass with forlorn expressions. Thorn and Riven stood next to the trees in the back. Thorn leaned on one with her arms crossed and her gaze at the stream. Riven studied her with a soft frown.

"What is it?" Thorn said.

Riven opened her mouth to speak, but only a whisper came, as if she had forgotten how to speak after being quiet for so long. "I... I wish I knew what you were thinking."

Thorn held her hands out to Riven. Riven took them and stared deeply into her oak eyes.

"I'm mourning, just as you are."

Riven smirked with her mouth closed. "I know you. You may be mourning, but you are plotting something. What is it?"

Thorn let her hands fall from Riven's. She crossed her arms and put her back against the trunk of a tree again. "I'm wondering what Kinsington thinks about Talkun's words."

"Kinsington used to believe in a united Folengower—"

"Yes, but that was long ago. I don't think he wants it to be united in the same way Talkun does. He sees a life of harmony between Amarda and Nniar, probably because he lived it, but what good is that to folks like us who have never known that life?" Thorn shook her head. "Kinsington wants to rule. To dominate Folengower."

"Maybe he will change his mind with Talkun speaking to him. It's better for Folengower if we are not fighting one another. He experienced a world that we only dream about."

"He didn't live long in that world." Thorn spit and wiped her lips.

"You doubt Talkun?" Riven scrutinized her.

"How could I not? Talkun is misguided in his thoughts. He relishes a world that couldn't last. We will change that with only Eltrist leading and…" Thorn stared into her eyes. "And then we will bring Nniar to their knees. They will beg for forgiveness, and we will grant them it only when they worship the true leaders of Folengower."

Riven's heart sank. She peered at Thorn as if she saw a storm cloud appear above her head. Her lungs felt tight, and even as her lips parted, she said nothing, as if she knew her words would be pebbles in Thorn's thoughts of boulders.

Guttural noises and a raucous sound of bodies thrown against boulders echoed throughout the mountains in the deep ghostly night. Thorn shot up, snatched her dagger and crept to the opening of her tent. She peered out. Others stared at her, they too holding their tent around them as if a blanket adorned their head. Then a lavender light streaked across the sky and another that collided with the other. Thorn gasped. She looked over her shoulder at

Riven murmuring as she rolled over, still caught by dreamland.

Thorn stepped out of her tent and ran to the narrow ravine that separated most of the Eltrists from them. A few others brave enough took the walk to where the Eltrists fought. Plants tangled around Thorn's legs with their needle-like spikes. She stared at her pant leg and plucked off what she could, wincing as the spikes stabbed her fingers.

Something darted out of her peripheral, and she spun towards it. Heavy winds whooshed around her, blowing her hair over her face in the gorge connecting the two camps. The others behind her fared no better. Their hands raised over their faces, gazing out of the slits between their fingers. An Eltrist tumbled to the ground, and Thorn witnessed the lashing tail of another curling away. Kinsington snarled at them, his maw dripping with strug, raising his paws, with piloerection on his back fur.

Sylin landed on his side, his smaller wing unmasking him even on the darkest of nights.

Thorn ran out into the open, her arms stretched out, her gaze up, and her mouth agape.

"*Leave us*," Kinsington seeped into her mind to say.

Thorn, almost breathless from the adrenaline, shouted back, "Let me help."

"You cannot settle an Eltrist's mind, not when it has already been forged."

Pavlyn swooped down. Her stern gaze was one that Thorn knew well. Thorn jumped out of the way, missing her footing and falling onto her back. Pavlyn charged past her, back to Sylin, who rose to his feet. He shook out his fur and stretched his wings. He didn't notice Pavlyn darting towards him until she held her paw out and snatched his leg. He twisted his body around until she released him. Wind whipped around.

With a stomp of his feet, as if done with the charade, Kinsington soared into the sky after Pavlyn. Thorn turned over, gasping as she tried to arch her back, but it felt as if she had landed on a knife. Her teeth clenched as she lifted her hand out to push up, but she quickly recoiled and tried with her other, crying out in pain. She turned herself over, desperate to push past the agony. She crawled on her knees to stand, and her hands stuck to the ground with the same plant that had caught her pant leg. Pinpricks of blood surfaced. She grimaced as she forced herself to push up, but she could only scream.

Someone grabbed her upper arm, and her fight instinct kicked in, but she had no physical capability to act on it.

O lifted her into his arms. "What are you doing out here?"

"I was just about to get up," Thorn said, her voice somewhere between a cry and fierceness.

"I could see that," O said sarcastically. He took her over to the side and let her slide out of his arms. Her nerves stabbed at her back. She winced, but tried with all her might to stand up straight.

"Why are they fighting?"

O lowered his voice and said, "I heard Talkun's words unraveled some minds." He turned Thorn around and plucked what he could see from her. Small holes riddled her shirt, as if moths had got to it. "Something that will need to be settled to advance in this war." He followed the thrashing from above with his eyes.

Kinsington reached Pavyln, who flew in circles to escape him. He stretched out his paw and clawed into her back. She shook and gnashed at the air. He drew faster and snatched her wing. She flapped her wings rapidly to get away, but he was stronger.

Thorn's gaze turned to the other Eltrist below, Talkun, who was standing in the shadows of a tree. "Does Pavyln trust Talkun?" she asked. Her eyebrow raised, her hands busy picking off the spikes she felt on her back that O had missed. "Or is it Sylin?"

"Sylin. He wants a united Folengower... a peaceful one."

Kinsington landed with Pavlyn in a thunderous thud. Pavlyn gnashed at Kinsington, strug tossing to the ground. Aylo and Esna raced to them. They shoved in between the two. Thorn turned back to where Sylin had landed and realized he was gone. Talkun's eyes were also now unseen where he had been hidden. She searched the crowd of Eltrists but failed to find Sylin's ashy-blue fur glowing.

"And who do you stand with?" Thorn said, not taking her eyes off the crowd.

O spit. "It's difficult, isn't it? Kinsington led us to Talkun, but stories of him have stayed." O patted at his heart. "I pray to the moon that they come to an agreement so we won't have to pick sides in our own camp. What are you thinking?"

"Kinsington knows the truth. The Eltrist have to conquer for us to finally be at peace. It's them who give us magic. They have always given, while the Ancient Ones take, take, take."

"You mean Korrigan."

Thorn glared at O. "One Ancient One is enough to spoil the hearts of an entire land. You sound like you've thought about his words more than you let on." She slapped his chest. "Have you stopped trusting me?"

"Of course not. If anything, I feel you've stopped trusting anyone but yourself. A lonely path—"

Thorn held her hand up. "Cursed soil, save your breath. Why is Kinsington fighting with Pavlyn, then?"

"You should ask him yourself. What do you need me for?" O grunted mockingly and left her side to join the Eltrists.

Thorn tossed a piece of plant at him that had been stuck to her, then crossed her arms. Kinsington and Pavlyn had calmed, and Aylo took Pavyln aside. He pushed her with his paws until she settled.

Esna landed directly in front of Thorn. "Return to your beds," she shouted in all the folks' minds who had wandered over to the other side of their camp. Folks turned and jogged away with concerned stares.

Thorn lingered. "And whose side are you on?" she challenged.

Esna's mouth hung open, seeping lavender blobs before Thorn's feet. "Side?" Esna glowered at her. The gold fur around her eyes looked like two crescent moons facing each other.

"Talkun and Kinsington have different views of our new Folengower. Something you already know."

"We would never disrespect the rightful heir of Folengower." Esna ran her tongue over her nose, like a dog wetting its snout. "I asked everyone to return to their beds. That includes you."

"Fine, but there will be talk throughout the camp of this. What should I tell them?" Thorn said with poison on the tip of her words.

Esna moved her head from side to side as she stepped closer, growling with a sinister smirk on her face. "You still think you have sway?"

Thorn backed up, her face neutral. "I know I do. They see me as a leader, and I know I can win Kinsington's trust back. They will talk, and it could destroy everything we have worked for. The moon will not shine on us if we can't even unite ourselves. Can you imagine the panic that will start? An egg hatching only to plummet to its death. I have bled, made mistakes and sacrificed my life for this." Thorn's chest rose and fell rapidly, and her eyes could have cut flesh. "I will not be cast aside." She twisted her pointer finger in front of Esna's face.

Esna slapped the side of her face. "You're marked." She tapped at the hole still in her cheek. It had grown smaller with the elixir, but even the light from Esna's belly could pierce through it. Esna pushed her other cheek to the side, where Theodore had left a diagonal scar. "The folks you believe will back you, would love to hear the truth about these."

Thorn swatted her paw away and clenched her hands at her sides.

Esna lowered her head to the ground, her gaze sending a chill down Thorn's back. "Get to bed."

Thorn's body twitched. A crazed and grotesque look devoured her normal self, but she walked away trying hard to move with ease as if she felt no pain. Esna relaxed her wings, keeping her focus on Thorn until she blurred from sight, then she joined Pavlyn and Kinsington. They stood several feet apart. Kinsington's head turned up, though his wings draped down like a cloak. His stance was that of marble.

"After everything, how could he trust that Nniar will care to unify?" Pavlyn's chest rose and fell, her claws scratching the ground. The fur on her forehead ruffled out, exaggerating the ridge of her brows and creating a menacing scowl.

Kinsington raised his head and sniffed the air. "His mind has not healed."

Esna's head cocked as she listened, but her gaze was stolen by Talkun.

"It is not my mind that hasn't healed, it is my heart that has refused to wither and harden as yours has," Talkun said as he landed beside them. They spaced out to make room for him. His wings were silent as the dead. His belly looked fuller and less of his skin sagged. "Have my words caused such strife that even our soil reeks of venom?"

"Forgive us." Kinsington bowed his head. "Our disagreement is tangled in fear. Most of us have forgotten or weren't born during the peaceful reign. Most of us were born to barren lands and starved until they allowed us to travel to the Earthen lands and feed upon the people there. We are told we are vile things with wings, yet they drain our magic to create their own. We cannot seek unity when our existence is feared. Domination! Then, like well-trained beasts, we will slowly allow them to join in harmony alongside us. But I imagine I will be long dead by then."

Talkun's mouth hung open. He said nothing for a long time, just stared up at the vast sky, where the stars glimmered. Sylin and the other Eltrists watched from a close distance, their faces plump with curiosity.

Talkun, without looking away, said, "I know that you all see the scars on my body, scars that will never vanish, but these wounds are nothing compared to what has festered inside. I understand the festering that has imprisoned your hearts as well. Do not think that I choose this path lightly." He scanned over his shoulder, then to Kinsington, Esna and Pavlyn. "This path you are choosing is the wrong one. One that will create more suffering and misunderstanding of our kind. You will have another war gnawing in every town for the freedom we are fighting for now."

Cold barreled down, as if Talkun's words commanded them. Snowflakes twirled onto their noses and melted into their fur. Some Eltrists held their paws up, hoping to catch one.

Kinsington shook his wings. "A storm could be coming. We must keep the folks warm." Eltrists took to the sky to land on the other side of the ravine. Then

Kinsington directed his words only to Talkun. "Mountains have less weight than your words."

33

Thousands of Cursed Knights stood in rows covering the entire castle grounds, holding as still as gargoyles with unsettling stares. With the windless day, nothing on them moved, not their web-like armor or even their lavender plume.

Korrigan peered out a window at the top of the castle. He could see the backs of his army standing as if elaborate grave markings. He dropped the curtains back over the window.

Queen Agden sat up in their bed with a silver book in her hand. Without looking up, she said, "And where are the others?"

"Off to recruit more knights. I sent Theodore to take a group to a few towns west and south of here."

"Do you only intend on killing our firstborn? More battles can break out at any moment." Agden slammed down her book on the covers. Her eyes met Korrigan with hate. "He should be here with us, with the rest of the knights, to protect us."

"I hardly would count a hundred knights and Bruthren with him as sending him to his death. Besides, he already escaped Amarda once and saved Eliza from them. Maybe you have less faith than you should in our son... and we already know he will use his magic if need be."

"They have rapture stones."

"Is he not wearing his crown or carrying his sword? It will protect him with the sunwaves on them."

"I know you don't care what happens to him. You have always treated him so harshly and—"

"And you have watched."

Agden's jaw dropped. She waved her pointer finger, and red flowed into her cheeks as if a tidal wave of rage crested. Shoving the blankets off her lap, she headed for the door.

"Save your dramatics. For moon's sake, *stay*." Korrigan's voice was stern and threatening.

Agden placed her hand on the door handle and squeezed. Hot orange and red bubbles emerged beneath her hand, as if she wished to turn it to ash. Korrigan placed his hand gently on hers and tugged for her to release.

"No reason to dwell on past mistakes."

Agden clenched her hand harder.

Korrigan sighed. "Focus on our future. We are so close to having a new Folengower. One where we won't need to negotiate with those flying parasites. We will own them, and the rest of the kingdom will rejoice."

"We?" Agden released the handle and charged towards Korrigan. He backed up. "I never wanted this for Folengower. I married you thinking that you were as kind and caring as your mother. She left a bright mark on Folengower. *You* are a scar."

Korrigan backed up to the wall, his eyes downcast as Agden stabbed her long fingernail into his chest. They glared at each other for several moments until Korrigan pushed her to the side.

"Theodore wants to fight. Maybe he's more like me than you think. Is he a scar too?"

"Theodore is nothing like you, and neither is Eliza. Thank the moon that our children are capable of things you never have been."

"You are worse than the morning birds"—Korrigan swished his hand in the air—"bickering away at each other for no reason except to antagonize those who have to hear it. Sit down."

Agden locked her jaw, as if she were a viper ready to attack, though she instead sat down on the bed.

"I need you to send a message to the sea towns by the Thornyarch Mountains to each of the three tolvins."

"A message?"

"I need you to convince them to let us camp in their towns. Amarda is camped on the Thornyarch Mountains close to them. We need to keep them safe from the battles to come."

"Convince them? You are their Ancient One. You hardly need permission. Unless—"

Korrigan put his pointer finger on his cheek, with his middle resting on his lip. "There is a strategy to the bloodshed. Don't pretend like you thought I haven't heard the whispers from some towns that curse the soil I stand on. If you send a message, they will trust you."

Agden pulled Korrigan down so his face was level with hers. Time stilled as she gazed into his eyes, as if scrying into a fire. In that moment, his eyes softened, and Agden felt a sliver of something. Korrigan lifted his hand next to her cheek as if to kiss her, but he looked away from her eyes and squeezed his hand. He rushed away, opened the door and said, "Send the messages." He walked out, shutting the door behind him.

Agden's hands trembled. She quickly sat at her desk and grabbed dried leaves, a bone with a sharp point and a bottle of black ink. She placed one leaf out and dipped the bone in the ink. It took her till morning to decide the right words to write. Once she sealed them with a strug mixture and the Nniar crest dried into it, she whistled faintly out the window. A hawk, a Steller's jay and a crow landed on the windowsill. Agden smiled and rubbed their chests with the backs of her fingers. "Now, I need you to head to the towns where the Thornyarch Mountains are."

They all pecked at her. The Steller's jay snatched at the first letter.

"Wait." She handed it to the hawk. "Here's one for you. Take this to Chant." He gripped it in his beak and soared off. "And you take this to Nilhorn." She handed the note to the Steller's jay, who waited for her to drop a seed before leaving. "Take this one to Corling." The crow barely waited for her to finish before opening his wings. Agden watched them turn to specks and then she stared down at the knights.

Nothing had changed from their mountainous stance. She closed the window and sat on her bed with her eyes heavy and puffy. She lay her head back, closed her eyes and soon fell asleep.

They had passed the Shadowvale Ridge recently. Theodore remembered it well. Cursed Knights in full armor walked ahead, with Theodore and Bruthren on chackles behind and more knights following. The town of Carlen was only a handful of chackles away now.

"I know this town and the folks. Let me talk with them," Theodore said to Bruthren.

"Friends? As long as it goes smoother than the last town."

Theodore nodded.

"Well, I also have friends here, and..." Bruthren put the back of his hand next to his mouth as he moved closer to Theodore's ear. "You will find many here for our cause."

Theodore clenched his hand on the reins. Tarmist tugged. "Now, now, Tarmist." Theodore scratched at Tarmist's neck. "I told you I missed you."

"He can smell the stench of other chackles on you."

"Then I should be mad that you allowed others to ride you in my absence." Theodore grinned.

Tarmist snorted, as if he understood.

They could see dull lights near them and hear soft laughter.

"It seems they were having a celebration," Theodore said.

"It would appear so. I think I know why."

"And what would that be?"

"Nothing to concern yourself with."

Theodore frowned and continued onto the path where the houses lined around them. A few folks gazed up with their mouths open. Most of them had disheveled hair full of twigs or petals. Theodore nodded towards them, crown upon his head, and the folks instantly fell to their knees and placed their fist in front of their eye.

"What cursed soi—" Art said, running down the knoll in front of the first knights to march through.

Theodore's friendly smile stole his gaze. Theodore jumped down from Tarmist and patted him. "Be well. I will return," he whispered in the chackle's ear.

Theodore touched the back of the closest knight and motioned with his hand for them to part. Each knight in front of that one parted for him to move through. Theodore rushed to the front and met with Art, nearly tackling him in a hug.

"What have I done to deserve your presence?" Art beamed and squeezed him tighter. "This is the moon's doing. I have prayed to her since you left."

Theodore patted his back and released the embrace. He raised one of his eyebrows. "I wouldn't praise anything just yet."

"Hmm... what brings you back to Carlen?" Art eyed the many knights. "And with the shadow of an army cast upon us."

"We can discuss everything shortly, but first I need to speak with your tolvin."

Art perked up and wiped down his clothes. "You are staring at him."

"You are the tolvin for Carlen?"

"Honored to meet you, Ancient One. They put me in charge when I was just a sprout of a man."

"Praise the moon for your humbleness. No wonder the folks here wanted you to remain in charge. Can we go somewhere private to speak?"

"Of course."

Art led the way to a building on the other side of the park. It had large stained-glass doors with finnixes in a leaping position, the other mirrored on the other door, with their paws meeting in a stunning mauve color and their small spiraled horns in gray. Above the doors were words from one of the old languages.

Art opened the door and let Theodore through. Bruthren followed to come, but Theodore held his hand up. Bruthren stood outside the door. By now, a crowd had gathered on the sides of the knights. Some children had tried petting the chackles, only to be halted by the knights.

Up on the knoll, Kalien stood with his hands in his pockets. The sun shined on his amber skin. It looked vibrant, as if healing all the blemishes he'd received since being captured. Bruthren cleaned his glasses with a cloth from his pocket, but then he tilted to the side and his eyes caught Kalien's, a faint smile on his lips. Kalien stilled, but he returned the smile.

Inside the building, a long hallway led Theodore and Art into a modest room with a towering ceiling. Above them hung a blown-glass chandelier with three finnixes chasing each other. A bowl with a strug mixture inside elongated out of the middle of their backs. In the middle of the creatures, the moon radiated. Art took out a satchel from a cabinet on the far wall and a step stool to reach the chandelier. He placed dry bits of plants into each one, and a white light illuminated the entire room.

There were two tables near one wall and two on the other, with chairs placed nicely next to them. In the back was a rounded bar table, and behind it, there were shelves of varying glasses filled with fermented drinks and wood mugs that hung off twisted iron hooks. There were two black stools at the table on the other side.

"Shall we drink?" Art led him to the bar and walked behind to the shelves.

Theodore climbed onto a stool. "Quite the selection you have."

"If you know us Carlens, we love our drink," Art said with a chuckle.

"I gathered that." Theodore grinned. "What's that yellow one?"

Art turned his head and snatched a bulbous bottle. "Sand songs, I call it. A collection of sea plants from the Sea of Calip. You can smell the sea on your very breath when you drink this."

Theodore shook his head. "I'll just have the local brew."

"This one, then." Art snatched one with silver liquid that shimmered like the stars, took a mug from the hook and poured. "From threadhare blooms. The last time I saw them bloom, my beard was only down to here." He put his hand near his chin.

"Quite rare, then."

"Indeed, and this is quite old." Art walked over to the other stool and sat down. "Now, Ancient One, tell me all I should know."

"Nniar is struggling to win the war, but that's not entirely why I'm here. I bring Cursed Knights because King Korrigan forced me to. He wants more knights recruited, but I want you to be a part of my army instead."

Art tugged at his beard. "Am I missing something? It sounds like you and your father are asking the same thing."

"I want to unite Folengower, and apparently, so do many other folks, but I have a separate army that began long before I even knew about them, and surprisingly, they have accepted me to lead. I want you to join me."

Art took a swig of his drink and set it down. Some of it dripped down the sides like molten metal. He wiped his mustache and beard of the silver bubbles. His eyes narrowed. "Are you speaking of The Choke?"

"You know about it?"

"Of course I do. I know all the folks in this town, and"—Art leaned over—"there are folks here who are a part of The Choke already. They have asked me to join in the past."

"You said no?"

Art gave a single nod. "I never thought there was a reason for it."

"I found out that we have not kept our promises to Amarda. I have seen their land of rotting trees and cracking ground. We take their magic and leave them with nothing, but that's not the worst part." Theodore clenched his fists and his lips parted but no words could come. He swallowed and tried again. "The whispers of my father killing Queen Callum are true. He was the Bloodtress, and he couldn't take that. He needed Talkun to take the blame, and so our history is written in blood and lies. Talkun is alive."

Art stood silently. He stared at the floor and teetered on his heels.

"I know it's a lot to hear."

"And does Korrigan know about The Choke?"

"He does, but he believes us to be small. I wish I could leave your town be, but this war is an infection. It has already killed too many, and I do not plan on it continuing into my old age." Theodore lifted his mug and drank. He held it in his hand and continued, "Will you fight alongside me?"

Art gazed at Theodore and tapped his fingers on the bar table. "What do you imagine happening if Amarda wins?"

"They are as desperate as my father. I assume they will want vengeance against us all, and part of me wouldn't blame them, but it will only bring more war. What will you do?"

"What kind of friend would I be if I said no? It's a good cause, but curse the soil, I need to have a town meeting."

Theodore placed his hand on his chest. "Praise the moon for your friendship." He clanked his mug against Art's. "Have the meeting after we've gone; not all the knights are part of The Choke."

"This is a narrow situation. I feel as if I've fallen down a hole."

Theodore placed a hand on his shoulder. "I will always get you out. I'm told someone is already here to organize the town with the current members. They will catch everyone up and know when there are battles brewing. If you need me, send a bird, but please write the note in a way that only I would understand."

"Is there a new battle brewing?"

Theodore nodded.

Art scratched the side of his head. "Oh, before you go, Kalien, that folk you asked about and spoke with his mother Luspy, made it home."

"He has? I need to speak with him."

Art and Theodore wandered back through the long hallway and out the doors.

Bruthren moved aside. "Finished?"

"Not quite. I need to speak with someone else before we go. It shouldn't take long. Ready the knights for the next town."

"We won't be making camp here, then?"

"Not when the day is young." Theodore leaned over to him. "The town is on our side," he said in a hushed voice.

Bruthren had a crazed smile. "I'll let the rest know."

"Ready?" Art said.

Theodore followed Art back up the knoll to Luspy's house behind the shops.

"Oh, there he is." Art waved to Kalien, who stood watching the knights. "Kalien, I have someone who wants to meet you."

Kalien froze, his eyes stunned. He knelt and placed his fist in front of his eye.

"You can stand. I need to discuss something important—"

"You want my earring?" Kalien peered up at him, still knelt.

Theodore's eyebrows knitted together as he reached his hand out. Kalien grabbed it and stood. "How did you know that?"

"My mom already told me about your visit."

"And what did she think you should do?"

"Give you it." Kalien wiggled the earring off and held it out to Theodore. "I understand why you need it, but know that this is the last thing my grandmother gave me. I have worn it since that day. Keep it well and do not make me regret giving such a gift to you."

Theodore opened his hand, and Kalien let it fall. "I will use it well, and I will not forget this gift."

"Important to everyone, it seems," Bruthren said as he joined them. He laced his fingers and pointed with his pointer fingers together at Kalien.

Theodore glanced at Bruthren and then back to Kalien. "What?"

"Kalien is already a part of The Choke, and he has something very important."

"How did you know about the earrings?"

Bruthren smirked. "We are full of surprises."

Kalien clinched his jaw. "This is between me and the Ancient One."

"What is he talking about?" Theodore said to no one in particular.

Kalien said nothing.

"Go on; you can't keep secrets from our leader."

"When the Eltrists came to the castle, they captured me, and one of their leaders, Thorn, made me a spy. I have this." Kalien brushed his hair behind his ear and turned his head to him. "When Bruthren found out, he decided to make me leave it in case it could be... I could be useful."

"It seems we have more to discuss, then, Bruthren. Kalien..." Theodore gave a single nod to him. "Tell your mother that I am in her debt. If she is ever in need of anything, send me a message."

"I will."

"Enjoy your first day at the grayden."

Bruthren and Theodore returned to the knights below.

"To the next town," Theodore said.

The knights in front marched forward and through the center of town. The folks stood at shop windows or outside of them. Some waved, while others whispered to one another and pointed at his crown. Theodore waved back to any who waved at him.

34

Leaves spiraled down like tornadoes to the insect kingdom. Eliza tilted her head up at them, her back resting on a lichen- and prancing-flower-infested stump. As the leaves neared the ground, they slowed and dispersed in every direction. One landed over Eliza's eyes. It was soft, like velvet. She could see faint light move through, and when she took the leaf off, the light flickered. She focused on what was cutting out the light above, and dropped the leaf as wings took shape. She swallowed and placed her hands on the ground to push up to run.

"Bloodtress." Cassin leaped over the stump to Eliza, his arms snatching her.

They barreled through the forest with her in his arms, Eliza's heart pounding against his chest. Cassin's deep green and blue strands of hair whipped wildly as he charged silently. The Eltrists' wings glided above the branches, the images of them coming like a slide projector.

Without warning, Cassin slid beneath a bramble of bushes into a hollow. He landed on his back with Eliza still secure in his arms. It smelled of warm berries that had fallen in on a hot day and slowly shriveled. Twigs, flowers, moss and shells wove together in an elongated sack next to Eliza's face.

Cassin glanced over at it. "Just a nest," he said in between his hurried breaths.

Ghastly sounds tunneled into the hollow. Eliza moved as if to look, though Cassin held her tighter and shook his head. The more sounds came, the clearer she could hear the shouting and magic exploding in the air. After a while, Eliza closed her eyes, and Cassin loosened his grasp. He warmed her back with his body heat, and her exhaustion soon took her into a deep slumber.

"Eliza... Eliza."

Eliza struggled to open her eyes fully. Cassin's face peered over hers.

"The sounds have quieted. I am going to check if it's safe. Stay here."

Eliza scooted away from the opening, and Cassin squeezed out. Eliza placed her ear against the soil near the exit, her body hunched over. She could hear faint rustling about from insects inside the dirt. She focused on her feet, waiting for Cassin to block the one ray of light that shined in.

Inaudible voices drifted in. No matter how hard she pressed her ear to the ceiling of the cavity, she couldn't make out what they said. A shadow flashed over the ray of light, and Eliza moved away from the entrance.

"Is everythi—"

Eliza gasped and shot to the back as something else dove in. It looked at her with its crown of green horns and red fur before diving into the hanging nest. Eliza laughed at herself. She placed her hand on her chest and tilted her head back, muttering, "Just a horned harling." A moment later, the horned harling poked out its head from the top of the nest. It tossed out several nuts that landed at Eliza's feet, as if it assumed she must be a harling as well even without the horns, fur and swishy tails.

Eliza moved to her knees and picked up all the nuts. The animal made a high-pitched clicking sound at her. She held her hand out, offering them back. It dove back into its nest. Eliza munched on the nuts till all was gone and her stomach growled as if it had forgotten she was hungry.

Cassin slid back in, nearly crushing Eliza, who sat opposite the hole. He moved his legs to the side.

"Cassin. What happened?"

"Eltrists were circling. Not many, and no folks with them that I could see. The knights fired at them, with no casualties, but..." Cassin scanned the ground.

"What?"

"We think one of them was Talkun."

"Talkun?" Eliza clasped her hands together and let them drop in her lap. "I won't allow you to hurt him. I am the one who released him. He is family."

"I know. We have spies from The Choke with Amarda. We've heard that Talkun wants the same thing; he wants to create harmony like he had with Queen Callum."

"O. O is the spy." Her eyes lighted like a lightbulb, remembering back to him mentioning it. "O," she repeated. How had this reveal landed and stayed in the back of her mind.

Cassin darted a look at her. "He's not the only one, but yes, he is. Did he tell you about The Choke?"

She nodded. "The day Theodore saved me and I met you and Palina, but he saved me before that... more than once. He didn't tell me any details though."

"He must have seen good in you." Cassin motioned his hand to the opening. "It's safe to come out, but just to warn you, Korrigan is readying knights to march to the Thornyarch Mountains to retaliate. Some will stay behind, and others are at the Anorphus."

"Why are any at the Anorphus?"

"I'll find out when the knights return. My guess would be they are collecting strug or other things that were left behind."

"Like the bodies?"

"You mean the bones. There are not many bodies that are whole. They will be tossed into the sea to be claimed by the depths." Cassin shrugged and held his hand out for Eliza. She took it. They climbed out of the hollow and walked back to the castle.

Cursed Knights hid in the trees near the castle. Eliza only knew of their existence when Cassin nodded up at them. The walls of the castle swarmed with seafoam and corpse-thistle-helmet-dripping knights, their swords resting in their scabbards.

They walked around to the front of the castle. Nia stood at the door with several other knights.

"Bloodtress." Nia bowed with a fist over her eye. "Cassin, you kept her safe?"

"Indeed."

"You will watch over the Bloodtress from now on," Hargrove said as she stepped out of the castle. "Follow me inside."

Eliza and Cassin did as she asked. They could hear Korrigan at the grand table with Lore.

"What are they discussing?" Eliza asked.

"The next plan of attack, probably," Cassin whispered.

Korrigan stood suddenly. "Eliza, there you are."

"Cassin hid her. I have put him in charge of her safety."

"What a job that will be."

Cassin jerked his head towards Eliza. "I promise to uphold my duty."

"Eliza, head to your room. Someone will bring your food to you today."

Eliza placed a hand on her hip and glared. "I can't leave my room?"

"It's too dangerous at the moment. Cassin will be at your beck and call for whatever you need."

"Where's Mom?"

"She's upstairs. Leave her be; she is sleeping," Korrigan said firmly.

Eliza threw her hands up. "How could she still be asleep after all the shouting?"

"Who knows? At least she is calm." Korrigan shooed her with his hand. "Now go to your room."

Eliza squeezed her hand that she'd had to magic back on and sighed as she sat at the window in her room. Many of the knights had left to march to the Thornyarch Mountains.

"Do you need anything?" asked Cassin.

"Elm... if I call her, will any of the knights say anything?"

"Why would they? She is your companion."

Eliza nodded and opened her window. It opened up like an awning. She hummed a song and waited. Near the towers, she could see great black wings. Eliza smiled. Elm swooped to her as fast as she could go and finally landed on her arm. "Elm," she said fondly, rubbing her chest.

"Cassin, do you know where Audrey and Ben are?"

"Yes. Why?"

"I want to send them a letter. Is it somewhere Elm can get to?"

Cassin nodded. "Though I wouldn't write to them. They are at the grayden, and the leader of the grayden would take your letter and it may never get to them."

"Theodore rides off to lead and I am here stuck with a knight to protect me," she muttered to mainly herself.

"You are a part of The Choke now. Right now, you may feel useless, but be patient. I know that you lost your hand and managed to mend it back together. A warrior never forgets how to fight."

Elm flapped her wings as a knock came at the door. Cassin opened it. A folk came in with a tray of food and set it down on her desk.

"Anything else, Bloodtress?"

"Bring something for Elm to eat."

The server bowed and soon returned with a bowl of carveberries and raw meat. Eliza ate as Cassin stood at the door.

"I plan to see my mom. You can come with me or stay here."

"I'm ordered to stay with you. I know that's not what you want, but I will stay out of your way."

Eliza finished the last bite and stood. "Then stay with me." Elm flew to the window, gazing down at the knights below. "Don't go anywhere, Elm."

Down the hall and up more stairs, they made it to the grand bedroom. Eliza knocked on the door.

"Who is it?" Agden immediately said, no just-woken-up tone in her voice.

"Eliza."

Agden swung the door open, eyebrows drawn together. "Are you hurt?"

"No, I'm fine. Dad said you were sleeping."

"Sleeping?" Agden snorted. "Who could sleep through all the shouting and firing sounds? Come in." She shut the door before Cassin could join them, then leaned her back against it, both hands on the wood, and whispered, "Another battle is coming. I believe it could be the end of the war."

"Why?"

"I sent letters to the tolvins of the towns near the mountains to allow our knights to camp there. I haven't heard back yet, but I assume I will hear something soon. Amarda's army lives atop it now."

"I have to go with them."

"Go with them?" Agden frowned. "To be covered in blood and consumed by strug?"

"Theodore is out there now, and at any moment, he could be taken again or murdered."

"He is the next Ancient One. He is trained for battle. You are not."

Her mouth twisted bitterly. "Ugh. Why do you say things like that?"

Agden moved away from the door to stare out the window. "What?"

"Act like I'm incapable of doing anything. You have no idea what I have done since Kinsington came to Harthsburg. I killed Wyatt while I watched Kinsington hold Theodore's limp body in his paw before he ripped him away back to this mess. A rapture stone gnawed my hand off when Amarda captured me because I chose to use magic regardless of the consequences. I was able to mend it back, but I still feel a constant pain in it." Eliza held her hand up and clutched her wrist. "You have no place to doubt what I can do."

Agden grabbed Eliza's hands. "I didn't know you have suffered so greatly, but I cannot let you fight in this battle."

Eliza took her hands from Agden's, and at the same moment, Korrigan opened the door.

"Eliza. I thought I told you to not bother—"

She glared at Agden, then Korrigan. "Yes, I am just a bother in this house, aren't I?"

"That's not what I was going to say. I told you to stay in your room at least until tomorrow. I need a word alone."

Korrigan stared at Agden. "Cassin, next time, don't let her leave."

Eliza charged into Korrigan's side as she moved past him, then grabbed Cassin's arm. "Let's go."

Korrigan slammed the door. "What did you say to her?"

"She's upset at me because I will not let her fight in the war."

"Why would she want to?" He sat on the bed and sighed. "If Theodore dies, she will take over and become the next Ancient One after my death. This is a good thing."

Agden moved to the wall furthest from Korrigan and eyed him. "You speak of this like you want Theodore to die."

"He wants to act as though I'm already dead. Why can't I assume the same for him?"

"I thought you two were getting along, and of course he doesn't assume you are dead." Agden walked over to her nightstand and took off her earrings. She placed them in a crimson box. "Why are you here?"

"The birds returned from the mountains. The tolvins have agreed to allow us to stay, but they want something in return."

"Give them whatever they need."

"I've already sent knights ahead to grant their wishes. They want their folks given a safe haven until the fighting has ended."

Agden's face remained devoid of expression, as if she'd presumed this to be the obvious wish anyway. "Where are you planning on putting them?"

"Well, I first thought Amarda since most of the folks are here, but then I thought that would cause conflict, so they will arrive in our forest in the coming days. You will be in charge of orchestrating their stay."

"Is that all?"

"I leave tonight with the Cursed Knights. I will leave some behind for your sake, and…" Korrigan grabbed his collar and tugged it as if it was too tight. "I… I…"

Agden's lips parted and focused on Korrigan. "I haven't heard you struggle with your words since before our wedding."

Korrigan dropped his head.

Agden placed her hand under his chin and lifted his head. "Have you tired of the blood?"

Korrigan's gaze was a thrashing sea hopeless to survive in. He brushed her hand away. "I am not thinking about blood. I'm thinking about when you looked at me with even a grain of sand of love in your eyes and how quickly that soured."

"You speak of love like you had any for me," Agden said with a quiver in her voice.

Korrigan took her hand. "All this time, I've forgotten those moments where you showed me light."

"It's only dimmed in your presence."

Korrigan dropped her hand, his nostrils flaring. He snaked his head to the side of hers. "Let me know when the darkness stays. I can smell it on your neck. You will hunger for me again." He dragged his finger down her throat. "Be well in my absence."

Agden turned away from him. He grabbed something from the drawer and left, though the bloodthirsty smell of him lingered on every surface he'd touched for days.

35

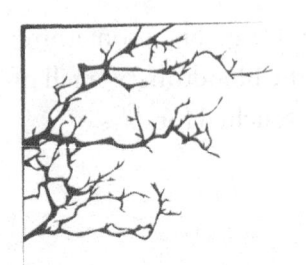

"We are to join King Korrigan in the mountains. They will need us for battle," a knight said with a note in his hand. He outstretched his hand to Theodore who sat atop Tarmist. Theodore took it. He had removed his crown after the last town, and it left an indent around his head.

"Is that all?"

The knight nodded.

"We will leave soon for the mountains, then. Send word that we are days away."

"Why not leave now? We have already started back that way," Bruthren said.

Theodore unrolled the note, his fingers moving with the words. "I have one more place to stop first."

Bruthren leaned over and said, "The moon will not shine upon those who hide."

"You mistake what I plan to do. I must see Audrey and Ben. You may not understand, but I need to."

"This battle that's brewing involves *us* too. Leave your heart out of this. I can give you something for that." Bruthren's eyes lit up with excitement.

"My heart is why you have asked me to lead. If you would like it removed, I would seek my father's side. We are going to the grayden."

Bruthren took his spectacles off and reached into his pocket for a small cloth. He moved the cloth over the glasses, wiping them clean. "And what do you expect the Cursed Knights with us that are not aware of The Chokc to do?"

"I will send them on ahead. They can make sure it's safe."

The chackles huffed as they walked. Tarmist walked awry as he tried to eat an insect fluttering by. Theodore patted his cheek to stop. Tarmist licked his hand instead.

"Ugh... you strange beast." Theodore flicked his hand in the air to rid the saliva.

"I suppose that would work... unless you want to force them into our army. Could you imagine the look on their faces?" Bruthren slapped his leg and then cupped his stomach as he laughed.

A few of the knights peered over their shoulders, their crimson eyes all holding the same curious expression.

"They're staring," Theodore mouthed.

That only made Bruthren laugh harder. His body hunched over his chackle's head. The chackle wiggled him off. "Alright, alright. Praise the moon for such moments," he said between laughs. "Send them off. Send them off."

"Gather the ones up that don't belong and take them to the mountains," he whispered.

Bruthren gave him a curious look. "You want me to leave?"

"It will seem less suspicious if you continue on with them; after all, you are the mastermind of everything, and I know my father will want you there to execute your grand plan against the Eltrist."

"Why does it sound like you have an issue with my plan?"

Theodore scoffed. Beyond them, he could see a grouping of tall trees that overlapped branches, creating a thick forest. Theodore kicked the side of Tarmist, and he cantered on. "I'm not sure how I feel about it, but I feel something. I hope you know what could happen if it goes wrong."

Bruthren grinned. "You think too small. When I plan something, it's revolutionary, and that is why it will work. It is not all that you think."

"What do you plan to do when they are controlled by you?"

"Don't lose the earrings; we will need them." Bruthren stared ahead, ignoring his question. "Oh look, Finnix forest is just ahead."

"Separate us."

"With pleasure." Bruthren pulled on his chackle's reigns and said something to it too quiet to hear. The knights behind him stopped abruptly, as did Theodore. The knights in front steadily stopped when Bruthren began to speak. "We will be splitting up momentarily. I will be choosing only the very best to journey to the Thornyarch Mountains, and the rest will lead the Ancient One to the last town before joining us. We must make sure it is safe before our Ancient One comes."

Bruthren jumped off his chackle and picked which knights to follow him and which needed to stay behind. Theodore watched them, hoping that this sudden change wouldn't cause them to wonder too much as to what it meant. Bruthren bowed to Theodore, hopped back onto his chackle and shouted, "*Halko.*" His chackle took off, and the knights marched with speed.

Theodore eyed the remaining knights around him. At least half were by his side. "All of you, then." They placed their palms on their neck. "To the grayden."

Hums of spirit wings and the creeping of fog wove between the trunks like strands of rags. Corpse thistles peeked out from below, adding sweetness to the air. Theodore breathed in, his eyes closed and his lips sealed in a grin. They traveled deep into the center of the forest. A finnix's deep howl called into the night, but it wasn't in sight. Then the knights in front stopped.

"We've made it," one of them said.

"Take me to Rew."

The knight nodded and slid into a crevice underneath a moss- and lichen-covered crag. Theodore followed and landed on his feet. The knight vanished in search of Rew. Carts rolling, axes slashing into the soil and rock filled the room with jarring noises. Everything seemed as it was before. The folks moved with such haste that no one noticed Theodore standing against the cavern wall.

"Ancient One." Rew bowed next to him. Theodore turned to him. "What are you doing here?"

"I came to see Audrey and Ben."

Rew's ears twitched. "They aren't here."

Theodore tensed. "What do you mean?"

"They are at Morrow's—the person training them. It's nearby if you would like me to escort you."

"I wouldn't want to waste your time. How do I get there?"

Rew explained where the path just outside led, and Theodore told the knights to be ready to leave at any moment when he returned.

Just as he was about to leave, he spotted Argwen. He turned to leave, but Argwen stood a few feet away speaking to another worker. Theodore waved to him. "Argwen."

The old man turned around, smiled at Theodore and walked over to him. "Well, and here I thought I wouldn't see you again."

"It's good to see you. How is everything?" Theodore bent out of the way of an axe swinging next to him.

"Collection has slowed, but we have harvested an incredible amount of dead magic." Argwen leaned over and picked up a ball of dead magic that rolled to his foot and tossed it into a cart.

"Has anyone decided how to allocate the magic to the fighters when the time comes?"

Argwen rubbed his forehead. "We have been sorting for several days, and so far, every grayden has a way to transport the weapons, and some have already started off to the Thornyarch Mountains by cart. On the eastern side, there is a mass of caverns that wind to the top. We are planning to lead them all there if Bruthren gives the word."

"The fighters will have to have the magic close by."

"It sounds tricky, but we are many, and everything will be in place well before the fighting begins."

"Is there anything you need from me? I'm traveling with Cursed Knights to the Thornyarch Mountains later today, but I can help before I leave."

"No, you have an important role to play. Just watch out for us when we join. Unity is upon us. I can feel it through every bone."

Theodore gave him a curious look. "Indeed. We all do. I will see you again."

Argwen bowed to him, and Theodore nodded before leaving the grayden.

Theodore walked briskly amongst the soft moss until he found the boulders, then he went down the steps until he saw the rounded house beneath the purple leaves. He stared at it for a long moment, fidgeting with his hands before he could step off the last stone and knock on the door. He waited for anyone to answer, but no one came.

He wandered around the side, peeking inside the window. He could see inside to the kitchen. A black bowl sat in the middle filled with clawnuts. Something rustled behind him, and he held his breath to listen, but as he turned to look, his feet lifted from the ground and he landed onto the damp grass.

"Theodore?" Audrey said. "That's Theodore."

"Oops," Morrow said, with her head looming over his. "This is the Ancient One you're with? I can see why." She licked her lips.

"Get out of the way." Audrey pushed her to the side, her face somewhere between happiness and concern. "Are you okay?"

Theodore smiled widely and pulled her down to him. He held the back of her head as her lips touched his.

"Wow. Hey, honey, come over and see this," Morrow called out to the back of the house.

Ben ran over with his sword in hand. His cheeks were red and his brow wet with sweat. "What's go—"

"Isn't it something? We can put on a better show, don't you think?" Morrow brushed her body against him.

Ben just laughed as he moved past to reach Theodore. Audrey sat up and pulled Theodore to stand.

"Come here." Theodore crashed into Ben with a hug.

"You always make an entrance." Ben patted his back.

As their hug ended, Audrey slipped her hand into Theodore's. "Do you have good news, then, or bad?"

Theodore squeezed her hand.

"Well, what is it?" Morrow said, tapping her foot. "Even if you look like that, you still need to spill your secrets here."

"I can't stay long, but I needed to see you both before I head to the Thornyarch Mountains. Amarda's army has moved there, and we are planning to attack."

Morrow's eyes turned dreamy. "Sounds like the place to be with all the blood and strong bodies moving about."

Theodore dropped Audrey's hand and stepped closer to Morrow. "You're *excited* at the blood already spilled? I have watched hundreds of bodies... innocent bodies floating in strug as their loved ones tried to save them, and now the Anorphus is dying."

"Well, it seems you've seen it all. A hero, I'm sure."

Theodore scowled. "I need time alone with my friends, and I will not take no for an answer."

"I wouldn't think of saying no to you," she said sarcastically. "You can have the house while I catch dinner." Morrow squeezed Theodore's biceps and gave a soft moan. Audrey shook her head. "Don't forget about me, honey," she said to Ben before taking off.

Ben shrugged. "Shall we?" He walked to the door and led Theodore inside. Audrey dragged him to sit on the couch. Ben sat on the fireplace bench across from them.

"I wish I could stay with you both. Morrow seems like..."

"She's something, isn't she?" Audrey said.

"She's not that bad."

Audrey shot a look at Ben. "You like her? Ben, don't say you've fallen for her."

Ben chuckled and brushed his hair from his face. "I didn't say that."

"Look at you; you're blushing."

"Leave Ben alone. He can have a crush. Honestly, after Eliza, I think it's great."

Ben lifted his head. "How is Eliza?"

"I'm not sure, but if I had to guess, everything is taking a toll on her. I know that she wanted me to keep you all safe." Theodore placed his hand on Audrey's leg. "I wouldn't worry about her, though. She will make it out of this alive. How has training been?"

"Morrow works us all day and sometimes nights. And, uh, Ben... is there something you'd like to say?" Audrey subtly mimicked waving a wand.

Ben choked on a laugh. "It's nothing, really."

"Nothing? More nothing than I have."

Theodore cocked his head. "What?"

"I have magic... somehow."

Theodore scooted to the edge of the couch. He stared at Ben with his mouth agape. "You are a magic bringer? How did you find out?"

"Morrow did an experiment with us, and I produced light or something, but I haven't been able to do it again."

"Praise the moon! I wonder how that's possible."

"I have no idea, but it's true. The problem is that I have no time to learn it well enough before we have to fight. Audrey is better at fighting than I am. She wields a sword now."

"You do too."

"I missed this. I missed you both." He smiled, though it faded with urgency like blowing out a match. "If you are to be forced into battle, find a place to hide underneath. The Eltrist have been drowning the fields in strug. You will fare better under a tree, or if you can, something more solid."

"Do you think we will?" Audrey crossed her arms.

"I would plan for it. The Choke need everyone able to fight if we want to win, and Bruthren does all he can to get what he wants."

"I hope he does in this case," Ben said.

The door flung open, and Morrow stood in the door frame, her hand raised, holding the legs of a long hairless creature with a pointed nose and long dirt-ridden claws. Its stomach had a gash in it that was still dripping blood. She skipped to the kitchen, blood trickling behind her. There was a thud on the counter as she placed the creature down. She poked her head out, with a knife pointed at Theodore. "Will you be staying for dinner?"

Theodore looked down at Audrey's hand in his.

Audrey smiled with her lips together. "You don't have to stay."

"Honey, when will you look at me like that?" The knife was now pointed at Ben.

Ben suppressed an uncomfortable laugh.

"I want to stay..." Theodore dropped his head.

"I know. We will be fine, but before you go, come with me." Audrey stood up and pulled him close. "Do you mind?" Audrey said to Ben.

"Please, go," Ben said with a smile.

"Woohoo." Morrow held up her knife and spun it around before returning to butchering the animal.

They ignored her and started up the stairs. At the top, Theodore walked around the small room.

"Do you remember our first date?"

Audrey sat on the bed and took her hair tie out. "Of course. Why?" She walked to the window and unlocked it. Wind rushed through, catching her wavy hair.

"My world shattered." Theodore rested his body against the wall on the other side of the window.

"Shattered?" Audrey mulled over his words like strong whiskey.

"Shattered. Completely. My world before was dull, regretful and shameful. But you, I would save you from the depths during an unforgiving storm. I would carry you to the ends of the realms if you asked me." Theodore took her hand, leading her to the bed. She sat on the edge, and he knelt before her. "But I know you are stronger and not in need of saving, so I will love every breath you allow me to feel against my skin." Audrey tangled her fingers in his hair as he moved his head between her thighs. "It is your face that I see when I close my eyes." Theodore lifted her shirt just above her hips, his lips teasing her. She threw her head back, with her hands planted on the mattress to hold herself up. He pulled her pants down inch by inch, with his lips following. "Your voice I hear to guide me to the right path."

Audrey pulled the rest of her pants down. "Fuck... stop teasing me," she said with a smirk.

"Gladly."

Crossing her legs over his neck, every inch of her body ached with euphoria. Rapturous moans released from her lips as rhythmic as the ticking of time. Time felt still and all-devouring at once.

Not even the rattling of the shutters nor Morrow's crude shouts that they could hear faintly between the bed creaking could take them out of the moment. Audrey uncrossed her legs and pulled Theodore forcefully up. Her hands worked to lift his armor off. Theodore helped as playful laughter ensued.

Audrey's fingers ran from his neck to his navel. Theodore held his gaze on her face. Then her fingers made it back up to his collarbone and onto his tattoo. "Did it hurt?" She touched each part that made up the crescent shape, every lavender circle and ended on the black upside-down triangle.

"Incredibly. When we get our tattoos, we must start with a clean slate. Our skin is burned where we choose to get it until it turns to ash." Theodore held her hand to it. "Then, after several days, new skin forms and our bandages are removed. We must create the tattoo ourselves with a takthorn spike and inks from plants in the Sea of Calip. It takes days to create the entire tattoo. It's mostly a solitary event, and one that I've never regretted, strangely enough."

Audrey mouthed, "Wow."

"I know... but you're pantless, and I'm"—Theodore moved his hand in a presenting manner up and down his chest—"topless. Shall we finish what we started?"

"If you don't, someone else will."

Theodore gasped at her jokingly. "We can't have that, can we?"

Audrey put her hands softly on his cheeks, kissing his lips. Theodore unbuttoned his pants and kicked them off as they stood on their knees. He moved down to her neck. Audrey pulled her shirt off, unclasped her bra, letting it fall, and pushed Theodore towards the headboard. He sat down, and Audrey straddled him.

Fragrant smells floated in from the garden, as if the walls of the room had left and the bed was covered in blooms and waving grasses. Audrey held the top of the headboard as her body grinded on his. Theodore's hands clenched her hips, his mouth parted.

Audrey slid her hand down and slipped her tongue into Theodore's mouth as she moved faster atop him. His mouth moved to her breasts. She closed her eyes, biting her lip and tilting her head back. As a symphony, they moved through the refrain with feverish lust until Audrey collapsed with a wide grin and the outro completed. Theodore brushed her hair with his hand as her head lay on his chest.

He smiled at first, but then his thoughts floated out the window. "Don't go."

Audrey tweaked her head. "I generally only leave after sex when it's really bad, but I can make an exception."

"No, I mean stay out of the war," he said with desperate seriousness. "I can hide you somewhere."

Audrey sat up. "I am fighting alongside you."

"I have this feeling deep in my gut... and it's not good for either of us." Theodore sat on the side of the bed, his feet touching the floor.

"We are all having bad feelings. This situation is an infestation that never leaves my mind, but I know that we"—Audrey moved behind him and placed her arms around him—"will get through this. It has to be done, and you need to leave." Theodore gazed into her eyes, and Audrey felt a tinge of tears waking. "Go."

Theodore put his hand behind her neck and kissed her passionately before clothing himself. Audrey watched every movement with a bittersweet feeling. "I love you," he said, lingering at the door.

"I love you."

Theodore closed the door and ran back downstairs.

Audrey fell back onto the bed, staring up at the ceiling. Cobwebs rippled faintly from the open window. She fixated on them as her heart sank and tears streamed down her temples, wetting her hair.

Someone knocked on the bedroom door, and Audrey wiped her tears and abruptly sat up.

"Audrey? Can I come in?"

Audrey looked at the door, as if she could be seen and her stare was enough of an answer. "Fine."

Ben opened the door partway and peeked his head around. "Morrow and I cooked dinner, if you're hungry."

"I'm fucking starving." Audrey pushed herself off the bed, opened the door the rest of the way and started down the stairs. "And don't think I didn't hear the part that you and Morrow were doing things together."

Ben followed. "Last I checked, we've cooked together too."

Audrey peered over her shoulder at him. "You know that wasn't the same. It's okay if you like Morrow. Just don't tell me any gory details."

"You're one to talk; we could hear everything."

Audrey smacked Ben's stomach with the back of her hand. "It's not my fault the walls are thin. And I deserve it."

"I didn't say you didn't."

The smell of cooked meat with wild herbs greeted them on the last few steps. Morrow busily worked to plate up for everyone. "Sounded like one hell of an orgasm."

"Fuck off. But yes, yes it was." Audrey stared up in a daydream.

"Good for you. Honey and I made dinner, though don't get too comfortable." Morrow set down a plate in front of the seat Audrey took. "We will be training again tonight. I received something from Bruthren." Morrow reached into her bright pink and black embroidered apron. She spun the letter around in her fingers and sat down.

"What does it say?"

A smile tugged at Morrow's lips, her face somber. "The Choke's big debut has arrived. Are you ready to get bloody?"

Audrey held her fork in her mouth with meat hanging off it. Ben tapped his leg.

Morrow ate, with her hands and elbows on the table. She clicked her tongue. "It's not all doom and gloom. I have no intention of ending up in the waters with the depths. And neither are you two." She pointed to them with her hands full of food. "Eat up before I drag you out for one of your last trainings. Maybe my honey will cast magic finally."

The night lasted into the morning, though even with the dawn emerging, the darkness felt thick as tar around them.

36

Chilling snowflakes dusted the ground and stuck on Cursed Knights' armor as they marched or rode upon a chackle to Nilhorn. Theodore ordered them to continue through the dead of night to catch up to Bruthren or risk freezing. Climbing through the treacherous Thornyarch Mountains made for grievous tales. One that Theodore refused to exist as.

The previous days after leaving the grayden had moved as swiftly as a bee, and now the memories of better days lurked above them like money on a hook, if only they could catch it.

Theodore brushed off the snow that gathered on Tarmist's head. "Be steady," he said to him. White covered Theodore's stiff dark hair, and drips ran down under his crown onto the tips. Snow tunneled down in flashes.

Something shined ten chackles away up higher than they were.

"*Fire*," a knight called back.

"Lead us to it. It must be Nilhorn." Theodore turned Tarmist to the side. "Rest is in sight; do not slow your heavy feet just yet," he yelled to those behind him.

The passing of time brought the smell of roasted meat and herbs as they journeyed up the steep passage to

Nilhorn. Theodore slid off Tarmist and wrapped his reins around his hand, leading him close behind.

Boulders the size of two-story houses were hollowed out everywhere you looked. In between the buildings were scattered trees with fawning branches with snow dust and the forming of icicles at the tips. Too many flurries made it difficult to see much of the town except for orbs of light, like stars that lighted the houses. The rest of the ground disappeared beneath the white. One door opened, and Bruthren stepped out.

"No heads missing or knights hanging from the cliffs?"

"As far as I can tell, we've all survived," Theodore said as he followed inside for warmth. Bruthren directed some knights to stay in the house and others to head for another one nearby where they could fit. "Is all the food eaten?"

"We've saved enough for your empty bellies, though I am surprised." Bruthren shut the door just as his glasses fogged. He took them off and rubbed them with a cloth. The knights inside took to the floor and bowed once they saw Theodore standing amongst them.

The house had curved walls like giant hagstones and windows that only a head or two could fill up in space. The windows had a perfectly cut circle of bark that could unlatch to peer out, and surprisingly, only a small pocket on them whistled with the presence of wind. Rugs covered the entire floor, and the ceiling hung so high that a sea glass chandelier could illuminate each room on the bottom floor if all doors hung ajar. Cooked meats covered all the counters in the kitchen, and a line of knights stood at the archway to it. A few of the knights worked to serve everyone.

Bruthren snuck ahead and returned with a plate of food for Theodore.

"I could have waited in line."

"Your modesty astounds me. I can't have you hungry and weak."

Theodore sat on a bench that had an embroidered cushion of crashing waves. Three benches lined a wall, and in between each one was a small wood table. Against one wall was a large black cabinet. Theodore ate with his plate on his lap. He stared at all the crimson eyes around him and all the dozens of helmets stranded on the floor or atop tables. He could see faintly into another room that looked to have a bed. Some knights sat on the floor against walls, and their bodies soon warmed enough for banter.

Bruthren shooed away the knight sitting next to Theodore and took their spot. He stretched his legs out and crossed them, as if he hoped to trip someone. "How were they?"

Theodore chewed and swallowed. He ate another bite and said, "Alive."

"Well... nothing to worry about, then. I told you they would be safe."

"Your idea of safe is caging a bird only to release it to a finnix. Their safety is temporary."

"As is all of ours. They wanted to stay. I find that when we see the true fighter in someone"—Bruthren's eyes lit up and his body shivered—"it can be most alluring."

Theodore cocked his head. "Alluring? Are you imagining Ben and Audrey as alluring?"

Bruthren clicked his tongue. "Not them, of course. You will see. When the snow clears, we will change the course of Folengower."

"Are you ready for it all? Even if it looks different from what you pictured?"

"I have planned this for such lengths that the image in my head has morphed with time; after all, this dream is built by many and my mind can only fit so much."

Theodore tensed as a chill ran down his spine. "How long has it been snowing?"

"When we made it to the mountain, flurries started, but we escaped the worst of it."

"Where's my father?"

Some knights clapped and laughed about something loudly.

"He's in the tovlin's home. It's the biggest. I did ask if he wanted to stay in one of the inns or other business buildings and I could have a bed made, but he declined." Bruthren rolled his eyes.

"Everyone safely evacuated, then?"

"Yes, for now." Bruthren reached his hand down and let a spider crawl atop his knuckles. He held it up to his face curiously before placing his hand against the wall behind him. Theodore didn't even notice. Not as he chewed away. When it crawled away he said, "I believe they are still heading to Nniar Castle. Chant left first, since they are the closest to Amarda's camp, then Nilhorn and Corling.

The other knights have taken over the other towns and are awaiting our orders by bird, but none of that is of concern."

Theodore raised his right eyebrow, holding a chunk of meat in his hand. "What concerns should I have?"

"Korrigan may squander some plans"—Bruthren bobbed his head—"but I just may let him follow through. It could make things easier for us. There are too many eyes in one space to say more."

"Is there somewhere else we can discuss this, then?"

"Rest... spend time amongst the knights. Tomorrow, we will find somewhere to go."

Theodore finished eating without continuing the conversation.

The treacherous weather continued for several days without much change, but even the snow knew it would be lost from time eventually. Theodore stepped outside and took a deep breath in, grateful to feel the wisps of snow fall on his cheek after being crammed inside the house for far too long. A group of knights stood in the city square next to a massive rock sculpture depicting a creature with many eyes amongst rushing waves. Theodore assumed it was representing the stories of the depths. The knights had a flickering fire and warm drinks in their hands.

Hargrove stood from the fire and ordered something to the two knights. Theodore watched the knights head over to him before stopping on either side of him. Specks of white became the passing of clear skies and the journey of the clouds to move on.

"Is there something I should know, or have you come to protect me?"

"Protection, Ancient One," they said in unison.

Spirit wings raced just past Theodore's face up to the slits of sunlight. Even the knights' gazes followed them, stripes of sun cast on their faces. Theodore blinked slowly, enjoying the warmth on his face.

"The weather turns while we prepare to burn," Bruthren said, joining their gaze towards the sky. "Korrigan would like a word with his son."

"You were in a meeting for a long time with him this morning." Theodore crossed his arms.

"Your observational skills are greater than the moon."

Theodore narrowed his eyes at him. "What was it about?"

"What it's always about." Bruthren turned to walk away. He waved for Theodore to follow.

Theodore sauntered behind him. The knights moved at a slower pace behind him. Bruthren led them to the tallest and largest home beyond the quaint shops and restaurants that still smelt of food as they walked past. The path to the homes beyond was being cleared of snow by knights who placed their hands above it and melted it with a fiery light, their feet crunching as they stepped on the remaining snow.

Ice-packed snow created short fences that stood up to Theodore's waist. The staircase was made of wood and rock mixed with a pale pink cement-like paste. The first steps led to a porch and then spiraled around the side of the house and up to a tower where a side door could be seen if you happened to be looking just right. Ice chandeliers hung on to the curved banister. Water droplets pattered against the lower steps, creating a beat with each drip.

Theodore grabbed the smooth black railing, careful with his movements to not slip. Bruthren cared not to grab the railing, and he slid on each step with a child-like smile. Three knights stood on one side of the door and three more on the other, standing in full armor and looking like hell. All of them had red or pink cheeks from the night's cold. Their bodies were stiff, but every now and again, chills came and shook them from their serious stature. Theodore stood at the doors.

"Please get them something warm to eat and drink. Surely we can put new knights at this post for now," Theodore said to the knights who came with him. One of them nodded and turned back towards the town.

Bruthren directed the other knight to gather more to relieve the knights in front of them and then knocked on the door.

The door swung open by Lore's hands. He stood looking more frail than usual, with a blanket wrapped around him that was pinned with a jeweled corpse thistle. "We've been waiting for you."

Theodore tried his hardest not to glare at him but briefly did so anyway. Lavish seating with shimmering threads, and enchanting chandeliers that had long, thin strands of glass as if a meadow flowed in the wind made up the downstairs, with art covering its grand walls. An inviting kitchen that Theodore only glimpsed was around the corner from them.

Korrigan was sitting on the couch, and in front of him on the coffee table was a map of Nniar. Lore sat down next to him. Knights stood at the frames of the halls and some sat at the table in the kitchen playing a game with nut shells, pebbles and bird bones. Theodore sat down across from Korrigan on the only patchwork chair that seemed out of place for the rest of the room.

"Now that the sun is well with us, we must make a move. Lore and I have spoken about diversions. Where's Hargrove?"

"A diversion of what sort?" Theodore asked.

Bruthren stood and hollered out the door for Hargrove.

"We want to invade the mountainside they're on, but as Lore and I have discussed, they pose a greater risk to us without a plan of secrecy. I want them weak. How would we do that?"

"Send the fighters away," Bruthren said, standing next to Theodore.

"That would need to be more than a diversion. How would we do that?"

"I have a few ideas." Bruthren leaned back and gazed out the window. It sounded like rain beating down as the snow continued to melt. Hargrove charged up the walkway.

"Have you managed to replicate a curse for Eltrist like the knights yet? We could capture one and use that to force the others to follow its lead," Lore said.

"I have, but I have no way of testing it. It could work if we can get one alone to do so and see what becomes of it."

"Couldn't we just send knights to all sides of the mountain they are on? Slowly, of course. We must outnumber them. They would struggle to fight each side with so many not able to fight," Theodore said.

"There are more than you think. We shouldn't underestimate their wings. Look at the Anorphus. We still have knights and workers pushing the bodies to the depths and even through portals to not anger the number of souls forced into the depths."

"Through portals? You mean to Earth?"

Hargrove walked in and bowed to Korrigan.

"No, of course not. At least not all of them, but some. You know the depths detest wars and plagues. Remember the last war..." Korrigan said to Lore.

Lore scratched his chin, pulling on his thin skin, nodding. "We had to have sent at least a few thousand through different portals then."

Theodore's eyes were wide, and his mouth struggled to shut.

Korrigan stared at Theodore. "We always send someone after to clean it up and to hush those who wish to speak about it."

Bruthren chimed in, "I will see about capturing an Eltrist or sending them away. Hargrove, do you have a plan to distract them?"

As she was about to speak, Lore cut in. "What about sending them to the castle, and when they leave, we take over their camp and keep the prisoners until their return?

They will have to bow to you then unless they want to witness a mass slaughtering."

Korrigan clasped his hands together and held them under his chin. His eyes stared at the ceiling, dancing from one side to the other. "Fine, send them off to the castle. Warn Agden about it. I wouldn't want her dying... she's much more favored than me."

Theodore tapped his foot. The room quieted around them. "That's what you care about? You wouldn't care if she died because you love her? Only for what gains she provides you?"

"Worrying about love in a time of war is like remembering to dust the top of cabinets. I can't have your mind concentrating on dust. We are ending this war... with or without you. Now, unless you have something to add to win, quiet," Korrigan said through gritted teeth.

Theodore squeezed his hands together at his side.

Bruthren nodded his head down subtly. "It will be difficult to make this happen, but not impossible. Hargrove and I can coordinate the plan."

"A few days too many could crush us," Lore warned.

"The snow is still melting; their camp must be suffering just as we were. Trust me."

"The moon talks when we sleep—do not let her befriend the Eltrists then. It will be you gutted if we miss our opportunity. Grab your things, Theodore and Bruthren. You will be staying here instead. I've had a work area set up for you upstairs, and, Theodore, you have a room to stay in as well. I can't have the folks talking as if I've cast out my son." Korrigan slouched, sitting on the edge of the couch.

Theodore and Bruthren stood to leave.

"And, Theodore, if you are to bear the Ancient One's mark, start acting like it, or I will cut it from you and feed it to the chackles."

Surprising to everyone, Theodore said, "I will."

Hargrove led them back through the town. The campfires dwindled to soot while the knights wandered around without their helmets. High spirits became infectious to all around. Theodore opened the door to their previous residence and grabbed the few things belonging to him. Bruthren took his time rummaging around until finally he held three bags. The house was empty of knights, as they all were basking in the sun. Hargrove returned to her dwelling.

"How do you plan to send everyone away?" Theodore asked.

"Our good friend Kalien," Bruthren said as he peeked inside a cabinet.

"Kalien? What could he possibly do?"

"Have you forgotten he has a vision meld? I can have him contact Thorn and tell them to attack the castle, then we can move on to their camp."

"But when do"—Theodore peered over his shoulder—"we get involved?"

"Tricky business, but the plan is all on you. You are the only one who can listen to the Eltrist anytime you want, and with that you can force them to listen to you."

"You are hoping they will just end the war?"

"I wouldn't be that naïve. No... I want you to get a meeting with Talkun. I hear he is wanting of our cause. The Choke will be joining the fight no matter what happens in this next battle. I want to hold off on the capturing of Eltrists for as long as possible. I find that when you use curses against someone, trust is further than the ends of the seas."

"You actually created it, then?"

"It really could be used on anyone, but yes, I believe it would work, though I never planned on using it unless things took a new turn."

"Like if Kinsington takes over and forces everyone not from Amarda to suffer for my father's wrongs?"

Bruthren slid his glasses back onto his nose. "Exactly. We have two vengeful leaders."

"Sending them to the castle still puts a lot of folks in danger."

"I can't fix every problem. We are in a war, and it will smell, taste, hear, see and feel like one whether we like it or not. I assume they will figure out soon enough that the knights are few and head back to their camp before too much damage is done."

"Then after you send a message to Kalien, I will find Talkun and see what I can do. I imagine he will stay hidden away from the fighting for now. He is their secret weapon."

"If he will side with us, I believe the war will end victoriously for us."

"What will you tell Hargrove?"

"Leave that to me. She will follow my suggestion."

Later, they returned to the new dwelling. A goling leapt towards Theodore with a tray full of tea and plumplings. Theodore gladly took one of each. Another servant with fair skin and long dark red hair bowed to Theodore, grabbed his bags and headed upstairs to the other rooms. Bruthren had another servant try to take his things, but he shooed the man away.

Theodore searched downstairs for Korrigan or Lore, but they were nowhere to be found. He took to the stairs and instead found where the servant had left his things.

"Is there anything else you need, Ancient One?"

"Have you seen where my father has gone?"

"I usually am not the one to take care of his requests, but I can find out."

"No, that will be all."

She drooped her head as if she had failed him and left.

The room was quaint compared to the rest of the house. Theodore lay on the stiff brown covers and wrapped himself in them. He stared at the ceiling, wishing he could see the painting of the forest, like he had in his room at the castle. His wishing soon faded to only a bath, and luckily, he had his own.

The bathroom hardly fit the wooden tub, glazed with a sea blue stain. Theodore turned the water on. The steam filled the room within seconds and covered the oval mirror in film. Theodore stepped in and slid down. His legs curved up to the other side, and his calves downwards dangled out. A basket hung over the side with sponges and bars of soap for washing. Theodore massaged soap into a sponge and lathered it onto his neck and chest. He paused at the sound of footsteps and then there was a knock on the door.

"What is it?"

Bruthren opened the door. "I've received word that a meeting with Talkun is possible."

Theodore rested his head back. "From who? When?"

"It doesn't matter. We need to leave tonight. Don't dwell too long in here."

"You cannot tell me who?" Theodore rubbed soap over his arms. His teeth clenched.

"Am I sensing ungratefulness? Because last I checked, you had no army without me. And—"

"Ungrateful is not what I would call it. I'm just angry. Angry at everything. My tongue reeks of it. It has since I returned from Harthsburg and it's only heightened. I am grateful for seeing what I failed to do."

Bruthren held his hands behind his back. His glasses were as fogged as the mirror, but he left them. "Good." Theodore cocked his head to him and squeezed the sponge. A puff of tiny bubbles seeped out. "I want that fire to burn as hot as the sun and as poisonous as a corpse thistle. It will subside when the war is over, but for now, use it. Soon, you will be the face of a united Folengower. I keep secrets to protect you or them." Bruthren dropped to his knees and wrapped an arm around Theodore, uncaring of the water or soap soaking his arm. He took his glasses off and held them out in front of him as he painted a picture with his words. "Imagine the kingdom whole. Statues will be built in your honor. Folks will faun over the Ancient One who restored the balance of our existence."

"I don't want any of that. And I am already fawned over." Theodore joked. "My thoughts cannot make it that far in the future, and wouldn't you want to have a statue?" he said with his eyebrow raised.

"No statues for me; I prefer to lurk in the shadows. The future is here. I have a feeling this next fight will be the end of it. I am never wrong about these things."

"When is the meeting?" Theodore rubbed the sponge down his legs.

"Whenever we arrive. We must race."

"How are we to leave without raising suspicion?"

Bruthren pretended to yawn. "Boring things, I promise. I have already taken care of it."

"And what of Kalien?"

"We have notified him of his new task. It's only a matter of time before I hear the exciting news and we join in battle."

"Then let me enjoy one last thing before I'm caked in blood and mud."

Bruthren stood and bowed before shutting the bathroom door.

Theodore wrapped his arms around himself, he gazed into the soapy water with downcast eyes. His finger traced the tattoo on his chest before splashing the image of himself into ripples. He washed his hair that almost reached past his shoulders and scrubbed his face, feeling his facial hair taking over. He rinsed off the soap and reached down for a towel that was rolled on a slab of wood.

He stared at himself in the mirror with his towel wrapped around his waist. His body bore more muscle than before, and his face was harsh. Harsher than he wanted. He turned away from himself and exited to the bedroom. Clean clothes were laid out on the bed with his armor beside it. Black cuffed pants with a seafoam green embroidery at the bottom of the waistband, the tunic jet black. He placed each one on and then his web-like armor. His sword and sheath rested atop the dresser with his belt, and his crown sat on the nightstand.

When he adorned it all, he stood tall with his head raised. His blueish gray eyes stood out from the darkness of his hair and clothing. He may not have crimson eyes, but they were the storm, and he was the commander of its reaping.

Theodore walked with grace down the steps. Bruthren stood off to the side, speaking with Hargrove.

"There he is." Hargrove peered over her shoulder and bowed quickly.

"Hargrove thinks it would be best if she came along." Bruthren ran his finger along his neck as Hargrove stared at Theodore.

"Come... why?"

"I am the leader of this army; I should be present if you are to capture an Eltrist."

"That is why you need to stay here. We are taking knights with us, but you are too important to take on such a quest. I will not allow another leader to be murdered, as Glaslin was. I order you to organize the troops for our imminent call."

Hargrove opened her mouth to say something, but Theodore cut her off. "Your task is too important to leave behind the knights that will be counting on your orders. Polt will be coming with us, and he will, by the shadow of his feathers, return no matter the consequences."

Hargrove placed her hand on the hilt of her sword. Her nostrils flared for a moment. "If I do not hear from Polt in three sunrises, the entire army will be behind me."

Theodore nodded. "As they should."

Hargrove stomped out of the house. "Have you discussed all this with Korrigan?"

"Why do you always assume I do things without thought?"

"I didn't suggest that..."

"Korrigan knows all there is to. He even left a gift for our journey," Bruthren said.

"And what's that?"

"The gift of surprise."

Theodore frowned. "Are our bags packed?"

"Everything we need." Bruthren grabbed two bags from the floor and patted them.

"Let's go. I want to be far from here before the night eats the sun."

Tarmist waited outside, licking at the ground and biting at any fungi he found. His honey eyes gazed at Theodore as he munched on his find. A servant followed them outside with their bags and attached one to Tarmist and the other to Bruthren's chackle. A pack of knights on chackles waited still as the dead.

Theodore climbed atop Tarmist. He lowered his head to Tarmist's ear. "Ride with strength and bravery, my friend. Death waits beyond those hills, but not for us. *Halko.*"

37

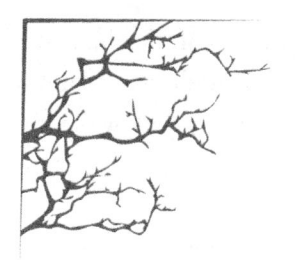

Dreamy clouds drenched in the sun's goodness glazed the sky with color on Elderberry Lane. Since Eliza, Ben and Audrey had vanished through her pond, life on the desolate road felt chillingly calm, yet several rooms felt haunted by their memories. Taylor sat out on the porch, with a mug in her hand. Her candy-apple red boots peeked out from under her long flowy black dress. Steam danced on her lips as they rested on the rim of her mug. She breathed in the strong notes of roasted almonds and sweet toffee and grinned. Her eyes darted beyond her mug at the sound of tires crunching on the rocky dirt road. Taylor crossed her legs and let out a groan at the silver car that came bustling up to her house.

"He's not back yet," Taylor shouted.

Gwen slammed the door. "Did you check the pond?"

"You could have just called." Taylor took a sip of her coffee and set it down on the table next to her. "I'm gonna need something stronger," she said under her breath.

"What was that?" Gwen thumped up the steps.

"Would you like a mimosa? Apparently, I will be taking up morning drinking again."

Gwen rolled her eyes. "If you're making one, I guess it would be rude to say no."

Taylor smacked her lips together, as if she had just applied her lipstick. A new row of dandelions sprouted through the slits in her porch with their yellow heads. Taylor squished one as she walked past Gwen to her front door. Gwen followed.

"How many times are you going to stop by looking for Ben? I told you I would call you if he was here. Why don't you take his car with you? I can tow it."

"He will need it when he returns."

Taylor stopped at the kitchen and turned on her heel. "What if he never returns?"

"Of course he will, and the least you can do is let his car stay here."

"The least? Then why do you keep showing up?"

"If I trusted you, I wouldn't have to. You've already lied to me before."

Taylor opened the fridge and shook a jug of orange juice that sounded nearly empty. She reached for a bottle of wine, glasses and Grand Marnier. She poured the orange juice into a glass and then lazily poured wine and Grand Marnier in. She stirred it and drank it.

"Sorry, hun, no more orange juice. Wine?" Taylor shook the wine bottle.

"I'm just going to check the pond."

"How many times are you going to check it before you stop coming to my home?"

"As many as I need."

Taylor slouched her head to the counter. "Gwen, Gwen, Gwen, you know I have to hand it to you. You are persistent."

"If I wasn't, I wouldn't have even known Ben left." Gwen snatched the wine bottle, poured it into a glass and took a swig. She made a sour face. "I've never cared for wine."

Taylor stood up. "Then why the hell are you drinking it?"

"Same reason you are."

"I thought you were going to the pond." Taylor swished her glass.

"I am." Gwen charged to the back door and walked out and down the steps. Tall grass consumed the ground and out to as far as she could see. Sunrays lit the tops of foxtails as if made of gold. Even the path that she had stomped over last time had resurrected, with only a few patches unrecoverable. She trudged through, forcing down what she could with her shoes. Grasshoppers bounced in every direction but hers, and other insects followed suit.

She neared the pond, but as she stepped forward, her foot lingered in the air and her arm covered her nose. Her stomach churned, and she peered back at the house. Taylor stood at the door frame and held up her wineglass as if to cheers her. Gwen's eyes bulged and her mouth filled with vomit. Her hand cupped over her mouth, but it wasn't enough to prevent the contents from escaping.

Taylor lowered her glass and frowned. "Everything alright?"

"No, it smells like something rotting out here." Gwen wiped her mouth with her sleeve.

Taylor walked down through the grass to her. "Oh... son of a bitch." She covered her nose. "That is foul. Something obviously died back here."

Gwen continued forward slowly, with Taylor almost touching her. Flies buzzed around and landed on them. Their hands moved to swat them until they made it to the pond. Gwen retched onto the ground again. Taylor blinked, as if that would make what she was seeing disappear.

Strug filled the pond in its lavender gelatin glow. A Cursed Knight stood with his waist in the strug. His skin touching the strug bubbled and popped, and he sank just half an inch more. There were bruises around his crimson eyes, and his jaw sagged. Flies flitted to him, landing on his tongue, but he wasn't the only one. At least ten other bodies floated in the pond, either as only a skeleton or with bits of flesh melted like the knight.

A woman's head and an unattached hand bobbed gently on the surface. Blood dripped onto the top of the strug and rested as if it were on ice. Taylor stepped closer and leaned over to peer in.

"Are any of them Ben?" Gwen said with a quivering voice.

"It's hard to tell, but no obvious sign of him." Taylor gagged.

Skulls poked out of the surface with bits of hair, and a sword stuck out with a skeletal hand still attached. None of the bits of bones or clothes suggested Ben, and for that, Gwen felt an ounce of relief.

"Who are all these people, then? What would they be doing here?"

"I don't know." Taylor shook her head, with her shirt pulled up over her nose.

Gwen crept closer to see for herself that there was no sign of Ben. "Look at that one's eyes. What caused that?" Gwen wrinkled her nose at the Cursed Knight and stepped back quickly, not wanting to see any more.

"Maybe they have red eyes in Folengower? This makes no sense. Unless they are trying to keep us away from the portal."

"Why would anyone do that? We can't even go through it." Gwen choked back tears.

"They were heading into a war, but this is only a couple handful of people."

"For now." Gwen placed her hands on each of her cheeks. "Oh, God. Soon you might have this entire field covered in their dead."

Taylor grabbed Gwen's arm and charged back to the house as Gwen repeatedly tried to pull her arm free.

"Let go of me."

"Why? So you can puke more? He's not in that pile, and I don't plan on sticking around to see who else comes through the portal."

Gwen relaxed her shoulders and followed Taylor back up the steps and into the house. Taylor moved Gwen out of the way and locked the door. For the first time, Gwen saw terror in her eyes. Something she imagined mirrored in her own.

"Does this mean those creatures are coming here like they did to Harthsburg?" Gwen said, almost out of breath.

Taylor pulled curtains shut, going from one to the next and even heading down the hall into the bedrooms to do the same. Gwen stood with her back against the wall, unable to do much else. Taylor returned with an antique gun with silver filigree. Gwen restrained from laughing.

"What do you plan to do with that?"

"Kill anything that tries to get in here, obviously. I don't see you with any weapons to protect us." Taylor scooted a chair over to the sliding glass door and pushed a sliver of the curtain aside.

"No, I don't have anything but some pepper spray in my purse, which might be better than that thing. Does it even work? It looks like you stole it from a museum." Gwen wrinkled her nose and pointed to the gun. "Anyway, I thought you could do magic."

Taylor fumed and stared at her. "Will you shut up? My magic died with Wyatt's death. This is serious shit, and I plan on *surviving* again. Now, either you help me or go the fuck back home."

Gwen raised her hands in front of her in surrender. "I couldn't leave you behind. Not after seeing all that. All of them were dead, so at least we have that. Maybe it was a mistake that they came through?"

"Nothing with them ever seems like a mistake. Go over to the other window and keep an eye out."

Gwen walked to the window and peered into the backyard. She jumped when the breeze moved the tall grass.

"Settle down over there."

"You're not the only one who is scared. My son could be in there. We should call for help."

"Help?" Taylor spit out a single sharp laugh. "No one can know about this. The second cops show up here, they would be pissing their pants with fear. And what story are we meant to tell them?" She paused. Her body stiffened as she listened. "Shhh, I think I hear something."

Taylor and Gwen stayed glued to the windows, mostly huddled behind a curtain, for hours. Somewhere in between, Taylor dosed off slowly, her gun dropping onto the floor, and Gwen slumped snoring in her chair shortly after.

With the sun high in the sky, it shined into the window onto Gwen's face. She covered her face with her arm the best she could, but the light stayed. She slowly opened her eyes and noticed Taylor. As if everything came back to her, she shot up. "*Taylor*, wake up."

Taylor groggily mumbled what sounded like nonsense to Gwen. Gwen got up and shook her shoulder firmly. Taylor burped, a stench of alcohol momentarily wafting into Gwen's face.

"Ugh," Gwen said with her upper lip pulled up. "We fell asleep."

"Shit." Taylor's eyes widened as she pushed herself to the edge of her seat and scanned the yard. "It's your fault."

"My fault? You fell asleep before I did."

"Yes, your fault." Taylor spit each word like a bazooka. "You had to come over here and now I will never be able to go to the back of my property."

"Last I checked, you were working with the people from there. It sounds like you dug that grave yourself."

"Working with is a bit of an exaggeration." Taylor scanned her yard quicker now, eyes seemingly bored of not seeing anything new. "What do we do now?"

"We could keep staring out the window, expecting something to come out and kill us, or we could eat."

"Mrs. Drewitt, you really are something. Fine... let me raid my pantries." Taylor picked up the gun and left it on the dining room table, then walked to the kitchen. "At some point, you will need to leave my house. I refuse to become your housewife."

"I'm the only one that has ever been a housewife, so if anything, you should be hoping I retire to help you."

Taylor chuckled. "Harper did like your wit." She held open a pantry, and her laughter faded. A bit of sadness drained the shine from her eyes.

"Harper loved everything about me." Gwen smirked.

"He did."

"I know he cared deeply for you, even if it didn't end up the way you wanted."

"No, I chose my path, and so did he. I bet he would have never expected us to be holed up in my house together. Could you imagine his face?"

"He would have been so confused." Gwen keeled over with laughter. "I can see it now."

Taylor couldn't help but laugh along with her. "I can see it too. Alright, enough of this. I have bread." She placed the loaf on the counter. "And turkey and cheese in the fridge."

"Perfect."

Gwen made both sandwiches, and when they finished, they sat in the living room.

Gwen uncrossed her legs and sighed. "Well, maybe I should leave. I'm not sure I want to find out what's going on with the portal."

"Yes, I guess you—"

Both ladies turned completely silent and exchanged a look of fright as loud footsteps sounded in the backyard.

"What is that?" Gwen grabbed her purse from next to her and reached in for the pepper spray. She held it out in front of them. Taylor stood up behind her. "You look out the window."

"You're in front; you do it."

Gwen rolled her eyes, but she crept to the window and pulled back the smallest part to look out. She gasped and dropped to the floor. Taylor grabbed at her but froze in her standing position.

The door rattled.

"*Go away*," Taylor yelled, stepping over Gwen's body and making it the few feet to her gun. She snatched it off the table, staying low to the floor, and looked out the bottom of the curtain. Goosebumps covered her skin, and her face flushed.

Midnight black boots laced in a carf-flower cord stood just on the other side. Further up, she could see black pants with embroidery on one side. Taylor's gaze followed past the armor and to crimson eyes. She barely noticed the helmet atop his head as she fixated on his eyes. Her hand covered her mouth to not scream.

Gwen finally came to, and for a second, she shook her head as if she couldn't remember what she had seen until she rested her hand on her racing heart. Taylor placed a finger on her lips to quiet her, but she never turned away. The knight hit the glass, rattling the frame.

"If I wanted, I could break the glass to come through, though I would prefer you answer me instead. I dare not draw my sword or use my magic." The knight pounded on the door. "Do not waste my time."

"What should I do?" Taylor mouthed to Gwen.

"Just let him in."

Taylor stood from her crouching position, her hand shaking as she unlocked the door. She ran to the back of the room, and Gwen crawled to the couch.

The Cursed Knight jolted the door open and stepped inside. He had a scar under his right eye, short ashy hair and golden-brown skin. The knight looked around the room. "It's my first time on Earthen land. If I say anything wrong, I swear to the moon, I am no cursed scum."

"Why are you here?"

"Did Ben send you?"

The knight's forehead wrinkled. "Ben? I do not know of a Ben. I understand that you know about the portal back there?"

Taylor nodded.

"You will see more bodies for some time. I cannot give you an exact day of when the bodies will stop coming—"

"My yard will be full of bodies. I want them all gone... *now*!"

"Lower your voice, or your yelling will be the last thing anyone hears from you." With heavy strides, the knight made his way to Taylor. "We will compensate your sacrifices when the war has ended." He reached into a pouch on his belt and pulled out a vial. "I wasn't expecting two Earthborns to be here. Praise the moon, I have more."

"More of what?" Gwen said softly. Her eyes squinted, as if she thought he would strike her down.

"Potion. This will make you forget. I advise you to take it only when the bodies stop coming."

"What am I supposed to do with the ones that are there?"

"The strug will break them down. I will be back with others to collect the strug."

"How is Eliza? The Bloodtress?"

"I cannot tell you such things. She is protected as a member of the Ancient Ones by Cursed Knights, like me. Folengower is not your concern." The knight's lip curled. "Take the potion when the bodies stop coming. You will forget about all of this and continue with your life."

"What will my compensation be?"

"That will depend on who reigns victorious."

"If the Ancient Ones win?"

"You will be gifted a small fortune." The knight turned to leave.

"Wait." Gwen placed her hand on his arm. He grunted at her. "Is there a way for you to send a message to someone in Folengower?"

"Do you not have birds here?"

"Yes, why?"

"Use your bird to travel to Folengower with your message."

Gwen went quiet for a second, trying to work out exactly which random bird from the sky could possibly be hers. "Can I just give you a letter to give to someone?"

"Do I look like a bird? I have no feathers, no way of flying or a beak," he said dryly. "Don't forget to take the potion."

The knight handed one to each of them, then vanished out of the house and back to Folengower. Gwen and Taylor sat together on the floor, unable to say a word as they stared at their vials.

Gwen breathed out. "I don't know if I want to forget."

Taylor shot her a look. "Why the hell not?"

"What if it makes me forget where Ben is?"

"Then you should definitely take it and stop showing up here."

"What will you do without me? I may not be who you want here, but at least you aren't alone."

Taylor clenched her teeth. "I will never admit to that."

Over the next few weeks, Elderberry Lane was as foul as a butcher shop. Gwen thought it best to buy a heap of mint plants and lavender to drown out the stench, but nothing can hide the smell of rotting bodies.

38

All over Nniar, below the surface in the company of soil and harmony spores, The Choke members worked tirelessly as the impending battle loomed over their heads. Carts of dead magic went out as quickly as it reanimated, and they all headed to the Thornyarch Mountains in secret.

Chackles led the carts to different locations inside the mountain, and the riders appeared to be selling food. They left just before the sun rose and before most of Folengower bloomed to greet the shine.

Kalien tossed a sack of dead magic ripe for using into the cart just outside the grayden in the Finnix forest. The bottles clanked together. A row of carts nearly ready to leave were on either side of him.

"Careful, we can't have them breaking." Camis glowered and kicked her hoof on the ground.

"I'm trying," he said, void of emotion. He placed the next sack down gentler. He inhaled the fresh air and his shoulders relaxed.

Camis eyed him, uncrossed her arms and left.

Kalien spent the entire morning loading carts with hundreds of other folks moving like machines. He fumbled for another bag that the folk behind him tossed to him. His arms felt heavy and too sore to continue, but there was no time to waste. Periodically folks barged in and out of the grayden with more sacks of dead magic.

"Kalien, where are you?"

Kalien stared around for the voice.

Rew leapt through the lines of workers. "I need to find Kalien. Do you know him?" he asked someone.

"I'm Kalien," he said as he loaded another sack into a nearly full cart.

Rew dashed over to him. "This line, move up. I need to borrow him."

The workers adjusted the line without Kalien.

"What is it?"

Rew pushed him forward by his shoulder. They stopped at a massive tree covered in vines. "Bruthren has sent a letter for you to contact Thorn."

"Now?"

Rew nodded. "You are to lead her army to the castle at once."

"The castle? And how am I supposed to accomplish that?"

"Tell her that the castle is weak and the knights are busy tending to the evacuated towns. It would be a painless end to the war."

"And what if she asks where I am?" Kalien held his hands out and spun. "Since there is no castle in sight. Unless I'm missing something."

"The mind can be fooled. We have a few Cursed Knights here, and they will suffice to give the illusion that all is true."

"How lucky I am," Kalien said under his breath. "Place me where you want me to spin this tale."

"Go right over there. Deeper in the forest, it will look like the forests of Nniar. She won't be able to tell the difference."

Kalien threw his head back and groaned. "Fine, leave me be, then." He walked over to a stump and slumped down next to it. The ground was slightly damp and cool beneath him, but the coolness calmed him. His eyes closed, and he whispered, "Thorn."

He could see Riven lying in a bed shrouded in a tent, her eyes closed. Everything stayed horizontal for a minute until Thorn grunted and grabbed a shirt to put on. She tore the tent flap open and jogged away from the space, down to a crevice in the mountain. She jumped down. Even though Kalien couldn't see her face, he could feel the heat of her glare.

"You're not dead."

"Is that a question?"

"An observation. What do you want? The sun hasn't even risen."

"I have an idea of how you could defeat Nniar."

"You've been scheming? And what exactly is your grand idea?" Thorn picked at the surrounding rocks.

"The Anorphus is dying, and I've heard that they are struggling to figure out their next move. The castle is weak from the past invasions. If you want to win this before Korrigan has a plan, invade the castle now while they are weak. End this war."

Thorn looked at her shoes and then at the sky. Faint rays of light shined onto her dark green hair and down her cheek. "Are you saying that it would be an easy battle?"

"I believe so. We are stranded here without a plan to retaliate." A Cursed Knight walked behind Kalien. He peered over his shoulder so Thorn could see and whispered, "What will you do?"

Thorn stared off into the sky. "I don't know yet. Goodbye, Kalien."

She vanished from sight. Kalien didn't even have to stand for Rew to know the conversation had ended. Rew wandered over to him, blending in with the mossy environment. If it wasn't for the pink glint in his opaque eyes, he would be camouflaged. He held out his hand to Kalien, who promptly waved it away in protest.

"I'm not ready to stand."

"What did she say?"

"Not enough for me to know what she'll do with the information."

"What did she say?" Rew repeated.

"She listened to what I said and said she didn't know what she planned to do. That was it."

Rew's pointed ears twitched up slightly. "We will plan on their departure, but for now, I need you back working." Rew grabbed his shirt and pulled. "Up, up. Whether or not the plan worked, the war is resting on the tip of our tongues. It's only a matter of time before we must swallow it."

Kalien placed his hand on the stump and pushed off it to stand. Bits of bark dusted the ground. "What will Bruthren do?"

"With what?"

"With me?" Kalien could not directly stare at Rew when he asked it.

Rew narrowed his gaze. "If you are asking if you will be punished or thrown to another's army for not getting a concrete answer, you will not. You did all that we asked. Now, get back to work, and soon you will be off with a cart to the Thornyarch Mountains too."

Kalien returned to his line, tossing the sacks in one by one, but he stared off and worked as if he had mechanical hands. The sun eventually came through the passing clouds, and all seemed steady and rhythmic for a time.

Morrow walked in front of Kalien's cart with Audrey and Ben. Kalien didn't so much as glance up. "You," Morrow said, pointing at Kalien.

He ignored her and worked, just as he had done for hours.

Morrow snaked her head next to his. Her hair poked his chin. "Can you squeeze another person or two in your line?"

Kalien shot back a step. "Why would you ask me? Go find Rew. He is in charge here."

Morrow cackled. "Where is he?"

"Does it look like I follow him around?" Kalien tossed another sack, filling the cart. "FULL."

"Well, you are quite a cursed scum, aren't you?" Morrow glared at him and grabbed one of Ben's and one of Audrey's hands as she stood in between them. "We will go find Rew." Morrow blew a raspberry at him, and she skipped away, dragging Audrey and Ben along.

"Let me go," Audrey moaned, trying to tug her hand free. "I can walk perfectly fine without your hand."

"I don't want us to be split up in this crowd," Morrow said. Audrey accepted her words.

Rew held two agor vines in each hand, pulling chackles behind him. He led them to the cart on the end and tied the blue lead firmly. Three folks sat atop the cart, squeezed into a narrow seat. There was a wood piece in front of it that hopefully would keep them from falling out forward, though it only went a smidgen above their knees. Once the chackles were secured, Rew yelled to them to go. They barreled away. Moss darted off the wheels as they moved through the woods.

Morrow flung Audrey and Ben in front of her. "I believe these belong to you," she said with a wide smile.

"Morrow." Rew looked her up and down, ignoring Ben and Audrey. "And why have you brought them here?"

"Are we not to fight for unity too? I will not stand here and let the carts roll off without me and them on one of them. Now, I would like to get in line and help load up the carts before doing so, of course, or are you going to stand there and deny me that right after being stuck training these two? I hardly would peg you as a cursed scum, but deny me, and even the moon will darken to you."

Rew stuck a leg out and put his hands on his hips. "Join the next line. You'll be heading off on the next full cart to the mountains." Rew beckoned Morrow closer with his webbed hand and whispered into her ear, "The Ancient One will have our heads if anything happens to those two. Protect them during battle."

"I intend to." Morrow turned around. "Come, adventures are to be had." She placed her hands on their backs and directed them to the line, squeezing them between two Choke members. Ben accidentally bumped into the man in front, and he turned and snarled, glaring through piercing gray eyes. He had six earrings going down one ear.

"Sorry," Ben said.

Morrow glowered. "No need for scum in the morning. You can see it was an accident. We are all working towards the same goal."

"You'll have to excuse him... he has barely slept," the woman in front of him, with cream pixie hair and skin like shining amber, said.

"We all aren't sleeping well."

"Just leave it," Ben said.

Morrow placed a hand on her side. The woman behind her tossed her a sack. Morrow narrowly caught it. "For you, honey." She handed the bag to Ben.

For what felt like all eternity, the sound of bottles clanking in the sacks drowned out anything else. The cart filled to the brim, the wood sides bowing out in the middle like a full belly.

The man in front yelled, "Full."

The last person in line set the sack back down. The man jumped into the cart, with Morrow following his lead.

Audrey and Ben climbed up after Morrow scooted close to the man. He eyed her like a fly had landed on him.

Rew joined them. A single sunwave stone necklace that hid beneath his shirt flopped out. He examined the cart and pushed on the bulging wood planks on the sides. They seemed to stay strong for now. "Fight well," he said to them. "*Halko.*"

The two chackles took off, following another cart that had left not long before. They jolted forward in their seat and felt the unevenness of the forest floor. Every rock and mound thrusted them side to side or forward and back.

As they rattled about, air cycled through, sending their hair in unpredictable directions. The man holding the agor vines merely blew his hair out of his face when it covered his eyes. Morrow's horns of hair stayed put except for a few strands that waved down, tickling the sides of her face. She left the strands dangling. Ben sat next to her with his hands clasped together, rubbing one thumb with his other. His eyes cast down, and his back arched a bit.

Morrow whipped her head towards Ben as loose dirt kicked up, and she cupped her hand over the side of her eye. Squinting, she noticed Ben's anxious hands and put her hand on top of his. He squeezed her hand gently in response.

Green fields returned full of tall spindly plants and opal blooms. Fluttering beings dashed around them and sometimes sat atop their hands or on their clothes for a short time before whooshing away again. It was better than dealing with the strips of dirt.

Audrey gazed out to the side, unable to stretch her tall legs if she sat straight. She let them dangle a bit out the side when the trail wasn't too bouncy. She had a dagger that Morrow had given her strapped to her leg. Now and again, she pulled it out and spun it like Morrow had shown her.

But even with all of them together alongside a stranger, they shared hardly a conversation the entire journey besides a curse word or telling the others they needed to piss. Even Morrow remained quiet until the sun descended behind the trees and the moon showed its face up ahead.

Slowly, the man pulled tighter on the vines, and the chackles shook their coats. They came to a halt, and the man tied the agor vines to a twisted iron bar that was on the front of the cart. He jumped down and massaged one of the chackles behind its ear. It moved its front hoof back and forth in enjoyment. He did the same with the other chackle before reaching underneath the cart and opening a compartment. He pulled out a large, faded brown bag.

Audrey stumbled out of the cart. Morrow and Ben scooted out after her.

"What is that?" Audrey asked.

"I don't suppose you expected us to carry on for the next few days without stopping, did you?" The man pulled out a long piece of obsidian fabric. "Grab a side, will you?"

Audrey walked over and picked up one end. It was a rectangle with white dots that appeared like stars in the dark background. He wrapped his side around a branch, and Audrey moved until she could wrap hers around a branch. "Now what?"

"I have one more to put up. You two"—he glanced at Ben and Morrow—"put it up unless you want to go out and catch dinner. Tall one, come with me."

"Audrey... my name is Audrey."

"Call me Ghalin. Now that that's over, let's go." Ghalin paused and called back, "Walk the chackles, will you? They have stomachs to fill as we do."

Dark green leaves swooped down as if a celebration commenced. Twigs scattered about the forest floor sounded like snapping bones as they walked on them. There were mounds of moss near most of the trees—a peculiar sight to most unless they knew about the creatures that tunneled underneath. Off to the left, a cacophony of a stream burbling and birds chirping felt like a dream.

The ember-like yellow of starberries speckled the ground, their blue anthers looking black in the dark. Audrey reached down to pick some up. Ghalin watched her curiously.

"Do you normally assume things are safe to eat?"

Audrey shook her head. "Do you normally assume what people know or don't know? Where I come from, assuming makes you an ass, and these are delicious."

Ghalin stroked his chin and grinned. "Maybe I am an ass... but how would a being of Earth know about these?"

"How do you know that?" Audrey plucked more starberries and placed them in the bottom of her shirt like it were a hammock. "You wouldn't believe all that I have done in Folengower. I... I don't believe most of it myself."

Ghalin unbuttoned a bag from his belt and tossed it to her. "Here, this is better than your shirt."

It landed at her feet. She picked it up and plopped them into the bag. "Thanks. What are we hunting for dinner, exactly?"

"Whatever comes our way, really. Praise the moon to grant us footfalls like falling leaves." Ghalin crouched as he moved, and a black flame emerged from his palm.

"If you know I am of Earth, you know I can't do that. We hunt differently." Audrey took out her dagger from the strap around her thigh. She stepped over a fallen branch and whispered, "Just so you know, I've never hunted before."

Ghalin, stunned, whispered over his shoulder, "How do you eat? Are you... What do they call it there?" he mumbled. "Are you of wealthy status?"

Audrey covered a laugh. "Not even close. I buy most of my food from the grocery store or at our weekly farmers' market in town."

Ghalin cocked his head but didn't reply.

"You know, like a shop or like that market by the castle you have."

He nodded and placed his finger over his lips. "Shhh, I hear something."

Audrey scanned the trees. She could see the outline of a bird overhead on a branch. It hopped up to the next branch, though just as it did, her eyes darted away. Something moved near them. Ghalin scanned all around, listening to the susurration of the forest. It sounded almost all around them and not at the same time.

He crept a foot or two forward, hiding his flame behind his back. Audrey stayed close behind, with her body low. Sticks snapped in front of them. Another snap to the side. No, behind or above. Audrey slowly spun around.

"Don't panic, but we are being hunted," he whispered.

Audrey held her dagger close to her body, her breaths hurried. "Fuck," she murmured.

A face emerged out of a hollow log. Audrey could see a black snout, and above its glass-like eyes were two short spiraled horns. The points looked sharper than Audrey's dagger. Her hand shook. "Is that a finnix?"

"Yes. They usually leave us be, but when they are in a stad, they can be quite aggressive."

"What's a stad?"

"When they live amongst many others."

"Like a pack?"

Ghalin ignored her question. The finnix bared its teeth, and a sound Audrey had never heard before bellowed out of the creature. Its growl extended low and long, as if it were a haunted imprint. Audrey shivered. Ghalin held his magic out in front of him towards the finnix. "Easy now. I hadn't planned on killing you."

Its head teetered from side to side as it drifted out of the log. Its body was long and its mauve fur thick and spotted with bits of lichen and moss that matched the fur on its paws. Its bushy tail flicked to the side. Then, all at once, six more jumped or charged towards them. Their drawn-out growl made them sound as if they were huddled in a cave, echoes trapping them.

Audrey moved around the circle that they had created around them. "What do we do now?"

"I would plan on not dying."

"Get, get!" Audrey kicked her long legs out and held her arms up high to make herself seem bigger. "Get, get!" The largest finnix gnashed its teeth at her, saliva dripping out. Audrey screamed. The finnix leapt to her foot and latched on. Audrey swung her leg and lost her balance, tumbling down. The finnix gnashed a hole in her shoe as she tried desperately to pull away.

Ghalin blew his black flame towards it. A burst of fire hit the creature's head, searing its fur. It writhed on the ground, smashing its face into whatever it could. The others narrowed the circle. One eyed Audrey and kicked its head up as if it were trying to get something off its horns. A hard breath whooshed out of Audrey as it pounced on her chest. She coughed and spluttered, one hand gripping its jowls and the other pushing its jaw back as its mouth snapped open and closed like an alligator an inch from her face.

"Audrey... try to shove it off." Three circled Ghalin while he waved fire at them with both his lit hands.

Her dagger dropped to her side.

Audrey spotted a glint of silver in the grass and already knew it was her dagger. "If I could, I would have already done that." She moved her legs up, trying to push under its belly. "Get the fuck off me." Her arms trembled beneath its strength and weight. The finnix pounded its paws on her chest. Audrey gasped.

Ghalin blew his fire all around him as he spun around, and the finnixes ran backward. He hit one of them directly in the face. Its eye bubbled and seeped down its cheek like thick, smoky water. It rubbed its paw on its face till the flame snuffed out. The others surrounded the finnix and nudged its body with their heads as it cried out.

"I can't hold it for much longer," Audrey yelled. "Shit... shit."

The finnix on top of her pushed its weight down on her chest until her hands slipped. Audrey screamed as sharp teeth penetrated her chin, and then a dark flame from Ghalin and fire from someone else out of Audrey's view connected. The finnix's body lit with flames, terror sparking into its eyes. It charged over Audrey's head and off into the forest. The other finnixes stared and growled before taking off after it, the one-eyed finnix the last in the line. Ghalin leapt towards it. He grabbed its tail and used it to whip its body back. The finnix scratched his paws on Ghalin's sides. Clamping his hands on its maw, he tore his jaw open sending magic down its throat.

Audrey lay limp, blood smearing her neck. Ben dropped to his knees and patted her face, moving it side to side, trying to see the bite mark hidden beneath. "*Audrey, Audrey*, please tell me you're alive." He gently moved her head onto his lap and cradled it. "Hey, come on. You can't die yet. Come on."

"She's breathing. Look at her chest. Probably just passed out." Morrow placed a hand on her hip and swatted at a bug that flew too close to her face.

"I have dinner." Ghalin held up what he could of the finnix by its legs.

"I wasn't expecting such a feast." Morrow licked her lips seductively.

Ghalin sighed. "Do you have any hallow nectar on you?"

Morrow reached into one of her small bags and pulled out a vial. She crouched down to Audrey and let several drops fall onto her wound. "She'll be alright. That will help."

Ben laughed, his eyes crazed.

Ghalin raised an eyebrow and frowned. "What is it?"

Morrow tilted her head to the side, her legs bouncing a bit as she stayed crouched like a frog.

"It's hit me that this... this is the beginning of our end. We can't fight an army. Audrey and I are not warriors."

"He's in shock." Ghalin pulled the finnix over his shoulder and trudged back to camp. "We should really get back before they decide to return."

Morrow pulled Ben's arm. "We can carry Audrey together until she wakes."

Ben moved his arm away. "Go on. I'll wait till she gets up."

"Don't be stubborn."

"Just go."

Morrow narrowed her eyes. "*Audrey*," she yelled next to her ear. Something waxy and thorny on the ground stole her gaze. She leaned over and ripped it from the soil. She pinched her nose with her other hand. "Oh, this could wake the dead." She put it right under Audrey's nostrils. Audrey jolted awake and scrambled out of Ben's arms. "See. It's time to go," she said dryly and snatched up Audrey's dagger.

Back at camp, Ghalin had a pile of logs and a fire swirling. His eyes looked like those of a Cursed Knight next to it. He stoked the fire with a long stick, then placed a black pot on top of the rocks in the middle. Next to the fire, the limp body of the finnix lay.

Audrey sat a few feet from it and slumped over. Her hand hovered over the bite, never touching it. Ben crossed his legs, ready to plop down next to her.

"You, come help me skin this."

Ben pointed to his chest, and Ghalin nodded.

Morrow wandered up a knoll a few trees away. Audrey dropped her hand and rested her face on the mossy and stick-ridden ground. She could faintly hear Ben and Ghalin talking about hunting and how Ben had fished with his stepdad, Harper, and done some hunting for food while camping. She could hear the scraping of the knife against the flesh of the finnix and even the tiny movements of spirit wings as they flitted onto another flower and then landed in her hair. She reached her finger out to it as if offering a perch to a bird. It stepped onto her hand and cleaned its antenna with its little feet. Audrey peered through its iridescent wings, as if she were looking through a bubble. It patted its feet on her hand three times, then floated off into the sky, leaving dusty white specks in its place.

Morrow came back as Ben tossed fresh meat into a sizzling pot. Ghalin walked over to the stream, passing Morrow as he went. She was holding long emerald shoots, and at the bottom, long crooked yellow vegetables dangled, with dirt hanging on to the roots. She set them on the piece of bark they had used to butcher the finnix. She placed her hand on Ben's neck fondly. "I'll be needing your knife."

Ben passed it to her, and she wiped the blade on the grass before chopping up the vegetable and throwing in uneven pieces. She sliced the shoot longways and then fine, and took pinches of it to season over the meat. Audrey sat up and watched them. She saw Ben laugh genuinely at something Morrow said and place his hand on her arm.

Ghalin returned with wet hands. He placed them over the fire until they dried. "Are you alright?" he called to Audrey.

"I've been through worse."

"Food is nearly ready."

Audrey pushed herself up and walked over to them. The smell of everything in the pot seeped out like a holiday dinner. Her stomach growled. "Smells good."

"Ugh," Morrow said, pointing to her chin. "Let me get you some more hallow nectar."

Audrey held her hand to it. "Does it look that bad?"

"Not exactly. It's stopped bleeding and a scab looks to be forming."

"I didn't bring any plates. For now, we will eat out of the pot as a family." Ghalin grabbed a jar of dead magic from the cart and rubbed it in his hands. He grabbed the handle of the pot, pulled it off the flame and set it down on the bark. "Grab your knives and dig in."

Morrow tilted Audrey's head to the side and put more hallow nectar on her. "Here, we grabbed your dagger for you." Audrey took it and stabbed a piece of meat out of the pot. She blew on it and then took a bite. Her shoulders relaxed.

They slept atop the hammocks they'd tied. Audrey joined with Ghalin since Morrow said she would rather be carved like the finnix than sleep with anyone but Ben. Ghalin was kind to scoot far away to give her lots of room and shoved a blanket in between them, though Audrey didn't care. For now, she wanted comfort of any kind so she could fall asleep, and so far, the plan had worked.

39

Thorn loomed over her own reflection in the stream. She placed her finger in the water and swirled. Ripples came to life. A few other Amardians sat on the other side of the stream or far away from her, softly chatting.

"Mourning over someone?"

Thorn saw the man she had trained with reflected in the water. "Are we training again, or did you come over to curse the soil I stand on?"

"It looks like something is weighing heavy on you. I thought you might want some company if you are sad."

Thorn picked up a pebble and sent it skipping. It sank after four bounces. "Everyone in this camp is sad. We reek of sadness."

"You certainly do."

Thorn shot him a look.

"Do you want to tell me about it?"

"I don't even know your name. Go bother someone else."

"Hyress." Hyress rolled up his pant legs and took his boots off and placed them to the side, the top parts slumping to the side without anything to hold up the fabric. He sat down and rested his feet in the stream, wincing for a moment. "Still cold." He chuckled. Thorn stared to the other side, ignoring him. "Now that you know my name, why are you down here alone?"

Two folks carrying a basket of pearly white vegetables and bright red feathery stems walked behind them, heading back up to the camp. They said nothing as they passed Thorn and Hyress. Everything felt still on the windless day.

"I'm not the only one alone. Why aren't you gallivanting with your friends?"

Hyress laughed. "Where is Riven?"

"Are we going to go around asking questions that neither of us answer?"

"What is crushing you? I know that look."

Thorn tapped her leg and sighed to the sky. "I have to make a decision. If I make the wrong choice, it could cost us everything."

"Us?"

"All of us. Amarda."

"Have you told Kinsington what it is?"

"No, I plan to. I should be there with him now."

"Then go to him. We don't have the luxury of time. Tell him what it is and let him decide."

Thorn eyed Hyress. "I will." She walked away.

Hyress called after her, "Happy to help."

Thorn charged up the narrow and steep path to the tents. Folks moved about sharpening swords and creating other weapons. Many trained with those weapons or practiced new magic with the more skilled. Clothing was being mended, children were chasing insects and picking plants to make more hallow nectar or other medicinal uses. Food was being prepared and packed in leaf wraps for the warriors at a moment's notice. They had holes dug deep in the soil to store the food and medicine that couldn't bear the drastic temperature changes.

Snow could still be seen on the highest peaks as it melted into jagged waterfalls. Thorn moved like a giant across the grasses that squelched beneath her feet. The sun was boastful of its conquest after many days hidden above the storm. Plants kicked up from her footfalls where too much water puddled. She made it to the mouth of the ravine. A shallow stream covered the ground. Thorn splashed into it, the cold water wrapping up to her ankles.

Sprouts of dicots vined up the wall, a coruscating shine on their petals and hazy gray leaves. The rocks reflected in the sparkling water, and Thorn could watch herself move through, though she turned her nose up. Small creatures moved around her legs.

The ravine curved like a dragon swishing its tail, and she rounded the last corner to see Eltrists speaking in groups. Kinsington stood next to Talkun, and, by the looks of his rigid stance, the conversation had taken a serious turn. Thorn stayed in the last bit of water and swallowed, her face hardening.

She slammed her foot onto the ground and charged over to Kinsington. She stopped a few feet away and placed her hands behind her back in wait. Talkun nodded towards her, and Kinsington continued with his conversation. Thorn impatiently paced in a short line. Talkun eyed her periodically.

"Your presence is not needed," Kinsington said in her mind.

Thorn stepped closer to him. "I need to tell you something. It's important."

Talkun stretched his wings and said something to Kinsington. He walked away, leaving them alone.

"Do not waste my time."

"Kalien told me that the castle is weak and that we squandered their plans to retaliate. Our plan to drive them off the Anorphus worked. It's time to strike now. We need to go to the castle and attack while they crawl."

"Korrigan has no plan? How would Kalien know this?"

"Apparently, the knights speak of it around the folks as openly as when rain will come."

Kinsington curled his tail in front of him. The end of it tapped lightly on the ground. "Do you believe him?"

Thorn picked at her nail. "Yes, I believe he is telling the truth. This could end the war. Capture Korrigan and make the folks of Nniar see the true heir. Talkun can tell the truth of what happened."

Kinsington held his stance, unmoving as the surrounding stones. "We will leave tonight. Meet with O on plans to send out our on-foot warriors first. The ones who take to the air with us will come shortly after. Talkun is to remain here. He will stay with any injured Eltrists unable to fight and the families until we have secured Korrigan."

"I will inform O."

"I trust you remember how to lead the right way?"

Thorn nodded slowly. "I could never forget."

"Then praise the moon for your memory. You will ride on me to the castle, and I expect no mercy."

Thorn bowed. "My duty is to you."

Kinsington stomped his paw. "Ready them all."

Thorn sprinted through the ravine, back to the other side, and continued until she made it to O's tent. She threw the tent door open and rushed inside. O sat on his bed with a book in hand. He tossed it to the side and bolted up.

"Fuck, Thorn. What are you doing in here like this?"

Thorn placed her hands on her hips and tried to speak as her breath rushed. "I... I just spoke with Kinsington. We are to gather the warriors and lead them to Nniar Castle, and I am a leader again. We leave at nightfall."

O shook his head. "Wait, what do you mean? Has something happened?"

"Nniar is crumbling. This is the perfect time to attack. The mission is to capture Korrigan and threaten death. Talkun will arrive after we have seized fire, and we will make the folks know the truth and show them that Talkun is alive after all these decades." Thorn spoke with her hands and let out a soft laugh. "We are going to win."

"When are we to leave again?"

"Nightfall."

"Then we should gather everyone now. The sun will be setting soon."

Thorn ducked out of the tent.

O grabbed a coat that buttoned down the middle with wood pyramid-shaped buttons. He held the middle of his long hair that he had braided in an intricate spiral and used a leaf-shaped clip to hold it together before placing it in the center of his back.

O met Thorn out in the middle of camp. With her arms crossed, she nodded to O.

"Amardians. Tonight, we execute our next attack in the hope of ending this war. We will rise up and change Folengower to how it should have been all along."

The crowd cheered at O's words.

"Warriors, gather below in your packs. Be ready with your armor and weapons. I will not allow time to become a cage. Thorn will command the order of the packs to leave."

Thorn noticed Riven standing just behind the first line of folks. All she could see were her piercing oak eyes and sandy blonde hair. The folks moved like a swarm of fish, gathering gear, filling bags and saying their goodbyes to the families that were to remain behind. Thorn lost Riven in the scuttling of the crowd. She started towards her tent, but Hyress stood in front of her.

Thorn abruptly stopped. "Hyress..."

"What is going on?"

"Did you not hear O?"

"I did, but why are we abandoning the mountain to fight?"

"I don't have time to explain any of this to you at the moment." She looked over his shoulder in a hurry to continue. "I will explain the mission more thoroughly when all the packs are below."

"Thorn." Hyress narrowed his gaze. "Are you confident in this plan?"

"Kinsington is." Thorn pushed past him and hurried into Riven's tent. Riven sat on the edge of the bed, placing a dagger into a holder on the side of her leg.

"Did you hear?"

Riven stared only at her own hands and the next pieces of armor she would be wearing. "That you are in charge again?"

"Yes. Kinsington trusts me again." Thorn lay on the bed. "I never thought he would come around."

"What did you do to make that happen?"

"Kalien told me that Nniar is crumbling. They had no other plan but the Anorphus to keep them safe. Now that the old being is rotting, we have a chance to take Korrigan hostage, and Talkun will take his place."

Riven clicked her tongue. "I thought you were against Talkun's idea of uniting Folengower."

"I am." Thorn sat up. "They should pay for what they have done to us. Sometime later, we can unite as one, but traitors should walk on fire before feeling safe. The same way we have."

Riven bit her lip. "I don't think that's the right way."

Thorn stood up and stomped around the tent, hands animated as she spoke. "And why not? You despise Nniar. You grew up there and were cast aside when your father fell in love with an Amardian. *You* should want them hanging from the castle walls for all to see."

"No, I want peace, I want love, and I wish..." She hung her head. "I wish you still did too."

Thorn grabbed Riven's hands and held them in hers. "I do... but there is a cost to love."

Riven pulled her hands away. She grabbed her helmet and placed it atop her head, an Eltrist's wings overlapping to protect her. She reached for her sheath that leaned against the tent's side and strapped it to her, the sword already snug in it. Potions hung from her belt.

"The cost you are expecting me to pay is too steep." Riven exited the tent and made her way down with the other warriors.

"Hmmphh." Thorn kicked a bag over, stones rolled out. She clenched her fists and tightened her jaw.

O barged in and frowned at the opalescent stones. "Are you starting down?"

"I just need to grab my gear."

"Do so quickly. Kinsington is already down with the other able Eltrists."

"I'll be there," Thorn snarled.

O held up his hands. "Whatever is causing this, straighten it out. If you are to lead again, you lead us all. Your emotions can wait."

Thorn put her belt on that had satchels hanging from it, glass baubles and her sheath. She reached for her helmet on the floor and put it on. "Where's your helmet?"

"Getting repaired. It was damaged in the last battle. Another random patchwork."

"I'll see you soon, then?"

"Yes, I plan to ride on Sylin when my helmet is complete."

"Sylin? You never ride on him."

"I didn't make the decision." O turned away. "I get along with Sylin well."

Thorn huffed. "See you when the skies are blazing."

O rose a fist and forced a smile. "To the blazing skies."

Thorn took off past O towards the creek. It was filled with folks waiting and more joining behind her to follow down. Packs had formed. She walked over to Kinsington and stood next to him.

"I want only the packs who are on foot to line up." Healers stood off to the side near a tree. "After the healers gift you a healing potion, head out to the base of the mountain, and from there we will continue to Nniar Castle. Capture Korrigan at any cost."

The lines moved in fast stretches as the healers gave a dry strug mixture for them to clip to their belt. It would heal them quickly if they became injured.

The light dimmed to a single sunray that strained to touch between the branches of trees. Warrior packs marched onward and down the dangerous mountainside. The trail had been claimed by nature some time ago, and they used their swords to clear anything that stood in their way, but it was better than taking the main road that led to the other towns. It was safer to be invisible.

Thorn stood on the ledge, watching as the Amardians cleared out one by one.

"It's time," Kinsington called to her thoughts. She stared for a moment more, placing her hand on her chest.

Kinsington waited alongside the other Eltrists. The twilight glowed in their presence. They appeared hidden even with their bellies, as if some other creature wisped through the mountains. She passed Riven, who mounted Pavyln. Riven turned away when she saw her walking towards them. Kinsington, whose fur could only be mistaken for the night itself, waited patiently for her to climb atop his back.

Kinsington stepped forward. Thorn held on as she always had before. His wings stretched and moved rhythmically as he rose off the ground. Esna, Aylo, Pavlyn and a dozen more pierced the sky. They were silent as they soared through the clouds. They chased the ending sun and turned gracefully towards Nniar Castle. Below, they could see silhouettes of the packs moving on the winding path at the bottom of the Thornyarch Mountains.

The Eltrists circled the area, keeping steady with the packs below. Near the mountain, orangey campfires sparked in the forest. Thorn scanned them curiously.

"Trouble?"

"The fires are too small to worry about," Kinsington said.

With twilight nearing its end, the moon hung over them, lighting their way. Thorn held her arms out, the breeze escaping between her fingers. Her head flung back, her face that of bliss. Kinsington teetered softly as the wind glided past.

The packs walked through the night until dawn approached, and they were lucky enough to stow away in a thicket. The Eltrist had a harder time blending into the surroundings and could not stay with their packs. Some stowed away in a cave, while others found places to rest atop hills. The tall grass and flowers engulfed half of their body.

Once they had all eaten, each pack staggered behind the other in case someone spotted them. Though they hardly heard anyone on the road save for a cart or two tumbling down it, they would head off the trail and wait for them to pass.

After several days, they made it to just below the castle during a cloudless night. The Eltrist spoke amongst themselves before Kinsington turned to the warriors, ready for battle.

"Once we head up that mountain, do not let anyone get in the way of finding Korrigan. Bring him to me alive."

The packs whispered together, "Above and below, watch them soar, hear them roar and speak, their magic runs deep, a bringer of gifts, a synchrony unlike others, we breathe together, we rule as one."

"Where is O?" Thorn said to Riven as they waited for the packs to sneak in to the castle.

Riven scanned the area, with her arms crossed. "I don't know. Did he go on foot?"

"No, he told me he would ride on Sylin since he was waiting for his helmet to get repaired."

"Well, I don't see Sylin either. Maybe they are still behind."

"Only the moon would know. It feels off though."

"You think something has happened to him?"

Thorn leaned against a tree. "If something did, it's not the best time to worry about it."

Magic cracked into the sky like lightning just above the castle.

Kinsington shouted to everyone near him, "Now!"

Thorn rushed to Kinsington and held on tight. The others did the same, and soon they were high in the sky, charging towards the castle. Another fiery light illuminated the castle. Thorn gazed down. Magic lit her eyes up as it scorched below.

The first pack drew their swords at the Cursed Knights standing at the doors. On each side of the castle, a pack ambushed, some climbing up the sides of the castle by the vines. Screams came from the camps of folks who had evacuated Corling, Nilhorn and Chant. Several adults shouted for their kids to run into the forest and hide as they drew their own swords and those who could lit magic in their palms.

Another pack joined the ones at the front doors, and before long, the knights slumped to the ground, dripping in blood. They tried opening the doors, but they wouldn't budge, they assumed barricaded. Cackling fire climbed up the doors, cracking them in half. The packs shot back at the knights who set the doors aflame just as the doors split open. Dozens of them flooded the room with confused faces and hushed footfalls, seeing the room empty of bodies.

They kicked at Korrigan's office, but magic kept it safe. Warriors continued to the other rooms and rummaged through every open room and cabinet. Many took to the stairs, some going to the right and some to the left.

Five Amardians stood outside Eliza's door. "One, two, three," the one in front mouthed before kicking the door wide open. The Amardians didn't get a chance to count the twelve pairs of red eyes waiting for them before black fire shot out of the Cursed Knights' palms, leaving them in temporary darkness. They pushed out of the room, their swords stabbing at the air as they did. The lead knight took his sword out and swung it towards the three Amardians in front of him. Their swords clanked together as both sides pushed. As the knight lifted his leg, his teeth clenched together and with a loud growl and kicked them down the stairs. Three of them tumbled down into a heap. He turned back to the others, still fighting with every inch of their soul with the other knigths.

On the level above, Nia guarded Agden's door, her hands held out to the sides as if she was stretching something out. Something that resembled clear water. Five Amardian warriors made a crescent shape around her, holding their swords out threateningly.

Nia glared. "Step any closer and I will release this," she said calmly.

"What is it?" one called out and spit at her feet. "Curse the soil you walk on!"

"Curse you," they grumbled as one.

"Who's behind the door?" a male with chalky white hair said, smirking. "I bet it's Korrigan." He charged at Nia and stabbed the magic towards her face. The sword ricocheted back into his forehead, flinging him backward. He toppled into three other folks, who managed to keep their balance as he hit the floor. His sword landed atop him with the blade across his chest and arms, the end pierced into one of his sleeves, just missing his skin.

The pack leader helped up the warrior who'd fallen.

"Go behind her and cut her," the man screamed.

Nia turned to the side as they shuffled that way. "Leave the castle now. I will release this if you come any closer."

The pack shuffled around her timidly, eyes always on what was between her hands, wondering what it was and what it could do. The white-haired man was the only one staring straight into her eyes, unafraid. He unbuttoned a jar of magic from his belt and threw it at her. Nia tossed the waterlike screen towards them. It bounced onto them like a bubble, taking his magic and his life with it. A bright lavender light puffed and released like a breath inside. Even as the pack placed their arms up to shelter themselves, the explosion came for them all, searing through their skin. Nia kicked the ball of dead bodies forwards till she arrived at the top of the stairs.

A group of Amardians halted in the middle of the steps as the ball loomed above them, gasping at the sight of their comrades' squished and distorted faces inside. Some let anger lead them, with the tip of their swords charging ahead. Nia gave a light kick at the ball. It roared down the steps, flying high and then low as it bounced down. Red streaked the surface and rained down onto the steps as the thing ripped in places until it crashed into the warriors like a water balloon. The bodies spilled out, drenched in their own fluids.

The warriors reached out from beneath the dead as more Amardians rushed over after seeing or hearing what had happened. They pulled the dead bodies off the living and placed them to the side of the stairs. The ones able charged up the stairs to Nia. Just as she shut the door behind her, another pack banged on the door. They gathered side tables from the halls that they slammed into the door.

"He's in here," the leader shouted. "We need everyone, *now*."

Cursed Knights fought with swords in the middle of the hall below the stairs. They moved swiftly against the Amardians, who fought nearly as skilled. The sounds of their grunts, curses and swords hitting echoed through the castle.

One Cursed Knight took to the stairs, grabbing warriors by their armor and tossing them over the banister as they tried climbing up. The knight reached into his pouch and took out corpse thistle extract. He held the bottle over the banister, dousing his victims' faces.

The warriors gasped, allowing the drops to seep into their mouths, eyes and noses. They clawed at their throats. The knight walked away without caring to watch them die.

He calmly ascended the stairs, reaching the group pounding on the door. The knight climbed onto the banister, silently balancing across all the way to behind the pack, then jumped down. He swung his sword across those nearest, five folks wailing and thudding to the floor. With the sheer number of pack members, they pushed the knight down and brutally took turns stabbing him. Dark blood sputtered out of the knight's lips, and the crimson in his eyes slowly dimmed.

More bodies thudded to the floor on the first floor, and a blow shattered the door above. Smoke whirled around the frame. Queen Agden sat at the window. Eliza held her hands of fire out with Nia in front, whose sword was at the ready. Cassin hid to the side with a black flame in his palm.

"Let them through." Agden sighed. She watched folks below battling with anything they could find as the Amardians took them hostage. Few knights had remained outside of the castle.

"We should have escaped," Eliza whispered to Agden.

"The castle is surrounded, and those folks down there came here for protection. Look at them." Agden gazed down at the folks fighting in the garden.

Nia and Cassin gripped their weapons as the door shot open. Agden rose from the bench.

"What do you all want?" Eliza asked.

The leader of the pack forced her way through. She placed her sword in her sheath, making sure her hand stayed on the top of it. "Korrigan. He is the one spreading lies and hatred towards Amarda. He will be the one to pay for the cursed soil he birthed. Give him to us."

Agden faced her with her hands laced. "He is not here."

The leader's eyes bulged, and she swiftly removed her sword from the sheath. Cassin sent his black flame darting towards her. The pack leader shielded her face with her arms, but Agden cast her own spell that hit the flame and disintegrated it.

"You may take me instead."

Uproarious shouts drowned out all other sounds.

The pack leader held up her arms. "Enough."

They quieted.

"Will you take us to Korrigan?"

Agden nodded. "I want this fighting to end here."

A thunderous crash came from above, and the pack fled the room to investigate. Nia and Cassin followed. There was a gaping hole to the haunted night in the middle of the ceiling.

Kinsington landed on the bottom floor, crushing several knights. "Korrigan, come out before your kingdom is but skeletons," he said into all the minds of those inside. Aylo came down beside him.

Agden pushed everyone aside.

Eliza ran after her and tore at her arm protectively. "Mom... don't."

Agden shook her head and slid Eliza's hand off her. She smiled, but there was something, possibly fear, in her eyes. "It is my duty to protect our folks."

Thorn stood up on Kinsington's back. "You heard him. Where is Korrigan?"

"He is not here," Agden said over the banister. A piece of rock from the ceiling tumbled onto the floor. It cracked open in hundreds of pieces. "As I told your army, I will come with you instead."

Kinsington glared up at her. "Where is he?"

"I will tell you if you leave everyone else be."

Kinsington paused, as if mulling over why she was giving herself to him so easily. He finally said, "Bring her to me."

The pack members grabbed her all at once, as if they had to be the one to capture the Bloodtress. Cassin placed his hand over Eliza's mouth and rushed her silently down the hall. Nia shoved folks to the side.

"I order you to let me go," Agden said to her.

"But—"

Agden smiled a smile that was full of weakness and strength all at the same time. "I need to do this."

Nia froze, and her arms dropped to her sides.

Agden moved down the steps with grace even as daggers and swords pricked her neck.

"Place her on my back. Thorn, put the rapture stone on her."

Aylo growled at her as she passed. Strug spilled out of his mouth and stained his white fur.

Four Amardians pushed Agden up onto Kinsington's back.

Thorn snatched her arm. "This will rip your fucking hand off if you use magic. Just ask Eliza." Thorn set the green stone on her arm. It slithered around her wrist and clamped down with pinching teeth. Agden sat down without a word or even a twitch.

Kinsington flapped his wings, scraping against the walls. Thorn squeezed her arms around Agden's waist. They soared out of the castle. Wind tunneled down, sending debris moving like a cyclone. Aylo stomped around, swinging his tail until the banister leading up the stairs toppled over. With one final growl, he followed Kinsington.

Kinsington circled the castle grounds. "Tell me where he is and then I will call them off and we will leave."

"He's in the Thornyarch Mountains."

Thorn's eyes widened. "No," she whispered. Her heart skipped a beat.

"Did you betray us?" Kinsington snarled in Thorn's mind.

Her cheeks warmed. "No, Kalien misled us. I'll kill him."

"Make haste back to camp," Kinsington said to all Amardians. "It is in danger."

Eliza clawed at Cassin to let her go. "I will not allow her to be sacrificed for my father's crimes. How could you allow this?"

Nia walked into the room. "She commanded us." Her face was stone. "We are not to disobey."

"Even under these circumstances?" Eliza shoved her palms into Nia's chest. "You call yourself a protector when you watched her leave to her grave." Nia didn't even flinch. Eliza balled her fists and stormed to the other side of the room.

"If Queen Agden wanted to fight back, we would have. She could have protected herself. Her magic exceeds ours."

"Not for combat. What battles has she been in?"

Nia and Cassin just stared at her.

"None. That's what I thought." With flared nostrils, Eliza paced around the room. "I'm going after her. If you try to stop me, I swear I will light you up like a sunrise."

"Then we will go with you," Nia said. "Cassin, put a knight in charge to keep watch over the folks who camp outside. I will prepare the chackles."

Eliza sighed and made a praying motion with her hands as she looked up. "Praise the moon. I will meet you outside the doors."

Nia and Cassin left the room.

Eliza quickly packed a bag and charged down the stairs. Bodies were sprawled across the floor. Her body moved through the speckled floor as if trudging through the mud. A trail of blood sparked her memory of the balls they would have, when she had her first kiss, right where a Cursed Knight bled out. She shook her head in disbelief at the shift in her world and pulled the knight into a sitting position against the wall. Eliza lifted off his helmet and armor and placed them on herself, then unhooked his sheath, placing it on her belt. She pulled at the stiffness of his fingers until she could wiggle his sword from his hand. For a moment, she stared at the dead knight. "Our bodies live above so the depths can take us below, for the waters have waited long enough for us to return home."

She placed the sword in her newly acquired sheath and continued to the front doors.

"Bloodtress." A knight bowed. "I will take you to safety; it is not safe here."

"Take care of the castle and the folks outside. I am leaving and do not need your protection."

The knight tilted her head. "It is my duty to keep you safe."

"I command you to do as I say."

Cassin made his way towards her. "The Bloodtress is under my protection. Meet the other knights in the garden for your orders."

The knight hesitated but left.

Nia stood outside with three chackles. "Are you sure you want to do this?"

Eliza climbed onto her chackle and shouted for it to run. Nia and Cassin mounted their chackles and raced off down the hill after her.

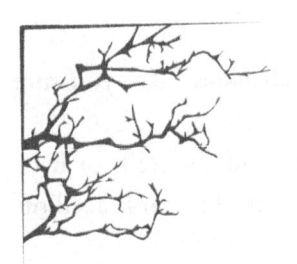

40

Tarmist lay in the grass, his long fur tangled with wildflowers and grass. His sleepy head rested on his paws. A rocky arch stood several yards away; beneath it, Theodore and Bruthren hid on the other side. Theodore balanced on the rocks that were scattered around.

O's hooves wouldn't have even disrupted the insects below with how silent and soft they moved through the meadow. "Ancient One," he said behind Theodore, "I have been eager for this meeting."

Theodore turned around, almost startled at O coming from the opposite direction than he'd assumed he would come from.

Bruthren hugged O as you would an old friend. He let a tear stream down his cheek. "It has been too long."

Theodore stared at them curiously. "How do you know him?"

Bruthren and O pulled away from each other. O's bushy tail twitched.

"Long ago, I caught O smuggling food from Nniar. His carts were overflowing, and he started towards the bridge that still existed at the Divide before it was blasted. When I caught him, he lighted my spark to help the Eltrist." He smiled at O, clearly thankful for him opening his mind from the naïvety most in Nniar unintentionally had. "He told me of the newly born faynes just birthed and how their mothers' milk had run dry and their bellies dimmed of any semblance of lavender light. You can imagine the horror I felt knowing the young Eltrists would die without his assistance."

"I can see your kindness is infectious."

"Where is Talkun?" Bruthren said.

"He is waiting."

Theodore leaned on his hip and crossed his arms. "Waiting for what?"

"I have told him about The Choke already and how we plan to create a Folengower that is in harmony with the old world. The Eltrist, beasts and magic bringers alike. He is unsure of what his kin has to say." O stared at Theodore.

"Why would he be unsure? He is the one leading us into a new era. Have you not received all my notes?" Bruthren said.

"I have, but I am an Amardian in my heart and to my core, so I need reassurance. After what your kalus has gone through, I imagine you would understand the trauma that still haunts him would need that reassurance as well."

Theodore stepped forward. "What can I do to ease your dismay?"

"Did you know Talkun was alive? That they imprisoned him for longer than the entirety of your being?"

Theodore shook his head. "No, I only knew of my father's crimes when I made a wish for the moon. When I saw what he had done, I decided to lead a separate army, but to my surprise, there already was one living in secret."

"You met the moon?"

"Esmeray. Her name is Esmeray. The stories are true—she is the keeper of our faults and accomplishments." Theodore rubbed his forehead. "I partook in the old rituals and walked on her surface. It's been a strange journey of understanding, but believe me, I am shocked to know the great lengths my father has gone for power even when my body has been subject to his hands of wrath."

O studied Theodore's face, his amber eyes bright in the setting sun. "I can see your compassion. I believe you. We will meet with Talkun now." He turned back from where he had come from. "Where are your knights?"

"On the road waiting, though they are all a part of The Choke," Bruthren said.

"I always told you that was risky... having knights unable to control what they are doing. The second Korrigan wants them to fight like mindless beasts, they have no choice."

Bruthren's lips tugged up, mischievous.

"What is it?" O frowned.

"I know the spell. It's merely but a few notes."

"How would you know it?"

"Korrigan gave me it at the Anorphus. He trusts me completely, if not the same as Lore."

O leaned onto a stone. Bits of moss stuck onto his back. "And what have you done to come here?"

"Korrigan believes that I made a potion to mimic a Cursed Knight for the Eltrist. We are supposed to come here and capture an Eltrist and force them to do as we say, then he can enslave them as he has always wanted."

"Did you?"

Bruthren shook his head. "It's an antidote for the knights to resist the curse."

O nodded, and Theodore's eyebrows raised in surprise. They walked down craggy rock steps left from a town that had existed long ago. White slabs poking out from the vegetation wrapped around them were whispers of the past. They twisted down the hill and into a cave. A brambleweep moved about at the entrance, its long arms dragging on the ground. They towered over the creature even as they came down the last steps. The brambleweep's illumination brightened when it saw them.

Theodore lit his hand in a white flame. "Talkun's down here?" he whispered.

"You know that Eltrist live in caves, right?" Bruthren said.

"Yes, but Talkun never lived in a cave."

O shrugged. "That may be true, but this is a safe space for him. Down here, the brambleweeps are kind and quiet for him to be at peace from all the noises that he had forgotten about. It's gentler in this space."

Water dripped from stalactites beyond their vision on the obsidian ceiling. In the back, a shadow with a twinkling lavender glow shifted. Theodore walked ahead of O towards it. His light brightened the back of the cavern, revealing twilight and hemlock fur. Theodore stepped up to Talkun, a deer to an elephant. Talkun lowered his head, their eyes meeting for the first time.

"Kalus," Theodore breathed. He dropped to his knees and bowed, his eyes wet from the rush of emotions.

"Cassus, I have wondered if I could bear your face after learning it resembles Korrigan. And now—"

Theodore shielded his face. "I didn't think about that. Forgive me."

Talkun placed his paw on Theodore's heart and smiled. "You do not need forgiveness; there is no wickedness plagued in your eyes. Praise the moon that I have met you and Eliza and see that the poison did not spread into your hearts."

"I vow to make sure that poison dies with its creator."

"Now what?" O said.

"We wait for the battle. Kinsington should be returning from the castle soon, and The Choke will already be here at the ready. If the moon is on our side, they will take our side and put down their weapons to align with uniting Folengower."

"The moon is on our side," Theodore said. "With hate deeply rooted in both camps, we should plan for battle. Unless you believe Kinsington will join us."

"We have tried to discuss unity with Kinsington. He despises the idea," O said.

"To the top of the mountain, where we will wait," Bruthren's words echoed. A brambleweep stopped in front of him, its head pointed towards the mouth of the cave. "It appears we've worn out our welcome anyway."

They headed back up the steps and into the meadow. Talkun flew up and touched the ground next to Tarmist, who slept soundly even as the ground trembled under Talkun's weight.

"The other Eltrists aren't far."

"They all stayed behind?" Bruthren asked.

Theodore slowed his steps.

"Don't worry. Only a few who are healing and a couple to look after the camp while the packs left for the castle stayed behind."

Theodore left Tarmist to rest. They came to more slabs of white stone smoothed down from the rain and snow that went around the hill. The middle steps had slivers of the same stone that O, Bruthren and Theodore had climbed.

"At the top, there is no turning back. I cannot guarantee peace."

Talkun flew up as the three of them walked up the staggering steps. The last two steps stood before them.

O held out his hand. "Let Talkun and I speak with them. They will not trust outsiders to not turn on Kinsington."

"I do not want them to turn against Kinsington, I want him to join us, as I have wanted this whole time. Everything would have moved smoother if we had accomplished such a feat," Burthren said.

"You do not know Kinsington. His beliefs are more solid than this ground. For some time, I believed he had softened to the ideas I shared, but..." O stopped and gazed at them both, his facial expression shifting. "When Haylin passed, it only solidified his stance."

"Her death has taken a toll on me as well," Bruthren said. "I know that her death has come as a shock to us all. She would have stood for what Talkun wanted."

O continued up to the plateau. Bruthren and Theodore waited behind.

Theodore reached into one of the bags hanging from his belt and pulled out two earrings—one green and one purple stone. He took out a thorn. "Will you?"

Bruthren clasped his hands over his mouth. "Oh... how many have made an Ancient One bleed?"

"You don't have to act so excited about it."

Bruthren held back a laugh. He grabbed the thorn and stabbed it through Theodore's ear. A prick of blood oozed out. Bruthren took the green earring and shoved it in. He did the same with the purple one and then he took a step back and studied him. "Anything?"

Theodore raised his eyebrow. "I don't—" He gasped and held a finger to his lips. "I can hear them."

Bruthren's eyes lighted as he waited impatiently.

"I can hear Talkun telling them that I'm here to discuss peace. One of them is angry..." Theodore looked around as if he were following a fly. "They are talking too fast. Someone just told the others to listen to Talkun."

"Time to make this work before Korrigan's army comes and Kinsington returns is fleeting. Hargrove said she would only give us three days."

"They might have already left."

O towered over them. "It's time."

"Deep breaths." Bruthren placed his hand on Theodore's shoulder.

"Should I remove my crown?"

"Leave it," O said. "It shows that Korrigan's rule can crumble."

Bruthren made it to the plateau, and then, with Theodore's chest rising and falling, his feet touched the top. He swallowed. Five Eltrists stood beside Talkun staring at him about a yard away, their mouths closed.

Theodore walked towards them. The last of the sun's rays highlighted his long brown hair as aureate. His hands glided atop the tall plants, letting the calmness wash over him.

"He comes with death following. He wouldn't do so unless he wanted Folengower whole," Theodore heard Talkun say to the Eltrists.

"Tell them why you have come," O said.

Theodore bowed to them, his fist over his eye. One by one, the Eltrists exchanged glances.

"Let him speak," Theodore heard one of them say.

Talkun gave a single nod.

Theodore rose. "I understand that my being here comes as a shock to many, though in my heart I find this to be the beginning of triumph. I come before you with dreams that I think we all share." He looked them each in their eyes, trying to ooze confidence he didn't feel. "Folengower is for us all. It yearns for our harmony. I can feel it aching for a time that I have only heard stories about, but one that Talkun has lived, if not for long enough. That life was stolen from us all. I was naïve before; I did not know the truth of how our land became divided. I want to right those wrongs even if that means at my own hands. If we can work together, that dream will be our future."

An Eltrist with nut-brown fur huffed. "What would he understand of our dreams?"

Sylin flashed her a glare. "Be quiet."

"My grandmother, Queen Callum, believed deeply in our harmonious way of magic, so much so that Talkun, my lost kalus, stands before me as an Ancient One. I never got to meet her, but I have felt my father's wrath, though I will admit, despite the constant beatings, I didn't believe he was heartless enough to have killed his own mother and framed his brother." He lowered his head and clasped his hands behind his back. "These are unforgivable acts, and the punishment is death."

"Praise the moon for your honesty, and I can see that my mother is with you even after death," Talkun said in all the surrounding minds. "Use those well," he warned Theodore as he stared at his ears.

Theodore nodded.

"Give us a moment to discuss," Talkun said.

O huddled with the Eltrists. Bruthren sat silently on a stump, and Theodore paced in front of him.

"The Choke has a camp just up there." Bruthren motioned with his eyes further up the mountain where sprawling trees grew. "Go there when the fighting starts." Theodore followed his eyes. He couldn't see anything but lush green. "Will you sit down?"

"Why? I can't sit still when we could be thrown off this cliff at any moment or melted to death if they see me unfit."

"You mean you." Bruthren flicked a bug off his shirt.

"What?"

"You see yourself as unfit, so you are assuming others do too."

Theodore stopped moving but couldn't get a word out.

Bruthren sighed and crossed his legs. "It's a tough job, but if you ask me"—he put the back of his hand on the side of his lips—"I think I'm the only one who sees it. That's great news, isn't it? A celebration will be in order."

Theodore shook his head. "It's not that I see myself as unfit. My intentions are thick as agor vines, but executing what I see in my mind is another thing. I expect you to get out of my way when my father chooses hatred over saving his head."

"Bloodthirsty are we?"

Theodore frowned. "Far from it, but if part of my body were infected and could be removed to save me, I would cut it off. I only want to cut off the infected parts, and you know as well as I do that if we don't, it will kill us all... or else you wouldn't have created The Choke."

"The infected parts..." Bruthren mulled over the words.

Talkun called Theodore to come up where they gathered after much of their bickering back and forth. Forbidding eyes stared at him. Theodore waited, holding his breath.

"From one Ancient One to the next, we believe in unifying Folengower, though by doing so we will be traitors to our sides."

Theodore's shoulders slumped and he bit his lip, wondering what was going to become of him. Even with his magic, he didn't stand much of a chance against multiple Eltrists.

"Despite the risk, we would rather fight for a fresh path than one that continues the cycle of hatred," Sylin said. "We will join you."

Theodore grinned, able to breathe properly again.

Bruthren clapped. "Then we have work to do."

O gathered the knights to station outside of the camp until the next day. He spoke with the folks left behind to join them and convince their loved ones to end the war by fighting at their side. Many tried fighting O at first until the Eltrists stepped in to convince them. Theodore even gave them a speech in the hope that their worries would dwindle. Most of them calmed down, and Bruthren handed out light gray ribbons to tie around their necks with their symbol. The triangle was dyed in lavender. It bled into the middle line leading from the point on the triangle through the back-to-back crescents, finally changing its color to a dyed green circle.

Bruthren sent O down the mountainside to check on The Choke, who had made the journey in their wagons to the caves on the cliff face on the other side. As the night prevailed, Theodore stood in the middle of the meadow with Tarmist at his side.

"Long ago, we had a tradition in times of turmoil to ask the moon to guide us, to watch over us. Now, we will come together as one with a harmonious wish. Gather hands with me." Theodore called to the Eltrists, "Join us."

The folks gathered in a circle, hands in paws and heads turned up to the sky.

Quietly, a child sang, "Above and below, watch them soar..."

Adults smiled. "Hear them roar and speak, their magic runs deep, a bringer of gifts, a synchrony unlike others, we breathe together, we rule as one," all their voices rang out in harmony to the moon above. They moved around the circle with their hands moving gracefully as petals in the breeze.

O stormed towards them shouting, "Kinsington returns. Hide Theodore."

The woman holding Theodore's hand clenched it and pulled him to follow her to her tent. "Bruthren, take Tarmist."

Bruthren leapt onto Tarmist and tore off to the main road where the Cursed Knights waited. Theodore reached the tent moments before the shadows of their bodies glided above the tents. The returning packs making their way to the top of the plateau sounded with relieved voices from those who had stayed behind. The women's eyes darted to the door of the tent.

"Are you waiting for someone?" Theodore whispered.

"Yes..."

"Then things could get chaotic fast."

The woman gave a twisted smile. "It already has."

"What do you—"

She pulled out bottle from her pocket that contained a strug mixture and shoved it into Theodore's face. He wiped at his face and winced. She turned to leave, but Theodore tackled her to the floor and flicked the remaining strug off his cheek onto her sleeve. He clamped his hand over her mouth.

"You have to do better than that to kill me. Folengower needs to be healed. This is not the way."

Theodore heard footsteps coming towards the tent and relaxed his hand as he looked up. The woman took the opportunity to try to bite his hand, but she only managed to pinch one of his fingers with her teeth. He reached into his pocket with his other hand and took out a root, scraping off bits of it with his thumb. Placing the rest of the root back into his pocket, he removed his other hand and quickly replaced it with the one with scrapings.

"Sleep."

Her head thudded down.

Theodore walked around her and over to the side of the tent door, where he waited. On a wooden stump next to a bed was a mug. He could see the white of the smoke rising in the air from it. A man made a joke just outside of the tent with someone whose voice was fleeting, then he opened the tent door.

"Raline, I am back. We were so worr—" The man tossed his helmet off and crouched beside the bed, next to the woman. "Raline, Raline... cursed soil. Wake up." He placed his head on her heart to listen.

Theodore strode over behind him, his footsteps silent on the fabric. "She's only sleeping."

The man stood up, his back still to Theodore. "And who are—" he started to say as he turned. His jaw contorted as he fumbled for his sword at his hip, immediately aware of who was before him. Theodore grabbed it first and pulled it out.

"I am here to bring peace, not death. Please sit. If you can't be discreet, I will have to put you to sleep too."

The man reluctantly sat down, glowering. "They will catch you and kill you."

"Like I said, I am not here to kill any of you unless I have no choice. I believed her to be on my side, on Talkun's side of uniting Folengower, but as you can see, after she attacked me, I sent her to sleep for a bit."

"Ancient Ones are why we are suffering, why Amarda is nothing but cracked dirt barren of water or life. It's not supposed to look like that." He leaned forward, knuckles white as he clutched the side of the bed. "The Eltrist give you the magic that you have. You would be nothing without it."

"I agree. Talkun is an Ancient One too, and I plan to rule alongside him once Korrigan is removed."

The man's lips parted, and he cocked his head. "You plan to kill your father?"

"If it comes to that, yes." There was a grim expression on Theodore's face as he put the man's sword on a wooden table. The man watched closely but made no move to grab it. "Folengower is sick because he has made it so, creating hatred towards Amardians. I see no future if he continues to breathe."

"Then why did Raline attack you?" The man motioned with his head towards the woman.

"I hope she can tell you when she wakes up. For now, I need a place to hide until Talkun has discussed the plans for unity with Kinsington. Can I have your word that you will leave me be? If things go to the depths, I will pretend that you tried to kill me."

The man's leg twitched. He stared up, as if he wished for Esmeray to fix everything. "Praise the moon that I don't end up dead because of you."

The sound of dragging across the grass and the smell of fire wafted into the tent. He could hear chatting and singing as someone shouted about food. "Go eat. Someone will wonder where you've gone to if you don't."

"They will only assume I'm busy with her." The man cracked a smile.

"Go; it might be your last meal for a while."

"I thought you were here for peace?"

"Not me." Theodore clicked his tongue. "My father is on his way here, and he does not want peace."

The man got up with a sigh. "Can you at least help me put her in the bed first?"

Theodore lifted her legs as the man lifted her by the head and placed her on the bed.

"I'll be back."

"Do not mention my name."

The man nodded and left.

Theodore could hear his heart thumping louder than the voices outside. With his arms crossed, he tapped his index finger on his upper arm. He had no way of knowing how long the man had been gone, but it felt like much too long. He thought about peering out, but then voices came jumbled and fighting in his mind.

"He came here to kill us."

"He could have helped us, but he chose to escape and leave his father breathing."

"Lies. More lies from his family."

"Kill them all."

"Fuck," Theodore said under his breath. Suddenly, he lost his balance as a roaring voice squeezed into his mind.

"Who decided to welcome the Ancient One with not a corpse thistle down his throat but an alliance? Stand before me with your treachery." Kinsington stomped over to the fire with pots of soup cooking over it on a branch. He struck the pots. They briefly propelled into the air before slamming to the ground. Soup splattered across the meadow. "Stand before me," he bellowed.

"He will not stand with us," Talkun said in Theodore's mind. "What now?"

Theodore let out a breath and stepped out of the tent.

Thorn snatched folks from the crowd and placed them before Kinsington in a line. She tore off one of their ribbons. "What is this? Cursed scum."

"The son wants peace. Isn't that what we are fighting for?" one of them said as they sat on their knees with their hands clasped together.

Thorn shook her head. "We cannot have peace without making them feel what we have felt. They will suffer as they have done to us and then... then we can speak on peace."

Kinsington squished Sylin's head with his paw. His smaller wing twitched violently against his blue fur. "Tell them to change their minds," Kinsington said to Talkun. "I will forgive you for your crimes."

Theodore could hear every word, as if Kinsington were speaking to him. He walked towards the front, moving in between the warriors who had returned. He heard gasps and shouts, but the Eltrists ignored it all until Theodore stood face to face with Kinsington. Thorn kicked the person she was interrogating to the side.

"Thorn," Theodore said. "Patience is not your strength, but I would practice it now."

Thorn took out her dagger, lunging towards Theodore.

Aylo grabbed her back and lifted her up. "Wait for orders," he said to her before dropping her to the ground.

"If you are willing, it would honor me to speak with you," Theodore said to Kinsington.

"Drown him in strug." Esna dragged her paw against the ground. Her claws ripped up the foliage.

"Your time is up," Kinsington said to Theodore for all to hear.

"Cursed Knights, Cursed Knights, Nniar is here!" A folk ran towards them waving his arms.

Everyone turned to see. Theodore thought it was only the few who had come with them until he saw the corpse thistle flags blowing in the wind and heard thousands of hooves barreling down the narrow road.

"We can end this now, together. I plan to do as you asked me," Theodore pleaded with Kinsington.

"Too late."

Theodore whistled, and Tarmist charged to him. Kinsington swiped at him, missing him as Theodore jumped onto his chackle just in time and rode off towards the other side of the cliff where The Choke hid. Bruthren ran up behind him, held a ribbon over the edge and dropped it. It danced down in the wind.

Theodore slid off Tarmist and peered down. "They will be waiting for that."

"Argh!" sounded behind them. Theodore spun around, taking his sword out of his sheath. His sword hit the Amardian's sword. Bruthren took off somewhere in the dark.

Theodore stepped forward and crossed swords with the man, who fought without a helmet and had black hair down to his chin. He had a sharp jaw and a crooked nose.

"I have no intention of killing you if you drop your sword."

The man roared a laugh. "I have no intention of killing you unless you..." He dodged Theodore's strike. "Wait, I do intend on killing you."

Theodore swiped his sword at his chest. The man failed to step back or block, and an angled line cut across his clothing, where a line of blood waited. The man cursed and spat before charging at Theodore. He raised his sword, making a cross.

"Drop your sword. You will not win this."

"Use your magic. I thought you were some incredible magic bringer... I guess that was a lie too," the man said with clenched teeth.

Theodore could see his face in between the gap of the swords. "Is that how you would like to die? I've heard dying by sword is much more revered."

The man grunted. Theodore pushed him off and swung his sword at him. The man dropped to the ground.

Theodore stood over him, sword above his throat. The man swallowed, unmoving.

"I told you I do not want to kill you," Theodore said and turned to walk away. When he heard the man's swift feet, Theodore spun around and sliced into his belly. The man's sword lowered as blood sputtered onto his lips.

"To the depths you go," Theodore said with sincerity in his words, putting his blood-covered sword back into his sheath.

Theodore climbed back onto Tarmist as the members of The Choke made their way up the side of the cliff. The first ones surfaced with a flag with the same symbol as on the ribbons. Jars of dead magic, swords or axes overwhelmed their belts.

Theodore rode over to them. "Nniar is here. We are fighting two armies, though some have come to our side from Amarda, including Talkun."

"We all fight two armies," one folk said as they charged into battle.

Several groups carried giant Y-shaped branches that had a woven cord in between and a pitted piece of carf flower attached in the middle. They positioned them a few feet away from one another, while two of them took out mallets. As they pounded them into the ground, they set sacks down from the next group of them coming in and sliced the bags open. Once all the catapult-like structures were set up, they each had several folks to fire them.

Theodore tore off into battle with Tarmist, zigzagging through danger. The Eltrists took to the sky and circled.

Hargrove led the crimson eyes into the meadow. Theodore made it to the head of Nniar just as they started on the soil.

"Hargrove, I need you to trust me."

She did a double take, her crimson eyes blinking. "You're alive?"

"Indeed," he said as if it was obvious he would be despite having strug thrown in his face, the standoff with Kinsington and his near stabbing. "I need you on my side. The side for unifying Folengower."

"What are you talking about?"

"This war will only create more of a divide. We must unite Folengower together. If you are with me, take this." Theodore held out a ribbon.

"What do you plan to do?"

"Kill the king." His arm remained out, unwavering, his jaw set in a determined line.

Hargrove's jaw dropped as she studied him as if he were possessed or not of sound mind.

"Lead my army to right his wrongs. The Choke. I know you've heard of it."

"Why didn't you speak to me of this before?"

"I didn't know if you could be trusted. Will you help me?"

"I... I..." Hargrove looked around at the other Cursed Knights, trying to gauge their thoughts, but all eyes were on her, faces devoid of emotion.

"We are in the midst of a battle," Theodore pressed. "Decide now."

"Yes." She nodded firmly, decided. "Yes, I will."

He handed her the ribbon. "Tie this around your neck. Welcome to The Choke. Spread the word to the other knights, and have them tie these around their necks." Theodore grabbed more that tied around his belt and handed them to her. "Where's my father?"

"Not far."

Theodore charged back into the fighting. Sweat lingered, as if everyone were trapped in a sauna. Guttural sounds and grunts filled the chaotic scene as bodies dropped all around. Dead magic whizzed through the sky and crashed down in grand explosions, hurling warriors in all directions to land with broken bones. Eltrists swooped down and snatched whomever they could before dropping them off the side of the cliff.

Bruthren called down from atop a boulder near the beginning of the ravine and screamed, "Get out of the chaos before all the knights flood in."

Theodore whistled at Tarmist, who then charged towards the ravine.

"Our blood bound or corpse thistles, we will drown," Theodore shouted.

The battlefield extended farther up and through the ravine. Cursed Knights flooded the space, many of whom still fought for Nniar.

The dawn approached with more bloodshed. Bodies were trampled by chackles, and magic soared to all. Theodore's crown marked him for dead. A mob of Amardians circled Tarmist, with their swords aimed at him. Theodore lit his hands black and forced Tarmist to move in a circle as he threw his magic out. The light boomed like a crack of thunder, their subsequent wails haunting. One man fell with a hole in his chest. He placed his hand over it, but Theodore knew he was for dead as he stared at the man's bloody ribs showing between his fingers.

Theodore rode through the ravine. "Fight alongside me," he shouted. "Halko," he said to Tarmist. "Get to higher ground, my friend."

Water sloshed and sprayed up around Tarmist's and Theodore's legs. Tarmist's long fur dripped beads back into the water. They made it to the other side. Choke fighters had made their way up with more giant branch slingshots. Eltrists rained down strug. Folks jumped out of the way, though some unlucky souls were drenched.

Theodore rode past, heading to the highest ground just beyond and up more ancient steps. Rew stood beneath a verdant canopy, hidden from the armies below and above. Tarmist stopped under it, and Theodore slid off him. Behind Rew, a modest camp came into view. Argwen worked behind him, handing out sacks of more dead magic to the warriors. Three healers moved feverishly to care for those injured.

"How did this all happen?"

"The first of us arrived days ago and set up camp. It was risky being so close to Amarda, but we could smell their unrest, so we went undetected."

"Where are the rest of the camps?" Theodore breathed heavily and wiped the sweat from his brow with a cloth.

"All along the side of the mountain. We have occupied the caverns on the western side. The rest of our army is coming in at a trickling rate. We are holding off as much as possible."

"Letting Amarda and Nniar exhaust their resources..."

Rew nodded.

"Where's Audrey and Ben?"

Rew crossed his arms. "They are in the last group to fight. I hope the war will end before it even gets to them."

Theodore exhaled, his shoulders loosening. "By the looks of the carnage, I don't think any side is willing to give up. The grass is turning to a red sea."

Rew's lip curled up. "Pray to the moon for bodies few and victory for us. Bruthren is joining us soon to discuss war plans with some of our other leaders. We ask that you join in the discussion and stay out of danger."

"I cannot guarantee that I will not fight. I have already bloodied my sword, and my hands are not free of blood."

"Korrigan is waiting on the road. If you still plan to kill him, be as patient as an owl."

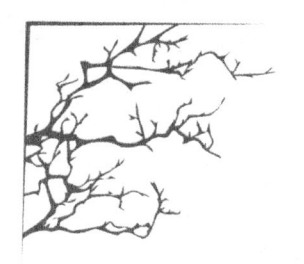

41

Agony drifted in the wind. Theodore sat upon a stump at a makeshift table of a fallen log with the top bark scraped off smooth. He had dark circles under his eyes and his hair was disheveled. His crown sat on the table next to him. Tarmist lay behind him, still speckled in another folk's blood.

Bruthren charged into the meeting area.

"Glad you could come," Theodore said sarcastically.

Rew handed Bruthren a note. Argwen sat across from Theodore, picking at the strips of wood coming up. Art had garnered a seat next to him after being appointed the geographical leader. Much to Theodore's surprise, it was Art's knowledge that had led them to make camps where they did on the mountain. Hargrove sat at the table, sipping on the potion that Bruthren had actually created that would counter the curse from affecting the knights of The Choke. Five other knights stood by them; Talkun, Sylin and three other Eltrists circled the table; and O and his sister Camis sat on the other side with a few others whom Theodore had only gotten to know the last few days.

Bruthren jumped onto the table. "Everything is going as planned—"

"The plan was for a crushing defeat," Theodore said sullenly.

Bruthren narrowed his eyes. "And now we shall have one. Amarda has lost many and Nniar drags their dead down to the beach, ready for them to be claimed by the Sea of Calip. We even gained a few warriors."

"And what of our body count?" Theodore asked.

"We will send in another group shortly."

Theodore placed his elbows on the table and rubbed his forehead with his fingertips. "How many injured?"

"We've brought in more healers."

"Is there anything positive you have to say?"

Bruthren sighed. He took a long stride across the table and then twirled back around. "We have spotted Korrigan just outside of the battleground."

Theodore hit the side of his fist on the table and stood up. "Tarmist, it's time."

"Woah... woah. Not so fast," Art said.

Talkun's wings twitched. "Patience."

Theodore glared at him. "I have been here for days listening to plans and helping the healers carry our injured back. They are dying while I sit here watching. If my father is near, I will call him out to a duel."

"Kinsington still flies. What about him?" O said.

"I have to hope that he will watch what unfolds and change his heart."

"Before you ride gallantly off, I have news," Rew said. "Please read the note, Bruthren."

Bruthren unfolded the note. "Kinsington captured Agden, and they will throw her onto the battlefield—"

Theodore slapped his palms onto the table. "What?" he shouted.

"Let me finish." Bruthren stomped his foot. "Eliza arrived this morning on a chackle. She is with a group of Choke warriors."

"Take me to her."

O stood up. "I can lead him down."

"We should all lead him down." Art rose from his seat and rubbed his beard.

"He can ride on me," Talkun said.

Rew tapped the table. "We need a plan. I will not allow anyone to aimlessly go down there and curse the soil."

"Talkun and I will fly down and find the queen. Find Korrigan and bring him to me. I need all the Eltrists on our side to stop Kinsington from getting in my way."

"How many Eltrists have died?"

"Three. They have the air to thank, though I imagine they are tired. Polt left to find out where they are landing to rest, but he is yet to return. Other birds are our eyes for now."

Sylin said to the other Eltrists, "Have you heard who died?"

"No," Talkun said. "Even though we have chosen a different path, we can still mourn."

A sudden sadness took the Eltrists, though only Theodore could hear what they were saying. He shared a glance with Talkun and gave a solemn nod, placing his crown on his head. As he walked up to Talkun, he whispered, "We will do something for all the lives lost when the time is right." He climbed onto his back. As if they shared a breath, everyone paused.

Rew's eyes were glossy. "It is time."

"Draw your weapons and light your magic; a new world waits for us," Theodore yelled.

Talkun closed his eyes, and when he opened them, the world moved in slow motion. His wings flapped, and they emerged into the sky. Theodore held on to Talkun's neck, watchful of what was going on below. They cleared the forest to where the others came charging down. Bruthren rode on Tarmist holding a giant flag with The Choke's symbol on, and Art held a three-headed ax filled with dead magic in the middle that lighted the middle and ends. Sylin left shortly after, and he and the other Eltrists flew in a diamond shape behind Talkun.

Fiery light whizzed past Talkun.

Theodore shouted, "Another one comes."

Crimson eyes gazed up at the clouds, the Cursed Knights' hands firing magic towards them. Kinsington, not far from Theodore, circled above knights, streams of strug raining down. Thorn was standing on him, throwing bombs down. Talkun swerved to the side as another comet-like ball hurled towards them and disappeared when it missed.

"Do you see my mom?"

Talkun tilted his body to the side, his massive wings pushing gusts of wind back. "Not yet."

They darted above the tents and gazed behind.

"Could they have been lying about having her?"

"It would be unlikely for her to be mistaken for someone else."

Theodore leaned over Talkun's back, his eyes laser-focused on the beings below. From above, the ground looked like a checkerboard of red and green. Even from up high, the sounds blared with chaos.

Talkun circled towards the eastern side.

"Wait. Do you see the boulders over there? Go towards them. Amarda has folks guarding them."

As they changed direction, Theodore spotted pink hair that shot up as horns. "Morrow," he said to himself. He lost his breath. "Wait... wait."

"What do you want me to do?"

"I need to make sure they aren't there."

"Who?"

"The love of my life and my best friend."

"Do you see them?"

Theodore squinted, but he couldn't make out many others. "Can you take us closer?"

Talkun dove. Gruesome bodies came into shape with cut-open bellies, bloody lips, twisted necks and hollowed chests. The smell of corpse thistles' sweet death was prominent.

As much as he didn't want to believe it, Theodore couldn't deny what he could now see. "No... no..."

"Do you see them?" Talkun asked again.

"Yes. They have arrived on the battlefield."

Audrey and Ben stood next to the catapult structures, filling the jars one after another. Just as Audrey reached for another one, Morrow flung her aside as a knight swung his sword at her. Audrey crawled back, reaching for her sword on her hip. She held it out and scrambled back up. Ben tossed Audrey a jar, then held his sword at another knight charging towards him.

"Let me down. Can you find out what's being guarded?"

"I will."

Talkun lowered himself a few yards away from Audrey and Ben. Most warriors ran from him, but the knights cared not for his size and came after him. Talkun flapped his wings, flinging tens of them to the ground. Theodore jumped several feet down as knights shot black smoke at him. One shot hit his front leg, and he flinched but continued up.

"It's the Ancient One. Get him," someone shouted.

Theodore ripped out a bushel of plants that came up to his waist. He rubbed them together, lighting both his hands in black fire before spreading them apart. The flame floated in between the space. A pack of Amardian warriors held their weapons out.

"Let me get him," one said, who had blood splattered on their face.

"Let the knights kill him," another said. "He's an Ancient One. He probably could kill us in a swift movement."

"Kinsington taught us. We could kill him."

"You should listen to your friend. You could even join my side." Theodore grinned.

"We won't listen to cursed scum." The man spit at Theodore's feet.

"Yeah!" the others said in reply as they hunched around him as if he were a rabid beast.

"Then I would run." Theodore lifted his hands over his head and violently struck them down. The fire flung towards them and knocked them down as if they were bowling pins. He ran from it, not caring to see what he had done.

He dodged combat from both sides of him and ran to the sidelines where he had seen Audrey and Ben. "*Audrey*," Theodore screamed, his heart racing. Time felt broken as he waited for her to turn.

Audrey gazed at him, her lips parted.. She mouthed his name and fled towards him. Theodore met her. She crashed into him and flung her arms around him before brushing his hair from his face.

"What are you doing down here?" he asked.

"I could say the same about you. I didn't want you to fight."

"Keep your sword out; I have a target on my back. Have you seen my father?"

"No, not over here at least." Audrey smirked. "Did you come down just to ask me questions?"

Theodore grinned, with his hand behind her head. "No, not even war could keep me from you." He pressed his lips against hers.

"*Watch out*," Ben yelled. A faint flicker of light emitted from his hand only for a moment.

Audrey spun to the side in Theodore's arm. The crimson eyes of a Cursed Knight were glaring and zoned in on Theodore. He swung his sword outwards, aiming for a side slice, but Theodore grabbed his face. The knight shook, dropping his sword as the black fire marked him for dead. Ben pushed the unsteady knight to the ground.

"Ben, good to see you," Theodore greeted in a rushed manner as he noticed more Cursed Knights turn to him. Audrey grabbed his hand and ran to the other side of the slingshots.

Ben loaded another jar and fired it. "Can we all just stay alive for a bit longer?"

"Indeed."

"For moon's sake, get the hell out. Unless you are going to start firing dead magic, leave. I don't care if you are our leader," Morrow shouted.

"Protect them," Theodore yelled as he charged out into the open. He took out his sword and swiftly slashed through anyone who came to attack.

Talkun's voice came into his mind. "Agden is tied up. There are at least a dozen Amardian's guarding her. Eliza is sneaking around to save her with two knights."

Sylin swooped down just above a row of Cursed Knights and opened his mouth. Strug drenched anyone below as he circled back to leave more on them. As Theodore walked around the bodies, he could see Korrigan's crown behind a group of knights on chackles. Theodore stared up in search of Talkun.

"Behind you."

Theodore held out his hand, gripped Talkun's fur and climbed onto his back. "Korrigan is straight ahead. The end is in front of us."

Talkun hurtled up and towards the knights that protected Korrigan. Kinsington soared just behind them like a storm cloud. Theodore heard him call to Thorn before he saw him. He peered back, and said, "Kinsington is just behind us."

"Let us kill him together," Talkun said to Kinsington.

"You betrayed us."

"You betray our home. It is for us all." Kinsington flew next to them.

Kinsington snarled. "Together, we take him, but I cannot guarantee what will become of you after." He darted down, his mouth wide as a bear trap. Talkun followed, snatching up knights and tossing those who were too distracted by Kinsington on the other side.

The knights upon chackles hurled magic up, blasting Kinsington's side. Kinsington dropped suddenly a few feet down before flapping his wings again. Thorn raised her hand, wet with a strug mixture, and squeezed it before hurling the magic towards them.

"Grab him," Kinsington cried to Talkun.

Talkun dove into the circle of knights as they tried to dodge the strug. There in the middle, Korrigan was ready and waiting with magic in his hands. He fired it up. Talkun dodged it and dug his claws into Korrigan's shoulders, lifting him from his chackle as he kicked and screamed.

"I should have killed you," Korrigan spit as he tried to pull Talkun's claws from his shoulders, but Talkun dug them in deeper.

Kinsington nodded at Talkun as his wings weakened and his side dripped with blood. "We've captured

Korrigan," he said breathlessly to everyone. "Nniar, drop your weapons, or you will drown in strug."

Talkun added to The Choke army, "Let us have peace for now." He flew to the other side of the ravine. Kinsington followed Talkun, crashing to the ground just behind where he'd landed. Thorn tumbled off him, her mouth wide with heavy breaths.

"Kinsington," Thorn cried as she pushed herself up from the ground, dirt streaking her arm and the side of her face. She held her hands firmly over Kinsington's gash, obsidian blood soaking her shaking fingers.

Theodore jumped off Talkun and rushed to Kinsington. Talkun's claws on his right paw didn't release Korrigan until O clamped a rapture stone onto his wrist.

"Healers, healers, we need you. Make haste," Theodore yelled, keeping his eyes on the fighting until the adrenaline faded like a ghost. Healers ran over or wandered through the battlefield to Kinsington and placed takthorn on his side. Theodore gripped one's arm as they jogged past. "Talkun is hurt too."

Gradually, the living started to journey over, many with wounds or carrying those injured. Theodore waited for them before speaking.

"Our minds may have forgotten the truth, but our hearts beat for it, our bones yearn for it and their voices have been silenced because of it." He pointed his sword at the Eltrist before turning it to Korrigan's neck as he walked slowly around him. "Make no mistake that this divide is not to protect us from Eltrist, it is to keep hatred alive. And for what?" He grabbed his father's hair and forced him to look at him. "Jealousy." Theodore released him, and Korrigan's face sagged. "Shameful. Folengower has no place for such feelings. Will you atone for this egregious crime?"

Korrigan raised his head, and his eyes wandered to the crowd. They stopped dead on Talkun. He snarled and said, "I should have killed you instead."

The warriors glared and clinked their weapons. Some threw bits of stinging magic at his face. Theodore held his sword out to his father.

"Theodore," Bruthren said gently, unmounting from Tarmist. He pointed to behind Theodore.

Theodore turned as the crowd silently parted, their heads lowered. Eliza pushed through with Agden lifeless in her arms, head lolled back, limbs dangling. Her blood left a trail like a red carpet behind them.

"Mom," Theodore breathed, his emotions catching in his throat.

Korrigan rose to his knees. "Who killed her?" he screamed.

Eliza set Agden down before him, and Theodore fell to the ground, his hands cupping her face, his tears dripping onto her chest. "*You did*. Everybody that lies upon the grass ready for the depths is at your hands."

He looked up at Eliza, the momentary tenderness gone. "My hands are clean."

Eliza took out her sword from its sheath and screamed as she raised it over her head, then forcefully stabbed it into his heart and twisted. "Mine aren't."

42

Around Talkun's Tower, great spiral arches were erected months after the war ended. Each one held the story of the divided kingdom and the fate of its creator so that all would know that not even Ancient Ones could get away with carnage. Below the arches were nameplates carved out of sunwaves of everyone who had died except for Korrigan.

Talkun and Theodore stood next to the first arch, which had The Choke's banner hung next to it.

"Thank you for joining us to mourn and also celebrate the first anniversary of the Rightful Heir War," Theodore said, smiling sadly at the crowd before him. All of Folengower had been invited to celebrate the change in history and honor the ones who had died. "The toll this war created is not lost on any of us. Some losses will never heal, but Talkun and I are ever grateful that you all stand before us with new achievable hopes and dreams. It is a new era of unity."

Eliza stood next to Agden's nameplate, placing wildflowers on top. Bruthren watched and bowed his head.

Talkun placed a paw on one of the nameplates. "Kinsington may have lost his way, but in the end, I know this is what he would have wanted. He suffered greatly, just as all Amardians and those taken by Korrigan's rule. Let us reflect on the work we have done to bring Folengower together as it always should have been."

Thorn stood in the crowd, she wiped a tear. Riven squeezed her hand and rested her head against the side of hers.

"Above and below, watch them soar, hear them roar and speak, their magic runs deep, a bringer of gifts, a synchrony unlike others, we breathe together, we rule as one," the crowd chanted. The Eltrist roared.

"Please celebrate."

Music played, and Theodore hugged Talkun as the crowd dispersed in dance.

"Can I steal him away now?" Audrey chimed in. She swayed her lavender floor-length gown with fern green ribbon crisscrossing down her back.

"Then who will keep me company?" Talkun said playfully.

"I was talking about you." Audrey laughed, grabbing Talkun's paw. "Do you dance?"

Eliza sauntered after them, holding her long dress up from dragging in the grass. "I'm coming too. Don't have too much fun without us, Storm."

Theodore smirked and watched Audrey head off into the crowd with Talkun.

Ben came up to Theodore with two drinks in his hand. "Here." Ben handed him a goblet. "I thought you could use one of these. It's a bit strong." Ben's face soured.

Theodore clinked his glass into his. "Aren't they supposed to be at events like this?"

Ben shrugged. "You're probably right."

"How is Harthsburg life going?"

Ben searched the crowd for Morrow. He found her sitting with a group of faynes, playing with their paws and rubbing their glowing bellies. They flapped their wings excitedly but could not fly yet. The adult Eltrists were close by, speaking with Morrow. Ben beamed at the scene. "Things finally seem normal except for Morrow. She is bored there and keeps begging me to move here. I can't blame her. This is a wonderful place, and after her meeting my mom..." Ben took a breath in and gazed up.

"That good?"

"Well, when we arrived back at the pond—which was dreadful by the way, bodies everywhere—we ended up helping the knights clean up Taylor's backyard. But I was confused to find my mom at Taylor's already. Apparently, she'd kept showing up there to find me."

"That must have been awful—the bodies. What did your mom think of Morrow?"

Ben teetered on his toes, his lips pursed. "At first, you know, it was rocky. Morrow takes a bit to get used to, but now they have morning mimosas once a week. Since we arrived last night, I think she is secretly scheming to keep us here."

"How dare she." Theodore took a sip of his drink. "Although I would completely support her scheme to keep you here."

Ben cleared his throat. "Of course you would."

Theodore stared off into the crowd. Thorn and Riven danced off to the side. Riven led in every step, and Thorn smiled. It was a curious display and one that Theodore would remember. Art held a meat skewer as he handed a piece to Hazy as Claire twirled on the dance floor with Luspy and Kalien. Hargrove stood next to Nia. She raised a glass when his eyes landed on her. He returned the gesture. O stood off to the side, his eyes on Eliza. A faint smile struck his face, but he remained distant.

Theodore turned back to Ben. "Audrey and I miss you. Even Eliza does."

Ben nodded and raised his glass. "Maybe I can split my time. For now." He stared at Audrey, Talkun and Eliza, who stole the dance floor.

Folks danced, played games, drank and ate until their bellies were stuffed.

Theodore stared up at the moon and smiled. For now, all was well in the kingdom, and Folengower could breathe as one.

The CURSED KNIGHT

Fig. 1 Cursed Knights are magic bringers for Nixia's army. Once joined in the army, they drink a potion that turns their eyes crimson. If a song is played from a three-headed flute, the curse will be enacted and they are controlled to only fight. They learn spells that are created with string and nature elements. They are also deadly with a sword. All folks are welcome to join.

Fig. 2 <u>GEAR</u>

Their helmet has corpse thistle carved on the sides with a plume made from fox-trot fur that is dyed lavender. Their armor is seafoam green and looks like an intricate spiderweb. Clothing and boots are black. They use a belt that has many hanging pouches and potions hanging off it.

About the Author

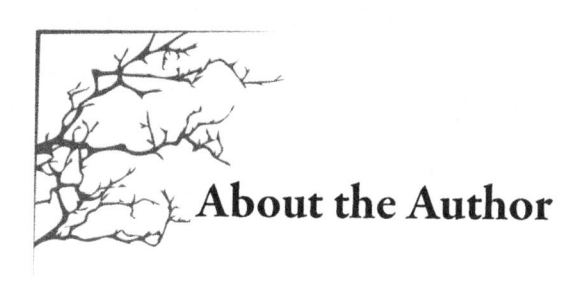

Candy D. Mitchell is an American author and artist. She mainly writes fantasy and horror fiction. Her inspiration derives from nature, the fairy realm, and traveling. Currently, she resides in Oregon where you can find her frolicking in the woods on a regular basis or talking to spiders. She is happily married to a weirdo and a proud mother to a rad kid and furbabies!

Leaving a review is hauntingly wonderful. Please, consider leaving a review and/or following the author for other book news.

Thepeculiarfairy.com
@thepeculiarfairy

Upon a Kingdom's Breath book 3

Made in the USA
Monee, IL
24 January 2024